# Breaking Ground

## Chris Towndrow

Valericain
Press

# 1

He was going to give her one last chance. After all, he wasn't a monster, was he?

He cared about her. Not as much as he did about the other stuff, but still.

He gazed out over Lake Vättern, where sailboats plied the calm waters. The sun was overhead, and the mercury was up. Not as high as it was in Washington DC, but it was early morning there. Eva would be heading for her pre-flight coffee stop—if she was on schedule. He never understood how she could stomach the coffee over there; too bitter. Yet, she'd emigrated to the land of the free, despite the beverage situation and the country's other shortcomings.

He picked up his Com and dialled. It rang and rang. He worried, knowing this chance was important for assuaging his conscience. Things were dragging on long enough, anyhow. He couldn't make the decision without speaking to her. Not Eva. Others, certainly, but she was one glimmer of brightness in a gloomy world.

He went to hang up.

'Mat?' came a familiar voice.

He smiled instinctively. 'Hej.'

'What's up?'

'Does something have to be up? You act like I never call.'

'Be honest, Mat, we're hardly joined at the hip.'

'You're the one who emigrated.' That came across too snippy. Not ideal when he was calling to ask a favour.

'For the millionth time, it was for my career—not to get away from you. Although sometimes....'

'Ho ho,' he replied flatly.

'Really, is there something? My flight is in two hours. If you wanted a sibling chat, there are better times, okay?'

He took a deep breath. 'I need your help getting through to Wilmer about this redevelopment thing.'

She sighed. 'Not that again. Look, I don't care, okay? It's his decision.'

'But he'll listen to you.'

'Because I'm the apple of his eye, I suppose?'

'More than I am.'

'That's not saying much.'

'My parentage and the matter of my birth are hardly my fault.'

'And what Dad does with his land isn't my concern.'

He made a fist. 'Why don't you care, Eva? The stubborn old fool is passing up a golden opportunity.'

'Then *you* talk to him, Mat. I'm all the way over here. Hell, you can pop in any time. Make your peace if this is so important to you. Have a word. You're the one who seems to care.'

'How can you not? You do understand that this is our future too?'

A breathy chuckle came down the line. 'I'm not sure it's yours too much, is it?'

'Well, that can change,' he sneered to an empty room.

'You mean if you make your peace. Give him a reason to add you to his inheritance. It's not my problem, okay? I don't care about the money. I came here to get out from under his shadow. I just want a regular job. I don't want to be a damn billionaire. Okay?'

'So you say.'

'Get lost, Mat.'

'So you won't talk to him? At least *suggest* he opens up to the possibility? This isn't about his life, his estate, his legacy—all that bullshit. Hell, you're in Fleet—you understand the importance of all this. Don't you want us to have better connectivity, more jobs, a growing economy? This is your homeland, Eva. Don't you want the best for it? You could transfer back home. Fly out of here instead, rather than be halfway around the world in a godforsaken country like that.'

'I like it here.' It sounded like she'd said it through gritted teeth.

He looked out over the water. He might sailboard later.

'And we're cast on the scrapheap, is that it?'

'I think you did that to yourself, Mat.'

'I didn't do a thing.' He wanted to reach down the line and pull her hair, like she'd done to him when they were kids. Not too hard, just hard enough.

'So you said. That's the problem with juries, right?'

He pressed his lips tightly together. 'Everyone is fallible.'

She laughed. 'Still with this "miscarriage of justice" bullshit? Move on.'

'My whole life is a miscarriage,' he grouched.

'Oh, puh-lease.'

He hated her adopted Americanisms.

'Stop being over-dramatic,' she continued. 'You've done okay for yourself despite that.'

'Humph,' he snorted.

'Have you talked to Anders?'

'About this? He wouldn't care.'

'What you mean is, you haven't bothered to ask.'

'He's never available—you know that.'

'Jet-setting entrepreneurs rarely are. Look, Mat, just talk to Dad, okay? Bury the damn hatchet if this development proposal is so important to you. God knows why. But I'm not fighting your battles. You're not my baby brother anymore. You're thirty-three, for Christ's sake. Now, I'm going. I'm not getting busted down a rank for missing my rostered flight. If you care about Fleet—and me—that much, don't drag me into your petty squabbles. Dad's a smart man. He didn't get where he is by making bad business decisions. Don't piss him off any more than you have—if that's even possible.'

Matteo Svensson took a deep breath. 'Right. I see how this river is running. I won't keep you.'

'Com me when you're in a better mood. Bye.'

He thwacked the handset down on the artisan pine table.

Well, he'd tried—he consoled himself with that. It wasn't going to go how he hoped, but it was going to go how he planned.

# 2

Inspector Kennet Carlsson wiped down the kitchen surface for the second time in half an hour.

Jana leant on the door frame. 'I wish you showed as much diligence when *I* have visitors.'

'I do,' he said, deeply unsure of his ground.

She strolled in and pecked him on the temple. 'Are you going to justify it by saying they are *our* friends anyway?'

'Are they not?' He stroked her cheek.

'I would be cruel to say they aren't, wouldn't I?'

'If you did, I know it would be a tease.'

'And you get teased enough anyway. You can't mind it too much if you are prepared to let her visit any time she wants.'

He patted Jana's backside. It came to something when he was gently teased about the subject of being teased. It didn't matter—he enjoyed it, whether it was from his wife, from his best friend and colleague, or even from *her* wife.

It would be another occasion of three-versus-one, but he'd learned to take it in his stride. Besides, this wasn't purely a social visit, although those were fine too.

The doorbell rang.

He scurried to the door.

Kayte saluted him—because, whilst being technically correct, it was very *her*. He poked out his tongue, which wasn't very *him*, but it's what she would appreciate.

'Oh God, hon,' Carey said, glancing at Kennet. 'You've finally done it. You've dragged the poor soul down to your level.'

'Then my work is complete,' Kayte joked.

'I don't know how you put up with her,' Kennet said to Carey.

'Yeah. You only have to work with her now and again. I have to live with her.' She mock-shuddered.

Kennet felt breath on his neck.

'Are you still screening the guests, sweet?' Jana asked.

Kayte pulled out her Polismyndigheten badge. 'We have a warrant to search the property for coffee, Mrs Carlsson.'

'And then drink the evidence,' Carey added.

'See—they are as bad as each other, sweet,' Kennet said. 'You have such odd taste in friends.'

Jana clipped his ear, then pulled him away from the door so the Americans could enter. Both pecked him on the cheek, then embraced Jana.

'No Charlotte?' Kennet asked, missing his goddaughter.

'We left her with the sitter,' Carey replied. 'This was hardly a fun trip for her.'

'You could have dropped her here while you did the interview, Kayte.' Jana began preparing the coffee.

'We lean on you enough, honey. Certainly, this past year or so. Always on the horn, asking advice about a million things.'

'Well, the authorities didn't have you deported, so we must have helped you to fit in.' Kennet patted the shoulder of Kayte's uniform. 'Which is a blessing.'

'Yeah—so long as I didn't waltz into the polis station on day one, acting like the foreign big city cop with all the moves.'

'Especially as we've had our share of serious crime in the last few years—even in Bollnäs.' Kennet feigned thinking. 'From the time I met you, I would estimate.'

Carey ruffled Kayte's hair. 'Yeah, she's a magnet for trouble, this one.'

They sat in the living room.

'And she always drags you into it,' Jana did likewise with Kennet's blond mop.

'At least we've not had any scrapes since we moved here,' Kayte said.

Kennet's ears pricked. 'Moved? This was a, what do you say, try-out?'

Kayte squeezed Carey's hand. 'It *was*. The year in Uppsala flew. Now, with this maternity cover in Söderhamn?' She did a so-so of the head. 'We like the pace of life. Staying is... tempting.'

'Even with my two-hour drive,' Carey said.

Jana sipped her coffee. 'Would they give you a permanent position?'

Kennet found it curious that Carey had chosen to work in the offices of the Uppsala Chamber Orchestra.

Since the doorstep attack in DC the previous year, when she'd lost her ability to play the viola at a high level, it might have been understandable if she had turned her back on the profession entirely. Instead, even though she could have felt frustrated or neutered by working alongside other musicians, she'd resolved to support the industry in her own way, taking an admin role and remaining in touch with fellow players.

She could still play the instrument, but not for extended periods, and lacked practice. Nevertheless, she gave violin and viola lessons locally as well.

As such, Carey was often at home, minding Charlotte, while Kayte worked at the polis station in Söderhamn, where they lived. It was a half-hour drive from Bollnäs, meaning the couple were frequently popping by, and she and Kennet worked on a number of cases together. There had been a few international cases through Fleet PD over the last year as well. Tom and Enna had visited Söderhamn once. Kennet rubbed his forehead at the recollection of the amount of drink they'd consumed. Enna's tolerance for brännvin was a standing joke.

'Someone in the office is retiring soon,' Carey replied. 'So, whilst we haven't properly decided, there's a good chance. Especially if Sarge here can nail down a posting. Can't raise a perpetually hungry toddler on my salary.'

Jana frowned. 'Isn't Sergeant Mikkelson transferring out of Bollnäs, sweet?'

Kennet nodded. 'Her husband has a new job in Göteborg.' He looked at Kayte. 'I would have told you, but it might appear I was trying to entice you into another move. It is much... slower here even than Söderhamn. Plus, there you have the sea.'

Kayte patted Carey's hand. 'We do have some stuff to think about. If we're staying—assuming the authorities grant us long-term residency—then we have to consider a school for Charlotte, whether to rent or buy, what we see our careers looking like.' She sighed. 'Much as it's nice to hang with you two—however close by we are—there's a lot to fix up. I know I seem like the crazy, impulsive type, but there are three of us in this family.'

Carey lifted Kayte's hand and kissed it. 'As long as you're not stomping around on the roof of a freight train with your sidekick here,' she winked at Kennet, 'then pretty much anything is less of an adventure.'

'That was no adventure,' Kennet said. 'Nearly dying is not my idea of fun.'

'Amen,' Jana replied. 'Stick with the kind of case you're working on. I think Carey and I have received enough heart-stopping phone calls.'

'Amen here too,' Carey said. 'I like excitement as much as the next gal, but getting shot into a coma really crossed the line.'

'Yeah. I prefer it when I'm following up on the shooting of a dog, rather than my wife,' Kayte said.

'Did it go well?' Kennet asked.

'Pretty good. The victim is pretty sure it was an intimidation tactic. Honestly, they're relieved that the perp—whoever it was—didn't kidnap their kid or do something worse. Sure, killing a family pet is not a lot of fun, but still.'

'Intimidation over what?' Jana asked.

She'd long ago abandoned the notion that Kennet or his colleagues would keep shop talk within the walls of the office. These days, she took an active interest in whatever he was working on. Sometimes it was genuine curiosity; sometimes, it was a risk assessment, so she'd be in a position to nag Kennet to take special care.

Kennet set down his coffee mug. 'Lena Ekström is on the selection committee for the new Stockholm Spaceport site. She's previously been offered a bribe in exchange for her vote. Now, that person—whoever it is—tried something more persuasive.'

'Probably,' Kayte said clearly. 'Nothing proven.'

'But, on the other side, anybody who is trying to interfere in this process needs to be careful. The more incidents and clues, the more likely we will find a pattern.'

'There will be thousands of people with views on this and opposition to it,' Jana said. 'It is always the way. Tearing up this beautiful country in the name of progress means walking a fine line.'

'Absolutely, sweet,' Kennet replied. 'But this development is good for Sweden. It will happen. The only question is where.'

Kayte chuckled. 'I think the bigger question is how many more protests, incidents, interferences and crimes will crop up along the way. Hell, you could put an entire squad of cops onto this. Keeping an eye on the OnePlanet nuts, rooting out bribery amongst the network of survey and construction firms, watching for any environmental protestors who go too far. Believe me, this kind of project stirs up feeling wherever you are in the world.'

'Maybe I should suggest to Chief Inspector Janssen that we focus on this. It will be at least five years before the site is operational. Plus, some could say it has an aspect which is appropriate for Fleet PD. Spaceport *is* a Fleet operation.'

Kayte held up her palms. 'Whoah, partner! I'd rather not be telling the boss what to do. Besides, I'm still finding my feet in Söderhamn. Let's not expect this whole thing to blow up into a crazy hotbed of crime. Hell—I came here expecting an easier life!' She laughed. 'Let's not invite ourselves—certainly me—into anything. I want our wives to have us around *more*. Plus, I want to get out and see this country.'

'You should,' Jana said. 'You dragged Kennet around the States. If you're here, let us do the dragging!'

'Technically, sweet, it was the Chief who sent me to New York that first time,' Kennet said.

She fluttered a hand. 'They get the point. We should recommend some places, let the girls take a weekend away. We'll look after Charlotte.'

'Oh, we couldn't impose,' Carey said.

'Nonsense. Besides, we might ask for a return favour sometime.' Jana winked.

'It's a deal,' Kayte said.

'We could use that voucher for the Narvik whale-watching tour,' Kennet suggested.

'Sorry, sweet. That expires this weekend.'

Kennet's face fell. 'I was looking forward to that. How time goes by.'

'We can take Tomas off your hands for a couple of days,' Kayte suggested. 'Go.'

'I can't. I have to cover for Sergeant Mikkelson. She is apartment hunting in Göteborg.' He waved it away. 'The whales will be there next year.'

'Ooh, we should make it a foursome.' Carey clapped her hands together girlishly. 'Whales are on my bucket list.'

'Maybe when Charlotte's old enough to appreciate it too,' Kayte said.

'You should go with Jana,' Kennet suggested.

For a few seconds, an odd silence bathed the room as eyes darted and brows furrowed.

'You're packing us off on a girl's weekend away?' Carey chuckled. 'Jana and I are hardly—'

'Oh well, it seems you can't even give these free tickets away,' Mrs Carlsson said good-naturedly.

'Oh God, that was horrible. I'm sorry. I meant I didn't want to take away your trip. Not that we're not friends, and I wouldn't enjoy it, and....'

'Stop digging, honey,' Kayte said.

'It was only an idea. You're probably busy anyway,' Kennet said.

Carey and Kayte exchanged a few expressions—and possibly some telepathy, Kennet reckoned.

'I *could* use a break,' Carey admitted.

Kayte met Kennet's eye. 'I could treat Tomas to something. Maybe the Flight Museum? Take him off your hands while you're on shift? Charlotte can tag along. They like hanging out.' She flashed him an encouraging expression.

Kennet wasn't sure. Yes, nine-year-old Tomas played nicely with Charlotte, who was approaching two, but it all felt a little... impulsive.

Yet, saying so risked Kayte trotting out her moans about what she called his "Swedish Reserve". Besides, Jana had been excited about this trip, it was out of peak tourist season, and it would be a good chance for the ladies to bond further....

'This is fine by me. We can make it work. Plus, I suppose it is good... payback for all the times Kayte and I were out having fun, leaving you two at home alone or looking after the children.'

Kayte shoulder-nudged him. 'When he says, "having fun", he means "kicking scumbag ass" or "getting shot at". The streets of DC versus a trip inside the Arctic Circle to watch whales? No contest. You two go. Have a blast. Drink too much. Moan about how your loved ones are never home enough and always worry the hell out of you. I think it's an awesome plan. Makes me wonder why we'd ever consider leaving this place.'

The trio of smiles made Kennet content. He'd always felt that Carey and Jana were dragged along through his and Kayte's rollercoaster of scrapes and high emotion. Now, they'd be able to make some memories, and if it cemented Kayte and Carey's decision to move here permanently, even better.

He couldn't imagine life without them.

# 3

Enna checked her wrist Com: there were a few minutes before she was due at the Gate.

She swore her bladder capacity had decreased since Lexie's birth eighteen months earlier. Or maybe it was merely ageing, reduced fitness, or she'd drunk too much coffee that morning.

A WPD Officer was standing outside the door to the Crew Rest Rooms at Washington Spaceport.

*Huh?*

Assuming the uniform's presence was coincidental, she went to pass by. The man stuck out his arm.

'Sorry, Lieutenant. Please use alternative facilities.'

She tutted loudly. This would mean retracing her steps, making her more likely to be late.

'Please, Officer, I have a flight. Armstrong Base, twelve-hundred.'

He looked her up and down. In a moment of sass, she reciprocated.

His eyes narrowed. 'I'm sorry, Lieutenant. Medical emergency in there.'

She frowned. 'Fleet personnel? They okay?'

'Need to know, Lieutenant. Please—alternative facilities, okay?'

As Enna opened her mouth to form a typically nosy follow-up, a familiar colleague arrived in a fluster.

'Lieutenant,' Gina Devine said.

'Likewise,' Enna replied with a lack of deference she felt she could get away with.

Firstly, no other Fleet personnel were present, and secondly, she was on first-name terms with Gina anyway. She'd mentored the perky blonde over the last two years, which may or may not have contributed to the woman's rapid rise to a rank that it had taken Enna twice as long to achieve in her own career.

'What's up?'

'Ask chuckles here.' Enna thumbed at the Officer, who wasn't amused.

'I got a ping from Purser Svensson. Said she was feeling ill, was going to the restroom. Probably wanted to apologise in advance for being late on deck.' Gina tried to look past the Officer. 'This must be her.'

Enna checked her Com. 'We'll all be late at this rate.'

'I asked the Captain to request a half-hour delay. If Eva's not well, we need to find a replacement cabin crew.' She addressed the Officer. '*Will* we need to find one?'

Enna smiled. It was a great way to ask about the condition of the person inside the WC without actually asking.

The Officer's eyes darted. He leant in. 'I think you will, yeah.'

'It's bad?'

He nodded solemnly.

Enna's eyes widened. 'Jeez.'

'Well, go on.' Gina nudged Enna with her arm.

'Go on what?'

'Flash your credentials.'

'I don't have any credentials, Devine. I'm a Navigator.'

'Fleet PD,' Gina hissed.

Enna laughed. 'That's all over. I'm just your regular, awesome-as-hell Lieutenant, supermom, and, frankly, pretty decent mentor.'

The Officer was eyeing her breast pocket name badge.

*Unless, of course, he's trying to undress me. Which would be flattering, as a forty-one-year-old mom who isn't as pert in the chest department as she once was.*

'Your name is credential enough, Lieutenant Dacourt,' he said.

'Oh no,' Gina said. 'Another autograph hunter.'

'Leave it out, Devine. That was the old me. Besides, this is an ill woman in the restroom. It's hardly a grand corporate conspiracy—which, as you know, was my stock-in-trade.'

'Are there suspicious circumstances?' Gina asked the Officer, ignoring Enna's desire to dump the whole thing. She needed a pee, and a hundred people were waiting to fly to the Moon.

'That will have to wait,' he replied.

'Lieutenant, we should be going,' Enna said.

The door to the restroom opened. A paramedic and another WPD uniform exited, looked around, then beckoned behind.

A gurney was wheeled out. On it lay a zipped body bag.

'Oh God,' Gina murmured.

A temporary hairline crack appeared in Enna's heart. A colleague—someone from the big Fleet family she adored so much—had left the world, and in all likelihood, much too soon.

She found herself grabbing the arm of a second paramedic as he passed.

The guy stopped on a dime and glowered at her. She flashed an apology.

'Sorry. We were... friends,' she lied. 'What happened to... Eva?'

*That was her name, right?*

'Ask the coroner.'

'She said she felt ill,' Gina interjected. 'She was flying with us today.'

The paramedic looked at them suspiciously, then lifted a plastic bag from the end of the gurney. It contained Eva's handbag and wrist Com.

'You're who she messaged?'

Gina nodded.

The guy stepped closer. 'There was no violence, okay? If that's what you're worried about. No assault. Maybe a heart attack. Hard to say. Look, we'd better get going. WPD crime scene will come down. That might help things. Call up the precinct later if you want. When you're back from,' he glanced up, 'work.' He smiled and then left.

'You should call Tom,' Gina said.

'Why?'

'Eva was Fleet, and there might be foul play.'

'That's a huge "might". And who am I to tell him his job?'

Gina shrugged. 'His wife?' She winked.

'Look, Devine, I'm the troublemaker around here. There's no room for two of us on that flight.'

Gina clasped Enna's arm. 'As a favour? Eva and I... had a drink now and again. She was sweet. It's probably nothing, but I thought Tom's job was butting into WPD any time of day or night?'

Enna looked at the door Officer, worried they might be insinuating that the regular PD couldn't handle something as simple as a woman falling ill, then dying, in a Spaceport cubicle.

'No comment,' he said. 'But I hear little acorns grow into oak trees, and then Fleet PD—often a certain Lieutenant Enna Dacourt of that parish—tends to come along and chop them down.'

'See—told you he was a fan,' Gina said.

Enna sighed with deliberate volume. 'Okay, I'll call the boss. Then, and I can't stress this enough, I *really* need to pee.'

# 4

The following day, Wednesday, Kennet was in the Bollnäs polis station when he took a call from a woman named Sara Lindström, who lived near Gävle, which was about 100km away. She'd been the victim of a graffiti attack on her vehicle.

He queried her for a few details and then put in a call to Kayte over at Söderhamn. Both PDs were equidistant from the crime scene—but there was another reason behind his call. Then he went into Chief Inspector Janssen's office, closed the door, and had a private conversation.

The logical transit plan was for Kayte to meet him at the victim's house, but it was a slow day, and his alternative gave additional time for them to hang out, which was never a chore. He collected her from Söderhamn, and they headed south.

'I spoke with Ulrik. About my crazy idea.'

'The one where you send our better halves off to enjoy nature while we're minding the farm?' She winked.

'No. My second crazy idea.'

'Two? *Crazy*?' she scoffed good-naturedly. 'From the King of Swedish Reserve? Surely not.'

He ignored the jibe. 'Chief Inspector thinks it *is* a good idea that all cases related to the Spaceport contract are sent to me. That way, I can spot any patterns, repeat offenders, any actions which go beyond legal right to protest.'

'Like the one we're going to see.'

'Exactly.'

'When you say, "sent to me", do you mean literally?'

A smile tickled his lips. 'I might involve you. If you are nice to me. For a change.'

She gently socked him in the side. 'I'm always nice to you.'

He considered the number of hugs and platonic pecks she'd given him. The conversations they'd had. The shared experiences. How they'd covered each other's backs. Been through emotional troughs and crests. They were arguably so different, yet he couldn't wish for a better duty partner.

'Of course, I'll involve you, Kayte. You are an excellent detective. The Polis is lucky to have you.'

'Enough flattery, Kennet. I'm still a big city girl in a small town, and I don't even speak the language. I'm making my way, at best.'

They were on AutoDrive, so he gave her a long, direct look. 'While I was in with the Chief, I mentioned Sergeant Mikkelson. I may have used your name. He said he would have you on the team in a heartbeat.' He looked deliberately away. 'So, I think you are more than "making your way" in our... slow little country.'

Her eyes narrowed. 'You're serious?'

'It was only to offer you... alternatives. Personally, I can't think of anything worse than having you on the team.' He maintained a commendably straight face.

'God, I hate you.'

'It is mutual.'

They roared with laughter.

Two hours later, they were heading back north.

Sara Lindström, early forties, serious demeanour, had had "Stop The Spaceport" scrawled in red paint down both sides of her car. It had happened overnight, and there were no security cameras in the vicinity. As the head of the Spaceport Siting Committee, she was a prime target. Arguably, however, the perpetrator had missed the logic of the situation.

The Committee wasn't behind the decision to *create* a new Spaceport—somewhere in the region north of Stockholm—merely the choice of location. Only a higher authority had the purview to cancel the project altogether. If a miscreant wanted to target Sara or her colleagues, it should be to seek to influence their ruling on which was the best site.

Whilst Kennet's view was nit-picking, Kayte agreed with it.

'This puts the Lena Ekström dog murder into context,' she said. 'That was clearly aimed at influencing a location decision.'

'And, you might say, implies the perpetrators of these two crimes are unlikely to be the same.'

'Unless they're less literal than you in interpreting the situation.' She winked.

'I agree. But why would the... graffiti artist not target Ms Ekström in the same way?'

Kayte held up her hands. 'Hey—I agree with you. Today's case feels like a OnePlanet stunt. An ideological opposition to mankind's development of spacefaring technology. It's typical non-violent action. Killing a dog? That's some local idiot who doesn't want fifteen square miles of interplanetary hardware in their backyard. And you know what? They have a point. I wouldn't like it either.'

'Nor would I. But I would either accept it or move house. Not commit crimes.'

'That's because you're a cop, Kennet.'

'Plus, don't forget being the King of Swedish Reserve.'

She laughed. 'Yeah, you wouldn't hurt a fly.'

He shook his head. 'Not true. I would very much hurt anyone who went after people I care about.'

'Like Linus Castle, Macario Balic?'

'Absolutely.'

An air of deadly seriousness and reflection held sway for a few seconds. Past cases coursed through his mind.

Kayte puffed a breath. 'So, what do we do about Lindström's car?'

'It's probably unsolvable, but we should send Crime Scene down anyway. Certainly, we should find a way to group all suspected—and definite—Spaceport cases on the system. Make sure we have accurate timelines and don't miss anything. It is unlikely to be the same person here as your Ekström case, but we cannot be sure.'

'It feels like you and I are like a new European arm of Fleet PD,' she joked. 'Especially with things like this.'

He shrugged, sober. 'Perhaps I'll speak to Chief Tom. Remember how this started—how you and I met? An American killer coming here to mess with Fleet matters. What is to say it isn't happening again? Tom should be aware.'

'Think this is the thin end of a new wedge?'

'I hope not. But we both know this Spaceport is a big deal—for many communities and businesses, not to mention Fleet and the local economy. It was never going to pass by without a few protests and hitches.'

'And now the decision is only a few weeks away—right?' she said.

'Yes. Interested parties won't go down without a fight. If they paint a few cars, that is a shame. If they do much worse, you and I—and maybe more polis—will be working long hours.'

She patted his leg. 'Then sending the wives off for a break means we get in their good books beforehand, right?' She beamed.

'I hope it won't be needed. You came here for an easier life, yes?'

'Easier, not easy. I still love the thrill of the chase. Except maybe not literally, and not when bullets are flying. I can't imagine Carey having to raise Charlotte alone.' Her smile was forced and pained.

'Nor Jana with Tomas.'

She shook her head vigorously. 'This is crap. We can't talk like this. You and I have to be damn careful, that's all. We owe it to them as much as we owe it to our uniforms to be the best we can. The two are *not* mutually exclusive.' She smacked her thigh. 'I will not be damn well cowed by assholes who have thrown punches at us in the past. I goddamn love my job. It's no different over here.'

She sighed hard. 'I was *over* this. One dead dog and a custom paint job, and suddenly I think there's a bullet with my name on it. What an idiot.'

He grabbed her hand and squeezed it. 'I've got your back, partner. Always. Look on the bright side. We are ahead of the game now, at least in our minds. We know there will be trouble—the signs are already appearing. We don't need to be surprised.

'And something else—it is likely to happen in our backyard. No wasted time racing across the Atlantic. Look at it this way—if Fleet PD get dragged into a local land squabble, you would be shipped over here anyway. The difference is you already have local knowledge. And you get to go home to Carey every night. I know I missed Jana when I was in Washington with you.'

She smiled. 'Lot to be said for home comforts after a hard day kicking ass, right?'

'True. So, do you think you should warn your Chief at Söderhamn that you might get pulled into more Spaceport cases if I need you, or if Tom and the team do?'

'That's an idea. And why don't you and I get some research done over the weekend while the girls are away? Take the kids out, get them exhausted, then pull a few hours in front of a screen.'

'Proactive policing. I like it. You know, on the Fleet PD cases, I always felt we were one step behind. It would be nice if we could be one step ahead this time.' It was an honest assessment of past failings.

'Yeah, but like you said before, I'd much rather be handing out parking tickets all week and home for dinner at six every night.'

'Me too. But I don't think criminals work that way.'

She waved it away. 'I'm kidding. But one thing's for certain. I gotta say the coffee over here really makes any hard work worthwhile.' She shuddered. 'That stuff Tom and Ellie drink at the office? Poor souls.'

Kennet beamed. 'I have been telling you that for so long. We are converting you! When you invite me over for home-cooked meatballs and lingonberries, I know you will finally be one of us.'

'Then I'll race you. Last one to break either of these cases cooks the four of us dinner.' She offered her hand.

He shook. 'Deal.'

# 5

T om Wagner had to applaud Enna. Not just because, in her adorable way, she'd demand it, but because things had gone exactly how he liked. It wasn't a difficult combination: she could use her nosiness and penchant for winding up in the middle of something, find an interesting case and pass it to him. Then, ideally, she'd butt out before things got dangerous. She'd already taken on the world plenty of times—and won. Now, he wanted her to be a mom and wife with a very cool job.

He'd visited the scene of Eva Svensson's death, talked to WPD, and been kept abreast of developments. When things started to look suspicious, he took the case to Fleet PD. Enna had said that would make Gina Devine happy. He didn't much care, but if it made Enna happy, that was important. Solving it was the key, though.

He took colleague Ellie O'Hara to Svensson's home address in Fairwood on the outskirts of DC. Eva's husband, Don Chadwick (she'd kept her maiden name), was understandably a broken man. They trod carefully through the emotional quagmire, but a few things were clear.

Eva was a dedicated Fleet employee with no apparent grudges against her. She was physically fit, bright, happy, and financially comfortable. Don had no idea why she'd fall ill and then die within thirty minutes. He asked about any news from the coroner, but Tom was unable to help as they weren't seeing the ME until later. Don gave them approval to investigate Eva's phone records, track her movements through security cameras, and talk to anyone they needed. He wanted answers.

On the way back to the Fleet PD office in downtown DC, Tom sought Ellie's opinion. She'd remained guarded during the interview, which tended to be her approach.

Tom looked across at her in the passenger seat. Her freckled, youthful face swam with microexpressions.

She'd come a long way in the two years since he'd poached her from Fleet. She had a nose for hidden motivations, absorbing what was unsaid as well as what was said.

It counterpointed office-based Han's data-focussed, analytical approach, which was a trait of his ASD. They were smart in different ways. Ellie was also different to Enna in that her theories were less wild, prone to hyperbole, and definitely devoid of an undercurrent of sass.

He missed having Enna on the team, and whilst it was arguably illogical that she was in less danger flying a spacecraft to the Moon and back at regular intervals, he wanted her in her comfort zone. Besides, it was like having a mole inside another organisation. Whilst Fleet PD was technically part of both SpaceFleet and Washington PD, Enna was the person with the greatest experience in Fleet, the widest knowledge, and the biggest network. She had certainly made a name for herself in the last three years, and much as she hated it, her reputation preceded her.

The car zipped along the DC urban freeway.

'There's something in there,' Ellie said finally. 'I get a feeling in my bones about Don.'

Tom hadn't seen anything beyond grief. 'How so?'

'Like maybe he's out from under something.' She faced Tom. 'Like there's a silver lining.'

'Because he knew she was ill already?'

Ellie shook her head. 'No. I mean, the coroner will tell us either way, but... I don't know. Feels like he lived under her shadow, and now he has space to be himself.'

Tom gave a faint smile. 'Because he has a regular day job, and his wife has a much more exciting life jetting around the planet? I can identify with that.'

'No. If I was being cruel and judgemental—and maybe a little jealous—I'd say that when he married a woman who was from a wealthy family, he maybe expected to live better than a townhouse in a pretty average neighbourhood.'

Tom's eyes widened. 'He was after the insurance payout?'

'Not that he was responsible—only that it cushions the blow pretty damn nicely.'

'Wow. So, you think we should talk to him again?'

'I think we should follow her movements, speak to the ME, and see which way the wind blows. Which I know was the agenda anyway, but still.' She chuckled. 'It's weird. Part of me always wants the simple explanation, the accidents, proof that people are generally good. The easy, quick wrap-up. But the nosy, suspicious girl—the budding detective you hoped you hired—wants a challenge. A labyrinth.' She eyed him. 'So I can show you my chops. Earn my salary. Make a difference.'

'Don't worry, Ellie. You're invaluable.'

They went to a coffee shop called Hot Stuff. Don had concurred that it had been Eva's last stop before the Spaceport. She was something of a creature of habit, always grabbing a takeout here before her flight shift.

Tom took the opportunity to get him and Ellie a coffee—partly to butter up the staff. Then he showed Eva's picture to the barista and asked if she remembered the woman coming into the café two days previously.

'I wasn't on shift,' she replied. 'I think... Brad was on. Were you, Brad?'

Brad came over. He looked at the picture, but it didn't ring a bell. He suggested Tom come back the following day to speak to a guy called Viggo, who was working on the morning Eva died.

Ellie took down Viggo's details in case they had time to contact him without waiting a day.

So, that had been a washout, Tom mused as they left. All the same, poor Eva had had great taste: the coffee was amazing.

They went directly to the ME's office.

Tom had had a few encounters with Dr Finkelman, a greying, wiry man with a dry manner overlaying a fierce intellect.

The three of them stood around the slab where Eva lay. Tom noted Ellie holding in emotion. It wasn't the first time she'd seen a body, but usually, they were of suspects or unsavoury people. Eva Svensson, a youthful and attractive forty, was neither.

After the usual, often redundant preamble, Finkelman gave them news which turned the case. Traces of a toxin were found in Eva's bloodstream. The doctor hypothesised—although Tom had confidence in the man's experience and knowledge—that the existence of the traces was an accident. The toxin was designed to be undetectable but had reacted with an agent which betrayed its presence.

He was pretty sure the poison had been mixed with coffee.

# 6

Matteo Svensson allowed himself a really good cry. After all, he wasn't a monster, was he? He and Eva *had* shared some good times, although they were long past. They didn't see eye to eye about many things, and being a OnePlanet supporter hadn't done her any favours. Those people were parochial idiots.

He mooched around his modest Uppsala abode. He missed the previous house. This place didn't befit him. If only that last investment hadn't gone south. This is the problem when you're too smart; everyone else is an idiot. Even people who are supposed to guarantee a cast-iron opportunity.

He gulped down the shot of brännvin. He excused its mid-morning indulgence as medicinal. Even modest grief needs attending to.

In the lounge diner, his tabletop Com bleeped.

He'd expected that a call would be forthcoming over the last day or so, but he hadn't expected it to be from Wilmer. Wilmer never called. But then, these were extraordinary circumstances.

'Dad.' Saying that word was difficult.

'Mat.' His father seldom used the word "son"—certainly not since Matteo's youthful indiscretion had ruined everything.

'What's up?'

'Have you heard about your sister?' Wilmer's lush grey hair was immaculately coiffured, as befitting a billionaire. Behind him, the long dining room of the family mansion stretched out.

Mat tried to conceal the wrinkling of his nose. All that wasted space, when he was living in a six-room apartment. What happened to families looking out for each other? "You did", Wilmer would say.

'No, what about her?' He'd decided to feign ignorance.

Dad told him she was dead. He pretended not to know. He fell deliberately sullen. He sympathised: she was always Dad's favourite. Anders was the one he was most proud of. Eva was the one he loved most. Mat? A poor third place. They both knew it.

'I'm surprised you called,' he said.

'We're still family,' Wilmer said.

'In name only.'

Wilmer scoffed and looked away. 'And whose fault is that?'

There were plenty of answers to this perennial question.

Mat knew his existence hadn't been planned; it was an accident after Mum and Dad got back together following Dad's stupid affair. So, arguably, Dad was at fault for Mat's birth. Yet, Mum was the one who'd foregone birth control, keen to have another child to cement the revival of their marriage. Dad always resented her for that. It balanced out her disgust at his affair.

Mat had done the maths to ensure he wasn't secretly the product of that affair. Years ago, he'd asked Dad straight, just to be sure. Dad remained coy, but Mum had confirmed he was hers. She'd loved him. Unfortunately, she was the one who hadn't made it this far: an unexpected heart attack had seen to that.

As if things weren't bad enough back then, Dad blamed Mat for her death. If there had ever been any chance he'd give his youngest son the time of day, that event had put paid to it. Aged sixteen, he'd fought with Dad after finding out about the affair. They'd kept it from him until then. He went ballistic, joining the dots to find reasons why Dad cared so little about him, and unleashed a tirade. Mum tried to break up the war of words, but the stress of the scrap pushed her poor heart beyond its limits.

So, here he was. His elder brother was a paranoid overachiever who looked down on Mat because he hadn't done enough to make his father proud. His sister was dead because of her stubbornness and refusal to see reason. His father had all but disowned him years ago. The only person he'd willingly turn to was his mother, and allegedly he'd triggered her passing.

This wasn't the first time everything had to be the fault of little Matteo Svensson. What happened at university wasn't truly his mistake, but the judge hadn't seen it that way, and six months in prison was the result. That was the nail in the coffin for any semblance of family ties. Dad, who could have posted bail or hired a better lawyer to defend the case, hung his unwanted son out to dry. Apparently, it was to show Mat that he needed to stand on his own two feet and learn from his mistakes.

All it achieved was to help Mat gain some useful friends, breed simmering resentment and suspicion, and turn his back on ever trying to make Dad proud. Wilmer wouldn't care. Anyway, sooner or later, Wilmer would die, putting Mat in line for a huge inheritance—so why waste years of his life working harder than he needed to? Why pay into a pension he'd never need?

The niggling problem was that he was never sure the inheritance was guaranteed. It would be just like the spiteful old man to write Mat out of his will—a parting shot from the grave, and proof that a son who lets down the family name deserves no reward. That would be a farce: there was more than enough money in Wilmer's assets to go around, even if it was split three ways.

Eva never cared about the money—she was an independent career woman who wanted to make her own way, not live off charity.

Anders was a millionaire already and didn't need a financial leg-up.

Matteo was the one who life had dealt a bum hand and the most in need of a break. He couldn't come right out and ask Wilmer whether he was named in the inheritance—that would seem disingenuous, especially now Eva had died. He'd come across like an ungrateful, whiney, money-grabbing cast-off. Unfortunately, that's exactly what he was.

The brief call with Dad lurched to a conclusion. He committed to attending Eva's funeral, which would take place when she'd been repatriated to her homeland. He wanted to remain on speaking terms with Wilmer for whatever came next.

He played loud music to exorcise the frustration of having to speak to his father. He cursed himself for not at least mentioning the development proposal. After all, the loss of his daughter might have softened the man's mind towards the sensible decision. Would it be so crazy to honour her memory by at least *entertaining* the advances of Fleet, the employer she worked for so diligently?

Mat scoffed; Wilmer was even more stubborn than she was. Perhaps Anders, as a fellow man of wealth, could be persuaded to have a word in Dad's ear. If Anders was as truly committed to collecting wealth as he appeared, wasn't it sensible to line his future with gold? If Dad received a huge windfall, some of it would trickle down. It might mean Anders didn't have to work so hard or travel so much. What man wants to labour unnecessarily when he can take an easier route to extra zeros in his bank account?

He called his brother, who at forty-two was elder by nine years. He didn't mention having spoken to their father—it wouldn't do any good.

Anders seemed pretty devastated; he and Eva got on so well.

'How are you doing with it, Mat? Bothered at all?' Even for a typically frosty and clipped manner, this was a new low for Anders.

'That is a hateful thing to say. It may not look like it, but I love you all and would never lay a finger on you. People die, Anders—it's a fact, whether it's explainable or not.'

'Well, the cops in America are saying it may not have been a heart attack. They reckon foul play.'

Matteo's heart jolted. 'Either way, it won't bring her back—and that's what's important. We've lost a sister.' He forced a derisory scoff. 'I always told her Washington was too dangerous. She should have stayed at home.'

'You're not the boss of her. In fact, you're not the boss of much.'

'Get lost, Anders. Just because you're the big I Am, running your little money-making empire, locked inside that prison you call a house.'

'Listen, *baby brother*, whilst nobody in the world gives a shit about a snidey disappointment like you—who, remember, is the one of us who's seen the inside of an actual prison—what I do has risks. You think I like having a bodyguard twenty-four-seven?'

Enough to hire him based on looks, then wind up sleeping with him, Mat thought. But this was an ideal opening in the conversation he wanted to have.

'So why not take the opportunity to get out of a risky line of work? Why the obsession with making things harder? For an entrepreneur, you're oddly good at looking a gift horse in the mouth.'

'What gift horse?' Anders asked.

'The Spaceport contract. Dad will listen to you. It's billions of kronor just for handing over land that's lying idle. Dad probably can't be bothered with the bullshit of contract negotiation. That's why he's turning a blind eye. *You're* the business genius. Tell him you'll handle the whole affair. Do it for... I don't know... in exchange for the interest payments. Free money—and I don't need to point out you'll inherit the assets later anyway.'

There was an odd pause, during which Mat believed he'd made a breakthrough. But it wasn't to be.

'Why do you care what happens to my inheritance? Especially as you'll be getting next to nothing. You think you're anything more than a footnote in Dad's good books? This is typical of you, Mat—getting other people to do your dirty work. You want to convince Dad to change his mind? You do it. Even I wouldn't stand a chance. You do *know* he still follows that OnePlanet mantra? Not openly, of course. But you think he'd want to sell half his land in direct counterpoint to his principles?' Anders laughed.

'So how come Eva was the apple of his eye? She worked for Fleet—which is the epitome of the enemy of the OnePlanet ethos.'

Anders tutted. 'Shades of grey, Mat. Fleet has been around for longer than you've graced this planet with your presence. You can't undo that. What people can do—or what those anti-development nutcases want—is to hold back *more* progress. Stop us where we are. Dad wanted Eva—and us—to be happy. She was. It doesn't mean he'll throw away a few square miles of beautiful Uppsala just to fatten his bank account.'

'He's an idiot.'

'No. He has principles. Now, I have to go. Don't make an ass of yourself over this. It's not your problem. Get on with... whatever it is you do.'

'Like you care.'

'Honestly, Mat, I don't really. I want you to stay out of trouble for once. That's something I know about.'

'More death threats?' Mat asked.

Anders had received oblique warnings before. It caused the man's paranoia. He prided himself on being untouchable. Impressively, given how much he travelled—and remained visible in the digital world—there had been no near misses. It lent credence to the belief that the death threats were no more than rants and jealousy.

'Not now. I've got things to sort. I've a meeting in Narvik on Saturday, and the guy is insisting I come out whale watching. Trying to make a social occasion out of a business proposition. You think I care about whales? You think I want to be standing on the edge of a boat where someone could recognise me and find it's an ideal opportunity to make an assassination look like an accident?'

Mat rolled his eyes. Anders was always living under the misapprehension that anyone truly cared what a random Swedish businessman got up to and would seek deadly force. At worst, he might be a target of kidnapping and blackmail if someone wanted to get leverage out of their father and demand a few million in ransom. Besides, that's why Anders had a bodyguard. Nobody ever got close enough to do something obvious, like push him overboard.

'You should go, brother. Take a break. You're always so tightly wound. Plus, you just had a family bereavement. Get some Artic air in your lungs. Chill—literally.'

'Whatever. You're hardly top of my favourite list of advice-givers. So long as I close the deal, I don't care. Anyway, please at least try to be sad about Eva. She did care about you. See you at the funeral.'

The connection ended.

Mat stood and paced. Amongst all that bullshit was a nugget of gold. There was urgent work to do.

# 7

Over breakfast on Thursday morning, while Enna fed Lexie, Tom called up Kennet in Sweden.

The time difference meant it was after lunch there. It wasn't unusual for Tom to work from home, and Enna never minded, but this time it was a bonus because she liked catching up with her erstwhile colleague too.

In the event, it was even better because Kayte also was at Bollnäs PD, and Enna really missed her. Since Kayte and Carey had relocated the previous year, she'd had limited opportunities to catch up.

Enna knew Tom's call was ostensibly work-related but couldn't help hijacking the first few minutes to catch up on gossip, ask about Charlotte, and comment on Kayte's uncharacteristically long hair. The peroxide pixie cut of the New York-era Kayte was long gone. Kennet looked unchanged, except maybe he'd put on a couple of pounds.

Kayte cooed over how cute Lexie was getting and asked Enna about her current flight roster. This lead nicely to the sad discovery that Enna and Gina Devine had unwittingly made.

'Did you get my message about Eva Svensson?' Tom asked.

He'd felt that, as the victim was a native Swede, he should keep Kennet in the loop. It hadn't taken much research to find out she was connected to a wealthy family, and whilst no motivation had yet been discovered for her apparent murder, one or more threads might lead back to Scandinavia.

'Yes,' Kennet replied. 'I have requested access to the file. If anything turns up here, I will keep you informed.'

'How are you getting on with any perps?' Kayte asked.

'Ellie and I are following up with this Viggo guy today. It's a long shot, but he may have been the last person to see her alive. Seems like she fell ill on the way from the coffee shop to the Spaceport. He may have seen someone suspicious hanging around—they could have spiked her coffee.'

'Why?'

'Million-dollar question. We can't find evidence of any debts, enemies or grudges. Yes, it could be random, but Ellie got an odd vibe off the husband, plus the elephant in the room is that her father is worth a few hundred million.'

'Too late for blackmail or ransom if she's dead,' Kennet said.

'Absolutely. But that doesn't mean it's not connected to Wilmer Svensson's life and business empire. Hence why I looped you in. Keep your ears to the ground.'

'He's not known for taking visitors, that man.'

'I'm not suggesting an interview. Just... making you aware.' Tom smiled. 'Can't have you bored over there, with the forests and clean air and laudably low murder rate.'

'We're keeping busy,' Kayte replied. She relayed Kennet's remit around the Spaceport project, plus their two potentially linked cases.

The call wrapped up with more pleasantries, then Tom and Enna took Lexie out to the car and drove to the Fort Valley town kindergarten. From there, they headed into DC. Enna had a free day and was going shopping. Tom was collecting Ellie from the office and visiting Viggo's apartment.

Enna studied Tom for a long time. It wasn't a chore—she fancied him as much now as she had done the first day they met.

'You do believe me, don't you? About what happened at the restroom?'

'Absolutely. After all, you've never needed to go looking for trouble—it's always found you first.' He beamed.

She socked him on the arm. 'Come on, Tom—law of averages. Fleet is a huge organisation. Spaceport is a huge place. Employees are going to die.' She fiddled with her wedding ring. 'I just wish it was only natural causes.'

He took her hand. 'Don't take it personally. That was your kryptonite for so long. You're over that. This has nothing to do with you. It had nothing to do with Gina either—other than they were sometime friends. Plus, you do have someone remarkable on the case.' He winked.

'I guess. Shame she's got you for a partner, though.'

As the car was on AutoDrive, and Enna's adorable cheekiness needed retribution, he pounced on her, tickling furiously.

Tom and Ellie arrived at Viggo Alban's apartment at eleven-fifteen. As he wasn't on shift at the café that day, and hence likely to be at home, they were disappointed when he didn't answer the door.

Despite patience, tactful queries, and then hammering on the door, they got nowhere. It sounded quiet inside, but that wasn't conclusive, so Tom called the office and asked Han to ping Viggo's Com. The handset was showing as located inside the apartment.

Ellie went down to the ground floor, fetched the building superintendent, and the guy cautiously opened the door.

Tom led her in, sweeping the way with his sidearm, careful as mice.

Viggo wasn't asleep or hiding. Fortunately—especially for him—he also wasn't lying dead. Tom knew that had been a possibility: the Fleet PD team had stumbled across more than one such scenario.

As the occupant was a legitimate suspect, they toured the four rooms, taking care not to disturb more than was necessary. An open, souring bottle of milk on the kitchen worktop indicated Viggo hadn't been home for many hours.

In the bathroom, they hit paydirt. In the cabinet, amongst various bottles and pills, was a half-empty vial labelled with a skull and crossbones.

'I'm guessing that's not shampoo for pirates,' Ellie said, eyes wide.

'No. Five bucks says it matches what Finkelman found.'

With any luck, they had the metaphorical smoking gun that had killed Eva Svensson. But where was the man who'd fired it?

# 8

Matteo woke in Sara Lindström's bed. He enjoyed the feeling because it invariably meant they'd spent the previous evening messing the sheets up.

For an older woman, she had great stamina. That was only the icing on the cake, however. Crucially, they were sleeping together, which meant they talked, which meant she had his confidence and he had influence over her. It was one of the key cogs in the vast mechanism he was running.

It had been a late night, but she'd left the bed early as someone was coming to assess the damage to her car: some prick had daubed "Stop the Spaceport" on it. She'd known that taking the position as Committee Head would open her up to potential vilification, but it paid well, she was admirably qualified, and the job was pretty much guaranteed for five years. Since her divorce, it was an ideal way to pay the bills.

Matteo took a shower. The divorce had also given Sara the motivation to have a fling with a younger man. He smiled. Sadly, she was getting much less out of their relationship than he was. If only she knew his real name.

After a late brunch in her kitchen, he made his excuses and left. While she'd cooked dinner the previous evening, he'd taken the opportunity to secretly scan her messages for any new information, then later asked her permission to use the terminal to check some information on the web.

As the AutoDrive took him to his next rendezvous, he made a call. It went to voicemail.

'This is Mat. It's a go for tomorrow. I'll send the details later. Get prepared. No screw-ups.'

At the jewellery shop, he carefully chose something which was more than he wanted to spend but which wouldn't raise suspicion that it was stolen or forged.

The next conversation had to be handled delicately: it was the lynchpin of the endeavour.

Afterwards, he found a café and killed time working on his day job. He sent a few messages, did more research.

Late in the afternoon, he drove to Anna Persson's house.

She'd just arrived home from work and was pleased, if not surprised, to see him. The gift of the necklace went down well, and she was appropriately grateful.

He wasn't as attracted to her as he was to Sara, despite being more his age. It didn't matter; he wasn't dating her for her looks. He cooked her up some dinner, then steered the conversation down a specific alley.

Over the past few weeks, he'd wormed his way into her confidence, feigning interest in her job and teasing out the mechanics of how flight crew scheduling was controlled. He'd said it was because his sister, "Karin", was considering the same line of work. He'd discussed hypothetical scenarios, asked her to recount some funny anecdotes about scheduling screw-ups, and methodically collected data which he filed away in his sharp mind.

They retired to the sofa. When the conversation stumbled, and he wasn't able to find the words to unlock her compliance, he buttered her up with compliments, morphed the embrace into a passionate clench, and then performed oral sex on her.

Within fifteen minutes, she was at her computer screen, providing him with the required information. As he watched, grateful and relieved that the pieces of the puzzle were falling into place, he saw an unusual, unseen beauty in her face. It worried him—an attachment was forming. He'd spent a long time debating what would happen after today—whenever 'today' ended up occurring. He was torn, and he didn't like it.

Killing her was too cruel and unnecessary, surely?

He put it out of his mind.

He wasn't sure that she believed the reason why he'd asked for the information, although he'd done his best to make it sound plausible. It didn't matter—the result was achieved.

It was nine o'clock in the evening, but not too late to pass on the details to the three contacts who needed to act. He excused himself into her small garden, so he could talk privately.

It was a clear night, and the stars were out. In a few short years, Fleet ships would be leaving from not far away and rising towards those stars.

When his tasks were complete, he found her in the kitchen, poured them a healthy glass of wine and then, because it couldn't do any harm, he told Anna Persson he loved her. It made her happy, which was all he really cared about, because her actions that evening were likely to make him infinitely happier in the long term.

# 9

On Friday morning, Kayte, Carey and Charlotte arrived at Kennet's house. Kayte was dressed for work, Carey for a weekend away, and Charlotte for preschool. They had grabbed a day's spot at the Bollnäs preschool that Tomas had attended when young.

Jana hadn't told Tomas that she was going away to see whales, so he didn't feel left out. She said she was visiting friends a long way away.

Kennet and Carey took both children to their respective places in his car. He could tell Carey was nervous about leaving young Charlotte in an unusual establishment, but he reassured her that they took good care of children: Tomas had loved it. Carey wasn't so sure—the preschool in Söderhamn was well-used to catering for Charlotte's need for English as a first language.

Kennet pointed out that Charlotte seemed to get along fine with gestures, play, and understanding a few key Swedish words. Children were sponges at that age, and if Carey and Kayte did choose to make a life here, Charlotte would have a head start with a second language. As her godfather and biological father, he always wanted the best for her—and was sure that Carey and Kayte knew it.

They loaded the weekend cases, Jana and Kayte jumped in the car, and Kennet drove to Bollnäs rail station. From there, the ladies were heading to Stockholm for their Narvik flight.

On the concourse outside, there were hugs all around.

Carey glanced at Jana. 'Think they'll cope?'

'What, the children or the grown-ups? I don't know which are worse.'

Kayte shot them mock daggers. 'Oh, don't worry, we'll all have a... *whale* of a time.'

Carey rolled her eyes. 'Sorry, Kennet. Hate to saddle you with this for three whole days.'

Kennet tagged onto her jibing. 'I can always talk to Tomas if I want intelligent conversation.'

Kayte whacked him on the arm.

A passer-by looked amused at the sight of two uniformed cops play-fighting.

'Play nicely,' Jana said. 'Set a good example to the children.'

Kennet mock saluted her. 'Yes, sweet.'

'Oh, God.' Carey tugged Jana's arm. 'Let's go.'

The weekenders wheeled their cases towards the station entrance, turned and blew kisses to their respective partners, laughed at an unheard private joke, then disappeared.

Kayte pulled her uniform jacket taut. 'Right, Inspector Carlsson. Let's go and fight some crime.'

In the Bollnäs polis station, they followed up on the first two incidents that Kennet had allocated to the new "Spaceport" folder. He hoped these would also be the final two—but held out little hope. Kayte had told him that the construction of the Washington Spaceport, which happened in her youth, had made the news weekly—and not always for the right reasons.

As Kennet had his own partitioned office, they brought in a second chair and terminal, so Kayte could work alongside him, and they didn't disturb the other four cops who busied themselves with the smattering of low-level local incidents.

Crime scene investigations on the daubing of Sara Lindström's car had turned up zero. The best Kennet and Kayte could do was assemble a list of known OnePlanet activists in Stockholm, Uppsala and Gävleborg counties. The Spaceport was going to be sited at one of three—possibly four—locations, most likely in Uppsala County.

A few activists had already been hauled in for public order offences at each of the three key greenfield sites. These names were top of Kennet's list. Kayte put together a contact sheet for key polis individuals in diverse locations across the region who they might need to liaise with.

Lena Ekström, whose dog was killed, had received previous intimidating communiques via post. Forensics had examined the envelope, paper and printer ink, but were unable to narrow down potential sources to any meaningful shortlist. They had tried to trace the bullet without success. Canvassing local residents had also come up empty.

Whoever was behind this attempted blackmail seemed to be more than a disgruntled citizen who was trying to keep a vast construction project away from his back door. Kennet sympathised: he'd hate to have the Bollnäs district torn up by endless machinery and then nights made sleepless by the roars of space vessels. It was ever thus: everyone wanted more convenient transport networks, but nobody wanted them built on their doorstep. The issue went back decades, if not centuries.

Shortly after lunch, Tom video-called from DC. That felt unusually early, EST, but quickly Kennet and Kayte discovered why.

'Viggo Alban was found dead last night.' Tom rubbed his forehead.

'Good news, bad news, I guess,' Kayte said. 'Proves he's the killer but doesn't help us discover why.' She sighed. 'This shit keeps happening.'

'First rule of assassination. Kill the assassin.' Tom thumped the desk.

'Or break as many links as you can. This means the rabbit hole goes deeper than a simple grudge.'

'Probably,' Kennet added. 'How did he die?'

'Contact poison. He was found on a park bench. No sign of what he touched. Maybe a fake payoff.' Tom held a crime scene photo up to the webcam. 'I'll send you all this. You have access to the file anyhow. CSI and Han are working through everything. Doesn't look hopeful. It's a fair bet that something orchestrated this well will be hard to trace.' He shrugged. 'Anyway, we'll turn over all the rocks.'

'Did Alban have history?' Kayte asked.

'Read his sheet, Connors. But... yeah. Start trawling known associates, the usual. At the moment, we have no clue why he'd target Fleet cabin crew—especially as there's been no collateral noise regarding her family. Ellie and I will go back to her husband again. I'd suggest you talk to Wilmer Svensson, but it's a long shot that you'd get in the door, let alone it's unlikely he'd have the slightest clue why his daughter was killed.'

'We could talk to her brothers,' Kennet suggested.

'Whatever you think best. Pretty sure the answer is in DC, not over there, but knock yourselves out—if you have time.'

'It's crime against Fleet, and she was born here, so it's easy to say that it belongs on our radar. We're not making much headway on the other two things Kennet and I are working on. We have a full weekend, but we'll look at this Monday. Alban's not going to be poisoning anyone else meantime.'

Tom peered hard down the lens. 'No, but whoever killed him might.'

Kayte nodded. 'Then let's hope they leave a clue next time. Or show a pattern.'

'Yeah. Anyway, Han is going through Eva's life with a magnifying glass. Maybe you do the same with Alban. I've requisitioned access to his life. I'll give you access. Right, Ellie is demanding donuts because it's Friday, and she's giving me the puppy dog eyes treatment, so I'll sign off. Shout if you get anything.'

Kayte fired a one-finger salute and ended the call.

'Coffee?' Kennet asked.

'Always.'

Midway through their coffee break, Kennet's Com pinged.

"I love you" was Jana's message. He smiled.

Moments later, Kayte's wrist beeped.

'Aw,' she said. 'At least we're not forgotten about.'

'They're probably making jokes at our expense already.'

'Can we help it if we're dedicated to our work?'

'Someone has to stay at home and watch the store.'

She laughed. '"Mind the store". Never a dull moment with you, Kennet. But yeah.' She checked the clock. 'Come on, let's look at this dead killer asshole before it's time to pick up the kids.'

They collected Tomas from school, then Charlotte from preschool, and went back to Kennet's. He helped Tomas with his homework while Kayte prepared Charlotte's dinner, then spoon-fed the toddler in the highchair that Kennet kept in the cupboard for such visits.

Charlotte had struggled to nap at the unfamiliar school, but around five o'clock she became bleary-eyed, so Kayte put her in Tomas' old crib in the spare room. Tomas went to his room to play.

'Do you want to stay for dinner?' Kennet asked.

'Yeah, but no booze. I'll take her home in good time. Whatever you can cook up is fine.'

He busied himself in the kitchen while she put her feet up on the sofa.

He smiled, seeing her act so at home. It was understandable; they'd been through a lot in this house. It was no different when he'd stayed at her place after Carey was shot—he fell into being something of an occasional housemate. Though there were few parallels with his first few weeks sharing an apartment with Jana twenty years previously, it turned his thoughts to her. He grabbed his Com and sent her a gushy message, then resumed cooking.

There was a noise of breaking glass.

At least she won't have spilt red wine on the pale sofa, he mused, hurrying in to check the extent of the mess.

Kayte was sitting bolt upright on the sofa, tremoring like she was in a deep freeze. Her breath came in irregular gulps, and her face was pale.

The tumbler was broken on the ground. She'd only spilt water. Things didn't compute.

Her head seemed to turn with extreme effort, like her neck was rusted up. Her expression was as if she'd witnessed Armageddon. A juddering arm reached for the distant media screen.

A reporter was standing in front of a scorched hillside. '...investigators on the scene here are refusing to speculate, but it seems unlikely that anyone could have survived.'

Kennet glanced at Kayte, his mind joined two dots, and his chest tightened.

'Flight AS166 from Stockholm to Narvik took off on time at fourteen-twenty with fifty-three passengers and four crew aboard.'

His legs weakened, and he sat hard on the sofa arm.

'Approximately ten minutes after takeoff, the aircraft disappeared from radar. It is not known whether any distress call was sent....'

Kayte's scream was so terrifyingly piercing, girlish and uncharacteristic that it tore through him like a gunshot.

He clasped at his tight throat, hands shaking, willing oxygen to enter his surely depleted bloodstream, to reinvigorate his brain, to flush out the hallucination that he must unaccountably be having.

But Kayte's detonation into appalling, hysterical sobs was unbearably real.

He collapsed to the floor, convulsing in withheld disbelief and despair.

# 10

Tomas appeared in the doorway, his young face writ with confusion and worry.

Kennet stumbled to his feet and wiped his sodden face.

'What... is it?' he asked.

'Somebody screamed,' Tomas said.

'Oh, I'm sorry.' Kayte didn't turn around. She clicked the remote, and the horrendous reality vanished. 'Sorry, Tomas,' she said brokenly and hoarse. 'I had the film on too loud. It was a nasty one. I'm so sorry.'

Tomas was glancing between the adults, unsure.

Kennet eyed the stairs in case Charlotte had been woken too. He hoped not. A sliver of paternal instinct fought through the incomprehension and devastation which drowned his soul.

'Come on, buddy. Show me what you've been doing.'

Still vibrating in shock, he led his son upstairs, mind reeling with the notion that the poor boy had probably just lost his mother. How would Kennet ever summon the wherewithal to break the news—assuming it was true?

He shook his head, parking that task, and gathered a few fragments of steely resolve to follow Tomas into his room and feign interest in the multi-coloured monsters he'd drawn.

There was no sound from the spare room, no toddler's cry.

Kennet worked hard to focus, but after five minutes, he couldn't bear to leave Kayte alone downstairs, surely rent with shock. The last time something like this had happened—no, infinitely easier than this in retrospect—she'd fallen apart, drinking, vomiting and making a stupid pass at him.

Now? He worried for her deeply. For a woman so tough, she broke with surprising ease.

He found Tomas a jigsaw to do, told the boy that he needed to help 'Auntie' Kayte clear up her spilt drink, and measured his wobbly legs down the stairs to the lounge.

She was curled on the sofa, foetal, quivering.

He left her for a minute, carefully cleared the broken glass into the kitchen—so they didn't have physical injuries to go with their mental trauma—and took the dinner off the stove.

He perched on the sofa arm. 'Kayte?' he said gently.

She rounded on him with scarcely believable speed and venom.

'You did this! I wish we'd never come here! You goddamn bastard, Kennet. Being all nice and welcoming. Putting a flea in my ear about how wonderful your country was. Now see what you did! My wife is dead!'

Her face was red, and her eyes blazed. 'I wish you'd never come to New York. You started this. You and your stupid country boy handshake. We come here to get away from killers and risk and death, and look!' She pointed at the blank screen. 'Stupid goddamn vacation. Stupid goddamn country. You've ruined my life! Go to hell!'

She stumbled to her feet, rapped her ankles on the coffee table and wailed in pain.

She hobbled to the stairs. 'I'm getting my daughter. Mine. Not yours. She's all I have left. Leave her the hell alone. We're going home. Don't ever call me again.'

She clattered up the steps.

Kennet's already splinted heart disintegrated.

Charlotte began to wail.

Kayte, herself on the brink of more tears, carried the protesting toddler down to the lounge, plonked her on the sofa, and hastily assembled their things.

'Look, Kayte—'

'Shut up!'

His life was over, and he had no choice but to let it happen.

Two minutes later, the door banged, and she was gone.

Broken, probably widowed, and without his best friend in the world, the shell which used to be Kennet Carlsson finished the dinner for two, didn't bother serving it up, but ate from the pans like a vagrant.

He wanted to speak to somebody, message somebody, but knew he'd never get past the first word without descending into a wreck. The house felt icily empty. He didn't dare switch on the news—he couldn't bear hearing the truth spoken again, the announcement of his apocalypse.

Robotically, he put Tomas to bed at the appointed time, conjuring his best impression that nothing was amiss. Mummy was still away. Far away. She'd be a while. She was with 'Auntie' Carey.

It took every ounce of strength to hold himself together.

All the while, the same mantra played in his head: it was, as Kayte had said, his fault. He'd suggested the women take the trip. He *was* trying to be nice. All he wanted was for his family and friends to get along, have fun and enjoy companionship.

No, he hadn't crashed that plane—he hadn't been directly responsible—but he'd pressed some kind of trigger. The cause of the disaster didn't matter; the outcome was the same.

Assuming the news and the correspondent were correct. Assuming the ladies hadn't missed the flight.

He scrambled for his phone. His last message was showing as undelivered.

Realisation gripped him.

"I love you" hadn't been a simple platitude from Jana. It was her final words. Probably as the plane was going down. Carey, too, in her message to Kayte, whatever it had said.

He broke out in sobs.

Ten minutes later, he dug out a bottle of brännvin and poured four fingers worth. He sat, sipping it, staring blankly, hollow inside.

Soon would come a phone call from the authorities. Possibly a knock on the door. He'd seen it enough times in his career. The sombre-faced messengers of doom:

"Mr Carlsson. It's about your wife. May we come in?"

He cried more, glancing upwards, hoping the noise didn't wake his poor boy.

He was drained, but there was no point in going to bed early. There was no point in going to bed at all. He'd never sleep. He might never sleep again, only stew on what had happened, curse himself for causing it, grieve to his marrow for Jana, and mourn the permanent estrangement from his friend and colleague.

He knew it had barely sunk in. Only hours without his wife, and he was already bereft. Even less time without Kayte, and he felt like he'd never in his life possessed a single friend.

He sought a grain of hope from somewhere. He wanted to call Arlanda airport or AirSweden and ask for details or clarification, but he couldn't face it. The measured, steadfast man was absent, possibly forever. The "Swedish Reserve" had collapsed in on itself like a dying star so that reserve and inaction were all he was.

On the side table was a picture of Tomas, aged five.

That was his grain of hope.

It was all he had left in life.

At nine thirty-five, there was a gentle knock on the door.

He fought back the sobs which wanted to flood his throat. He needed to face the visitor as, at the very worst, a shocked but together Inspector. Otherwise, the word might get back to Chief Janssen, and Kennet would be put on compassionate leave. That was the last thing he wanted. Besides looking after Tomas, he'd need to throw himself into his work if he was to retain his sanity and get through the hours and days which would seemingly stretch out forever.

His shoulders fell: he'd be working alone now. Fun wouldn't be a part of his day job. His shadow, mirror, partner, confidant, sounding board, and the devilishly angelic thorn in his side wouldn't be working cases with him again. If she had any sense, she'd be on the next plane back to DC, her life in tatters.

He took a deep breath and opened the door.

The person on the step was indeed a Swedish policewoman. He knew her.

He knew her birthday, her favourite song, her waist measurement, her daughter's middle name, and that she wasn't really a *Swedish* policewoman.

She was American.

# 11

Tom, Ellie and Han spent Friday combing through the life of Eva Svensson.

There were no obvious flags. She'd visited nowhere suspicious nor taken any calls which couldn't easily be traced. Still, they contacted everyone she'd called or messaged in the seven days before her murder.

They called Fleet HR and obtained her employment record. It was squeaky clean.

Han had trawled her husband's life and found nothing. Yes—killing a spouse in order to claim the insurance was a classic trick, but there were no warning signs. All the same, they supplemented the To Do list with a dig into her will, his employment record, his phone records and his browser history.

Tom had never liked this part: essentially eavesdropping on the minutiae of people's lives—usually innocent people. He hated to think that anyone would ever have access to his Com records, but at least the endless banter and smooching with Enna would keep them amused and heartened.

They hadn't uncovered any link between Eva and Viggo. He was a barista at a place she frequented: that was the crux of the connection. It was logical that anyone who knew her and her preferences could use the coffee shop as a potential site for instigating her murder.

Viggo was ideally placed. He probably took her order, then slipped the toxin into her drink whilst preparing it. He'd worked at the café for many months, so it was unlikely he was specifically implanted by his future killer. Not impossible, though. Something this carefully planned might have been in the works for a while. Perhaps Eva's visits and Viggo's shifts hadn't coincided before the fateful day. That was another, apparently tedious, job for Han—cross-referencing the two variables. Han would love it, assuming nothing more pressing came across his desk.

There was still no luck identifying how Viggo had been killed and by whom.

A thought occurred. 'Why didn't the killer target Eva directly? Why go through an intermediary?'

'You said yourself—to add a breakable link in the chain,' Ellie replied. 'Look at us—at a dead end.'

'They must be smart,' Han said. 'Well-connected. This rules out a random killing. Viggo was dead before he was hired. He was a tool, nothing more.'

'Why a toxin delivered via an intermediary?' Tom asked. 'In a place where Viggo could be spotted? Why not a doorstep hit at midnight? Why not mow her down at the crosswalk?'

'Because this was designed to look like a heart attack. The residue of the toxin was a mistake. An oversight. This was meant to appear an accident.'

'Someone *really* doesn't want to get caught.'

'Or they want it to look like natural causes so they can claim insurance or inheritance.' Ellie raised her eyebrows.

'You have a thing against the husband, don't you?' Tom said.

'A hunch. But hunches can be wrong.'

'I'll prioritise analysing his data.' Han gave a rare smile.

Tom had a feeling that Han was developing a crush on Ellie. He checked the clock: the Swedish contingent hadn't come back with anything, and it was almost the end of the day there.

'Yeah. Let's cover all angles. I don't want to get hung up on boxing anyone in yet. For starters, I want to get more on the toxin that killed Viggo, places where he could have sourced his own agent, and any record of those substances being used elsewhere in the state. Meantime, I'll take a ride out to Don Chadwick's place, break the news that his wife was killed by a hitman—and assess his reaction.' He eyed Ellie. 'You going to browbeat me into coming along, seeing as you're the team expert on human behaviour?'

'I never said that.'

'I know. But four eyes are better than two, right?'

'You're the boss, boss.'

After the visit to Eva's husband, which was largely unrevealing, Tom dropped Ellie back at the office and then headed home to Fort Valley. Enna had a two-day break between flights, and he wanted to squeeze in as much family time as possible. He was getting much better at leaving the detective work to the young bucks, rather than micromanaging everything and taking on too much of the legwork.

The town was bathed in warm June sunshine. The French house and garden, less than eighteen months on the plot, were maturing nicely. Enna was on the front step. Could life be any better?

As he walked up, it was clear something was amiss. There was no nascent kiss on her lips, no sparkle in her brown eyes. He darted glances around, heart rate accelerating. Had something happened to their daughter?

Enna reached for his hand and squeezed it. 'No, Tom. Lexie is fine. I'm fine. But come in. Something else is very not fine.'

# 12

'W hat did you forget?' Kennet asked.

It was the only explanation that came to his fractured mind. He glanced around behind him for an item of Charlotte's that had been forgotten in the rush.

Kayte stepped closer, frowned, then spluttered a half-sob. 'Nothing. Except my goddamn manners.' A tear ran down her cheek. 'And that if there's anyone in this country, in this world, in my *life*, that can get me through this, it's you.'

'I am not sure I can get through it myself.'

'And I take it back, Kennet. Every word. And I am so, *so* goddamn sorry for what I said.'

'I forgive you. We are not ourselves tonight.' His head fell, and a cloak of blackness enveloped him. 'We will never be again.'

'Yeah. I know.'

Silence. A car glided down the suburban street. The streetlamps, triggered by twilight, flicked on. Night was coming. He felt like it would never be day again.

'Charlotte's in the car,' Kayte said. 'Can I... can we...?' She shook her head. 'I don't deserve it. Sorry. I'll go.' She turned.

He reached out tentatively, fingers twitching. 'Come in. Bring her. Do you want help?'

'I brought a bag. Goddamn presumptuous, right?'

He shook his head. 'No. Now I know you are fine—well, not fine, but....' He forced a weak smile.

'Not in a ditch somewhere, stoned, wasted or worse.'

'Something like that.'

'I've done this before. When Mom and Dad died. It's not easy. Like, *really* not easy. But I survived.'

He pointed. 'Put her in the spare room. I'll bring your bag.'

'You're a lifesaver.'

'Don't speak too soon.'

They quietly settled Charlotte down, grabbed a bottle of wine, and convened on the sofa.

Kayte looked like she'd been hit by a tornado.

The atmosphere was unlike anything he'd experienced. Perhaps redolent of living in a bomb shelter, either after the apocalypse or in imminent expectation of it. Certainly, a large aspect of both their worlds lay destroyed. He didn't know where to begin or how to even consider making sense of things.

She played with the stem of her glass. 'I messaged Enna.'

He was taken aback by her ability to take any logical, practical steps. He'd done nothing. He'd been a zombie.

'We don't even know for sure that—'

'I called the airline. They made the flight. It's true. It's real. They're—'

She managed to get the wineglass onto the table before the flood came.

Tears cascaded from her, and quickly he erupted in sympathy. They reached for each other, hugging tightly, survivors clinging to a life raft amidst the deluge they'd created.

For five minutes, they rested there, unashamed and conjoined in their grief.

He retrieved a box of tissues from the bathroom. They dried their eyes, then moistened their throats with the wine. He knew it was merely the first of many such episodes.

'They said... the airline said... they could only confirm the girls were on board. Nothing else is being said. I don't know about you, but I'm not going to be stubborn about this.'

He exhaled hard. 'No.'

She clasped his hand. 'Something else too. I'm not going to get drunk and make a pass at you. I'm not doing that shit again. I already nearly kicked you into touch.'

'It's understandable. You were—are—in shock.'

'Still—'

He found a faint shrug. 'If you want to think about butterflies flapping wings, I can't say there isn't sense in what you said. Coming to New York started all this. But I never came for friendship. I came as polis.'

He took a big slug of wine. 'But this week? I suggested this trip. I *did* put them on that plane. So don't feel bad for accusing me of having a part in this—however logical or fanciful the argument.'

She shook her head firmly. 'No. You can't think like that. I won't let you. Besides, I was as guilty of encouraging Carey to go along with it. You can put a pin in the timeline at any point and make a case *that* is the reason. Hell, if Jay hadn't been called away that day, you would have talked to *him* about the... what was it... Lindt murder.' She laughed hollowly. 'Lot easier if we blame Jay for triggering this chain of events. At least he can't answer back.'

She looked heavenwards, and that line of thought took her to Carey and Jana, and in moments she was crying again.

He pulled her to him, stroking her unkempt hair.

'I'm all alone, Kennet. We don't... didn't... know anyone here. Not really. Not made friends in Söderhamn yet. Couple of parents at preschool would smile, but....' Her sigh was warm breath on his neck. 'What do I do? How do I go on without her?'

'How? By using the fire and steel we know is inside you. By holding onto the child Carey carried for you both. By leaning on the people, even person, you *do* have here.'

She explored his face, curious. 'How do you have the headspace for logic and insight at a time like this?'

He chuckled sadly. 'While you were gone, I did nothing. I barely had the strength to breathe. You took *action*. Logical, practical action. Do you think you are a mess? I am very much a mess.'

'I also messaged my Chief at Söderhamn.' She bit her lip. 'And Janssen. Sorry—did I step on toes?'

His eyes widened. 'Of course not. I should have. To... warn him, I suppose, that I won't be myself for a few days.'

'All in good time.'

Silence fell.

'Thank you for letting me... us... in.' She flashed a weak smile.

'I can't kick a woman when she is down. Plus... a problem shared is a problem halved, yes?'

'And this is an absolute doozy. The worst.' Her face creased. Sobs came.

They embraced. He cried. His shirt became moist with both their tears.

After a while, they dried their eyes again, and she leaned into him.

'I've got your back, partner,' she said into his shoulder. 'Or I'll try.'

'And I have yours. And I think some people will help. There will be support. I have seen it happen.'

'Hmm.'

More silence, barely tempered by their breathing.

'Charlotte is too young to understand,' Kayte said.

'Tomas isn't.'

'I don't envy you.'

'I think I will... see how best to proceed.'

She frowned. 'Lie? That's unlike you.'

'Let's say... find the best time for the truth. He is a smart boy.' He swallowed hard. 'I only hope I can do a good job with him.'

'I'm sure you'll be amazing. You rise to challenges, Kennet. More than you think.'

He picked at his fingernails. 'Anything before was a... "cakewalk"?'

She nodded, smiling. 'Finally, of all the times, you nail an expression. God, I hope you can still make me laugh through this. That'd be a damn gift.'

'I can't promise.'

'And I can't promise not to be irrational, angry and incredibly hard work.' She plucked a tissue and blew her nose. 'Or a snotty, blubbering mess.'

'You do you. That is fine. I will do my best. But I think it will get worse before it gets better.'

'I guarantee it.' She stifled a yawn.

He glanced at the door. 'Do you want to go in with Charlotte, or use the sofa?' He swallowed. 'Or....'

She patted his knee. 'I won't make you feel awkward and uncomfortable. Knowing I have a *literal* shoulder to cry on is enough. I couldn't do tonight in that house. Not without... her. But I don't need to do the bed thing again.' She fixed her gaze on him. 'That was a goddamn lifeline last year, and I'm not saying I won't need it again, but I think we need our space tonight, huh?'

'I agree. But if you need me, you shout, okay?'

'You too.'

'I have some spare things in the cupboard. I'll bring them down.'

They made up a bed on the sofa. The atmosphere was tense and maudlin. They switched off their Coms, not wanting disturbance, bad news or well wishes.

After a welcome goodnight hug, they retired to bed, shorn of their dearest, bereft, and wishing that morning would deliver news that it had all been a bad dream.

# 13

Enna had a disturbed night. The news from Sweden was so awful. First, she felt devastated for Kayte and Kennet, then worried for them, then she pondered how she'd deal with something like that happening to Tom.

She kidded herself that she was a strong person, but she'd previously gone to pieces over things which were ultimately less serious or fatal. She ached to offer support.

At an earlier-than-normal breakfast, Tom appeared less than sprightly.

'Bad night?'

'Yeah. It rips me up,' he replied.

'Wish I knew what to do.'

'I'll make it easy. I'm pulling rank. I know I'm not your boss, and I'm damn sure you wear the pants in this house, but my people are hurting, and damn if I'm standing by. I need to know what shape they're in. The team has a lot on its plate. Stubborn people—mentioning no names—would throw themselves into work and bottle their feelings. I don't want Kayte or Kennet ending up in a psych ward because they made the wrong decisions. They are great detectives and wonderful people.'

He set his coffee mug down with a thud. 'So. You have thirty-six hours before you're next rostered. You're staying here with Lexie. I'm taking the SkyRun to Stockholm at eleven. This is not an item for debate. I'll be back tomorrow. If you want to give me the world's best and longest hug, I'll pass it on.' He smiled. 'Probably not so much of it to Kennet, though.'

Enna opened her mouth for a rejoinder, realised nothing whatsoever was wrong with Tom's plan, then closed it.

'Bring me back some brännvin?'

He nodded, impressed. 'Thanks for understanding.'

'Just one thing, Tom.'

'There had to be, didn't there?'

'You're doing this because we love those people, right? As well as they're in your team.'

'Absolutely.'

'Accidents happen—I get that. But if there's anything the slightest bit fishy, I want to know.'

He frowned. 'A plane crash? Honestly, honey, I think you're looking down a telescope the wrong way.'

'OnePlanet blew up a Moon shuttle six years ago. They're not beyond anything.' She pressed in close to him. 'And Kayte is my friend.'

'She's not Fleet,' he pointed out. 'Eva Svensson, fair enough. But you promised to stay in your lane. Be Lieutenant Dacourt, Navigator. No ass-kicking needed.'

'The Stockholm Spaceport is Fleet. You're Fleet PD. You said Kennet is majoring in Spaceport-related incidents. This is an incident. In Stockholm.'

He clasped her shoulders. 'You're joining dots that aren't there. I'm going over to give condolences and support. I'm not walking into the Scandinavian Air Crash Bureau, flashing my credentials and looking for evidence of malfeasance that isn't there.' He kissed her. 'Even though my wife, who has a track record most regular cops would envy, says so.'

Her eyes narrowed. She growled.

'I love you with every fibre of my being,' he continued. 'But please butt out. I'll tell our friends we'll do *whatever* is needed to help them—and I know it will run and run. But I'm not turning their grieving into a witch hunt. Yes, if something smells rotten, I'll be on it like a shot. For now, we wait to see what comes out in the wash. Probably, hopefully, nothing.'

She stroked his cheek. 'Okay.'

'Good. Now, how many bottles do you want?'

Tom was subdued on the two-hour SkyRun flight. He wondered what kind of emotional mess his colleagues were in. He recalled visiting his mother after they'd heard that his father had been shot and killed.

When he reached Kennet's house by taxi, the time difference meant it was after nine: not ideal, but the rotation of the Earth is no respecter of loss and circumstance. They knew he was coming—there had been no point in making it a surprise visit. Kayte was at the house too, and both wore very casual attire—something he was unused to seeing. As expected, they appeared weighed down by sleeplessness and emotional fatigue.

He was surprised to find Chief Inspector Janssen there too, so he shook hands with everyone and decided to pass on Enna's hug when the Chief left.

'Chief Wagner, I'm indebted for your support. I know sometimes I complain about you stealing Lieutenant Carlsson away for your cases—notwithstanding that you allowed Sergeant Connors to bolster our polis with her talents—but we are a big family at heart, and I am sure you feel this pain as much as I.'

'Very true, Chief Inspector.'

'I am leaving now, but you should know the respective departments have granted four weeks of compassionate leave.' He rubbed his jowly chin. 'I am not sure Kennet will be able to resist the temptation to do even a little work in that period—probably Sergeant Connors too, by reputation—but it is not expected. This is a time for family. To bring their spikes down. We both want focussed polis on our team, but in due course.'

'They'll get nothing but understanding from Fleet PD.'

Janssen offered a casual salute and then Kennet showed him out into the growing dusk.

In that interval, Tom took Kayte's shoulder and pulled her into an embrace.

'This is from Enna, with deep love and sadness.'

'Thanks, boss.'

Kennet re-entered the lounge, and Tom passed on a similar but briefer clasp.

Kennet pointed Tom at the sofa.

'One question. What can I do?' Tom took the beer he was handed.

Kayte chuckled sadly. 'Take up the slack. But the Spaceport cases here? They'll have to wait. That project's not going anywhere soon. We didn't get to the Viggo stuff. Sorry.'

'You just had the rug pulled from under you. Violently. Don't apologise for anything.'

'You didn't need to fly all the way over,' Kennet said.

'Yeah. I did. Wish I could stay and take the load off you.'

'You can't take the emotional load away,' Kayte replied. 'And the school runs, the feeds, the bedtimes?' She glanced at Kennet. 'That's about all that'll keep us sane, yeah?'

'I think so,' he murmured.

An uncomfortable silence fell.

Tom didn't want to discuss work, and he couldn't bear raising the subject of the plane crash. What else was there left? Did they have so little in common? Were they ever colleagues but never real friends? It saddened him further.

'How's Enna?' Kayte asked.

'She hasn't taken on the world in the last couple of weeks. Which is a change. Think she's getting itchy, to be honest.'

There was laughter, verging on polite.

Then Kennet asked a follow-up. Soon they moved on to a discussion about Lexie, Charlotte, then Ellie and Han.

A few beers were drunk.

Tom called it a night at eleven-thirty and took his hired AutoDrive to a hotel in town.

He didn't see any sign that Kayte was leaving. That was a wise move, he considered. He'd hate to be home alone when consumed by grief. Kennet and Kayte could lean on each other; a mutual support group so they'd get through this quicker or with less soul-crushing despair.

It was unlikely. He couldn't conceive of life without Enna, so could never truly understand how they felt. At least he could immerse himself in work. Maybe he'd spend an hour tomorrow finding out more about Eva Svensson.

There was still plenty of mystery in what that case was hiding.

# 14

Matteo called Wilmer. It was the right time to hold out an olive branch. He couldn't imagine what it was like to lose both a son and a daughter in the same week. Losing a brother and a sister wasn't the same somehow—certainly not for him.

It couldn't hurt to speak to his father. It would hardly worsen their relationship.

'How are you doing?'

'What does it look like, Mat?'

It looked like Dad had been hit by a truck. He hadn't shaved in two days. It made him look like a bum. All that money, all those facilities at his disposal, and he probably hadn't even had a shower either.

Mat experienced the tiniest prick of guilt. It didn't last long. He'd done his mourning. After all, he wasn't a monster. There had been good times with Anders; they just felt so distant. Besides, accidents happened, didn't they? Surely Wilmer must appreciate that? Especially for someone like Anders, who travelled so much.

Yes, he resolved; that was a good argument to make.

'It looks like you lost your son. I get it. You think I'm not sad?'

'You don't seem sad,' Wilmer replied.

'Well, I am.'

'I'm mad too. Things like this shouldn't happen. I tell you, human error is often to blame, and when I see whatever comes out of that crash report, I'll pursue any individual to the end of the Earth. I'll ensure they get the full force of the law for incompetence, negligence, missed procedures, whatever it may be.' He scratched his grey stubble. 'Not that it will bring Anders back.'

'At least he has—had—accomplishments. Which is more than I have, I suppose. You accuse me of not being sad? I bet you won't cry for me.'

Wilmer leant in to the camera. 'Of course, I will. You're still my flesh and blood.' He screwed up his face. 'Maybe all I really have left now.'

Apart from your money, Mat thought. And your stupid OnePlanet ethos. And your refusal to see reason. And your lack of forgiveness, your narrow-mindedness, and your intolerance.

'Then I'll be taking extra care that nothing happens to me. They say bad things come in threes. I'm the third. If there's a vendetta against us, a curse, whatever, then I won't go down without a fight. That would break you, right? Losing all of us. The two apples of your eye, and then the rotten one.'

'Don't talk like that, Matteo. There has been a lot of bad water under the bridge, but at least we are talking.'

'Yes. And all it took was two tragedies. How sad is that?'

'Very sad. Very.'

Mat took a gamble. 'Are you able to handle all the arrangements? Legacies and things? Admin. I mean, Anders had no children, no wife.' He feigned curiosity and innocence. 'What heir does he have?' He sighed. 'That would be so sad, so ridiculous. Such oversight for a smart investor like Anders to be *in testate*.' He waved it away. 'But it's none of my business. I'm being insensitive. Sorry.'

Wilmer's hard expression softened. 'Knowing Anders, he left it to his bodyguard. Silly fellow. But, whatever the case, I—we—must respect his wishes.' His head bowed. 'And mourn him. And those other poor souls. No one person on that plane was worth more than another. A life is a life.'

'Except one was your son. My brother. It's perspective.'

Wilmer nodded. 'Anyway. I'm more interested in Eva. The police in America say it was murder. If there is anything which will get the full force of my legal team, it is the inhuman reprobate who is behind it.'

'I had a message too. I asked to be kept informed. See—I do care about Eva. They know who killed her.'

'Yes. This Viggo character. But he was a hired ruffian. And he is dead.' Wilmer clenched a fist. 'Which is not ideal justice for the fiend, but it is better than permanent impunity. Now the matter is who is behind this despicable act.' He threw his hands up. 'Against my darling daughter, who never hurt a fly.'

'Let us have faith in the authorities and that things work out as they will. There will be a solution to this. An explanation.' He grimaced deliberately. 'Let's hope we are alive long enough to discover it.'

Wilmer's eyes widened. 'You do worry so, Mat.'

'It's too much coincidence, Dad. I fear for myself. You should know I'll be managing my affairs more warily for a while. Being less public. So, if you don't hear from me, it's not that I don't want to support you at this time—that I don't *care*—but I need to be safe. I mean, a lot of responsibility for your legacy hangs on my shoulders now, I suppose.'

'I suppose.'

Mat didn't know how to take that. It wasn't an explicit sign that events meant he'd been de facto returned to the family fold. Equally, it was the most extensive, productive, good-natured conversation they'd had in years.

Things were looking up.

Exactly as planned.

# 15

The weekend had been a mercy—plenty of time with the children—but Monday meant it was time to adult, and Kayte didn't feel like adulting. She didn't want to go back to the rental place in Söderhamn where she and Carey lived—had lived—but she couldn't stay under Kennet's feet forever.

She took Charlotte to preschool, then went to the shops. She filled the larder to the brim. She found an out-of-date yoghurt at the back of the fridge: Carey's favourite flavour. She cried.

She brewed a series of mugs of coffee. She devoured a pack of chocolate biscuits. She tidied. She tidied again. She checked the clock. Carey had chosen it. She cried.

She messaged Kennet. He said he was coping. She didn't believe him—because she certainly wasn't. She thought about Jana and Carey, side by side, on that small local plane. She got a vision. She cried.

She prepared a huge lunch, ate it all, got emotional and vomited it back into the toilet bowl. She cried.

She made another lunch and managed to keep it down. She thought of Kennet, dearly wanting the biggest bear hug, and for him to lie convincingly, telling her everything was fine, and it would all be over soon. She accidentally caught a news report about the crash investigation. She cried.

After an eternity, it was time to collect Charlotte. She pulled herself together and kept superficially cheery until the toddler's bedtime, then gave her the biggest goodnight hug ever. The poor thing still didn't know or suspect that her birth mother was dead.

Kayte sat on the sofa with a bottle of wine and cried.

On Tuesday, she debated keeping Charlotte home for company, but even the smile of a beautiful toddler couldn't nourish her for twelve hours straight. Besides, she'd slept so poorly that she had little energy to entertain her daughter for long periods.

She dropped Charlotte at preschool and went to the salon. In an effort to rip Carey—and the associated grief—from her mind, she instructed the hairdresser to shave her head. Her hair had been short when she met Carey. Removing the hair would be like ripping ten years from the pages of history.

At the last moment, she stopped the carnage. She asked for a pixie cut, as she'd worn for so long. Certainly, at the time, she met Kennet. It made her think of him, and a shudder of empathic grief went through her.

She composed herself. The hairdresser moved in with the clippers.

Kayte's hand shot up. She asked for a trim and tidy instead.

Then she cried.

After the debacle in the salon, she enjoyed an indulgent lunch in Söderhamn, then bought some new clothes. She considered driving to Bollnäs but didn't. She had coffee and cake in a café, then collected her daughter.

In the evening, a counsellor from AirSweden came to the house. Kayte asked the woman to leave.

She played with Charlotte, smothered her with love, put her to bed, ate an entire apple pie for four, curled up on the sofa and fell asleep.

By Wednesday morning, she was starting to hate the house. It felt like a ghost walked. The air seemed stagnant, empty of Carey's voice and laughter.

Kayte showered before dropping Charlotte off, afterwards, and then again after spilling chocolate mousse down her blouse and chest.

She forced herself to watch the news. Shots of the wreckage and scarred hillside were mercifully brief. Most of the content was graphics, speculation and interviews. The consensus was that sabotage or mechanical failure was unlikely.

Still, she cried, though much less than the previous days. She was probably numb now. A shell, walking through life in a stupor.

She tidied up the day's contingent of discarded wrappers and packets, considered going unannounced to Bollnäs, then messaged instead. His replies were pleasant but brief.

She wanted to hold his hand. A crippling pang of loneliness gripped her.

She collected Charlotte early and took her to the harbour. They counted the pretty boats and had an ice cream.

Carey's favourite had been strawberry.

Kayte held in tears.

Kennet called on Thursday. Hearing his voice was like ambrosia. She wanted to say she missed him but didn't. Kayte Connors wasn't weak; she was strong. Yet her wife was dead, and she was essentially alone in a foreign land. Chasing a dream had resulted in a nightmare.

There was nowhere in the house without Carey's belongings or personality somewhere. She dearly wanted to gather everything together and put it in a crate, a shipping container, or a hole in the garden. She couldn't bring herself to. It was too disrespectful. Besides, it would be an admission of the truth—she'd never see her again.

Should she find another place? Stay in a hotel for a while? Charlotte had grown used to her little room. The absence of Carey was undeniably getting noticed: more change might upset the girl too much or at least foster questions that Kayte couldn't bear to answer nor know how to frame.

It made her think about Tomas. Had Kennet told his son yet? Quickly, her mind's eye turned to the diving plane.

She tugged a handful of tissues from the box on the coffee table and filled them with her tears.

She spent three hours at the Söderhamn café on Friday. Their pastries were delicious. She watched people. She surfed the web on her tablet Com. She didn't once get emotional.

Two polis came in. She knew them. They offered their condolences. She held herself together with alacrity. Then she sat in the car and cried. As she did, she wondered whether she'd ever have the strength to return to the cop life again. Currently she was a mess, not fit for the uniform.

She experienced a few minutes of wishing she'd never left DC, then shook that away. The past couldn't be undone, and the trajectory of her and Carey's life hadn't caused the crash. It was a coincidence, bad luck.

Yet a worm wriggled in her brain—something any regular person should feel in the same circumstance: a need for answers. What happened on flight AS166? What failure, event, mistake or oversight had caused the loss of those lives, one—if not two—of which were so precious?

This was difficult, harder even than something like investigating a child's murder. She would have to dig deep to put aside grief, regret and anger, focusing purely on closure.

She went home.

The place was so quiet. In an hour, she'd need to collect Charlotte. Could they get through the weekend? The time would drag.

Kayte wanted time to leap forward. Six months, ideally, bypassing all this melancholy bullshit. Skipping the delivery of Carey's remains—if there were any. A wake of some kind. The disclosure to Charlotte.

If she felt minded and was true to her calling, she'd be back in uniform, doing what she loved, working alongside people she cared for. Trying, in a tiny way, to make the world a better place—even if someone, something, had made hers a much worse place.

She came to a decision: she was damned if she was going to be miserable when there was the chance of something marginally less draining.

She messaged Kennet, drove to preschool, then onwards to Bollnäs.

# 16

Y ou cut your hair.'

'Half an inch.' Kayte was taken aback. 'How the hell, after everything, do you notice that?'

That embarrassed him. 'Come in.'

He helped her inside with the large suitcase while she carried Charlotte. He pecked the toddler on her forehead. It was an odd moment of normalcy in their devastated lives.

Tomas came in, took the youngster's tiny hand, and walked her into the small playroom. It wasn't the first time the boy had exhibited such maturity, compassion and pragmatism, but Kennet was still buoyed. It was as if Tomas, without knowing the true horror of the situation, sensed that his father and not-truly-an-aunt Kayte were having a hard time and needed help.

Kennet had needed to field questions about Jana's absence in the past week but told Tomas she had decided to stay away a little longer because they hadn't seen any whales yet, and it was a long way, but she'd be back as soon as she could, and she loved her boy so much. Kennet felt awful for withholding the truth but revealing it would be even harder on Tomas.

Kayte brought more of Charlotte's things inside, plus a shopping bag of food. Kennet poured her a glass from the bottle of wine he'd opened as soon as Tomas was home from school.

'You look... better,' he said.

'Hard to look worse.' She examined him. 'You being lazy, or deliberately growing that?'

He scratched his chin. 'Growing it,' he lied.

She set the glass down. 'Have you been a mess too?'

He forced the smallest smile. 'I think it is allowed, no?'

'It's okay being a mess *together* for a couple of days?'

'I thought about visiting. I did worry.'

She tentatively reached out, then squeezed his arm. 'Me too. Every day. Because doing this alone is hard enough, right?'

'Almost impossible.'

She swallowed and pinched her lips together. He recognised that sign, so he drew her in and rested his chin on her head. Her body convulsed with dry sobs. Despite the reason for the embrace, the proximity to solace and shared experience was like a bandage on his fractured being. He squeezed her tight. She hugged back.

'Don't stay away, Kayte. Not if you need someone. You can be weak now. It is allowed. I have been.'

She eased away and looked into his eyes. 'What I need—what we need—is our wives back. But they're... irreplaceable.' She wiped the wetness from her cheeks. 'This is the next best thing. If there's one crumb of comfort, it's that it happened here and now.'

She pulled away. 'Did the support person visit?'

He nodded.

'I sent her away.'

'I let her stay for ten minutes,' he said. 'But we can go to a group if we need to, yes?'

'Sure.'

He waved at the sofa. 'Sit. Tell me what you've done. Is Charlotte okay?' He drank. The wine was nectar.

He listened to the ups and downs of her week. She listened to his. She put Charlotte to bed in the spare room, then he read Tomas a bedtime story and tucked him in.

When he came downstairs, Kayte was preparing food. Beside her on the surface was a large bag of potato chips, half-empty.

'You didn't have to do that.'

'I'm borrowing your roof and sofa. Did I overstep, partner?'

He laughed—a rare commodity lately. 'No. Go ahead.'

They finished the wine and dinner. She changed into slouching clothes and tucked herself up on the sofa beside him. The conversation inevitably came around to the plane crash.

He'd been avoiding the news. Chief Janssen had called midweek to say that his cousin worked for the Investigation Bureau, so he'd keep abreast of developments and pass them on. Kennet feigned interest and gratitude; in truth, he couldn't look past facts for causes. Jana wouldn't come back.

Kayte, unsurprisingly, was more terrier-like, possibly using the investigation—although it wasn't hers—as a lifeline to some kind of explanation, a way of making sense of the unbelievable. It was clear that he should leverage any possible means to allow her to find closure.

'They found the black box,' she said. 'Some guy—maybe a leak—said the plane nosedived. A witness saw no flames. A lot of talk about the pilot. A colleague said he was unstable. Another guy saying it was nonsense.'

She fiddled with her glass, then her hand began to shake, so she set it down.

Again, he knew that sign. He slapped his glass down just in time before she folded into him, sniffling.

'You really are a hugger, aren't you?' he said.

She sat up, pain on her face. 'I'm sorry. You're always saying what a rock I am, and here I can't even get through five minutes without blubbing like a girl and running to you for comfort.' She sniffed. 'I'll try harder.'

'Holding it in is worse, I suspect.'

'Probably. So long as I don't do anything stupid again.' She put her shoulders back. 'But I learned my lesson. Imagine if I'd broken us then, and I wouldn't have you now. I'd really be in the shit.'

He took her hand. 'So would I. Shutting everything out was stupid. At least you have sense. At least you went out. All I did was buy a new dressing gown.' He hung his head. 'I've been living in it.'

She pushed in and laid her head against his. 'Oh, poor Kennet. You should have called. Or visited. This is a two-way street, you know. For however long it takes.'

'I suppose.'

'I know so.'

Silence for a moment.

'I... never loved another woman. Or was ever without someone. I... don't know how...' He broke into tears.

At ten-thirty, they called time on the evening. It was the best day of the week because he wasn't managing alone. He took a healthy measure of brännvin into his room. Her gaze followed his hand.

They assembled the makeshift bed on the sofa and said goodnight.

When he turned off the bedroom light, the darkness closed in like a demon, as it had every evening. He shivered, although it was a warm night. The space beside him was cavernous, empty of his lifelong love. He'd washed the sheets and pillowcases to rid the room of her scent, but there were tell-tale signs everywhere. This had been their house for many years.

The invented image of Jana and Carey's horror-stricken faces burned the inside of his eyelids again. He swallowed down the grief, pining deeply.

There was a gentle knock at the door, startling him from maudlin introspection.

'Yes?'

'Are you okay?'

'Yes,' he lied.

A pause. 'Are you decent?'

He sported a night tee and shorts. 'Yes.'

'So am I.'

The door opened. 'Are you really okay?'

'No.' It caught in his throat. He gritted his teeth to hold in tears.

'Nor me.' A dark shape sat on the bed, depressing it.

He felt lame and needy, weak and hollow—much like during the whole week.

'What do you need?' she asked.

'My wife,' he spluttered.

'Me too. But that's not possible.' Her sigh was deep, audible and broken. 'Second best?'

'Hmm.'

The sheets moved, so he scooted away. She slid in behind him.

'This is payback for what you gave me, okay?'

'Okay.'

She pressed in, loosely spooning him. First, he tensed, then, as she rubbed his arm, he relaxed. He let out the stiffness in his neck. Yet his eyes remained moist.

'Do you want to talk?' she said after a while.

'No. Do you?'

'No.'

A pause. 'Do you want me to go?'

He thought. His conscience said Yes. Unidentifiable guilt said Yes. His reserve said Yes.

'No.'

She moved slightly closer. 'I've got you.'

'I've got you too. Partner.'

'Try to sleep.'

'You too.'

Time passed.

'Kayte?'

'Yeah?'

'I'm glad you're here.'

'I'm glad I'm here too. Think about tomorrow. Let's take the kids somewhere. Work on that. Think about how amazing the children are. Focus on that.'

'And how amazing you are.'

She kissed the material of his shirt between his shoulder blades. 'Back at you, partner. Go to sleep. You need the energy. Charlotte's a handful.'

'Like her mother.'

Kayte snickered. 'And her father—remember?'

'I am not a handful,' he protested jokingly.

'I'm teasing.'

'Some things don't change.'

'Good. I'm still me inside. Even though my heart feels like it's gone.'

'Me too.'

She patted his arm. 'Back up. No wallowing. Kids, plans, happiness, sleep. Okay?'

'Yes, Sergeant.'

A faint titter. 'Good. Night, Inspector.'

'Night.'

# 17

Enna was getting worried about Kayte. She hadn't heard from Connors in a week.

When Tom came home from work, and she'd put Lexie down for the night, she joined him in the kitchen, and they prepared dinner together.

'Any news on your cases?'

'No. Viggo has previous, but no trace of the toxins. Han is combing prison records for anyone he might have met. Nothing on his Com records. Or nothing that leads anywhere. There was a call from a Swedish number, but it was a burner. Chances of getting anything off that are slim. Eva's husband comes up clean. I sent Gina a message because I know you'd ask me to.'

She rubbed his shoulders. 'Thanks.'

After a pause, she casually asked, 'Heard from Kennet or Kayte?'

'No. Giving them space. I'm in touch with Janssen, as he has a finger on the pulse of everything.'

'You mean the crash investigation?'

He stopped chopping vegetables and met her eye. 'What's this about?'

'Answers. We all want them, don't we? I bet K and K sure do. Closure. I damn well would if you were on a plane that went down. A shuttle. A boat. Hell, even a malfunctioning AutoDrive.'

He sighed. 'Janssen's across the plane crash. Has a connection.' His eyes narrowed. 'Have you been looking at conspiracy theories, Dacourt?'

She held up both palms. 'I'm not butting in. Just... interested. Concerned. I haven't heard from Connors. It's unlike her. Ever since they moved there, not a week has gone by when she hasn't sent pictures of beautiful sea, or blue sky, the cute harbour, or an even cuter child. She's going through *hell*, Tom.'

'She strong. Smart. Resilient. And she has support. She and Kennet are like... not peas in a pod but... inseparable. A dream team. They have compassionate leave. They have two kids to take their minds off things. They—'

'Have lost deep, long relationships. When Pascal died, I was a wreck. And you know what? I damn well wanted closure. Teksys said it was an accident, but we both know it wasn't. It was a cover-up. And justice? Too long in coming, and, yeah, very imperfect, but damn cathartic.'

She pressed close. 'So, look me in the eye, Tom Wagner, and tell me you don't think there's a tiny, *tiny* chance that what happened in Stockholm wasn't an accident. Ignore your butt-in wife and her crazy ideas. Tell me you *don't* care what happened.'

'I do care. Deeply. I want those two ladies back because I don't like our friends' lives and careers being compromised. Honestly, I *do* want it to be ruled an accident because I hate to think what will happen otherwise. I know you were knotted up inside for years about Pascal. I don't want that for Kayte and Kennet. I want them to be able to move on—if they can.'

She kissed him. 'I never consider you heartless. I didn't mean that. But....' She sighed. 'Look, I have a crazy idea, okay? Not a "causing trouble, poking in my rather beautiful nose" idea. A practical, caring... very "Enna" idea.'

He cupped her cheek. 'Go on.'

'Let me go visit.' Her hand shot up. 'Hold on. Give the defendant a chance to plead her case. I'll take Lexie—don't worry. You can stay here and be Chief, catch some bad guys. I'll give K and K all the support I can for a few days. See some sights. Hang with the kids—if they'll have me. Maybe stop by Mom and Dad on the way back, show them how Lexie is getting almost as beautiful as her mother. Oh, and I promise not to browbeat Janssen, AirSweden or anybody along the way.' She held up a palm. 'On my honour, Your Honour.'

She watched his eyes flicker.

'Thinking of reasons to turn me down, aren't you, Wagner?'

'I'm assessing whether you'll be a help or hindrance.'

She whacked his ass. 'Look at it like this. Kayte pulled me out of a freezer last year. She saved your unconscious ass too. Both she and Kennet covered for us when Lexie was taken. Hell, they *demanded* they support us. I'm just giving back. I've spoken to Fleet Resourcing. After this week's tour, I have leave I can take. Think of this as a vacation.'

'Without me,' he said, half-joking.

'So, come along. If not now, later. Ellie and Han can hold the fort, right?'

'I guess. Let me see how things go.'

She assessed his expression. 'There's something going on, isn't there? Tell me I'm wrong.'

He rubbed his chin. 'Ellie is latching onto that Swedish burner phone. Eva was Swedish. Two potentially activist-induced incidents. Now a Swedish plane crash?' He resumed chopping, but pensively. 'I don't want to butt in over there, but Kennet and Kayte are seconded to my team, even if only part-time. They have cases. And they might be accidentally caught up in something.'

She laid her head on his shoulder. 'At minimum, they'll be in pieces. And I've flown six billion miles since we last had a vacation. Lexie can keep Charlotte company. I can drink—'

'Okay, okay. Deal. Just tell them you're coming. They've had one nasty surprise already this week.' He winked.

'On second thoughts, don't come along. *Rat*.'

He smacked her ass. Then took a handful, pulled her in, and kissed her like she was leaving forever.

# 18

Kennet woke alone. He was relieved. Being proximate to another woman—even though it was only Kayte—so soon after Jana's loss felt... odd. Immensely comforting, valuable and nonsexual, yet... odd.

He smiled. Had Kayte felt the same after he comforted her likewise in DC? It was a milestone for their relationship, certainly, and arguably this time, there had been much less tension and anxiety.

He lay there, studying the plain white ceiling, allowing his mind to wander over the good and bad of everything—mostly the bad. His chest felt pressed by an anvil.

A knock at the door.

'Yes?'

She entered, carrying a mug of coffee. She wore sweatpants and a top. She'd showered.

How late was it? He checked the nightstand. It was 08:44.

'Oh. Tomas?'

'Up, breakfasted, playing. Same with Charlotte. I guess you slept.'

He frowned. 'I think so.'

'I didn't stay. Didn't want to make you uncomfortable. Socially, I mean.'

He grimaced. 'I can't deny it. If someone walked in—not that they would—'

She sat on the bed. 'And noted two friends helping each other, in some small way, cope with the loss of loved ones? Without a trace of impropriety? I should be the one more on trial. Hugging a man?' She mock-shuddered. 'Bleuch. I'd be kicked out of the lesbian community in a second.'

'That is more than true.'

She looked him straight. 'The medicinal power of hugs is proven and legendary. And right now, I could use *any* medicine to make this unbearable, godawful bullshit feeling of loss a mite more manageable. I reckon you could too. And I'll hold my head high if anyone makes any insinuation. Still, I've no desire to make you wring your hands or question your morals. You have a damn comfortable sofa, and there are plenty of daylight hours if either of us needs a quick hug to get over a downslope. Okay?'

'I didn't mean....' He sighed, then drank. 'I'm sorry. It helped. That was the best night I have had. Maybe it was you being in the house. Or talking. Or even,' he eyed the covers, 'being here.'

'And I had a decent night too. Much needed.' She stood. 'So, what are we doing today?'

First, they went to Lilla Bolleberget, admired the views and watched the children run around. The clear air was welcome and blew away a modicum of his pain—until he remembered this was where he'd proposed to Jana. Kayte noticed his sudden melancholy, prised the reason from him, and rested his head on her shoulder as they sat on the bench.

She pecked his temple. 'These moments won't go away overnight. Don't fight them, okay?'

Then she welled up, so he held her and focussed on Tomas, who was helping Charlotte look for creepy crawlies.

They had lunch in a nearby café. Despite Kayte having chomped on a chocolate bar all morning, she devoured a hearty meal. He made a note to watch her like a hawk.

In the afternoon, they went to a soft play centre.

The plan to tire out the children worked, and by early evening both were sound asleep.

'We make a good team,' Kayte said over dinner.

He drained his beer bottle. 'Like at work, no?'

She fiddled with her cutlery. 'Is it wrong to miss work?'

'No. But I don't think Ulrik will accept me back. Though I could do with the distraction.'

'Me too. But let's give it another week, okay? We should try to get the worst out of our systems.' She pursed her lips. 'I'd hate to make a mistake on a case because my mind wasn't in the game. I don't want to be thrown out for incompetence.' She swallowed hard. 'I have to provide for Charlotte. There's no backup now.'

Her lip quivered, so he reached across the table and clasped her hand.

It didn't work, so he pulled her up and held her tight. Soon, he was in tears too. He'd passed the point of fighting these episodes. There was nothing wrong or weak in them. They were necessary steps.

She made him play card games. They needed to avoid work, their loss, or debating the future.

They emptied six beer bottles between them. He enjoyed being loose and letting the good and the bad of circumstance wash over him, giving in to the need for some kind of release.

She noticed his yawns grow more frequent.

She tucked a leg underneath her and faced him on the sofa. 'Tough talk time, partner. You and I are in the doldrums. We're hurting. That's not news. Today was a *good* day. You're great company. Invaluable. I hope I am too.'

He nodded. 'A lifesaver.'

'But some of this is awkward as hell. Damn unconventional. Friends sharing a bed?' She pulled a face of mock horror. 'But it works, right?'

'I did sleep well,' he admitted.

'Because it's about sleep. Comfort.' She took a deep breath. 'So I can make up the sofa tonight. Or... not. One hundred percent your call. Because I know it sometimes doesn't sit easily with your....'

He smiled. 'Swedish reserve.'

'Right. And you are what matters. In here and here.' She tapped his forehead and chest.

'It's just....' He frowned.

'I know. I absolutely know. In our DC apartment, something like this would make the neighbours' doors crack open. Whispers. And you know what? I wouldn't give a shit. In this situation, where we are—rock bottom—I don't give a shit. You may have realised that about me.'

He laughed. 'Very much.'

'So, the sleeping—*sleeping*—arrangements. Don't worry what others might think or say. They aren't in your position. Or mine. Don't think about how this would be odd or inappropriate if things were different, as they aren't. Only listen to what your gut tells you about whether *any* action is, on balance, positive and helpful for you. I *will* call you out on any behaviour I think is wrong or disagree with. I hope you'll do the same to me.'

He rubbed his chin. He should probably shave. 'Yes.'

'I want you and I to be as happy and comfortable as possible, given how goddamn unhappy and empty we are at our core.' Her eyes darted. 'Apocryphally, a boy once stuck his finger in a dyke and stopped a flood. Some hugging is *such* a small gesture when what we *really* want is our loved ones back so we can hug them instead. You're *so* unlike Carey in many ways—not least physically—but god*damn,* you give good comfort and hugs, and I feel safe knowing you are a deeply honest, kind, non-threatening person. I'd like to think I am the same to you.'

He squeezed her hand. 'You are.'

'I have *no* idea what we're doing. This is such uncharted territory. Not just the misery but the task of putting my—and your—hearts back together. Finding a path that works. Solving the case of the two broken cops.'

'You have such steel and insight, Kayte. I don't know how you find it amongst all this.'

She shrugged. 'Survival instinct. You and I have gone through near death more than once. We found a way out, and a lot of it was down to the bond we have, openness and practicality.'

'Undoubtedly.'

'Then let's not get hung up on conventions or wondering whether our wives are looking down on us, riddled with shock. I *know* Carey would want me to be suffering as little as possible. I expect Jana too. So let's suffer less. Okay?'

'Okay.'

'Good. Let's hit the sack.'

Under the covers, both duly dressed against embarrassment, he let her embrace him from behind. It was much less awkward than him spooning her. Still, his mind whirled with the emotional uncomfortableness, the almost anaesthetic quality of holding a good-looking woman, and knowing that comfort was nearby if his mind insisted on pummelling him with grief.

Mercifully, the day's travails—and the effects of booze—took him into sleep.

On Sunday, they ate lunch in town, bought Charlotte a few new clothes, then spent the afternoon in the house playing games.

There were no tears, but when Tomas asked about his mother—not for the first time—Kennet had to invent a creative answer. Kayte backed him up. How he wished that Tomas was as young as Charlotte, not needing an explanation nor able to process one in any case. The girl would grow up barely remembering her birth mother.

That situation formed a conversation after dinner, punctuated by supportive embraces.

Kayte decided to stay over, then drive directly to preschool in the morning. Kennet didn't fight it.

On Monday morning, they were up at seven, then had breakfast. Kayte's appetite was again oddly full. She gave him a warm hug, then a sober smile, took Charlotte to the car, and they were gone.

He closed the door slowly, feeling like a rug had been pulled from beneath him, and went to get a drink.

# 19

Kayte moped through Monday and Tuesday without much of any consequence—good or bad—happening. A few people at preschool, and the woman at the supermarket with excellent English, asked about Carey, heard the news and shared their sympathies.

Each time, Kayte swallowed her sadness, made it to the car, and allowed herself to have a teary moment.

On Wednesday, something wonderful happened. Enna messaged to say she was flying over. With the school holidays starting the following Monday, she suggested that Kayte and Kennet might be grateful for childcare support, on and off, for a few days.

She told Kennet, who seemed unusually distracted and low, but this cheered him a little. She worried for him. Should she have popped around to visit more often? Men are worse at revealing their emotions. She wondered whether he'd truly gotten to grips with the enormity of the loss or let out as much sorrow as he needed.

On Thursday, she had an unexpected visitor. Chief Inspector Janssen travelled all the way to her house, making her feel cared about and a real part of the Swedish PD family.

He bore two pieces of bad news. Firstly, the plane crash didn't look like an accident. He gave her the details, but when she'd had enough of the gut punch, she asked him to stop. It was making her annoyed and melancholy.

'What was the other thing, Chief Inspector?'

'I don't think Kennet is coping.'

'I thought he was... not too bad.'

Janssen fiddled with his tie. 'Someone at Tomas' school spoke to me. When they were offering condolences to Kennet, they smelled alcohol on his breath. In the morning.'

She closed her eyes, heartbreak spiking. 'Okay.'

'I called in to his home. Later. He had a beer open. I suspect.... Well, you are an excellent detective, Sergeant Connors.'

She nodded, sombre. 'Okay. Best it comes from a friend.'

'I have seen you together, you and Kennet.'

Her pulse raced, feeling like she'd been found out, despite having done nothing untoward.

'As a team,' he continued. 'You have excellent understanding—despite your clear different backgrounds, methods and personalities. I know he took part in your wedding and that you give each other succour. Now, more than ever, this man, this colleague I value deeply, needs someone in his corner.'

'We are in each other's corner, Chief Inspector. And your support is... much appreciated. I think we both want to be back at work as soon as possible. What you've told me about the...' she swallowed hard, 'crash means we're even more invested in helping out the inquiry.'

'You need to process this—and your emotional state—for as long as you need, and in the way you see fit.' He sighed. 'I hear your colleagues from Fleet PD are visiting.'

'Yeah.' That prospect brightened her.

'I'm sharing information with Chief Wagner. More so now. Yes, it is a domestic issue, commercial airline, but I will grease what wheels I can if it helps you and Kennet lay things to rest in your mind.' He scratched his head. 'None of us can stop our curious instincts, yes?'

'I've had to hunt down two people who nearly killed my wife before. This time will have a reason too, and a culprit. A lot of people want answers. We'll be there, helping.'

His typically modest smile appeared. 'Good.'

On Friday, she formed a plan. Tough love from Kennet had gotten her through the last trauma. This time, her approach would get him fixed.

She put on her metaphorical detective's cap, collected Charlotte from preschool early, and drove to Bollnäs. She waited down the road from Kennet's house until he left to collect Tomas. Then she pulled up outside, trotted to the rear of his house, and went to his waste bins. The glass bin was overflowing.

She clenched a fist in annoyance and sorrow, then returned to her car and drove to a café in town.

Towards closing time, and with Charlotte needing her dinner, she went to Kennet's house, being careful to park across his driveway, blocking his car in.

She was polite in her greeting, enthusiastic about seeing Tomas again, but surreptitiously gathered micro-evidence.

When the children were in bed and dinner was in the oven, he invited her to the sofa and brought her a beer. She took two gulps. He downed half the bottle.

'Okay. Enough,' she snapped.

He frowned.

She took his hand and led him into the kitchen. There, she pressed him into a stool at the breakfast bar.

'Sit down. Don't move a muscle, okay?'

He grimaced. 'Yes.'

She opened the cupboard under the sink. The waste bin was piled high with empty bottles and cans. She tugged it out, sailed it across to the table, and clattered it down.

Worry and fear covered his face.

She pulled up a stool and sat opposite him, their knees touching.

'Do you know what an intervention is?' she snapped.

He hung his head. 'Yes.'

'Well, this is one. It's my first. It will also damn well be my last. Are we clear?'

'Yes.'

'This is unacceptable. Do you hear me? What part of "I'm here for you" wasn't clear?'

'I....'

'Goddammit, Kennet, I've given you my shoulder to cry on. I'm in the same position too. Drinking? Drink-driving? With your *son*? Oh yeah—you've been noticed.' She curled her lip. 'Jeez. I really thought better of you.'

She shoved the chair back, dug out a bin liner, emptied the bin, and then put the full bag outside.

She put her hands on her hips.

'I'm not swearing you off drink, okay? I'm not a bitch. I'm swearing you off being a drunk. We'll have a drink now and then, okay? In memory, in sadness, in happiness, whatever. But don't *ever* do that again, Kennet.'

'I'm sorry.' He wasn't far from tears.

'Now, where's the booze? *All* of it.'

She followed him around the kitchen cupboards, collecting full and half-full bottles and cans, emptying the dregs down the sink and gathering the usable booze into another bag. Then she went outside, dumped the bag in the trunk of her car and locked it.

One bottle remained on the kitchen worktop, plus two beers in the fridge. If he wanted more, he'd have to go to the store—and his car was immobile.

She gave herself a metaphorical pat on the back.

He was still hunched in the chair. She could smell the booze on him. He hadn't shaved in two days.

'I love the bones of you, Kennet. Please don't make me regret that.'

'It's too difficult.'

'Damn straight it is. But strength in numbers. You and me against the world, the slings and arrows of outrageous fortune.'

She poured the remaining inch of whiskey into two glasses, then tossed the bottle into the empty recycling bin.

She raised her glass. 'To two amazing ladies. Wives, mothers, friends. Gone, missed desperately, but not forgotten.'

He tentatively raised his glass. 'Yes. And... thank you.'

'No problem. Now, let me beat you at cards. Again.'

# 20

The clock on the nightstand read 03:09.

Kayte reached out but touched only sheets.

She listened for the sound of the ensuite or the family bathroom across the hall. Nothing. She tried to discern any sounds from the kitchen—a midnight snack perhaps. Nothing.

She grew worried. What had woken her? Kennet getting up?

She padded out of the bedroom. Perhaps Tomas or Charlotte had woken and cried out? Yet as she passed their rooms, all was quiet.

She went downstairs. A single light was on. There was a shape slumped on the sofa. Had she snored and driven him away?

There was a bottle in his hand.

Anger and crushing disappointment gripped her.

He jolted, yet sloppily. 'Kayte?'

She ground her teeth, stamped her foot, then went to the kitchen. 'Hiding bottles?' she murmured. 'Jesus Christ.'

She made up the drink, strode into the lounge, and helped him to his feet. He was trying to do so anyway. She wondered how much he'd had.

For a good cop, she was lousy at conducting a thorough intervention.

She hauled him to the downstairs bathroom and closed the door.

'Drink this.' She thrust the glass towards him.

'What is it?' he slurred.

'Saltwater. Drink it. Now.'

He frowned, eyes wandering.

'God. Damn. Now. Kennet.' She held it to his lips.

Together, they poured it down his throat. The gag reflex fought it. She persisted, then whipped the glass away.

He began to retch. She yanked up the toilet seat, helped him collapse to his knees, and watched, revulsed and dejected, as her best friend puked copiously.

When it was all done, she eased marched him upstairs to the ensuite, barrelled him into the shower—still in his puke-stained tee and shorts—and closed the cubicle door.

She jabbed a finger at the faucet.

He'd regained sufficient sobriety to understand reason.

She watched as the water cascaded over him for two minutes, then told him to cease, opened the cubicle door, and threw a towel at him.

'I'll wait downstairs. I'm showing you some courtesy and respect, even though you showed me none. Get dry. Then get an explanation ready. It better be goddamn impressive.'

He lay in her arms on the sofa, in his dressing gown, and cried for five minutes solid. He hadn't given an excuse for his behaviour.

When he was done, she gave him a tissue. He wiped his eyes and downed a glass of water. She brushed damp hair from his temple and stroked his cheek. She cared so much it physically pulled at her insides.

'Jeez. You poor soul. What did I say? Lean on me, not a bottle.'

'It was because of what you said. I realised I let you down.'

'Damn straight. Listen here.' She held his face in both hands. 'If you drink yourself to death, you leave me behind. Ever think of that? You're all I have. Did you not *get* that? Huh?' Her lip curled. 'Stop being so goddamn selfish. I feel bad, too, okay? I feel bad for you and for me. We are friends. More than that. Much more. You *know* that.'

She rested her forehead against his, feeling his breath. 'If you care about me, live and help me live. We must stay strong and catch whatever sonofabitch did this. Okay?'

'Okay,' he murmured.

'You must do the right thing for Jana. To take care of Tomas. You aren't doing that by being a drunk. We can't get our wives back, but at least we can do what they would expect. We help each other, okay? We do the best for our kids.'

'Yes.'

'Talk to me. Any hour of the day or night. And I tell you what, I'll make it easy. I gave you a chance this evening, and an ultimatum. You blew it. You let me down. I am *so* disappointed. Yeah—I get why—but you're better than that.' She searched his face.

He nodded.

She reciprocated. 'Here's the thing. I'll be honest with you. Living in that rental, with Carey gone and her stuff everywhere, is really getting me down. Okay? I'm sharing. Speaking up. See—easy, right?'

'Okay, okay, I understand.'

'So, because this is a crazy idea and I'm this crazy chick, plus the fact you need to be watched like a hawk, so you don't reoffend—prisoner 42991 Carlsson K—I'm moving in. Charlotte and I are.' She held up a finger. 'Just for a while. Until the worst is over. Until you've gotten used to the new life.' She sighed hard. 'And me too. Mutual support network.'

'Hmm.'

'I believe you meant to say "Yes". Or "Yes, Sergeant" if the real Kennet is still in there somewhere.' She offered a smile.

He cupped her cheek. 'You are incredible. Sergeant.'

'Yeah, I believe I am. Now, pull on some underwear, because sleeping in your robe is a recipe for disaster.' She waggled the V of material across his chest. 'If that comes undone, the neighbours *will* talk. And I'll see you in a whole new light. Which will make being your housemate awkward as hell. Okay?'

'Yes. Partner.'

She gave him a few minutes in the bedroom and ensuite, scouted around for any more nasty surprises, then joined him in the bedroom. He was under the covers.

'One more thing. Yes, this part is *very* crazy, and I'm only going on my history as a cop, not on your six hours of alcoholic deceit, which, for clarification, don't fundamentally detract from your high degree of incredibleness.'

'Okay?'

'Where's your standard-issue firearm?'

He opened the nightstand drawer and pulled out the pistol.

She took it from him. 'Now. One single chance for honesty. Do you have any other weapons?'

He shook his head.

'Good. Because we don't want any stupid ideas, even if they are spur of the moment. I'm not saying either of us is suicidal, but equally, we're off duty, so don't need them. I'm hiding this somewhere. Then on Monday, I'm taking it, and mine too, and leaving them at your PD. Agree?'

'Agree.'

'Good.'

She secreted the weapon behind the books on the high shelf in what was temporarily Charlotte's room. It mostly contained chick-lit—Jana's staple—and neither child could reach it. Kennet wouldn't go looking for it—he wasn't stupid, and she'd probably scared him into complicity anyway.

Then she slid into bed beside him, being careful not to touch. This was companionship, care and the act of a guardian angel.

It was 03:44. She was exhausted.

'Night, roomie.'

'Night, Kayte. And... thank you.'

# 21

Kennet found her in the kitchen at 07:55. Charlotte and Tomas were at the table, eating nicely as if they'd been siblings for years. That was a small mercy amongst this mess—they weren't making things harder.

He felt humbled but buoyed after the night's events, a demon exorcised. He was blessed to have someone to keep the emotional wolf from the door.

There was coffee on the side and an open bag of chocolate cookies.

Kayte was still in her night things. 'Hey.'

'Hey.' He sat.

She reached to a high cupboard, fetching down a new bag of coffee. Her top rode up a couple of inches.

He frowned. Her belly wasn't as flat as he remembered. That, plus other evidence....

He marched her into the lounge. 'What do you weigh?'

'Huh?'

He fixed a serious look. 'It's important.'

She folded her arms. 'About one twenty-five normally. One twenty-six at the Söderhamn physical.'

He took her hand again and led her to the upstairs ensuite. He pulled out the scales.

'Kennet—'

He held up a finger for her to shush, then waved her onto the foot-square platform.

The display read 131.9.

'Look—' she began.

'No. I don't want to hear it.'

She tugged her strap top down like a petulant teen. 'What do you care about the way I look?'

'You're snacking. Bingeing. Over-eating. It's compensation.'

'It's... a little comfort food.'

He clasped her bare arm. 'And mine was a little *comfort drinking*. So I will have *that* back, yes?'

'You will not,' she snapped.

'So it's one rule for you, another for me?' He lasered his eyes on hers. 'I'm doing the intervention now. You stop this. It is not about your *figure*. I don't mind that. I am judging your behaviour, not your body. Protecting your health and your mental well-being. Don't hide like I was. I'm not letting this go, Kayte. I care too much.'

Her head fell. 'Shit. I knew, but... I didn't....' She looked up. 'I'm sorry.'

'Fine. I will trust you. I won't make you drink saltwater or have a shower or throw out all the delicious food. Especially as most of it here is *my* delicious food.' He smiled. 'But no sneaking. And no withholding sadness. Yes?'

'Yes.' Her eyes twinkled. 'Inspector.'

He pulled her in and kissed the top of her head. She embraced him.

'Maybe this is another good reason for you to stay. I can watch *you* too.'

She broke off. 'You don't mind, right? I thought about it so hard. This isn't my space. It's yours and Jana's... and Tomas'. I'm not trying to come in like a new broom and sweep away her memory.'

'I know. But it is a sensible decision. Why be single parents far apart? There is room here. The children get along. I have access to the polis system. We can do a little... sneaky work. Put our minds together. Maybe achieve a small victory.'

'Yeah. But one thing's definite. There'll be awkward moments. There must be ground rules. I know it's your place, but privacy is privacy.'

'Indeed.'

'So, we always lock the bathroom door. We share chores. We don't assume it's okay to walk around half-naked—even for middle-of-the-night emergencies.'

'We don't eat cookies alone.'

'We don't drink alone,' she retorted.

He nodded. 'It is a... house share.'

'Exactly. And I have a crazy idea that when Enna comes next week, she can crash at my place. Save her the hotel bill—pay her back for doing this visit.'

'You are very smart.'

She mock curtsied. 'Absolutely. But there *will* be mistakes here. Not the withholding, puking and showering kind—at least, I hope not. We get on together, but this is uncharted territory. Honestly, I'm a little scared, though it's for the best. We're too close—and too dependent right now—to let small problems derail us. We have to find a new normal.' She glanced around the ceiling. 'After the sky has fallen in.'

They returned to the kitchen.

Tomas looked up. 'Daddy? Is Auntie Kayte staying with us again?'

Kayte flashed embarrassment.

'For a little,' Kennet said. 'Is that okay?'

Tomas beamed. 'Of course. She's nice.'

'Yes, she is. And she's a bit lonely without Auntie Carey here, so we are... hanging out.'

'Because she is from America, and it's a long way away?'

'Exactly. Plus, I think she likes you a lot.'

'I do, Tomas,' Kayte said. 'You're a very good boy.'

'Charlotte is nice too,' Tomas said.

Kayte smiled and kissed her daughter's head. Charlotte looked up from creating a mess on her highchair tray. Kayte tapped the button nose with a fingertip. Then she frowned, glancing back and forth to Kennet.

'What?' he asked, stepping to her, concerned.

'She has your chin. I never noticed before.' She fingered the dimple in his chin. 'And she has your eyes.'

Her fingers entwined with his. 'We made a *person*.' Her expression was earnest, almost adoring.

'Carey did the hard work. I only—'

Her hand shot up. 'No imagery, please. You provided your *input*. I provided my *input*. You gave Carey and me something special. And her nurturing and care gave Charlotte the best start in life. She is the product of three amazing people.'

Kennet held himself against the emotion of that.

He changed the subject. 'What shall we do?'

'Take a trip to my house, bring some more things back? Take a walk at Segelvik?' She pinched her nose. 'Carey liked it there.'

He clasped her shoulder. 'Come on. Let's make it a place that you like, too. I think Tomas has been there. Let's get some air.'

Given the pervading circumstances, it was a joyous day. Bright, sunny, and sprinkled with laughter.

However, one awkward wrinkle had happened, and as they sat on the sofa, dinner in their bellies, children asleep upstairs, Kennet sensed something preying on Kayte's mind.

'What is it?' He hoped it was the same thing as he was pondering.

Kayte bit her lip. 'When that... woman said what she did, the way I reacted was....' She shuttered her eyes. 'Hurtful. I'm sorry. I was thrown—you get that?'

'Of course. I understand. I must have gone bright red.' He flashed an embarrassed smile.

'I mean, I can see why she said it. The kids were happy. We were happy. Man, woman, two kids, out for a walk.' She shrugged. 'I might just as well have slapped you, right?'

He took her hand. 'We can't go around being miserable. Nothing will stop comments, good or bad.' He heaved a sigh. 'Many people in Bollnäs have passed on good wishes. It is nice, but it hurts, you know?'

'I've had that. Can't stop these reminders popping up.'

'So today we seemed like... "a lovely family". I would rather such words than pity and solemn looks. It makes me hopeful that Tomas and I *will* look happy—and *be* happy—again. Perhaps not soon, but someday.'

'And I reacted like a bitch. Like... "Ohmygod, I'm not with *those* people. No *way*. Married to *him*? Yuk.".' She punched her thigh.

He calmly placed her palm on her leg, so she wouldn't repeat the gesture.

'It was a gut reaction. A... "curve ball"? You are right to set that woman straight. I don't feel insulted. We don't want people getting the wrong idea, isn't that so?'

She sighed hard. 'I guess. Only... it isn't *yuk*. Hanging with you and Tomas. It's good. And pretty damn necessary. But you will tell me if I'm treading on toes?'

'Of course.'

'Your support and company are... the difference right now. I know we did this before. When Carey got shot in DC, I thought it was the *end of the world*, but it was nothing compared to this. Back then, I treated you bad. Overreacted—like I did today. Hell, I made a pass at you—which is *not allowed* when we're both married—potentially pushing you away or losing you as a friend, as a colleague.'

He smiled. 'So I should not worry you will do the same again?'

She shook her head. 'No. I need you—even if it is because you're sharing my pain.' She rested her head on his shoulder. 'Plus, you give such damn good hugs, and that may be my one outlet to expel pain and loneliness.'

His throat tightened. Just when she and Carey—and he—thought things couldn't get any worse, they had.

'You suffered so much. You never get any luck in your life.'

She put an arm across him. 'Yes, I do,' she murmured. 'I got you.'

# 22

Sunday was tough for Kennet because his parents visited. Kayte made herself scarce, taking both children into town for ice cream.

It was an emotional couple of hours for him, but there was no point in suppressing it. It was the first time they'd visited since Jana died, having given him space until then. They asked about the presence of Kayte and Charlotte's things but seemed to take his explanation at face value—which was a mercy. The last people he wanted to get the wrong idea were his relatives.

They offered to examine the possibility of selling their house—which was a four-hour drive away—and moving somewhere closer. Or perhaps Kennet and Tomas could make a new start in Örebro?

He declined: Tomas was settled at school, and he didn't want to have the additional burden of transferring his job to a new PD. He didn't mention that it would leave Kayte isolated, nor that she might be moving to Bollnäs PD soon. Yet, it had factored into his thoughts.

Mid-afternoon, after his parents had left and Kayte was entertaining Charlotte, Chief Janssen made a surprise visit.

There were handshakes all around, Kennet brewed coffee, and he encouraged Tomas to play in his room. Janssen was unlikely to be here socially, which meant that sensitive and unsettling matters were on the agenda.

Janssen eyed his hosts warily as if torn. 'Because the two of you are not suspended, only... taking a rest, it is not improper to share details with you.'

Kayte nodded. 'That doesn't mean we're—I'm—not grateful, Chief Inspector.'

The man waved. 'Ulrik, please. Rank is unimportant in matters where colleagues are at a low ebb.'

Kennet toyed with his mug. 'Kayte is right about our thanks. But it is also the case that I—we—would not want you to make your circumstance difficult—'

'Put anyone's nose out of joint, tread on toes,' Kayte interjected.

Kennet nodded, reflecting on the almost telepathic connection he had with her. 'Do not make a nuisance, Ulrik, for us.'

Ulrik wrung his hands. 'Well, amongst this horrible situation, there is one piece of luck. There is some investigation about the pilot. He was a Dane, Aksel Hansen, now living in Gävleborg. I have secured authority for Bollnäs to be involved with the case.'

Kayte sat up straight. 'What investigation?'

Janssen's gaze flicked between them. 'The black box was found, but it did not record the last minute of the flight—in the cockpit. The data....' He shook his head. 'It can be interpreted that the plane was deliberately put into a dive.' He held up both palms. 'But I am not an expert. I am only relaying evidence. The conclusions are for the crash investigation unit.'

'Ulrik, how do you have this information? Surely it is not public?' Kennet frowned.

'It isn't. But I have opened a conversation with Juhani Koskinen, the Team Leader. They are, of course, a Finn, but the team is Nordic regional, so we are all part of one happy...' his head fell, 'or maybe not so happy family.' He rubbed his chin. 'And by chance, my niece is marrying their son.' A heavy sigh. 'I didn't want you to be in the middle of this—'

Kennet swallowed down sorrow. 'We were already in the middle of this.'

'—but Bollnäs and I will be lending our help, though our time is short.' Janssen forced a smile. 'The little things of police life still go on amidst this madness.'

'You know that Lieutenant Dacourt is visiting?' Kayte said.

'She made me aware. She also vowed to... "butt out"?'

Kayte smiled at Kennet. The stab at foreign colloquialisms wasn't uniquely his quirk.

'With respect to Enna, she often says that but seldom manages it. This time? She's probably dying to help.'

Ulrik finished his coffee. 'I received a call from Chief Wagner. He asked that I keep him updated. He said he would visit soon. I think the news about the pilot has motivated him. Plus, we did not yet solve between us the Eva Svensson murder. I told Tom that Wilmer Svensson does not take interviews. Tom said he would not be the hotshot from the big city and try to bully our citizens.'

'All the same, citizens of both countries and more were on that plane,' Kayte said. 'Tom has many years as Fleet Liaison. He's tactful at getting what he wants, which is answers.' She coughed. 'Enna, maybe less so.'

Ulrik stood. 'If you have your friends and colleagues nearby, that is good for you. And if anyone can add weight to solving any of this, we will all be grateful. Nobody wants noise about flight safety when we are at the point of adding more flight traffic in this region.' He fastened a loose button at his ample midriff. 'If I were a suspicious man—'

'Isn't that all our jobs?' Kayte queried with a smile.

'—true so much—then I hope for a simple explanation. If the pilot was in the clutches of OnePlanet, then this incident would be a way—a horrible, excessive way—to damage public confidence and turn the tide against the new Spaceport altogether.'

Kennet shuddered. All this for an activist protest? Ulrik was right—it was a quick, logical, easy connection to make. At this point, any answer was better than no answer.

'Spaceflight and commercial airlines aren't the same, Chief Inspector. If the idiots at OnePlanet crashed a plane to stop a rocket, they've lost the plot.' Kayte shook her head in disbelief.

Ulrik threw his hands up. 'A lot of people do a lot of crazy and strange things. For causes, for revenge, for greed. We will get to the bottom of this—somebody connected with this investigation will—and then I hope you and Kennet can sleep sounder in your beds.' He checked his wrist. 'Anyway, Mrs Janssen expects me home for dinner.'

He shook their hands. 'Please, above all, remember you are on leave, and any logins to the polis system will be frowned on.'

He went to the door, turned and winked. 'But valuable.'

# 23

Enna was a bundle of nervous energy as she took the hired AutoDrive car from Arlanda airport up to Bollnäs. It was a gentle three-hour drive—no rush, a chance to enjoy the scenery and call Tom to tell him she hadn't got up to any mischief yet. Lexie dozed or watched the landscape slip by.

She'd never visited Kennet's house before. As she approached, Lexie holding her hand and toddling unsteadily, her mood dipped. She'd barely known Jana, yet the loss was keenly felt.

Kennet opened the front door, so Enna found a smile.

He offered his hand, but she pulled him into a loose embrace and murmured her condolences. Kayte appeared behind him, and it was clear that her smile was forced. Still, Kayte scooped Lexie into her arms, cooed for a few moments, then passed her across to Kennet.

The women embraced. Enna felt the suppressed emotion in Kayte's frame, so she let go.

'Where's Charlotte?'

'Napping.'

'Tomas is in his room,' Kennet said.

'I'll have to tell him he's grown. It'd be rude not to.' Enna winked.

'Come on in. Coffee's on,' Kayte said.

'My favourite words.'

They sat in the lounge, all very civilised. Periodically, Enna surreptitiously glanced around. Some of this was to assess Kennet's home, some to see whether he'd begun to hide away any reminders of Jana—he hadn't, and some was curiosity that Kayte's presence appeared more than fleeting.

Enna had imagined that the two grieving friends would stay closely in touch, but when Kayte led her into the spare bedroom to see a waking Charlotte, things seemed different.

*Has Connors moved in? This bed is slept in. Those are her clothes on the rail.*

Kayte must have seen her curious, even judgemental expression.

'Whatever you're thinking, Enna, I wish you'd say. I don't believe for a second you've turned into a shrinking violet in the last six months.'

'Look, Kayte, it's none of my beeswax—'

'He was drinking.'

'Aw, shit.' Enna recalled her own less-than-stellar behaviour when the chips were down.

'I think it's over now, but someone has to watch him. I needed to be here. And... I was comfort eating. Low. Lonely. I don't know anyone outside Söderhamn PD. We've only lived in the area a little while.'

'Hey—I wasn't insinuating anything. Some decision, though.'

'Not at all. This is temporary. A week or two, maybe. Until the worst is over. Actually, moving in with Carey was scarier. We'd been dating just eighteen months. I've known Kennet three years. Plus, there's nothing to lose by being roomies for a few days. We can't *break up* because we aren't dating. And my relationship history is hardly replete with the male of the species anyhow!'

'Yeah, you're right. Sorry.' She felt a heel.

'Plus, remember you and Tom were only working together—I mean that loosely—after your asteroid adventure for, what, a couple of weeks before you started dating?'

'What can I say? It was love at first sight.'

'You really felt like that?'

Enna beamed. 'I was talking about Tom.'

'Don't ever change, Enna.'

Enna took Kayte's hand. 'And I hope this godawful thing doesn't change you too much either—doesn't rip your heart out. A blip is fine. I blipped like crazy when Lexie was taken. And you and Kennet were there for me. That's why I'm here. Because I know what it's like to have a loved one ripped from your life.' She held her chest, suddenly emotional on her friend's behalf. 'Except I know there's no way back for you.'

'No. But there's a way forward. And I'll find it. Kennet too.' Kayte took a deep breath. 'Let's get this baby girl up and fed.'

Enna fed Lexie alongside Charlotte as the two toddlers sat at Kennet's kitchen table.

She watched her colleagues busy around. It was understandable that Kennet took such an interest in Charlotte's welfare—the circumstances of the baby's conception had been disclosed. Yet the cops' coexistence reflected how well they partnered at work, and Enna was sure there wouldn't be any fallouts from cohabiting for a while. All the same, incalculable grief can unsettle the strongest of relationships.

After Tomas ate, Kennet made the three adults an early dinner. Enna had a tot of brännvin, conscious that the AutoDrive would take her and Lexie safely to the hotel.

In a few quiet moments, she missed Tom. The spectre of potential accidents—happening to anyone, anytime, regardless of circumstance—suddenly made her feel very vulnerable. She shook it off, knowing it was only a light being shone on current events. After all, she'd cheated death on many occasions.

*Maybe you're invincible, honey? If so, I hope Tom is too. And Lexie. And everyone here. We could use a collective break.*

'Enna?' Kayte said.

'Hmm?' She focussed.

'I know you're already accommodated in town, but if you want somewhere a bit more spacious and personal, you're welcome to have the keys to my place. Save yourself the hotel cost. It's a half-hour from here, but the harbour's nice, and honestly, I'd like to do something to thank you for coming all this way.'

Enna debated that. 'Maybe we'll look tomorrow, okay? Whatever helps.'

'Ulrik said Tom is coming over,' Kennet said.

'In a couple of days. Wants to throw his hat in the ring, help turn over some rocks. But part of this is supposed to be vacation time. And to take the kids off your hands for a few hours. They don't seem to be too hard to handle.'

'Tomas is a good boy. Plus, he can show you some sights.'

Enna toyed with her glass. 'I had a crazy notion to see if they wanted to go stay in a real castle for a few days?'

Kayte's eyes widened. 'You'd take them to your parents' place?'

Enna shrugged. 'We're in Europe anyhow. Mom and Dad haven't seen Lexie for six months, and boy, has she changed. Plenty of space for them all to run around. Moat pool for Tomas. Sunshine. Plus... it might show me that one bundle of joy is enough.' She smiled. 'If I'm at my wits end with three children after the first day, then on goes the chastity belt, and Tom will have to ditch any hopes he had of a son to knock around with.'

'We couldn't ask that. Could we?' Kayte looked at Kennet.

*"We"? Interesting.*

*Cut it out, Enna.*

'The children aren't under our feet, Enna. They keep us—me—grounded. Without them? Would we lose a touchstone? Mope around?' Kennet rubbed his chin.

'Or you might be free to focus on the case?' Enna suggested.

'"Case"?' Kayte replied. 'It's all curious as hell, but Ulrik didn't call it a case.'

'You mean you don't get the impression there's anything fishy, you don't have the time or headspace to get involved, or you're not interested in helping? Don't think it's the latter—if I know you, Connors.'

'It's personal, I get that, but Janssen reckons—sensibly—that emotional involvement in a case—if there is one—isn't ideal. Probably doesn't want me conducting a vendetta on foreign soil. Though, by the sounds of it, if it's all Aksel Hansen's fault, he's beyond the reach of anyone anymore.' She swallowed hard. 'So, until it's undeniable there's malice—or external agents—then I, for one, am staying out of the office.'

'Okay. Understood. But some time off, away from this place?' Enna bit her lip, afraid to voice the idea. 'Or—please tell me this isn't insensitive and inappropriate as hell—you might go over to visit the site? A chance at a crumb of closure. It's right for some people, but....' She waved it away. 'I want to help, that's all. You know me—always sticking my nose into things. Speaking my mind. Usually winding up getting taken down a peg by the brass—or Tom. Or waking up in a hospital bed.'

Kennet and Kayte exchanged a look.

Enna saw his hand move towards hers, then retreat.

'It has crossed my mind,' he said.

Kayte bit her lip. 'Mine too.'

Enna drained her glass. 'Let me know, okay? I need to do something to keep busy, or I'll be tempted to make a nuisance of myself somewhere.'

# 24

Kayte stayed in the spare room that night after Enna had left. There were things to consider, and Enna's curiosity, even inference—although it was barely that—regarding her and Kennet's... house share... caused self-consciousness and made her examine her deepest insecurities.

She slept fitfully, made worse by a keenness to have the comfort of Kennet just inches away. She'd created a crutch for her emotional needs—and now, to at least one visitor, it was making her appear inappropriate. She could even be accused of disloyalty to Carey's memory, able to all-too-easily brush off death and a vanished marriage.

Her fist clenched: it wasn't like that. She missed Carey deeply.

She allowed herself to cry—quietly so she didn't wake Charlotte nearby. This was impossible: it seemed tricky to do something which kept everyone, especially her conscience, happy. Still, she had to try—to look deep inside for guidance on how to get through this without incident, heartbreak or potential ostracization.

Over breakfast on Tuesday, she and Kennet discussed Enna's suggestions. They knew it would be hard to visit the crash site, but it felt timely. It was already painful enough having to wait so long for the recovery of remains. Only funerals could draw some kind of line under things, but this was the next best step.

They told Tomas they had some work matters to attend to, then took him and Charlotte to meet Enna at Kayte and Carey's house. Tomas had been there before, so it wasn't a stretch for him. Unfortunately, he asked when Carey would be back. Covering that up was a tough couple of minutes, but Enna gamely jumped in and saved any tears.

Showing Enna around also required Kayte to corral her emotions. The outcome was that Enna was happy to move in for a few days.

Kayte gave Charlotte a big hug and said she'd be back from "work" as soon as possible.

It was a two-hour drive to the site, and conversation was spartan. As they drew nearer, butterflies of sorrowful apprehension besieged her belly. Kennet's expression indicated he was suffering likewise.

At the waymarked entrance to the taped-off site—a mile in circumference—they showed their police and civilian credentials to the official gatekeeper, clasped hands firmly together, and walked to a pre-ordained area where loved ones were allowed to observe and grieve.

They declined offers from support staff, found a spot as remote as possible, gazed at the carnage, and then dissolved into a long tear-soaked hug. It was barely enough to distract from the eerie calm of the battered hillside. Knives scraped at her insides.

She dried her eyes. 'I think we deserve a drink.'

'Not too much, just enough, yes?'

'And your best-ever meatballs, if you can manage it?'

'I will try. Jana's special recipe.' He swallowed hard.

She looped her arm into his. 'Take me home, Inspector.'

'Yes, Sergeant.'

They collected the children from Enna—a good few hours had passed—then went to Kennet's house. After the usual routine of getting through mealtimes and bedtimes, they worked together in the kitchen on their own repast.

Before they sat at the dining table, nearly a full bottle of wine had disappeared. What had also nourished her was not needing to return to an empty house, put Charlotte to bed, and then sit alone in silence, contemplating the day's milestone.

The dinner was exceptional, and there was fun during its preparation—shoulder nudges, mutual teasing, and he'd even spoon-fed her a couple of taste tests of the sauce. That was unexpected, a softening of his natural reserve and historical embarrassment at things like bodily contact with her.

They retired to the sofa, wine glasses in hand. She was nicely lubricated—not maudlin but pensive. The last couple of days had shone a light on the past, present and future. It made her think about things, some of which were awkward.

'Kennet. Have you thought about whether you'd ever consider another relationship? Have someone in your life again, sometime?'

He toyed with his glass. 'No. I have not thought. But if I did, I wouldn't want to replicate what I had before. Maybe not even search for someone like Jana. There would always be comparison, which is unfair to... whoever.'

'I think that's very self-aware.'

He shrugged. 'But I would... consider it. I like company. Need it, probably. As long as they were intelligent, and they made me laugh. They were nice to look at—for me, anyway. And they accepted my flaws. And me being a single father. And being polis—which we know is not the safest thing sometimes.'

'Sensible, grounded expectations. Very *you*.'

'Hmm.' He sipped, offering an almost furtive glance. 'What about you?'

'I'm positive I couldn't carry on alone. Being with Carey for so long, and now with you all this time, has shown me I need somebody in my life. Someone to hold onto at night. Hug.' She beamed knowingly. 'You may have heard that about me. Experienced it too. Anyone new wouldn't have to be a clone of Carey.' The smile vanished. 'Up front, they'd have to one hundred percent accept that I was a widow. They'd have to understand I might think about her sometimes. And get kinda down—only for a spell, I guess. They'd never know how hard it was—this period, getting through it.'

'Unlikely.'

She brightened. 'But so long as they were kind, and smart, and caring, and funny. They'd have to be a good parent to Charlotte. Understand she had a father who might want to visit.'

'I'd be flexible.'

She patted his knee. 'I know.'

He smiled. 'Would they have to be American?'

Her heart thumped. 'Not necessarily. Kinda tough anyway, if I stay here.' She offered a sober smile and took a brave pill. 'Would your... person need to be Swedish?'

'I don't think so.' He stroked his chin nervously. 'Would yours need to be...' he swallowed hard, 'female?'

She looked away. 'Not... necessarily.'

She drank hastily. Something unidentifiable crackled inside her. Was it nerves, embarrassment, or discomfort? No—it was fear. Fear that she'd realised a truth which couldn't be.

It was the wine, she resolved. That, and the hyper-real sight of life-changing destruction. The void inside her had swelled during the day, and she was hastily filling it with the best option available. She was making herself believe, even admit, that Kennet's presence in her life was, although perhaps a poor second best to what had gone before, a very fine outcome to have.

He was looking at her, and she met his gaze.

Rogue synapses fired, and she leaned towards him, aiming for his lips.

Mercifully—and hopefully even before the gesture was screamingly obvious—she halted. Inside, she cursed: damn alcohol. Damn circumstance. Those two had got her into a mess once before.

He glanced away, drank, and closed his eyes briefly.

'I....' Then she wished she hadn't started. She might have got away with it otherwise.

He coughed. 'It's okay.'

'It's not okay.' She rapped the glass down on the table in self-admonishment.

He winced. 'It has been a difficult day. And I know that wine takes away the pain. It also takes away....' He frowned.

'A layer of good sense?' She cursed herself again.

'It can make you believe things that aren't true.' His chuckle was nervous, forced.

She nodded hard. 'We need to deal with what *is* true, professionally and personally. Facts, however bad they are.'

He quickly took her hand, which was a surprise. 'And however good they are. I mean that we have people looking out for us, our health, our children, and the knowledge that tomorrow cannot be worse than today.'

'You're a smart guy, Kennet.'

Then he did something even more wild and uncharacteristic. He lifted her hand and pressed it against his cheek. 'I forgave... silly outbursts before. Emotions are high—bad and good ones—right now.'

'Blood alcohol levels are pretty up there, too,' she joked.

'And we did say mistakes will happen when we are being... roomies?'

'Roomies, yeah. Yeah, we did. Thanks for forgiving me. In advance of... nothing.'

'If you walk through the valley of death, I expect there will be stones to trip on, no?'

She beamed. 'Poetic, even when you're boozed up. Pretty amazing—yet again.'

He winked. 'Well, Enna is here now, so we need to... up our game... on being amazing—if we want to compete.'

She shoulder-nudged him. 'She's alright, I guess, but she's no Kennet.'

Then, having sized up his mood and judging the atmosphere and intent to be wholly different from sixty seconds before, she calmly leaned in and pecked him on the lips.

His wide-eyed response was relatively tame. 'And that was very... Kayte of you.'

'That's something, I guess—that I'm still me.'

'And does this "me" snore after she has drunk a lot of wine?'

'I don't think she does. Does this Kennet?'

'I was told yes.'

Her heart sank a mite. 'Separate beds. And hopefully, clear heads tomorrow. We should investigate what Ulrik said—I mean, if you're able.' Her shoulders fell. 'I think if today did anything, it made me want to start turning over some rocks.'

'I suggest we take Enna up on her offer. There is work to do, and Tomas has many weeks' holiday. I can't imagine I can put on a brave face—and keep him entertained—for so long.'

'I don't envy you that. At least Charlotte's more immune to... the shock. The loss.' She put her shoulders back. 'Anyway, enough wallowing. Doesn't do any good. Can't change the past, only make a future. Plus, you know, the boss arrives Thursday, and we can't have those damn Americans coming over here, solving Swedish cases, right?'

She winked, and he returned it, which pleased her booze-soaked mind.

# 25

On Wednesday, they hung out with Enna and Lexie. Enna was great with Charlotte and Tomas, but Kennet was nervous that three children were a lot for her to handle, especially on a journey, despite Enna's self-proclaimed superwoman status.

'You forget, Kennet, that my parents will be at the chateau too. And my sister is coming over for a few days. There'll be Theo and Honorine to play with.' She patted his shoulder. 'But if things get crazy, I'll call you up, and you can come relieve me of the burden. Deal?'

Kayte was looking expectantly at him.

'I suppose so,' he said.

Enna crouched down in front of the eight-year-old. 'Hey, Tomas. How would you like to go to a real castle? With a swimming pool and suits of armour and an orchard full of apples and more children to play with and an enormous bed to bounce on and—'

His eyes lit. 'Yes, yes, yes!' Then he looked up at Kennet, who ruffled the boy's hair and nodded.

'Will mummy come? And Auntie Carey?' Tomas added.

Kennet's throat tightened. 'No, not this time. They are still... away.'

Tomas fell sad. 'Oh.'

Enna tickled his tummy. 'But there will be me, Charlotte, and Lexie. We can climb the tower and play hide and seek. Okay?'

Kennet was filled with gratitude.

'Daddy?'

'I have to stay here with Auntie Kayte and do some work. Very important work. Enna... *Auntie* Enna... will look after you.'

Enna winked.

'Okay,' Tomas said, bounding off to catch up with Kayte and Charlotte.

Kennet hugged Enna. 'I wish things were different, and I didn't need such kindness.'

'Me too. I'm only trying to make a silk purse out of a sow's ear. And if you've seen my sewing, you'd never let Tomas anywhere near me.' She winked.

On Thursday, Enna collected Tom from Bollnäs station, and all seven ate lunch in town.

Then they went back to Kennet's house, and the adults gathered around for an early evening pow-wow.

'Pretty brave, letting Ellie and Han mind the store,' Kayte said.

'She's really coming on,' Tom said. 'Besides, things are quiet. Arguably I'm better off over here, poking my nose into a few things.'

'Amen to that,' Enna said. 'It's been three weeks. It's past time for answers.'

'I had a long call on the train with Janssen. A few answers, but more questions.'

'Well, don't keep us in suspense,' Kayte said.

Tom took a deep breath. 'The cockpit voice recorder doesn't have the crucial final minute. I think you knew that. The box is being forensically analysed, but the current theory is that it was switched off. Maybe by the pilot. Maybe because he didn't want the conversation or the alarm being publicised.'

'Which means this was no moment of madness. It was planned. Almost...' Enna shuddered. 'Cold and calculating.'

Kennet pinched the bridge of his nose.

Kayte rubbed his shoulder. 'Come on, partner. We've got days of this. It won't be easy.'

He blew out a breath. 'I know. I am sorry. Go on, Tom.'

'They've found the pilot's remains and are doing analysis. They've spoken to the family. Apparently, Aksel Hansen was on standby and was called up to take the flight after the rostered pilot couldn't make it. The person who interviewed his wife said they suspected she was hiding something but had to go steady with the questioning because of the sensitive nature of everything.'

'More questions, like you said,' Kayte murmured.

'I've requested the flight manifest. If you want something to do, you can go through that. We should check if Aksel had a... I hate to use the word... accomplice on board.'

'OnePlanet?' Enna asked.

Tom shrugged. 'Our job is always to search for motive as well as a perp. If it was purely Hansen wanting to commit suicide—in the worst way possible—then that's a simple explanation and doesn't leave much room for any follow-up. If it was a horrendous OnePlanet act of sabotage by a lone wolf, we're at a dead end. If there were other parties involved—who can meet justice—then that's what we all want.'

Enna gritted her teeth. 'And if I find who ruined Kayte and Kennet's lives, I'll tear them a new asshole.'

Tom shot her a hard stare. 'That's not your job.'

'Then you do it for me.'

He rapped the chair arm. 'I'll go by the damn book, Enna. I'm pulling so many strings, calling in all my favours to be involved in this godawful thing. Don't for a second believe I'm not as emotionally and professionally invested in this as you.'

'We know you are, Chief,' Kayte said.

'Yeah. Sorry.'

Enna sighed. 'No, I'm sorry. I said I'd butt out, but seeing the hurt up close and personal, and getting a damn scary feeling this was no accident? Hard not to get this gal's hackles up, that's all.'

'Then you need to chill. Take the kids and skedaddle!' Kayte winked. 'Go have fun. No point in all of us being riled up and hurting. I'm jealous as hell. Would I rather be eating French pastries and swimming in the sun? Hell, yes.'

'Take your holiday, Enna,' Kennet said. 'Hopefully, this will be over soon, and we can all rest.'

'There's an open invitation for you to come out to Fort Valley, or Frogerie. It's damn nice round here, Kennet, but I'm biased—the Loire is always better.'

'If I can go to your parents' house without either Kaye or I being assaulted, that will be a start!' Kennet laughed at his recall of previous near-misses.

'I think we've all used up more than our fair share of hits and near-misses.' Enna raised her glass. 'Here's to plain sailing, friendship, and throwing a few more assholes in jail.'

# 26

F riday turned out to be a watershed.

During the morning, Kayte helped Kennet to gather the children's things in preparation for their impromptu French holiday. Tom would accompany them to Stockholm, take the flight to Paris, drive to Chateau Frogerie, stay a night, then return alone on Sunday, ready to begin work in earnest on Monday.

Kayte was already suffering separation anxiety—it would be the longest time she'd been away from Charlotte—but they could videocall any time, and the change of scene plus the available play and activities would do the child no harm at all.

Tomas put his favourite toy in the suitcase. 'I'm sad mummy can't come to the castle.'

'I'm sad too,' Kennet replied.

'When will mummy come home?'

'I... don't know, buddy.'

Kayte saw him purse his lips. The silence was horrible.

'Daddy?'

'Yes?'

Tomas gazed up at his father with wide blue eyes. 'Did mummy die?'

Kayte's heart fractured. She breathed deeply, centring herself. I must be strong for my pal, she mused.

Kennet swallowed hard. 'Yes.' His voice cracked. 'Mummy died.'

Myriad emotions swirled on the boy's face. 'Oh. I'm sad now.'

'I'm sad too, Tomas. But mummy loved you so much, and we need to remember that. And she is in heaven now, and it is nice up there, so we must try not to be *too* sad, okay?' He ruffled Tomas' hair. His hands shook.

Kayte held in tears.

'Okay, daddy. I'll try.' Yet the lad chewed his cheek.

'Good boy.'

He looked at Kayte. She tried a smile, but it came out more like a grimace.

Tomas' little eyebrows furrowed. He looked at Kennet. Clearly, he'd joined the dots.

'Did... did Auntie Carey die too?'

Kayte had to turn away and steel herself so hard. Kennet's hand took hers. She squeezed like a vice.

'Yes, buddy. Carey died too. Auntie Kayte is very sad. But she loves you too and knows you can be grown up about this. And deep down, she is happy because she has baby Charlotte, and her friends. And she wishes she could come to the castle with you, but the work she has to do is very special, and she also might want to be sad for a while. So it's *really* important you look after baby Charlotte in France and make sure she has the best time. And when you come home, we will go out for the biggest-ever ice cream, and you can tell us all the things you did. Is that a deal?'

Tomas raised a palm, and they high fived.

The window into Kennet's paternal bond was instrumental in brightening Kayte's spirits, but when Tomas trotted off to watch cartoons, she barely lasted five seconds before collapsing into Kennet's embrace.

They cried. Water was shed at this watershed.

At three o'clock, Tom arrived, and they gathered in the lounge, making sure Tomas was out of earshot. Charlotte innocently played with blocks.

'I went with Sergeant Mikkelson to see Hansen's widow. She's a fine cop, your colleague.'

'Yes. It will be sad to lose her to Göteborg polis,' Kennet replied.

'She led the interview. Woman to woman was a good plan.'

'And?' Kayte felt like Tom was deliberately drawing this out, possibly to make it easier to digest.

'Hansen was ill. Terminally ill.'

Kayte covered her face. 'Hence suicidal.'

'No. No indication of that. He was a good pilot, excellent record.'

'Does she receive insurance?' Kennet asked.

'Yes, he was covered. If I was being cruel, I'd say Mrs Hansen was spending it already.'

'Any sense of infidelity, marriage problems, custody issues, gambling—the usual suspects?' Kayte asked.

'No. But what I don't like is that she said neither of them had anything to do with OnePlanet. He was very pro the Spaceport. All the same, she'd noticed him being quite guarded recently.'

'Introverted or subversive?'

'Less open. Resigned to things, maybe. He'd made sure his affairs were in order.'

'He knew this was coming?' Kennet asked.

'He knew there would be an end, but maybe not when.'

'But he might have decided how—by taking a few dozen other people with him.' She swallowed down the rank taste in her mouth.

'The selfish, cruel—' Kennet ground one fist into his palm.

Kayte rubbed his back. 'Come on, partner. Box it up, file it away. Solutions, not recriminations, okay?'

He forced a smile and took a deep breath. 'Yes. You are right. Professional detachment.'

Tom gave them a few seconds. 'So my thinking is—why like this, specifically? Why that week? Why that day? Why that flight?'

'Because it had to happen sometime, and we just got unlucky,' Kayte said.

Tom did a so-so of the head. 'Absolutely, it could be random. But he was on standby. Something called Priority One. Last line of defence. You know how often they get called off Priority One? Less than once a year.'

Kennet bent forwards on the sofa, elbows on his knees. 'There's a dog buried here,' he murmured.

She patted his arm. 'To translate—Inspector doesn't like it, boss.'

'I don't like it either, Kayte. I need to talk to Crew Resourcing. And I got you the flight manifest. See if there are any... dogs buried in that.'

Kennet smiled. 'Thank you.'

'And I put a call in to Koskinen on the crash team. They'll keep me updated on black box forensics, pilot autopsy. Janssen has requested the pilot's medical records, digital life, bank records, the works. And the co-pilot for good measure. If there was a conversation, or worse, on the flight deck, there's nothing saying who was at the root of it. But the word is that technical malfunction has been ruled out. It was pilot error or something else.'

'The big question is why,' she said.

'Something pushed Hansen over the edge. Triggered the decision to act at that specific time. I suggest you spend the weekend coming up with as many wild theories as you can. We'll talk on Monday.' He stood. 'Now I need to go and see whether my troublemaker wife has trashed your house, Connors.'

'If I know her, she'll have tracked down the best chocolate pudding in Söderhamn, found the brännvin shop, and be filling the car with provisions for your trip.'

Tom rolled his eyes. 'If that's the worst she gets up to, that's a result. See you in the morning. Drop the kids over around eight. It's going to be a long day.'

# 27

Kayte knew that this goodbye was harder for her than it was for Charlotte. Her daughter's separation anxiety was always worse regarding Carey. She spent more time, and unarguably had a closer natural bond, with her birth mother. Plus, Kayte was away from the house much more, so Charlotte was used to her absence.

What the girl needed was the person who would never return.

The car was packed, Tomas had bid farewell to Kennet, and Kayte locked Charlotte's baby seat into the back.

'Need Mommy,' Charlotte said.

'Mommy's not here. Mommy's gone. I'm here. Mom's here.'

'Want Mommy.'

Kayte painted a smile over her concern. 'You've got Auntie Enna, Uncle Tom. And Lexie—look at Lexie. What's that she's got?' She pointed at where Lexie was sucking on a stuffed cat.

'Cat,' Charlotte said.

'You'll see some real cats at the castle. And horses. And chickens.' She pecked her daughter's forehead. 'Have a lovely time. Mom loves you. Mom loves you so much.' She forced down the emotion, ruffled the girl's hair, and closed the car door.

Tom, standing near, got the message that a swift departure was wise, gave her and Kennet a knowing nod, and slid into the driver's seat.

Kennet came to her shoulder. She wasn't doing this alone, she reminded herself.

The car purred away.

When it was way down the street, she allowed herself to take a familiar hug, let a couple of tears dribble, and then puffed out a breath of composure.

'Take me to coffee and unhealthy pastries, partner.'

They went into Bollnäs and had an indulgent brunch. It nourished her stomach, mood and soul.

Walking back to the car, she spotted a gap in the traffic, grabbed his hand and led them quickly across. It momentarily felt like joyful truanting.

As they continued down the pavement, she became aware that she hadn't let go, and the hyper-real surroundings leapt at her. She released his hand as if it was hot.

'Ohmygod. I'm sorry.' She cupped her mouth, glancing around nervously.

He frowned. 'What?'

'This is your town. I don't want people talking. I don't want to spoil your reputation. What if anyone sees?' She grimaced. 'Jeez, we already live together—which is major fuel for gossip!' She screwed up her eyes. 'No! Not *live*! I'm *staying over*. Jeez.'

He cocked his head, clasping her arm. 'First, I don't care. I'm in mourning for my wife. I have the company of my best friend to get me through—and vice versa. We are *housemates*. Besides, if they accuse me of impropriety, it's easy to deny because there is nothing going on. Is there?'

She chuckled, playing nervously with her hair. 'Hell no. Absolutely not. And I suppose any people whose opinions you cared about—*real* friends—would want you happy, above all.'

'Or at least as happy as I can be in the circumstance.'

'Which is the point of this. All the same, hand holding does give off a... *vibe*.'

He wrinkled his nose. 'That is true.'

'So, agreed. But I can do it at home, okay?'

'Absolutely. Where we won't be in the newspaper for shocking breaches of public decency.' He winked.

'Well, now there really is a problem because you just made me want to hug you.'

He frowned. '"Rain check"?'

'Wa-hey! You nailed one!' She chucked him on the shoulder. 'Good job!'

They noodled around for the afternoon, tidying.

She tentatively raised the topic of what to do with Jana's things.

'Is this because you want to steal some more wardrobe space?' he asked.

'Do I seem like the type of gal who has sixteen pairs of everything?'

'I suppose not.'

She waved it away. 'Sorry for asking. I took the easy way out—walking away from reminders of Carey. The fact you've chosen to stay in this house? Pretty impressive.'

He toyed with a picture frame whose contents depicted their wedding day. 'It is very difficult to look at these things. But also hard to throw them away.'

'Not throw,' she clarified. 'Put them... in the garage. Or store.'

He scratched his chin. 'Or at your house?'

'Combine our... shrine?' She grimaced. 'I don't plan on paying rent on a place I'll never live again.'

'So you will move?'

This topic had been resurfacing in her thoughts.

'If the job is still open at your PD, and I pass muster, I can't think of a good reason not to take it.'

'And you would move here, you and Charlotte? To Bollnäs, or nearby?'

'Dumb to commute, right?'

He brightened. 'That would be a project. For me to help you find a house.'

She narrowed her eyes mischievously. 'Not too close by, okay? I can't be living in your pocket twenty-four-seven.'

'It's not so bad. You didn't annoy me too much yet. Or load the dishwasher wrongly.'

She clicked her fingers. 'Damn. I must try harder.'

He poked her in the ribs.

The house felt oddly empty that evening, and it brought a sense of an almost illicit union. It was ridiculous, but it hadn't stopped similar notions from popping into her head over the past three weeks. It felt wrong to be happy when she should be sad. To have company when fate dictated she be alone.

They lounged on the sofa.

He threw increasingly querulous looks in her direction.

She patted his hand. 'What is it, roomie?'

He took a deep breath. 'What *are* we, Kayte? Truly? What are we doing, you and I?'

'Is this about the handholding before?'

'And the hugs, and the sleeping over. And maybe more things.'

She nibbled her lip, thinking. It wasn't as if this question hadn't crossed her mind. 'You know the expression "friends with benefits"?'

He eased back. 'Yes.'

His alarm made her smile. 'I didn't mean.... Look. Hear me out. We are friends with benefits—but not like *that*. We are colleagues and friends. That's inarguable. Close friends. The difference is I get companionship. We work well as a team with the kids. We support each other logistically, physically, intellectually and emotionally.'

She took a deep breath. 'And, honestly, being with you makes me feel like the darkness will stay away. Being in a house with you means I have a touchstone here. And—this is going to sound odd, maybe—at night, holding you or having you hold me makes me feel safe.' She gritted her teeth. 'And after the worst accidents and incidents have stalked my life lately, safety is a damn high priority.' She took his hand. 'When I'm with you, I'm content. It feels... natural and *right*.'

'Me too.'

'Usually, "friends with benefits" means two people who hang out plus have sex. Nothing in between. No true closeness. No deep bond. It's a cheat. A way to have your cake and eat it.' Her eyebrows flickered in a recall. 'Carey and I knew a couple in New York. Shallow people who didn't have the balls to commit to a relationship—not that it would have worked anyway—but still wanted some free, uncomplicated... *action*.'

He smirked. 'That doesn't surprise.'

'We have *all* of the in-between stuff, which is a damn sight more valuable than something like sex, which can be empty if it's between two people who don't truly love each other in that way. I could never do that. I like to think I'm too respectful and three-dimensional.'

'Certainly, you are.'

'The bad news is that I'm a huggy, kissy person who, for ten years, has had someone to offload affection on. Now she's gone, if you keep letting me hang around, you're in danger of getting that part of me.'

'I am the... rebound person, yes?'

She laughed. 'Yeah. And very much second best to a curvy sleep monster with lips to die for.' She patted his leg. 'But a damn fine second best, all the same.'

'I am your comfort blanket.'

She nodded. 'Aren't I yours?'

'Absolutely.'

'Is that okay, Kennet? You must say if not.'

'It is okay. And I will say.'

'Good. I don't take you for granted, not for a second—which is why openness is vital. What we have isn't fragile, but I would hate to break it. Especially now.'

'Especially now.' His eyes explored hers. There was happiness and warmth in their cool blue. 'Do you want a hug?'

'Always.'

He took her in an embrace.

Everything was okay, she mused. More than okay.

# 28

He awoke on Sunday to find her still in bed in the spare room. He did miss her company—even the proximity of her body—at night, but it had been a temporary arrangement to allow them to get over the horrors and the gaping hole in their lives.

She was right—the days were getting easier, certainly in terms of coping with the grief. Coping with and understanding whatever it was they were doing? That was harder.

While he was having breakfast, she walked in, bleary-eyed. Her hair was askew, her feet bare, the sheer cami top and shorts accentuating her pleasing figure.

He shook away any hormone-induced interest. For many days, they'd managed to coexist without his libido being spiked. After the previous evening's conversation, something had changed—but in some ways, it had worsened the situation. He was experiencing unwelcome twinges of curiosity. It was an echo of the first few seconds in NYC when they initially met—when he saw her for the first time and noted how strikingly pretty she was.

Now, such notions were inappropriate. He was living with loss. She was too. It wasn't ideal to feel even the tiniest thing—yet he wasn't in control of his masculinity.

The situation was too perfect to spoil, like juggling Fabergé eggs or walking on fresh snow.

'Hey.'

'Hey,' he replied, emerging from a haze.

'Can you... um.... What do you think about teaching me Swedish?' She poured a glass of orange juice.

He processed that. 'Why suddenly this?'

She fiddled with her hair, checking her reflection in a table knife. 'Just an idea. The way my mind is, I can't see myself going back to the States anytime soon. Plus, you know, a distraction from... everything.'

'That feels like a decision to be taken when the circumstance is more... normal. When you can think about matters without the baggage of what happened. Without being affected by living in this bubble of sadness and,' he gestured around, 'pleasant cohabitation.'

'You kicking me out, roomie?' Her eyebrows darted up. 'Wait. I should be paying you rent.'

'Now you are being ridiculous. You are my... guest.'

'Okay. If you insist. Then get your guest some coffee. And quick sharp.' She clicked her fingers.

He poked her in the side. They laughed.

Starting the day with laughter was infinitely better than the alternative.

A cold front had brought rain, so they huddled around the PD system and attempted to make progress—the space created by the children's absence needed to be used productively rather than for enjoyment. Certainly, Kennet was finding it odd to be in his home without anyone from his family.

He accessed the flight manifest that Tom had acquired, then printed it so they could annotate at their leisure.

The first thing he did was to take a thick black marker and put a solid line through two familiar names—names which had everything to do with their lives but not their investigation. They exchanged a sober expression.

They started at the top, treating each passenger with equal diligence.

It was somehow heartening and anchoring to get back to working as two cops, an island of normality in a storm-whipped ocean of unfamiliar challenges.

They trawled the PD system, linked to the worldwide database, for evidence of crimes and misdemeanours. They undertook internet searches, following up on social media profiles and posts, articles and blogs, employment listings and anything else in the public domain. If they needed to access further data, they'd subpoena for the relevant records, but the first job was to search for anything suspicious or connected to other elements of their investigations.

After eliminating six people—it was tiresome work—they took lunch.

Kayte munched on a sandwich. 'How about we call Enna?'

'I'm amazed you waited this long.'

'I miss Charlotte like crazy, but she's in good hands. Besides,' she winked, 'I've got other, bigger, hugs on tap if needed.'

They videocalled Enna and spent half an hour catching up, cooing over the toddlers, feeling jealous at the convivial atmosphere, and getting sidelined by discussing police work for a few minutes.

Tomas was taking everything in his stride, and whilst Charlotte more than once displayed longing for Carey and Kayte, Enna reassured them that the child was coping splendidly.

When the call ended, Kennet fell quiet, wishing it could have been a holiday for the entire family rather than a convenient diversion to allow him and Kayte some space.

She patted his hand. 'Come on, partner. Answers won't find themselves.'

In the afternoon, they got through eight more names and turned up nothing untoward. Then, as his stomach was issuing reminders that mealtime was approaching, he happened upon something.

'Emil Falk served time for murder. Freed on appeal and good behaviour.'

'So? Anyone going to cry about that?'

He tapped the screen. 'The victim's husband campaigned furiously for Falk to get a life sentence with no release. Protested at the courthouse every day.' He clenched a handful of his hair in frustration. 'Because his wife was killed.'

She gently took his hand down and held it. 'And he maybe doesn't feel he got justice?'

'Or am I projecting?'

She bit her lip. 'Doubt it. I think you have a point. History is replete with vendettas.'

'But to crash a plane to kill one man out of frustrated revenge?' He shook his head. 'It's a very long shot.'

'There are a lot of crazy people in the world. Look, it's a start. A glimmer of a motivation here... somewhere. This is good, Kennet. We're getting our mojos back. Let's absolutely follow this up. You see if there's any way Falk could be connected to the pilot, the co-pilot, the flight, OnePlanet—even the Spaceport. But tomorrow, okay? I don't want us burning out by working until midnight. We're not even supposed to be working at all. Plus, there are plenty of people covering other angles.'

He made a fist. 'I need to *contribute*.'

'Hey, take it easy.'

His mind flashed with images of the plummeting aircraft. 'I can't do this. I can't do it. Why that day? Why them? Why my wife? Why yours? Why not me on that plane?' he rapped. 'Then I wouldn't be in this mess. Nor you.'

She grabbed his shirt and hauled him up. 'You cut that out!'

'I can't go on.'

She clasped his hands. 'That's enough. We've cried for this, hated this, and plumbed the depths. Not again, Kennet.'

'Bring Jana back. Take me!' he implored the heavens.

'Now you're being ridiculous.'

'Then make it stop,' he said, body fizzing.

'I can't. But you know what? *You* damn well can.' There was disbelief on her face. 'How can you wish you were dead? You have a son, a daughter you helped create, a career, and the chance to get justice for Jana? You being dead would disappoint and grieve plenty of people, especially me. It's dumb as hell to wish for that different timeline. You might as well wish the crash hadn't happened. It's a waste of time, Kennet.'

She rattled his hands hard, as if to shake sanity into him. 'We must deal with *reality*. And the reality is that we get on with our lives. We find a future, and we be the damn good cops we are—together or apart—and we find answers, and causes, and culprits. Okay?'

He forced away the despair and feeling of inertia. 'I will try.'

'Yes, you damn will.'

He rubbed his forehead, sheepish. 'I'm sorry.'

She pulled him into an embrace. 'Come here. It's okay. Neither of us can stop the demons from coming. Only cast them out as quickly as possible, send them packing, and know we're on a path. Cry—fine. Regret and rail? No.'

She let him go. 'Now, let's make dinner, then let me whip your ass at cards.'

As the evening passed, the card games descended into mock cheating, real cheating, teasing and good-natured prods.

It took him back to similar days with Jana, on the same sofa, in equally high spirits. That nosedived his humour, and Kayte had to give him another pep talk.

She buoyed him with hammed-up pronunciations of the handful of Swedish words she'd picked up over the past year. Then he took the mickey out of her soft New York twang, and laughter was soon back.

She was looking at him unusually intently.

'What?' he asked.

'You have a nice smile, Kennet. You should smile more.'

'You make me smile. So do Tomas and Charlotte.' His head dipped. 'Jana did too.'

She gently raised his chin. 'Oh. The smile has gone now.'

'Hmm.'

She softly ruffled his hair. 'Remember the mantra. Tomorrow will be another day. A better day. Every day will be a little better.'

He gazed at her, around the room, then at her. 'If I have you.'

'And I have you.'

His brow furrowed. 'Are you worried about this... co-dependence?'

She managed a half-smile. 'No. Besides, you don't take a plaster cast off until the wound is mended.'

# 29

A single day hadn't been enough for Tom to relax at Enna's parents' Chateau de la Frogerie in the Loire. Still, that wasn't his job. His role was to ferry Enna, Lexie, Tomas Carlsson and Charlotte Kayte Maddison to their vacation getaway, settle them in, then turn around and retrace his steps alone.

Luckily, parents Mimie and JP Dacourt had laid on an amazing spread, and Enna's childhood four-poster bed proved both comfortable and a playground for enjoyable nocturnal *activities*.

After an early train from Cholet to Paris, he took a lunchtime flight to Stockholm, then collected Enna's rented AutoDrive from Arlanda airport and cruised upcountry to Bollnäs.

On the way, he called Ellie and Han, who were sipping the first coffee of the morning in the Fleet PD office in Washington DC.

They were coping well, with banter developing—Han was beginning to open up. Tom knew people with ASD often struggled to socialise and had small friendship groups. Perhaps Ellie was joining that select group? She was a smart young woman herself, on the shy side, driven, curious and occasionally mischievous.

Tom congratulated himself on those two hires. With Kayte and Kennet temporarily sidelined, the youngsters needed to pull their weight.

Sadly, there were no developments on the Viggo Alban and Eva Svensson cases, the trail going cold. Unless Viggo's movements could be traced via thousands of hours of security footage, or a thread of foreign DNA turned up in his apartment, it would be tough to find who'd hired then killed him, and hence why he'd killed Eva.

Their best hope seemed to be the burner phone Viggo had been in contact with. It was a Swedish number, so far untraced—surely as planned. All it did was give Tom confidence that the root of the problem was in Sweden, which allowed him to feel relaxed about spending a couple of weeks there.

After all, when they found the owner of the burner phone, would that necessarily be the end of the trail? Also, what was the collateral impact of Eva's murder—what had been the aim? No ripples were evident, but that could be because they didn't know where to look.

As the AutoDrive whirred through the Gävleborg countryside, his thoughts turned to the plane crash. He called up team leader Juhani Koskinen and had a productive conversation. Things were moving on—and not in a pleasant way.

He pulled up outside the iconic falu red detached house on Alftavägen. Kennet came out to meet him, appearing less weary than he had two days earlier. Kayte wasn't far behind. Both were attired in comfy house clothes, clearly relaxed in each other's company.

Enna had posited that something unspoken was going on between these so-different characters. He'd chastised her, saying that supposition and gossip helped nobody. Besides, if alternative realities had presented themselves—for example, if Jay DeLeo hadn't been murdered, and Tom hadn't survived the factory fire at Project Mercury—wouldn't Enna be seeking comfort in a close friend or colleague? Maybe even Jay himself?

She'd laughed that off. Why stay in DC if her parents would welcome her to the chateau? She could grieve in peace whilst stuffing her face with chocolate pudding and bottles of fine French wine.

Tom had said that would make her very fat and unattractive. She wondered why he cared—*he'd* be the one she was grieving over. He reflected on what would happen if either of them was ripped from the world. For sure, he'd want her to have a happy life without him—marrying again if necessary. Would he move on if Enna died? He couldn't conceive of anyone being able to fill her shoes, for many reasons.

It was a maudlin, silly way to pass the time, so he parked the notion. However, it did throw Kayte and Kennet's situation into focus and strengthened his hope that each would move past their loss, carving out whatever future they best saw fit. It wasn't his place to judge. As long as they were happy and ideally remained a vital component of Fleet PD, then he'd be content.

'How is Charlotte?' was Kayte's first question.

'Having a whale of a time,' he replied. 'Honestly, don't worry. Enna's parents love her to bits.' He faced Kennet. 'And Tomas too. Pauline is taking them swimming in the moat pool today. I could have stayed a week. Nothing beats the innocent joy of kids playing.'

'Well, now you made *me* jealous.'

'The door is always open. We all want to wrap up this investigation, then the two of you deserve a hell of a vacation. How are you doing? Really?'

Kennet shrugged. 'Tom, to be fair, it is up and down. With us both, I think. But doing work helps.'

'Plus having me around to annoy him, pick up his dirty laundry, beat him at cards....' Kayte winked.

'Ah. Sounds familiar,' Tom said.

Kennet gestured to the house. 'Come on in, Chief.'

They sat around the kitchen table.

'So here's the news. I'm not tiptoeing around anymore—okay?' Tom looked at them. 'I know that, at some level, parts of this are hard to hear. You're not yourselves yet. I feel for you every day, and I can't imagine how hard it is, but I don't think you need soft soap. From what I can see, you're pretty good for each other when it comes to shoulders to cry on.'

'That's fair,' Kayte said. 'He's a rock.'

'No, *she's* the rock,' Kennet replied.

'You're both damn lucky, I reckon. Anyway, while I'm over here—for a few days, maybe more, depending on how things go—I'm going to focus on the day job. Janssen and I have pulled a lot of strings, as you know. Part of that is to support you two and help you get to the bottom of how your loved ones were lost. A bigger part is that there's something to uncover, deskwork and legwork to be done, and all roads seem to lead to Sweden. Fleet has given its blessing for me to poke my nose in anywhere it's wanted. I only had to *suggest* the plane crash was maybe designed to kibosh the Spaceport, and I was given the green light. But with all this, the bottom line is Koskinen and the crash team are running the show. I'm not butting in, trying to steal their work. Neither will you.'

Kayte nodded. 'Agreed.'

'We'll take anything that's a potential criminal offence. In conjunction with the Bollnäs team, anyone at AirSweden, and any local forces.'

'I have no desire to get a reprimand for overstepping,' Kennet said.

'Sure. The good news is that Koskinen will meet us tomorrow, give it to us from the horse's mouth. I briefed them on you two and your situation.'

'That's kind.'

'Not a bit of it.' Tom drank from his mug. 'Listen, here's the headline. The cockpit recorder was sabotaged. There's evidence of a tiny explosive charge on the data connection.'

Kayte's mouth fell open.

Tom flashed wide eyes. 'Yeah. This was pre-planned. Who, why, when—don't know. But Hansen had already decided to dive the plane, and he—or someone—wanted to make sure that any words on the cockpit were never heard.'

Kennet frowned. 'What kind of words?'

'Search me. Either the co-pilot, Paulsen, would try to intervene—telegraphing the situation. Or they were in it together, and collaboration needed to remain secret.'

Kayte pinched her lip. 'Or we're making wild guesses, joining dots that aren't there. Maybe the point is to vanish the evidence—whatever it is—so nobody can prove it wasn't an accident. I'll bet the ramifications for insurance pay-outs, litigations and whatever are a damn sight different between murder, sabotage, act of God, and accident. Perhaps someone is simply trying to muddy the waters.'

'Then our job—the whole network of investigative parties—is to make that water crystal clear, so we can see to the bottom, find the who and why, and get this tied up.' Tom drained his coffee. 'Because there's nothing to say there isn't more of this kind of shit going to happen, and nobody wants any more dead bodies.'

'Especially innocent ones,' Kennet said.

'Exactly. So I need a fine night's sleep after today. I'll stay at your place, Kayte, and see you at Bollnäs PD at ten hundred, okay?'

Kayte did something unusual for her relationship with Tom. She leaned over and pecked his cheek.

'Thanks, Chief. You're the best.'

He coughed, hiding a modicum of embarrassment. 'No problem. Nobody screws with my team and escapes justice. And without Lieutenant Supermom Mischief Dacourt here to lead the line, it's my job. This is taking a damn sight longer than I'd want, but we'll get there.'

# 30

Kennet felt odd on Tuesday morning, buttoning up his polis uniform. It was as if he was drawing a line under everything, getting back to normal—or whatever this new phase of his life looked like. Yet that was a mind trick, a way to feel self-conscious, create stupid guilt, or see this false dawn as anything other than precisely that.

It was also strange to see Kayte back in uniform. He'd got used to her in civvies, even in nightwear, but it was unarguably good to reaffirm that she was, underneath it all, a colleague. Today, certainly, there had to be professional distance.

They arrived at Bollnäs PD at nine-thirty, seeing all his colleagues together for the first time since the crash. Respectful, encouraging words were uttered, followed by a private chat with CI Janssen in his office.

Tom arrived, a four-way chat ensued, and finally, Juhani Koskinen arrived.

Kennet found them to be a less officious individual than he'd imagined, about his height, with strong shoulders, neck-length hair and a softly spoken voice.

Janssen showed the quartet to the meeting room, had coffee brought in, and they got down to business.

'This is the situation with the voice recorder,' Koskinen said. 'It was rigged to be disconnected on command. We are searching for evidence of a trigger mechanism in the cockpit area. Possibly it was on the person of Hansen or Poulsen.'

'We think Hansen,' CI Janssen said. 'Poulsen comes up clean. We've been over his life with a rake. Nothing. Not so for Hansen.'

'Hansen was ill?' Kayte recalled.

'Yes. And he kept that from his wife, but his consultant confirmed.'

'Is there anything on the voice recorder which is useful?' Kennet asked.

'No,' Koskinen replied. 'All normal up to that point. The same with technical data.'

'How would the black box be sabotaged?' Tom asked.

'It would have to be removed, tampered with, and refitted.'

'By Hansen?'

'By an engineer. One of a few with that speciality. Unless another individual gained the knowledge—and access to the aircraft—by stealth.'

'Or more than one person was involved?' Kayte asked.

'That's for you guys to find out. We'll hand off—or collaborate on—any criminal investigation. I just want a material cause. Hansen is notionally in the dock for diving the aircraft. If there was no other mechanical interference other than breaking a data link, there's no contributing technical or operational factor beyond pilot activity. Yes, I want to know why he did it—assuming he did—but that doesn't alter the underlying cause of the loss of those lives.'

'What's happening about locating the engineer?' Tom asked.

'Stockholm polis are investigating now, getting the duty rosters for ground staff and conducting interviews. I've asked them to share results with you.'

Kennet drummed his fingers on the side of his mug. 'Wasn't the pilot on standby duty?'

His boss nodded. 'We have to speak to Crew Resourcing to find out what happened there. I have a name—Anna Persson—if you want to take that on. Honestly, I'd prefer Tom did any interviews.'

Kennet's spirits fell. 'I understand.'

Under the table, unseen, Kayte briefly pressed her knee against his in emotional support.

'How are you getting on with the manifest?' Tom asked.

'Thirty-six down. A few more to go.' Kennet explained his theory about Emil Falk. He tried to read what was in Janssen's eyes—was the man humouring him, or did he feel the line of enquiry had merit? He thought the latter.

'I'll get Sergeant Mikkelson to follow up,' Janssen said. 'To check for any link between Falk and anyone on the plane or ground crew. Go through all his records.'

'Thank you, Chief Inspector.' It was curious to again be referring to Ulrik by his rank—as Kennet had done for years—when lately, their relationship had developed into friendship and support.

'Was the flight path unusual?' Kayte piped up.

'No,' Koskinen replied. 'Why?'

'Just grasping at straws. You know—in case Hansen wanted to use the aircraft as a missile and take out a ground target. Wild theory, I know.'

'Wild theories are welcome,' Tom said. 'Certainly by me. I've had my ear full of them since a certain, singular member of the team started throwing her hat into the ring on cases. All the same, if Hansen was aiming at something, there was nothing to hit for miles—right, Juhani?'

They nodded. 'He'd be a pretty poor pilot. There are no large targets in the area. If it was about causing maximum damage, he'd have done better to circle back and aim for a terminal at Arlanda. Due respect, Sergeant Connors, that's a non-starter.'

'So, you think suicide?' Kayte said.

Koskinen looked at Tom. 'It's not my area. Suicide, via temporary insanity, hopelessness or whatever, wouldn't be new. But also, talking to Chief Wagner, neither would be extreme activism. A statement.'

'Murder-suicide?' Kennet asked.

Koskinen held up their hands. 'I'll leave that to you. For my part, we want to be absolutely sure there were no mitigating technical malfunctions, confirm that sabotage didn't go beyond severing a data link, and support any efforts to find out which member of staff is at the sharp end of this.' They glanced at Kayte and Kennet. 'We don't want to be in the way any longer than needed. Funerals need to happen.'

Kennet slid a hand onto his knee and gripped hard, repressing a spike of sorrow. In a moment, Kayte's fingers were there, squeezing in mutual understanding.

Kennet masked his social uncomfortableness, checking whether anyone had noticed the movement of her arm towards him. He didn't think so, and relaxed.

Koskinen stood. 'I need to get to the site.' They all shook hands, then Janssen showed Koskinen out.

Kennet eased into the chair.

Tom drained his mug. 'I'm going down to Stockholm to speak to this Anna Persson. On any other day, I'd want one or both of you there—as cops. But right now, anyone could be the lynchpin, and I don't want personal feelings clouding any interview, spooking someone, or giving a risk to call foul and ring their lawyer.'

He patted them on the shoulder. 'Because believe me, if someone had a part in killing my wife, I'd be ready to haul them to the electric chair with my bare hands.'

Kennet gripped Tom's hand unusually hard. 'Thanks, Chief.'

'No problem—again. We've got this. We're a step closer. We find that engineer, we could be home and hosed.'

# 31

Overnight, settled in Kayte and Carey's erstwhile home, Tom pondered the day's events.

Anna Persson, a crew resourcing operative at AirSweden, had been taken into custody. It had been a good news, bad news outcome from her interview. She'd admitted rostering Aksel Hansen onto flight AS166, despite there being higher priority crew available. Undeniably, he'd been specially preselected. But who by?

Anna was initially forthcoming in her interview, then clammed up when motivations were raised. When Tom discussed the matter with the Swedish polis Inspector also present, both agreed she hadn't acted alone or on a whim. Someone had ordered, incentivised, or coerced her into making the roster change.

Was it the engineer? That was logical. That person must have worked with Hansen—the black box tampering *had* to be linked to the specific flight and pilot.

Now, with Persson lawyered up and tight-lipped, their best bet was the engineer. If they located him, they could establish any link between him and Persson. In the meantime, Tom asked Sergeant Mikkelson at Bollnäs to comb Persson's life for clues.

Waking on Wednesday and not having brought many provisions—work had taken priority—he walked into Söderhamn and had a late breakfast.

Afterwards, he drove the half-hour to Bollnäs and updated Kayte and Kennet—who were working at home—on the Persson issue. Then he went to the PD to discuss with Sgt Mikkelson and CI Janssen.

While he was there, crash investigator Koskinen called. For a moment, Tom struggled to place the name. With various parties involved in this sprawling investigation and many Scandinavian names, they were starting to blur into one. At home, things were usually anchored by names and faces he knew within

Fleet, Washington PD or NYPD. This time, the learning curve—for personnel, organisation structures, and technical matters—was unusually steep.

'Chief Wagner, Inspector Koskinen.'

Tom cursed under his breath—the Finnish accent was identifiable if you listened carefully.

'Inspector, is this good news?'

'Yes and no.'

'I'm familiar with those. Go ahead.'

He ate lunch in a Bollnäs café and then went to Kennet's house. They'd had a fruitless morning, partially due to an unexpectedly long call with Enna. Everything was fine; they were merely missing their kids.

On the sofa, Tom toyed with his mug. 'Okay, this is a big step, but a frustrating one.'

Kayte closed her eyes. 'Don't tell me. Someone's got to Anna Persson. Killed her, so she doesn't talk.' She thumped the chair. 'Dammit, if another suspect—'

'Whoah. Kayte, Kayte. No. It's fine. The Fleet PD curse of the nobbled witness hasn't struck.' He chuckled, though hollow. 'Maybe because our... *petite dame de calamité* is out of the country.'

'So, spill!'

'They found the aircraft engineer.' He sighed. 'Well, not found. Identified.'

'So, *he's* dead?'

'Jeez, quit on the downers. No, he's alive. Or... he was at the last time of being seen.'

Kennet leant in. 'Come on, Chief. How bad can it be?'

'He's on his way to Mars.'

After Kayte had turned the air blue for a couple of minutes, and Kennet had curiously expelled his frustration by sorting and folding clean laundry—including Kayte's clothes, Tom noticed—they reconvened around a fresh pot of typically rich Swedish coffee.

'How do we know it's him?' Kayte asked.

'Because everyone else comes up clean. Because he has the know-how. And, tellingly, because he booked the Mars flight the day before AS166 and took off the day after the plane went down.'

'Sheesh. Fleeing the country? Fleeing the planet is a pretty big red flag.'

'Who paid for the flight?' Kennet asked.

'He did. We'll dig over his financial records as soon as we can, but it was his payment device,' Tom said.

'And look at his entire life. Movements. Reasons. Everything.'

'Absolutely. We're on it.'

Kayte was scouring the ceiling for something. 'Can we get him back?'

'I'm assuming you don't mean call up the ship and ask them to put it into reverse?' Tom beamed.

'Extradite?' Kennet said.

'I'll schedule a meeting with Lincoln Pike at Fleet, Stockholm PD, and AirSweden. My feeling is we have to be careful as mice.'

'What's the name?'

'Frans Olsson. This is new territory for me. Different from when Enna had to escort that OnePlanet asshole back from Mars for the shuttle sabotage.'

'Because how?' Kayte asked.

'Because he thinks he got away with it. We've already put an intercept on all his Com traffic. If he's in contact with anyone while he's on the flight, he'll never receive that message. If any AirSweden colleagues try to warn him that the cops were sneaking around, he'll never know.'

'Why would they warn him? Or care?'

Tom shrugged. 'Almost certainly, they wouldn't. But I don't want to take risks. Neither does Janssen. So, it's essentially radio silence. His being a suspect isn't in the public domain. As far as AirSweden staff are concerned, the interviews at Arlanda were about finding technical malfunctions. Word is getting out that Hansen dived the plane. That's hard to suppress. But the black box thing is being kept under wraps.'

'What happens to Olsson?' Kennet asked. 'Mars PD interview him?'

Tom shook his head. 'Again, not entirely my call, but I vote no. It would spook him. In an ideal world, we'd leave him alone, let him get to Mars, then find a way to bring him home asap but without raising the alarm.'

Kayte stood, whistling a soft, 'Phew. Good luck with that.' She paced.

'I don't need luck, Connors. I've got you and Kennet and all the other brains who are involved in this.'

'How long?' Kennet's face was stern and focussed.

'Well, that's the "good news" part. Mars is almost at closest approach. It's about four weeks each way.'

'And he left over three weeks ago?' Kayte asked.

'Yep. So he's almost there.'

She flopped into the chair. 'But still, like, five weeks before we can question him? Jeez. Isn't there a better way?'

Tom held up his palms. 'I'm all ears. Sure, I'd rather find another path through the maze, but right now, he's our hottest lead.'

'And he's a million miles away. Wow. Redefines "good luck", I guess.'

'It's a break, Connors. I wish I had better news, but I don't. Hansen hired Olsson to do the sabotage, or someone else did. Or someone hired them both.'

'Why?' she asked.

'Billion dollar—sorry, kronor—question.'

'You can't stay here for five weeks, Chief. And I can't be apart from Charlotte for that long.'

He met her eye. 'Don't worry. Neither of those will happen. We'll work out a plan. But one thing's certain. I'd bet a few thousand of those kronor we can find some other avenues to pursue in the meantime. And I doubt many of them will lead back to the US. So you might be stuck with the boss for a while longer.'

Kayte mock sighed. 'Just what we needed—more bad news.'

# 32

Kayte slept badly, or at least she struggled to get to sleep. The conundrum of the engineer Frans Olsson plagued her mind: his motivations, the identity of his potential paymaster, and his flight from justice. She sought solutions to getting him back to Earth quicker, lines of investigation to pursue, and how to do all this without raising the alarm—either with Olsson or whoever else might be part of the puzzle.

It pushed her sleep cycle into mid-morning, when she was woken by light flooding into the room. The door was open, and Kennet was standing there.

'Huh?' she mumbled, barely compos mentis.

In three purposeful strides, he was at the bed and sat down at her waist. If she was to guess his demeanour, she'd say "excited".

'What?' She brushed hair from her eyes, licked her lips.

The clock said 09:54.

'I have something. Oh, and good morning.'

She wriggled upright. 'Morning, partner. You haven't brought me a wake-up coffee, so what gives? I deduce from your cheeky smile, the news isn't bad.'

'For a change, no. But do you want a coffee?' He glanced at the clock.

'I couldn't sleep. The detective in me is back. Which is a good sign, I guess.'

'It is. You get decent, and I'll bring coffee.'

She looked down. Her attire wasn't indecent. She was comfortable in nightwear—he was no lech. Yet when she looked up, he didn't avert his gaze from her chest in time.

She said nothing, but warmth shimmered in her tummy.

'You mean "get up, lazybones, I've broken the case"?'

He grimaced. 'Sorry. I was meaning "wake up properly". You aren't indecent. You're only in bed. I shouldn't have come in.'

She grabbed his hand as he made to get up. 'I'm joking, partner. As usual. And on another morning, you could just have rolled over to have this conversation, right?'

'Yes,' he replied sheepishly.

'Indecent is buck naked,' she clarified, winking to show she was yanking his chain—and to put him at ease.

What had caused his flutter of embarrassment? Perhaps because this was the first time he'd come into 'her' bedroom? At least he was understanding and deferential—many people might not have been. Yet his eye line...?

She dismissed it.

'I'll go to the bathroom and come through.'

She perched on the sofa, now in a robe.

'Is this about the engineer?'

'No,' he replied. 'The manifest. I reached the third to last name and got something.'

'Better than Emil Falk?'

'I think so.' He gestured her over to the dining table, where they'd set up the large terminal screen a few days before.

'Oscar Gustafsson,' she read.

'Except that's not his real name. It's an alias—legitimately registered but not in the public domain. From what I can see, he uses it when he is flying, sometimes when he is in a hotel.'

Her eyes widened in encouragement. '...and?'

Kennet tapped the display. 'It's a smokescreen for Anders Svensson.' He gave a smug smile.

'Nope, you got me.' She sipped her welcome brew.

'Eva Svensson's brother.'

She rested the mug on the table. 'What are the chances, right?'

'I would say the chances are high. Especially if we consider that the plane crash was possibly a cover for murder. And Eva was just murdered.'

Her palm instinctively laid on his shoulder. 'Sheesh.'

'But nothing is proven, yes? All I am saying is that Anders Svensson is a potential target.'

She shuffled closer to the screen. 'Tell me more about him.'

By noon, they were in the Bollnäs PD meeting room with Tom and Janssen.

The consensus was that Svensson was certainly the most likely target for a disguised assassination. The guy had a persecution complex, assumed an alias so that many of his movements weren't easily traced, had a bodyguard, and was a wealthy and successful businessman—not all of whose interests were morally upstanding.

He was also Eva's brother—and it was accepted that she'd been the victim of a well-planned hit. Both were children of billionaire Wilmer Svensson. Future heirs. Potential blackmail pawns. And, if that wasn't enough, one of the shortlisted sites for the Stockholm Spaceport was on a few thousand acres of Wilmer's land.

Kayte's mind whirled. After days of scant progress, this was a paradigm shift.

'Kennet, this is stellar work,' Tom said.

'It was just a list. I didn't solve anything yet.'

'No, but you gave us something very real to grab hold of. Unless anyone has objections, I'll make this our key line of enquiry.' He raised a finger. 'Not to exclude all others, though. I don't want us all crowding down the same alley and finding it's a dead end.'

'Agreed,' Janssen said. 'We will take the list and check for any other potential leads from the passengers. Also, check the two names Kennet didn't reach yet. Oversight would be an embarrassment.'

'Especially as Wilmer Svensson won't like all telescopes pointing in his direction if the connection is not certain,' Kennet said.

'He must know his son was on that flight?' Kayte said.

'Probably. As would anyone connected with the family.'

'Except, like we said, Anders wouldn't go around telling anyone he didn't need to. For some personal and business acquaintances, they're probably wondering where he is, but thinking he's just crawled into a hole for self-preservation,' Janssen said.

'But the passenger list is public now,' she pointed out. 'If someone wanted to find it on the web.'

'And one of the names *isn't* Anders Svensson, remember?'

She sighed. 'Oh. Yeah. It'll get out eventually, though, right?'

'That's not the issue,' Tom said. 'Or our problem. We want to know *why* he was killed—again, going with Occam's razor.'

'So we have to probe all his business dealings, his entire life—which won't be easy because he was so secretive. And try to find out who held a grudge.'

Tom patted her shoulder. 'Remember, we have five weeks until the engineer is back. Who knows—he could be the one who can lead us to the grudge-holder. Giving you and Kennet—us all—ample time to explore all avenues. Look on the bright side—we actually *have* avenues to explore.'

'True.'

Kennet was stroking the table pensively, almost dispiritedly.

'What's up, partner?' she asked.

'Someone would really crash a plane to kill one man? That plane? *Our* plane?'

Janssen, on Kennet's right, clasped his junior's arm. 'Sometimes, innocent people are in the wrong place at the wrong time. We all feel your pain—both of you. But now we look for guilty people, yes?'

Kennet patted his boss' chubby, empathic hand. 'Yes.'

'Now, Inspector Carlsson—and Sergeant Connors perhaps—in light of excellent work, you are granted a day's leave. I know this news, while good for our police work, is less palatable as relatives of those passengers. To be collateral victims of something so heinous. Please, switch off your terminal. Tom and I will progress things.' He looked through the window. 'Good weather this weekend. Did you go to Ago hamn ever, Kennet?'

'And the lighthouse? When Tomas was small.'

'Very quiet. Enjoy nature. Show the Sergeant some more beauty of the country she has chosen.' Janssen's face fell serious. 'Because one cruel act does not break God's glory or man's spirit, yes?'

That perked her up. 'Picnic?'

Kennet nodded. 'Tiny islands. Trees. No cars. No tourists. Peace. Reflection, maybe?'

She beamed. 'It's not got the big city bustle I used to crave, but what the hell.'

# 33

They spent Friday taking care of probate and administrative affairs—not fun stuff and not without tears.

On Saturday, the emotional uplift was huge, travelling to the handful of tiny islands off the coast near Vâtnas, about an hour's drive from Bollnäs. It was soul food. Kennet provided wonderful company, and it was a glimpse into a world of possibilities—a new dawn beyond the dark clouds of loss.

However, Sunday morning dampened their spirits again.

Noticing the date, she told him it was one month since the crash. They allowed themselves to shed tears, then formed a plan.

'We'll raise a glass tonight,' she said.

'And let ourselves be sad. But not get drunk or maudlin. Okay?'

'Agreed.'

It felt like a good time to draw some kind of a line under very tangible things, so they cleared some of Jana's effects into boxes and took them to Kayte's house in Söderhamn. Out of sight, out of mind. There, she took ahold of her emotions and boxed up Carey's things. They'd decide what to do later, but this was a step.

In the evening, as they cooked together, a thought struck her—a much-needed positive one after the resonances of the day.

'Hey, you know what's weird—and a damn sight happier? This is also another anniversary for us.'

'In what way?'

'First day we met in New York.' She set down the wine bottle she was uncorking, and pleasant reminisces tugged at the corners of her mouth.

'The innocent, blond country boy. The fish out of water.' She waggled her eyebrows.

'Oh yes, pigeonhole me again.'

'Man, I was cruel.'

'You were... a change. A welcome introduction to a new city.'

Her face lit, and she extended her hand. As he offered his, she retracted hers, and they recreated the "hand dance" they'd done at One Police Plaza. It seemed a lifetime ago.

They laughed heartily.

'See? We should be happy because we have each other to help us through. Imagine if we didn't have that.'

'But that's a silly thought,' he replied. 'Without meeting, we'd have no friendship, no move to Sweden, no accident, no deaths.'

'So why did the universe throw us together in work and life? Not for tragedy.' She shook her head hard. 'No. We did *good,* Kennet. We solved crimes. Had some scrapes. But had fun. Laughed. Hell, even had a baby together.' Then her face fell. 'Not just the two of us, though.'

He held her shoulder. 'Actually, Charlotte is the product of *four* people.'

'How do you figure?'

'You and I for the... ingredients. Jana, for allowing me to even go ahead with it. And mostly Carey for nine months discomfort, a few hours of terrible pain, and then many weeks of love and nurture.'

Kayte quickly poured the wine and raised her glass. They toasted.

'To our wives. Beautiful, amazing, caring people. Irreplaceable. Never to be forgotten.'

Kennet was breathing deeply. 'Yes. All that and more.'

Before things went awry, she quickly took a gulp, he did too, then they set down their glasses, embraced and cried.

After dinner, lounging on the sofa was the habitual wind-down. It felt oddly normal—not just for the two of them in the current situation, but in general. It felt like normal *life.* Attainable and undramatic, like the glorious smell of petrichor after a storm. She was getting used to the close company of a man and enjoyed his proximity. It was preying on her mind, mostly positively yet running with an undercurrent of unease that she wished she could shake.

She looked across. 'What are you thinking?'

'Honestly? About you and I. Comfortable here. And what brought us to this.'

'We're nothing without those we loved and lost.'

'Yes, we are. We are us. We have a duty to them to have a future, to raise our individual children and ideally be friends—they wouldn't want us to break up.'

'But would they be happy if things... developed?'

Fear swam on his face. 'That is unanswerable. Besides, I will remind you that we each loved a *woman*. Maybe in future, I can love another woman. As much as I loved Jana? Who knows. But it's harder for you to love a man or at least have the same kind of holistic relationship as I would. That would be... uncharted territory.'

'This is all uncharted. There's no map for how this goes, or a cure for a mind, heart and body full to bursting with a million things. And for the record, I *can* love a man. I love *you*, Kennet, in a way I can't even explain to myself, let alone to you, nor even know what to do next, if anything. Maybe this is peak *us*.'

He kissed her forehead. 'I love you too, Kayte, in the same blizzard of impossibility, unfamiliarity and fear, yet in a life-affirming way. Not the same as how I loved Jana, but if there never came anything better than what we already have as friends, soulmates even, and each being the rock we'd want to hang onto when drowning, that is fine.'

'Then we won't drown. We'll swim to safety and find a desert island to live out our days.'

He nodded. 'As whatever the universe tells us to.'

'Whenever it tells us.'

'I hope it tells us soon because my insides want to settle down and get on with life.'

She examined his face, her heart pattering. 'You know, don't you, what you want it to tell you and us?'

'No. I only know one thing. Well, perhaps two. The decision, the journey, everything is harder for you because of who you are. So, patience is key, and this thing will evolve—if it is going to—over a long time. Or it will stay the same, and we will be friends, maybe housemates for a while or longer. As a status quo, that is fine, better than fine.'

'One hundred percent agree. What's the other thing?'

He stroked her hand. 'I suppose you want honesty. Then you are a smart, funny, mischievous, loyal, steely woman. And—for true honesty—a beautiful and desirable one.' He held up a hand against her interjection. 'That is on one side of the balance. On the other side is that circumstance is impossibly difficult and unusual, we both have immense baggage, and, most importantly, you are gay. These things I have known for a long time. The things in the room we spoke about. Things that could not be said aloud because we each had the strongest of marriages and lives we did not want to tamper with.'

'Fate tampered with them.'

He pulled a face. 'Something did. A person, maybe. Who needs to be found.'

'The outcome is the same. But anyway. You say very kind things, Kennet. And you have tremendous qualities—which I'm not shy of telling you. You're also right—there were barriers, and there still are.'

'Barriers are only seen if a journey is wanted or expected.'

Her expression told him he'd hit the nail on the head. 'We *have* been on a journey. From hand dancing, through gunshots and hugs and setbacks and partnership, and now death. I think fewer things hold us back now.'

'Hold us back from what? You speak like you have an end in mind.'

She shook her head. 'I don't, because it's... the undiscovered country. You're right. It's easier for you because you're naturally drawn to women. Not that it's all about physical attraction.'

'More than true. Personality and the ability to coexist without falling out is paramount.'

'We've done fine sharing a house—especially under emotional duress. In fact, if we can bootstrap each other through things which, honestly, do lay waste to some people or relationships, then we might have a damn fine foundation.'

He drank. 'We always did. But I can't walk this journey in your shoes. Only you know your insides, what you think and feel, and what you are predisposed to, driven to, or even can guess at.'

She took his hand and kissed it. 'Okay, here's my journey so far. The part we're talking about—because I know we're tiptoeing around it. You know it too—it's like going in that room again.'

'I suppose.'

'A long time ago, I kissed a boy. More than kissed. Then I kissed a girl, then more girls, then one girl repeatedly. Millions of times. And all those times were great, and they felt real and natural.'

'I've understood that.'

'Then, in Paris, I kissed you. Mainly because I was drunk and grateful and possibly because you reminded me of a boy—*the* boy—I kissed. Then, when Carey got shot at our house, I was drunk—again—and screwed up in the head with grief and worry, and I kissed you again. A lot of that was probably raging hormones and an attempt to derail the whole world. Maybe to see what happened, in case I lost her.' She looked down, suppressing sadness.

'And I kissed you—to prove you were being a fool.'

'Which I was. Because destroying two marriages would have been the summit of stupidity.'

'Amen.'

'Then I was sober and gave you a thank-you kiss because you were the best friend in the world. And you held me tight against the night terrors and left me alone—I stayed away, too—because the alternative was dumb. Even though it would have been a car crash, what with me being gay and all.'

He shrugged. 'Very likely.'

'Pretty soon, you woke Carey up from a coma, and man, was I grateful then.'

'That was a kiss,' he conceded.

'As was yours.'

'I was trying to be less nervous around you, remember? And maybe give as good as I got.'

She raised her eyebrows. 'And maybe a little bit because of all the good things you just told me I have?'

'Those good things are what made it scary. They blurred the lines between friendship and... beyond that.'

'But you never overstepped bounds.'

He smiled. 'Because of all my *good qualities*. And I am sure you felt the same, from guilt and self-hate, because it is—was—wrong.'

'Wrong to cross boundaries, yes. And in the train car? After we killed that man?'

'Not killed, but yes.' He pondered. 'Saving your life? I understand your appreciation. But I wondered if you really were as detached as you claimed.'

'I don't know. I think part of me knew I could kiss you and... get away with it. No—that's not right. Perhaps not feel guilty or awkward. Because we'd gotten closer. Except *relief* was the main thing. Being alive and finding the bastard who hurt Carey.'

'And we'll do the same again.'

She nodded firmly. 'Absolutely. And we're even closer friends now than we were then.'

'I should prepare for another kiss, then.'

'Let's hope—as that will be our victory dance.'

'I'll look forward to it. The victory, I mean, closing the case. Doing right by our family.'

She played with her glass. 'Yes. And... the kiss? You'll look forward to that? It's alright to say, Kennet. If I hear you, it'll sit easier because you won't be consumed by worry or regret.'

He pondered. 'I suppose I will be able to take it at face value.'

'You'll be *allowed* to be happy—overjoyed—that we've served justice. I won't mind if you kiss me because I won't have any guilt either. We won't damage anything. We won't have to lie or cover it up. Explain any sense of... infidelity.'

'All the same, you'll still be who you are, and I'll still be a man, and those two things are... not wholly compatible.'

She toyed with his hand. '*That's* the journey. The one I don't know where it goes, how and when it ends. But I'll say this, Kennet. If the first time in Paris was curiosity, and maybe even the second time, the times after that, I *knew* what I was getting into. And the gay police didn't come and throw me in gay prison. If they did, I think I'd have to spin the Brandon story and tell them maybe I'm... not the real deal.'

'You certainly seemed like the real deal.'

'The universe is a mystery. I'd never imagine I'd wind up here, in this situation.'

'A widow,' he said gravely.

'I meant talking about kissing a guy. For whatever reason.'

'It's mostly gratitude and comfort. And, like you say, a glimmer of memory or inquisitiveness.'

'Don't do yourself down, Kennet. One of your qualities—which I skipped over—was that you're a good-looking guy. I'm sure a regular girl would say so. This girl? Probably shouldn't say so but will. I can't deny that if you had a beard, I'd be less... physical in the lip department.'

'You too,' he joked.

She laughed—much-needed medicine which covered her nerves. 'As it is, that barrier's not there. Like the guilt.' She laid a palm on his cheek, stroking.

'There's still a lot to deal with or get over—if that's the way things go. And I will not predict or suppose how things *will* go. Especially because I could never have predicted most of the past three years... and certainly the last few weeks.'

'"The journey of a thousand miles starts with one step".'

He gently cupped her jaw. 'We have a lot to be grateful for and curious about. I won't tell you which fork in the road to take, or how fast to walk, or take your hand and drag you along. That's a recipe for disaster. And we don't need another one of those.'

She sighed with melancholy. 'I agree. But walk by my side, okay? Baby steps while I work it out.'

'Definitely.'

'Okay. Then this is the first step.'

She pushed her face close to him, watched his eyes dance, then put her lips to his. He held station—walking by her side, not running ahead or holding her back. It was what she imagined a Hollywood screen kiss was like—for show, not for desire—like it had always been until now.

She kissed a little harder, and then he broke off.

She frowned. 'What did I do wrong?'

'Nothing. But the step was yours to make.'

'Sorry. I'm being insensitive. You don't have to take the steps if you feel uncomfortable.'

'I don't. I feel... not too bad.'

'Not too bad,' she joked. 'Thanks for the vote of confidence.'

'I mean, I'm not having a mental crisis. Only I am feeling like I'm in a car being towed by a truck with no headlights.'

'You know what, for all your quirky Swedish phrases, that may be the best analogy yet. Just one problem. I don't want you to feel like you're being towed along.'

'Alright, by your side, like you said. Or maybe a small pace behind.'

'Don't worry, we won't run off the road. I only kissed you, and we've done that before. And, if I understood you, if we ignore what was in your head, the actual kissing was not so bad? I passed muster?'

'You did. And you do.'

'That's something. You know, for a novice at this weird heterosexual form of the art.' She smiled.

'A kiss is a kiss, is it not?'

'I suppose.'

'And if I don't have a beard or bad breath or cold sores, then it is not a whole universe different. Or horrible.'

'It's not horrible. It's perfectly fine.'

'Thank you.'

'It makes me believe the world is a better place. That I have a safe harbour.'

He stroked her cheek. As with many times before, his touch was immensely pleasant to experience, and with each additional contact, she awaited the next one.

'Good. That's all that matters.'

# 34

The highs and lows of the weekend had made Kennet completely forget there was normally someone younger in the house, too, so mid-morning on Monday, he videocalled Enna. Kayte joined in, and they chatted with the gathering of adults and children. Tomas had caught the sun, and he even showed off a few French words he'd learned.

Kennet tried to keep the conversation away from the polis investigations, but Enna was a terrier, and he was encouraged to reveal the key points to date. Mercifully, Enna had the foresight to take her Com to a remote place in the garden so young ears didn't hear uncomfortable details.

'Tom was right to come over, then,' she said.

Kayte chimed in. 'You mean that you were smart to drag him over here.'

Enna pawed at the camera. 'Aw, since when did I ever try to take credit for anything?'

'Honestly, you never did—certainly not something you didn't do yourself. Largely because you're a one-woman army anyhow.'

'*Was* a one-woman army.'

'Is all that sunshine, cuisine and cohort of youngsters turning you soft?'

'No way. But I told Tom I'd butt out, and I'm trying damn hard. Problem is, you just made it harder.'

'How is that?' Kennet asked.

'Because I've babysat a prisoner on a colonial flight. I've had to keep someone under wraps. I've had to chase down people who screwed with my family and people I love.' She shrugged. 'Offering my two cents whenever it's needed, that's all. I mean, I'm not on vacation indefinitely. Certainly not five weeks.' She glanced around. 'Though I'm sure your two munchkins would gladly stay all summer.'

'We cannot impose. Certainly not on your sister and parents, Enna. Kayte and I are...' he flashed his partner a smile, 'Coping much better. We are in the groove of work too, which keeps the sadness away.'

'And I miss my girl like crazy,' Kayte added. 'So, talk to Tom, and bring her home when you can.'

Enna fell silent, her pupils gyrating in thought. 'Okay. That could be a plan. Tom and I will go back to DC for a while. He'll have to watch Lexie while I do some more shifts. Then we can come over to you in a few weeks. But if you have...' she closed her eyes, 'the funerals in the meantime, you shout, okay?'

'That's kind,' he replied.

'No, that's friends. Besides, we might leave Lexie with you for a weekend and go explore Sweden.' She winked.

'It's a deal,' Kayte said.

Kennet invited Tom over for a working lunch, and they set a timeline and shared out the tasks.

Ellie and Han would comb through Anders Svensson's life and business dealings, and look again at Eva. If there were interviews needed in Sweden, Tom would take these. Kayte and Kennet would follow up on the engineer Frans Olsson. Janssen would seek full access to every scrap of the man's life.

Tom would liaise with Fleet—like his job years earlier—to work out the best way to keep Olsson inside a bubble of ignorance. Then together, they'd plan for how to cajole the man into returning to Earth on the next spacecraft. The flight crews in both directions would be briefed, and an undercover Mars PD officer, or preselected Fleet uniform, would babysit Olsson from a distance on the ship home.

'I'm nervous, Chief.'

'You, Connors?' Tom said. 'Didn't think you knew the meaning of the word.'

'A lot of moving parts, that's all.'

'True. But when we learn Olsson's life, see his pattern of Com traffic, understand his goals and motivations, we can create a reality to protect him—and us—for a while.'

'Did you ever consider why he emigrated?' Kennet asked. 'Was it choice or coercion?'

Kayte tinkled her short fingernails on the table. 'Kennet's right. If this crash was about murdering Anders Svensson—for whatever reason—then could it be that because he was a high-profile hit, Olsson was paid off handsomely? Or alternatively, he was provided passage to a new life? Whoever hired Viggo to kill Eva wasn't interested in a luxury payoff. They wanted Viggo dead—quickly. Why is Olsson different?'

Tom scratched his chin. 'Because he isn't a hitman? He's not a career criminal who might get revenge or be a liability to his paymaster further down the line? Because he begged for mercy? He cut a deal? Maybe he knows the person who hired him—there's a bond—but Viggo didn't?'

'Except there's no loyalty amongst thieves,' Kennet said.

'You know what? We could sit here all day theorising. Hell—nothing says that the same person is behind Anders and Eva. Sure, it would be the coincidence of the century, but let's not go pinning everything on finding what connects those two. We need to rule out—as best we can—any *other* credible reason for downing that plane. We're putting a huge operation into ring-fencing Olsson, and we're skirting the border of Wilmer Svensson's empire. Both require a careful touch. Let alone that this whole thing could be a OnePlanet scheme—and they're a slippery bunch at the best of times.'

Kayte shook her head. 'Sorry, Tom, I still don't buy OnePlanet influence being behind this. They never attacked commercial air traffic before. If they wanted to stymie the Spaceport, they'd be better off continuing with the personal attacks. Lena Ekström's dog. Sara Lindström's car.'

Kennet nodded. 'I agree. There is much more leverage they could achieve by targeting members of the Planning Committee or even the stakeholders for the potential sites. They could whip up local fervour to such an extent that the project slips into endless delays.'

'Well,' Tom said. 'Peaceful protest is one thing—police can't interfere in local planning issues, legitimate business projects or democratic process. But we can investigate, ideally stop, anything nefarious. I don't think any of us care how long this Spaceport takes to come to fruition, or even where it's sited, but we want any bad actors caught—whatever the reasons for their actions. If this is nothing to do with the Spaceport and... I don't know... someone paid off Hansen and Olsson merely because Anders Svensson reneged on a business deal five years ago, they need finding.'

'And we'll find them,' Kennet said.

# 35

Whilst Tom had insisted no line of enquiry should take precedence over another, there was a feeling in his bones that the deaths of Eva and Anders Svensson were simply too coincidental. When you added in that their father was a wealthy landowner with an interest in the Spaceport decision, it crossed the line into the 'suspicious' category.

The ideal step was to interview Wilmer to discern what family secrets and squabbles might be bubbling under, but he was a hard man to pin down and had a history of complaining about police and media intrusion on his life. It was far from ideal.

The next best approach was to speak to the remaining member of the family—Matteo.

Having researched the man online, Tom was familiar with Matteo's spell in prison as a young man, the death of his mother, and his moderate achievements. He'd neither grown wealthy and suspicious like his brother nor taken a mainstream career like his sister. He had no known OnePlanet associations, no recent alarming coverage on the web, and carved out a living running a small software business. He had no wife or family. Perhaps he was biding his time in search of a bride—there would be plenty of 'gold diggers' who only saw Matteo for his potentially vast inheritance.

His house was a sizeable place on the outskirts of Uppsala.

Sergeant Mikkelson accompanied him to the interview. She was an affable blonde mother of one, mid-thirties, with excellent English. As they drove to the location, she recounted her peripheral involvement in the Steffen Iversen case, which had brought Enna and Tom to the area for the first time and catalysed their meeting with Kennet.

'It's a shame I won't get to work with Sergeant Connors. She seems like a fine detective.'

'And a damn fine person, too,' Tom replied. 'Neither of them deserves what's happened. But then, who does?'

'Nobody. Not even the worst criminal. Such scum should suffer personally, even if it is only jail time. Not by taking away their loved ones, people who have done nothing wrong.'

Tom sighed. 'By killing Anders Svensson, for whatever reason, Aksel Hansen has deprived Matteo of his brother. The question is what Anders ever did wrong—if anything.'

Matteo appeared older than his thirty-three years, but perhaps that was the weight of recent history. He'd reluctantly agreed to the interview, citing mourning and that he had nothing to offer. His welcome seemed forced, and his manner guarded. Perhaps a chip off the old block?

They sat in his airy living room. While Mikkelson did the preliminaries, Tom glanced around. He couldn't see any family photographs. Having spoken to Eva's husband, he'd gleaned that the Svenssons weren't a close-knit family. He speculated how much was due to Wilmer's patriarchal reputation.

All the same, Matteo, Anders and Eva did communicate: their Com records indicated as much.

Matteo was open about having spoken to Eva on the morning she died.

'What was it about?' Tom asked.

'I wondered when she was next over here. We don't see much of each other. And I heard she was up for promotion. I wanted to know how it was going.'

'And did she sound stressed? Like she had worries on her mind? Did she terminate the call abruptly? Had she seen anything suspicious—like a stalker?' Mikkelson asked.

Matteo frowned. 'Nothing like that.'

'You're aware that there was surely a motive behind her killing?'

'And if I knew what that was, I would say.'

'Could she have been having an affair with this barista Viggo?'

Matteo laughed, yet emptily. 'No. She was happy.'

'And her husband? Any thoughts?'

'No. As long as he made her happy. I met him maybe only twice. He seems fine.'

'Do you think he married her for her inheritance?'

Matteo shifted in his seat, sipped his coffee. 'I think he married her because she was a nice person, and beautiful, and... principled. She wouldn't be pushed around.'

'She moved there to be with him,' Tom pointed out.

'She moved there because Fleet is based in DC. She loved Fleet. Like your wife, if I understand right.'

'The Lieutenant is passionate about it, that's true. Anyway, Anders. Did you see eye-to-eye?'

'We spoke. Of course, there's rivalry—I'd be stupid to admit there wasn't. We're brothers. There's always something, isn't there? There's always competition. Maybe it's for parental love. Maybe for bragging rights.' His head dipped. 'If we argued about anything, it's because I told him he was paranoid. Now look—he's dead.'

'Accidents happen,' Mikkelson said in a mollifying tone. 'Anders was unlucky, that's all.'

Matteo lasered his gaze on her. 'Let me ask this—are you interviewing *all* the crash victims' families? Asking *them* about relationships and motivations? Are you?'

'You're... one of the first,' Tom blustered.

'It's because of Eva as well, isn't it? You think the two are linked?'

Mikkelson held up a palm. 'Look, Matteo—'

But the man was on his feet, rattled. Tom worried that things were getting away from them: they'd barely begun to delve into Anders' life. However, the response wasn't what he expected.

'Do you think I don't see beyond coincidence, Chief Wagner? My two siblings, to all intents, were murdered. If you are suspicious, I certainly am. And, I'll be honest, pretty scared. What comes next? I'll tell you—me.'

The man's fists were clenching and unclenching.

'Mr Svensson—' Tom began.

'I'll bet that you're not here to offer me protection. Are you? I thought not. Well, I tell you, I'll be getting some. I know it didn't save my brother, but I won't be taking any chances. Somebody is targeting this family. Did you speak to my father?'

'We haven't pursued that line yet.'

'Let me guess—he doesn't want visitors. Or is that just me—the boy who disappointed him?'

'It's not our place to judge family politics,' Mikkelson said.

'You know what? I can't even be sure it'll be safe to go to Anders' funeral. Especially if Wilmer is there. If some crazy person is trying to taunt, fracture or even erase this family, then am I safe in the same place at the same time? Two targets for a sniper's bullet? Absolutely not.' Matteo's eyes were wide.

Tom trod carefully. 'So you think there was something behind Anders' paranoia? You understand now?'

'What, you're going to laugh at me like I laughed at him? Point out that the boot's on the other foot now? Is this what polis do?'

Mikkelson gestured calm. 'Look, we know this is a difficult time. We were only interested in insights as to who might have a grudge against your brother.'

'Throw a rock, and you'll hit someone,' Matteo scoffed.

'But anyone *specific*?' Tom asked, on tenterhooks.

Matteo fluttered a hand. 'You'd have to look into it. You have the means, yes? All I know is he was going to Narvik for a meeting.'

'Under his alias.'

'Well, it's not like he doesn't use that alias every week. It wouldn't be hard for someone to track him down. Someone determined. Someone who wanted to teach him a lesson.'

'A lesson for what?'

'How should I know?' Matteo thudded into the seat. 'The bottom line is there's only Wilmer left. Not ideal. And all this crap about the Spaceport circling? He's lucky that the OnePlanet nutcases don't come after *him*.'

'Because his land is under consideration?' Tom asked.

Matteo pulled a face. 'It'll never happen. OnePlanet would be attacking one of its own. Wilmer won't agree to sell up. He should just come out and say so publicly. Get any potential aggravation off his back before it starts. You've seen what they are doing—those dumb protests.'

'Your father is a supporter?'

'That's a private matter, Chief Wagner. Please keep it out of your reports. His objections, too. And our history. The people who died are my siblings—and they don't directly have a thing to do with the Spaceport. The most they are—were—is pawns in some game.' He stood. 'And I have to live with never seeing them again. Plus, the spectre of ending up like them very soon. So, I have matters of personal security to attend to.' He waved towards the door.

Tom conceded to his instinct that they were done for the day. It hadn't been a great fact-finding mission beyond getting the measure of the remaining Svensson heir.

Nobody was going to hand them answers to this mystery. Fleet PD would have to grind out a solution the old-fashioned way.

# 36

Wednesday was an unproductive day in the makeshift Carlsson/Connors household. The big news was that the kids were coming home on Saturday—Tom was heading to the chateau on Thursday, taking a couple of personal days off... though he'd be using the long travel time to let the cases percolate in his mind.

Kayte and Kennet held a joint update call with Ellie and Han. It was good to catch up for the first time in weeks. It felt strangely like the crash had happened barely a few days earlier—but that was because it was such a huge event that it overshadowed the relative minutiae of recent history.

They went to the supermarket and loaded the trolley with supplies, ready for two extra mouths to feed again.

Kayte announced a big decision: she wanted him to speak to the Bollnäs preschool about available space for Charlotte.

'You will take the job at PD?' he asked.

'I don't see why not. I spoke to my CO at Söderhamn, and they're happy for me to move. It was only a cover position anyway, and with my recent absence,' she shrugged, 'They learned to live without me. Honestly, I'll never live in that house again, so why stick to that town? Part of it was because it's an easier trip down to Uppsala for Carey and... that's not necessary now.' Her lip quivered.

He gripped her shoulder in support. 'Whatever you think.'

'You have to help me find a place in town, okay?'

'Of course. We'll talk to Ulrik about the job. I'll speak to the preschool. We can look for a rental house next week.'

She searched his eyes. 'Moving on is the right thing to do, yeah?'

'Absolutely. You're in limbo. At least I'm settled here. You don't need more things to worry about.'

'And I can't crash out in your spare room forever. If nothing else, Charlotte needs to feel at home somewhere. You know—pretty walls, all her things around.' She chuckled. 'Not her mom cramping her style.'

'And she needs to socialise. Preschool was excellent for Tomas. Really helped his development.' His brow furrowed. 'Now I think of it, Sergeant Mikkelson has her daughter there. Perhaps there will be a space when the girl leaves? We should act quickly.'

'We'll go tomorrow, okay? I want to be there. Don't need you as my messenger boy. I can't avoid whatever's necessary to make a life in this country.'

'Staying is your decision?'

She nodded. 'Yeah. And you were smart to make the crazy suggestion that I—Carey and I—come here in the first place. Ease up the pace of life. I'll tell you something else. I won't be cowed into returning to the US by the actions of one deranged individual. That was a blip. A goddamn awful, life-changing one, but I *know* that all the things I loved about this place before are still here.'

That night, Kennet felt like he was barely asleep before something woke him—a noise or merely a sixth sense? Either way, Kayte was in the doorway.

'What?' he asked gently, convinced there must be a problem.

Her dark form approached. 'Oh God, Kennet, I'm starting to forget her already.' The words were surfing silent tears.

'Come here.'

She sat on the bed. It trembled.

'What do you mean?' he asked.

'Today was our anniversary. Me and Carey. And I only just remembered. That's appalling.' She sobbed.

He sat up and held her vibrating shoulders. 'No, it's... understandable.'

She sniffled. 'No. It's cruel and wrong and disrespectful.'

In the half-light, he brushed away her tears. 'Alright, Sergeant. This must stop. Get under the cover. This matter is one for a night hug, yes?'

'I think so.'

He allowed her room, she slid in, and he took her in a familiar spoon position that was neither embarrassing for him nor alarming for her.

'Tell me,' he said.

'We met eleven years ago today. We always celebrated it. Now, I've... erased it.'

'I think you are wrong and chastising yourself for no reason. Events mean that your brain is full of other things. Memories, regrets, worries about the future. Also, any uncomfortableness about what is happening between you and me, how much of it is right and wrong, what other people will think. Frustration that we haven't solved the cases yet.'

He kissed her bare shoulder. 'It is okay to have blind spots, Kayte. But the fact that it's upset you so much shows that, deep down, you *do* remember and care. And that life event memories will never leave you. Things like your wedding—when Carey probably looked the most beautiful you have seen her, and you loved her the most intensely—will be the strongest memories. And it's *good* that you have those highlights to hold onto because it's better to remember the good times than the day you lost her. Don't think of the day of the crash as an *anniversary*—never make it that—because anniversaries are supposed to be good things.' He smiled in the gloom. 'Like the day I met you.'

She lifted his hand and kissed it. 'That's a good memory for me too. While I don't want to worm my way into your life and memories, you're inextricably linked with my past, and I can't imagine the future without you in my life in some form.'

'I feel the same.'

She wriggled, so he released his spooning, and she rolled to face him. Her features were dimly lit, the whites of her eyes picked out, the curve of her shoulder. 'Hold me.'

'I was.'

She pulled him close. 'Like this.'

He wrapped his top arm over her and held the small of her back, stroking the fabric as she pressed her head into his shoulder. His heart thudded at this new proximity.

'Thank you,' she murmured.

'You're welcome.'

After a couple of minutes, their bodies relaxed, and she let go.

'Stay if you want,' he said.

'Thanks.' She rolled over and arranged the pillow. 'Night.'

'Night.'

As he flickered into consciousness in the morning, the nerve endings on his chest told his brain there was a hand laying there.

He slowly opened his eyes.

Kayte was close by—not quite touching—with her head lolled towards him and her left palm on his breastbone.

His pulse quickened. Now he became hyper-aware of the skin-to-skin touch. He churned with guilt, comfort, and a frisson of desire, then dismissed it as wanton and wrong—though it wasn't the first time the thought had appeared.

A tear formed as he felt like his mind was betraying Jana's memory, even if his body wasn't. He didn't want to ever forget her or do wrong by her, yet he needed to let go and move on, even if not romantically, even if not with Kayte.

His troublesome cogitation was brief, interrupted by her waking. There was something deeply enchanting and intimate about the experience of watching her come into the world.

She saw his face, jolted at how close they were, then looked down at her hand as if it was an alien limb. She whipped it up like his chest was a fire.

The expression in her eyes was that of a startled rabbit. 'Ohmygod. I'm sorry.' She grimaced, clenching a fist.

'Hey, it's okay.'

'But... but I.... How long was I like that? Touching you?'

'I don't know. I just woke.'

'I must have.... Sheesh, I'm sorry.'

He was in a quandary. If he told her he didn't mind, it would overtly telegraph—correctly—that he found it pleasant, which could be regarded as forward. However, it was important that she knew she hadn't overstepped the mark, offended him or made him uncomfortable. He didn't want her to feel guilty or embarrassed.

'Kayte. Honestly, it is fine. It's a... gut reaction. It's because we're comfortable together. And remember what you said? We are each so used to hugging a partner in bed. It is a... sense memory, that is all. Maybe even a wish for that to happen again if the universe grants it.'

'Even so....'

'Hey. I know you are not "trying anything on". You said there would be... mistakes. Think of it like that, if you want.'

She sighed. 'Okay.'

'Besides, it could have been worse. We could have woken with *my* hand on *your* chest.'

She laughed. 'Okay. Agreed. That would be a whole different conversation.' She puffed a breath. 'So, we're good?'

He took her hand and pressed it onto his chest again. 'It is no big deal. Okay?'

'You're the best.'

'Yes. Yes, I think I am.'

She pecked him on the cheek. 'Sometimes, you're damn funny too.'

'Yes. Yes, I think I am.'

She pressed a longer kiss to his cheek. 'Stop, okay?'

'Yes, Sergeant.'

'Well, now you're just too much.' She threw back the covers.

As she left the room, heading to the shower in the main bathroom, he found himself watching her locomote away.

He scrunched the duvet in self-recrimination. This wasn't the time for flights of fancy.

# 37

Matteo Svensson spent many hours replaying the meeting with the two cops, assessing their motivations and his own level of concern.

He concluded that it hadn't gone poorly—in fact, he'd done well to magnify his fears. True, his fears weren't in the domain he'd mentioned, but he wasn't immune to anxiety. After all, he wasn't a *monster*.

He felt cushioned from the investigations yet not dissociated from the deaths. He'd attended Eva's funeral, but could he attend Anders'? What if the cops happened to turn up and saw him there, in direct contravention of the paranoia he'd voiced?

Seeing Wilmer at Eva's wake had been tricky, but they'd managed to hold a civil conversation—for show if nothing else. The condolences of family friends, which were murmured in his direction, were hard to take—not least because it showed how much she was missed by other people.

Still, she'd had her chance. As had Anders.

He'd have to get a bodyguard now for show. At least part-time. Very part-time. He didn't want anyone unduly shadowing his moves or eavesdropping on his calls.

Mat cursed his quick words.

Feeling tense, he went for a walk in the nearby woods. He sucked clear air into his lungs, tried to fuel his mind for solutions to current problems, and gathered strength for the next stages in the process. There were more challenges ahead; this was never going to be an easy plan. Time was short: the Spaceport decision was due on 1 September, less than two months away.

Wilmer needed to see reason.

As he listened to the birdsong, something like the tap tap of a distant woodpecker knocked at the inside of his skull. Things the old man had said over the years. Rumours had flitted in and out of Mat's peripheral vision. A drunken night, years ago, with his siblings—one of the few occasions they'd relaxed and sociable together. Or rather, one of the few occasions they'd accepted his presence without disgust and mockery.

Wilmer never truly opened up about the wilderness period, the three years during which he'd conducted an affair. Eva was still young, Anders older than her by two years—as ever. Mat hadn't even been mentally or physically conceived.

What had happened during the time Dad was with the "other woman"? None of the family had ever seen her nor known her name. Dad had drawn a thick black line under his "mistake".

Mat scoffed. Three years is a damn long mistake. There was clearly something significant in the relationship; it was more than a fling, a one-night stand.

He found he'd come to a stop, so parked his backside on a fallen tree.

He'd done the maths—and confronted Mum—about his parentage. He'd been passionate about it at the time, before the prison stretch, but now he considered deeply, it didn't really matter if he was Mum's son. So long as he was Dad's—because that's where the money lay. And, of course, even if he was the product of that affair with a nameless birth mother, he was still part of the Svensson line.

The question was this: what if there *was* a product of the affair? An undisclosed, denied, perhaps even expelled individual?

Mat's pulse raced.

That would change the game. Open up a whole new world of problems.

He steepled his fingers. Matteo Svensson doesn't panic. He explores all avenues, he calculates, and he sees an opportunity when others see issues. He leverages everything at his disposal—intellect, resources, contacts—to get things done.

He began to walk home, cogitating on the best way to approach this.

# 38

Kayte struggled to concentrate on work the following day.

She was preoccupied with what had happened overnight—or at least in the morning.

Unless... had something happened in the night? Waking up with her hand on his chest was a first, but was it an echo of earlier contact? Had she snuggled too close this time? Had she unwittingly brushed into his... nether regions beforehand? He'd never mention it, likely crippled with embarrassment and not wanting to make her feel awkward.

She gripped the coffee mug tighter.

She hoped nothing untoward had *happened* because she didn't want him to be uncomfortable around her—and he'd been doing so well. She was fortunate to be able to trust him, move around the house in nightwear without being ogled, and share a bed with him without the fear of being groped.

Undoubtedly, it was a faint echo of her time at college with Brandon.

Sweet Brandon, who treated her like a sister, each so innocent in matters of the flesh. She'd hugged him many times, offered girlish pecks. Then, of course, they'd slept together. Well, not slept... not like she truly slept with Kennet.

She frowned, casting her mind back, dredging for a sense memory of her one time with a man. It had been enjoyable—she hadn't been scarred! —but what has it *felt* like? Was it relief because she'd lost her virginity? Was it a natural step in the evolution of their relationship—although they were only friends and never dated? Or was it because she was intrinsically attracted to him as a boy, a male?

She sighed hard.

Perhaps she'd woken in the morning after that long ago night, comforted that Brandon was still in the bed and hadn't treated her like a plaything, and snuggled up to him, her hand on his bare chest, playing with his skin?

There was never a time in her life when she regretted the occasion, nor any sense that she'd found the experience anything less than pleasurable.

Yet, soon came her first time with a girl. Then a couple more. Then Carey. Those were all pleasurable, too—the companionship and the physical side of things.

Kennet was purely muddying the waters—but in a good way. Tendrils of doubt were creeping in. What if girls were the phase and not boys—or boy, singular? What if that first time with Heather had been an... experiment, a reaction? Yes, it was very fine, and different, but....

She picked at the material of her trousers.

What if the person in the bar, those ten years ago, had been a man? Would she have flatly turned down any advance purely on principle? Would no male—armed with wit, intelligence, charm, care and good looks—have stood a chance? Had Carey been her destiny, or simply a wonderful person at the right time?

She was on a dangerous and redundant path of hypothesising now, but she couldn't stop, wouldn't stop—because it might provide a breakthrough. Answers to questions that had pricked at her for longer than she dared admit. After all, she and Kennet had already explored the "alternative universe" scenario and recognised that it was all hot air because things were what they were and couldn't be changed.

All the same....

Had she married Carey after meeting Kennet to prove to herself that she *didn't* want him, to signpost her unavailability, to remove temptation, as she'd already experienced the Brandon echo and was attracted to Kennet?'

She scoffed, yet worried.

Would all this trawling of conscience, motive and sexuality have happened if she'd not kissed him in Paris? But she could ask plenty more "what ifs": if Kennet hadn't come to DC, if she was only dating and not married to Carey. If they hadn't come to Sweden, then the wives not gone away together and not have died.

She clenched a fist—she'd examined this already and resolved that looking back was wasted time.

She might as well ask what would have happened if Kennet had come to DC ten years earlier, or if she and Carey had broken up, or if a youthful Kayte had pursued a relationship with Brandon rather than essentially a one-night stand.

There were a million questions, but she could only draw a line under things and move on from *this* point and what was current and true.

The easy way forward was to fall into a relationship with Kennet, because he ticked so many boxes, while at the same time offered a significant hurdle.

Going into a new relationship with *anyone* would, at minimum, have the hurdle of her feeling bad about it—the guilt of it being too soon, or inadvertently compared to Carey. Kennet's specific hurdle was that he was a man. If Kennet was female, she would have asked him/her out in a heartbeat as he/she was exactly the kind of person she could see herself with. Was the only hurdle physical intimacy and romantic attachment?

Except waking up in Kennet's arms made her happy. Perhaps touching him was merely the next step on the journey they'd acknowledged. Considering a relationship with him was *good* because it wasn't primarily based on physical attraction, but a bond and rock solid platform of personality.

She chuckled quietly. It was better to debate it and examine her conscience than to be shallow and pick up someone—man or woman—in a club for a superficial drunken fling! That wasn't her style. Besides, it would probably disappoint Kennet, and he'd lecture her.

Well, that's some kind of revelation, she mused. She *cared* what he thought of her and her actions. But that wasn't news—he'd repeatedly shown that he cared deeply for the welfare of her and her family. Another reason why he was... a catch.

So what was the right path?

Kennet was in his study, solemnly working through admin for Jana's affairs.

'Are you okay?' She had to enquire.

He looked up, sombre. 'I'm trying to feel lucky—that I had such time with her. That I have Tomas because of it. I told you to think of the good things, so I must do that.'

She perched on the small desk. She considered her own conundrums. 'And don't wish things were different. Or ponder what they would be. Life will never go back to normal. The world has shifted. No, the universe.'

He patted her knee. 'And I have my best friend to help me through.'

'You know, I'll have to go back to DC for some of my... stuff.'

He stood. 'I'll come. I mean, if you want me there.'

'You can't pull Tomas around the world for the sake of being there for me to lean on. I'm a big girl.'

'So, I'll stay?'

That's a question, she thought. 'I didn't say that....'

'Okay. Will you *let* me come?'

It was hard to resist the care and empathy on his face. 'I guess.'

His hand came to her waist. 'It is hard to stay away from you. Do you know that?'

'I'm getting the picture, yeah.'

A couple of butterflies danced in her stomach. She pressed her lips hard to his cheek.

'Damn, but this journey is hard.'

'Nothing worth having is easy. Fate will show us, events will shape us, and we will discover how to carry on our lives. There will be a sign, a moment, which pushes us together,' he smiled ruefully, 'or more likely, keeps us as friends. Hopefully, not blows us apart.'

He frowned, then cheered. 'And our heads and hearts will be in unison for the correct way to act to have the *best* future—not only for us but Tomas and Charlotte too. If that's two single parents as house neighbours—'

'That could work,' she suggested.

'—who help each other out, so be it. We are smart and hopefully know each other well enough to turn away from a slide or fall into a chasm which would mark the end of... us.'

She put a hand on his chest. 'Besides, we voted to save each other from the hospital, excess, indulgences, insanity or whatever. So, surely neither would take an action which would be personally self-serving but destructive to the other.'

'Not in a second.' He pecked her cheek.

'I know that my journey is about working out what's right and wrong. I've got to examine conscience—we both do—and how we each *really* feel. There's no booze nor heated emotional situation—I honestly think that's passed.'

He frowned. 'Has it? Who is to say? We are still grieving, aren't we? There's not a day I don't think about Jana.'

'And it's okay to look back. I don't mind you talking about Jana. I'm not offended. I'll talk about Carey, but, like we said, it's wasted time to wish it was different. We can remember fondly, not sadly.'

'That is true. We have emotional needs, and maybe now I'm plugging that gap for you and any... attraction... you feel is possibly not real. Don't judge what you need in the *remainder* of your life—the type of love, support and physical closeness—by what you feel *now*. *Now* is not "normal".'

She processed his words and earnest expression. 'But I've always known there is *something* there—even if it's simply bond and care. You know—our "parallel universe" heart-to-heart. More and more, with every step on our journey—my rollercoaster ride—I think there's attraction too.'

Now her heart was pounding, so as a firm underline to that sentence, that sentiment—so she could drop the damn subject and get a grip—she kissed him, not quite on the mouth, not too quickly, not too extensively. Not too hard, not too soft.

Then she blew out a breath that said, "right, to business".

'I'll make coffee. How long do you need here?'

He shook away whatever was on his mind. 'The rest of the morning. This afternoon I want to check the engineer's Com records. See who he talked to. I doubt that a lead will magically pop up, but we have to try.'

She nodded. 'I only wish we didn't have to wait so long to talk to the guy.'

'Agreed. If our luck was different, Enna would be on that return flight from Mars, and could spin her magic.'

'Well, let's roll with what we have. Ellie said Olsson's taken the bait, and he leaves the red planet tomorrow.'

Kennet stroked his chin. 'It puts me in mind of the Dr Iversen case. Trying to keep his return and his work secret until we could use him as bait to catch Alaric Layton.'

She patted his shoulder. 'And that worked a dream. So we have a track record, right?'

# 39

On Friday morning, buoyed by the prospect of Tomas' and Charlotte's imminent return, Kennet attacked his travails with gusto.

When he came across a number in engineer Frans Olsson's call log, which he traced to a Swedish burner phone, his suspicions were piqued. Burners weren't something he often came across, but they were usually a sign of underhandedness.

However, this bolt of lightning had struck twice.

Almost jittery with excitement—not the measured cop he normally was—he rushed to Kayte, who was on the sofa, engaged in her Com. He perched nearby.

She set down her mug. 'What?'

'I have something,' he said, eyes wide, holding up the palmtop Com.

She came to him. He showed her the split screen, which displayed two lists with one number cross-referenced.

'Olsson had repeated calls from a burner, one in this country.'

She frowned. 'Makes sense, I guess—criminal activity, a plan, a payoff—'

He tapped the screen and held it close to her face. 'No. Look. Viggo Alban was in touch with the same number.'

Her hand came to her lips.

'The same person hired them both. I am sure of it. Eva and Anders' deaths *are* connected.' He smiled hopefully.

'God—that's it! It has to be.' Her face lit with cheer. 'You're a genius.'

'It's only a theory.'

'It's the damn finest thing I've heard in a while. If we could get to the bottom of this, find the bastard, get some closure....' Her mouth hung open as she gazed around, almost in wonder.

Then she stepped to him. 'Kennet, I could kiss you.' The joy leaked from her tone.

He smiled. 'I think that's been repeatedly proven.'

She laughed. Her eyes explored his, so briefly. In moments the air crackled with heightened tension which tingled on his skin.

Then she kissed him, as forewarned. It had a glow to it, a positivity, a sense that this was no journey's step, no tentative exploration. Was it relief, happiness, or expulsion of tension?

He only knew that there was a difference. Previously, the kisses had been merely an act of contact—like a press of a button. They were borne of friendship, gratitude, comfort or relief. Now, as he eased back, expecting the end, she held the pressure, so he reapplied the touch, and their lips remained together. They didn't hold still but slipped, moist, warm and supple.

Endorphins radiated from the bond and crashed through his body like a surfer's dream waves.

They parted. He caught his breath. What was in her eyes? Contentment?

Instinctively, he put a hand on the small of her back, so she couldn't leave, not quite yet. This couldn't go undiscussed.

She cupped his cheek, stroked it. He had a million things to say and nothing. Plenty to ask, but her posture spoke volumes. She daintily licked her lips, and her eyes danced as she sought those million unspoken words. She moved her fingers to the nape of his neck.

'Is this a... thing now?' she murmured.

'I don't know. It could be... something. I don't know that I should be the one to decide.'

She swallowed. 'I don't know either, but....'

Her smile, though nervous, was warm and delightful. Suddenly she was more impossibly beautiful than ever, like a veil had been lifted.

'Okay.' It was barely a whisper, his nerves battling with the possibility that this *could* be more than a step, perhaps a stride.

Something told him that the worst outcome was the status quo. They were at... not an impasse but a gate, and he believed she wanted to open it, yet something held her back. If he barged through it—as part of him wanted to—then rusty hinges could cause the gate to buckle and be unusable. They'd never be able to go back the way they'd come.

Caution, as if not to risk a squeak.

He kissed her gently, yet in a way that was transparently not one of friendship. He supported her chin and kissed her again, three, four brief times. Softly, so the nerve ends of his lips crackled with the feel of her. His chest hammered in youthful desire.

When he broke off, she said nothing, only looking at his mouth. His dating years had long since passed, but he recognised that sign. With his arm, he drew her close and offered his lips to hers again. She met him halfway.

He lost track of time. The kiss was long, full of motion and emotion.

The end only happened to allow breath.

She beamed, then lay her head on his chest. 'I think this is a thing.'

'I think so too,' he replied.

She took his hand. 'Come.'

They sat on the sofa. He didn't hesitate to put an arm around her—that act was hardly unusual between them.

'That was some breakthrough,' she said.

He frowned. 'On the case, or the... relationship?'

She laughed. 'Both. Don't know which I'm happier about. Actually, I don't know which is the clearer cut, more likely to be the truth.'

'Do you want to talk about either one?'

'Maybe the case.'

'Okay.' He picked his mug from the table.

She helped him set it back down.

'What?' he asked.

'Are *we* okay?'

He frowned. 'Yes. Or is this... not a thing?'

'Have I changed my mind? No. Have you?'

'No. Just... processing, maybe.'

'That it's real.'

She kissed him briefly. 'Does that feel real?'

'Very.'

She cocked her head. 'I get it. I get the... "processing". Doesn't mean you're not sure, right? Just... getting used to the idea?'

He nodded. 'Of it being real, yes.' He scratched his cheek, then gently caressed hers. 'Kayte, I refused to admit to myself—for so long—that you were pretty, and that I was attracted to you. I forced it down. I certainly couldn't say it aloud. It would have been betrayal. Weak. Neanderthal, perhaps.'

She smiled. 'I get it. Really. Being honest, as I never got hit on by many men, *I* wondered if I was attractive to them.' She played with his shirt button. 'And to you, specifically.'

'You are. Very much.'

Her eyes twinkled. 'I got the feeling.'

'Good.' He blew out a happy breath. 'So, the case.'

'In a minute.'

She leant in, offering her lips, and he took them gratefully.

Her moves were exploratory, like she was trying him on for size. As if he was a pair of shoes that fit so well, you wish they would never wear out.

After two minutes, she eased back, a gentle query on her face, gaze exploring his eyes and mouth.

He didn't know what the question was, so instead of an answer, he made a statement.

'I very much enjoy kissing you. Sergeant.' Though his facial muscles fizzed with nervous joy, he managed a wink.

Very gently, she ran a fingertip across his lips. 'You too. Inspector.'

He couldn't wait this time and kissed her with greater passion. Still, his hands didn't stray, a guardian angel on his shoulder whispering caution, reminding him that nothing should be taken for granted, even at this stage. While there was a chance that circumstance, or curiosity, was driving them forward—rather than pure desire—there were still many lines which should not be unilaterally crossed. He still had to walk beside her, not ahead, on her journey.

He knew this episode would go one of four ways. Either she'd pull away, embarrassed, tearful and apologetic, saying she couldn't do it, that kissing like this—and the prospect of any further steps towards physical intimacy—she couldn't consider, even on a basic impulse level.

Or it would go fine, but she would come back the next morning saying it was a mistake, a blip, and she couldn't consider a romantic relationship any time soon because it was cruel to Carey, let alone being innately anathema to her sexual preferences.

Alternatively, irrespective of *her* decision, he'd lie awake, torn, and then conclude it had been nothing more than wish fulfilment, and he couldn't move on—so quickly, opportunistically and disrespectful towards Jana's memory.

Fourthly, everything might be fine tomorrow—no inquests or reservations—and this extended lip-locking marked another step on the journey towards, hopefully, happiness. And the more she kissed him, and her fingers toyed with the hair on the back of his neck, the more she matched his moves beat for beat, the greater became the likelihood of this outcome.

He took the invitation gratefully, unshackling another layer of want, holding her to him, letting the moment evolve until they were partially reclined on the sofa's cushions, imbibing each other.

Kissing so openly with her was a heady cocktail, and he stopped before he feared passing out due to the volcano of hormones. She had started this, but he had to end it.

As they caught their breath, her eyebrows furrowed and relaxed.

'Did things just get simpler or more complicated?'

He thought. 'Simpler.'

'Because?'

'Because nothing is hidden. Some things are more obvious now.'

'I guess so.' She picked at a nail. 'Being honest, I have thought about it. Maybe for a couple of days. Have you?' Her gaze burrowed into him.

'For a few days,' he lied.

'Just a few?'

His shoulders fell. Lies were unacceptable. 'Maybe longer.'

She rubbed his shoulder. 'It's okay. Honestly, it is.' She screwed up her eyes. 'Enough post-mortems for now. Too damn stressful.' She took a slug of water. 'Do you want to discuss the case?'

'I think we should. Before our minds are washed by... other things.'

She beamed. 'Like what just happened.'

'I think that is a... "morning after" conversation, is it not?'

She laughed. 'I suppose so. But honestly, we do need to think about... this. And I don't know about your schedule, but mine's wide open around breakfast time, so let's be grown-ups and say we'll sleep on this. You know, do some mental detective work, put the clues together, check for red herrings....' She looked him up and down. 'Examine the physical evidence and decide how we want to pursue... the case.' She raised her eyebrows.

'The case of the curious relationship.'

'That's about the size of it. Partner. Roomie. Friend. Friend with *significant* benefits.'

He stroked her cheek. 'Please stop being so adorable. We have a case to discuss.'

She mock saluted. 'Yes, Inspector.'

He pressed a brief, unusually hard kiss to her lips by way of jokey admonishment, then backed off and put on a serious face.

'The case.'

She put her shoulders back. 'The case.'

They successfully set aside matters of the heart and worked through theories about the plane crash. Then came dinner and lounging in front of the TV. There was no more kissing, as if they'd returned to being merely roomies again.

It was an odd change of pace, like a savoury sorbet after the sweetest dessert. Yes, Kayte was right to suggest a timeout from the unexpected crescendo in their physical relationship. Sharing a bed after what had occurred might lead to hasty decisions which were informed by lust alone. The careful journey could be ruined by a headlong dash for the finish line, only to trip and fall, or realise the tape was a mirage and the race had been misguided all along.

Was she fundamentally reconsidering their marathon kiss already?

At eleven-fifteen, they called it a night, took to their bathrooms, washed and changed.

He worried that he wouldn't sleep, his mind blazing, hormones raging, and guilt tickling his conscience. Still, he had to try.

As he turned off his room light, she appeared in the doorway.

His sharp inhalation was a kneejerk reaction. Empirically, she looked no different to previous nights, attired in plain camisole and shorts. Yet it was as if this was the first time he'd seen her as a *woman*. A woman he was unapologetically attracted to and desirous of.

She frowned. 'What?'

'Nothing. Just....' A stupid lump appeared in his throat. 'You look... nice.'

'I look the same, Kennet. So do you.' She tapped her head. 'It's mind tricks.' She moved closer. 'Maybe a sign of... hope? Or something undefinable.'

'Relief?'

'I don't know.' She fluttered a hand. 'Anyway.' She stepped into touching distance. 'Today was a good day. In a lot of ways. A damn good day.'

'Agreed. Significant... developments.'

She smiled. 'Yeah. Developments.'

The silence clanged.

She sighed hard. 'Look, just a goodnight kiss, okay? Being honest, it'd be nice.'

'And *acceptable*.'

'Sure.' She moved close.

He stroked her cheek, his nerve endings crackling. Her eyes glistened with affection.

He kissed her, slowly at first, then with more want. He held her so tight, fingers on the soft material covering her back, her hands on his waist, their chests pressed together.

All too soon, it was over, as if by unspoken mutual agreement that despite a desire for continuation, the sensible thing was to stop before things escalated.

She stroked his chin. 'Goodnight... my sweet... friend.'

'Goodnight, my... roomie.'

She laughed, pecked him on the cheek, gave a little wave, and sashayed out.

He collapsed to the bed, emotionally drained.

# 40

Kayte pulled a robe on before going to the kitchen for breakfast. Whilst Kennet was a discreet and honourable man, exemplified by his restraint during the evening's romantic interlude, excess temptation was unnecessary.

He was at the breakfast bar, also in a robe—which made her smile.

The first few seconds were a nervous standoff, then she realised she was being an idiot, stepped in and kissed him on the cheek.

He embraced her, eyebrows working in apparent concern.

'What?' she asked.

'I don't know. I...' He took a breath. 'Nervous, I suppose.'

'About what I'll say?'

'Yes.'

She smiled—his apprehension warmed her. 'Good. Means you didn't take yesterday to mean things are a slam dunk.'

'I don't.'

'Do you... regret it?'

He squinted. 'No.'

She let the tension leave her frame. 'Me either.'

Then his fingertips were tenderly on her cheek, so she gave in to temptation and kissed him.

'Here's the thing. Kissing you last night was a joy. Unexpected but a joy. As I lay awake, I wanted more. Then I hated that I wanted more. I hated that I felt... unshackled... for the first time—because it meant that being with Carey *held me back.*'

She grabbed a handful of his robe, trying to squeeze away the guilt—or at least the *notion* that she should feel guilt. 'Which isn't true.'

She eased away, a few tears dribbling down her cheeks. Chivalrous as ever, he wiped them away.

She took a deep breath. 'I mustn't think it was wrong to be with Carey. It's *so* not true and hurtful to her memory.'

'I felt the same—that anything we did would be disingenuous.'

'Carey *was* the best person to spend my life with. I knew for a while you were—or would be—the second best... if I could come to terms with my new—no, probably my real—sexuality. Or at least accept that I can fancy men and women.' She shook her head. 'It was all moot. It was the parallel universe. A scientist would say that parallel universes only meet at some insane, catastrophic, unexplainable thing like a black hole.'

She chuckled a little mournfully. 'Well, we've had to go through a life-altering, perspective-altering thing like a black hole. Now we're in the universe we, jokingly, spoke about not long ago. And we *have* to make a future here. Here, where you're no longer the second-best person to be with but the first.'

He held her. 'The first you know of,' he clarified.

'I've no inclination to seek out someone better. It's probably a waste of time. To strike lucky twice in a row is long enough odds already.'

'Me too.'

'So, whatever happens, I don't want to be compared to Jana or expect to be loved as much. Whatever our new future, I only want you to *love* me—in whatever way—to the best of your ability. For who we are *now*—that's enough.'

'Likewise.'

'So I need to... think. I have to know if this is real, or a reaction to grief, or an impulse, or gratitude for support. Or a heterosexual blip. What I'm saying is I need time. I know that's not what you want to hear—'

He put a finger on her lips. 'Perhaps I need time too. Because it is very easy to accept your proximity and... affection. But that doesn't mean it is the *best* thing.'

She kissed his finger, then traced her own fingertip over his lips. It was enough to catalyse a hug which morphed into a long, tender kiss.

'I'm glad we agree on things, Kennet. Let's... take some space. Reflect.' She beamed. 'See if having the children back breaks the spell. We've been in a bubble. An enforced period of just us two. And it was damn fine. But if yesterday was a kind of... honeymoon, we have to remember that a marriage is more than that. Whatever you and I decide, it has to work in the real, day-to-day world.'

'Smart, grounded and practical as ever, Sergeant.'

'Thanks. Roomie. Now, I might skip breakfast here, take a ride into town, stare into a coffee for a couple of hours, then bring back the shopping and wait for the chaos to descend.'

'You are talking about Enna, yes?' He beamed.

'Right on the money.' She gave his backside a firm pat. 'Honey.'

She went to her favourite coffee house in Bollnäs, had two coffees and two pastries, took a long, pensive walk around the main streets, shopped, and then returned to Kennet's.

Tom, Enna and the children arrived late in the afternoon. It was an emotional reunion for everyone.

While Lexie and Charlotte napped, and Tomas played in the garden, Kayte and Kennet discussed case developments with Tom and Enna. The latter was predictably bullish, nosy and fired up. Tom had to remind her that she was a Navigator. She poked her tongue out.

Kayte wondered whether to steal that move to use on Kennet, but their relationship—whatever it was—was in its infancy, so she shouldn't plan ahead. She was careful not to appear too cosy around Kennet yet was certain Enna's mind was whirring.

At an opportune private moment, she set the record straight—"nothing is going on". Enna denied she was even thinking along those lines, but Kayte wasn't sure.

Tom, Enna and Lexie left around six, taking the keys to Kayte's place. They'd head off to DC the next day.

As Kayte and Kennet put Charlotte to bed and then kissed Tomas goodnight, the young boy's mind was clearly whirring.

'Will Auntie Kayte be staying longer?'

Kayte glanced at Kennet. 'Yes, for a while.'

'Is that okay, Tomas?' Kennet asked.

'Yes. It's good. I like her.'

'That's a kind thing to say. I like her too.'

'Okay! Night!' He hugged Kayte, then was led upstairs by Kennet.

They cooked together and then ate. Conversation was oddly spartan—both had a lot on their minds. She did have one specific point to address, however.

'Listen, I suggest we don't share a bed for now. It could influence our decision.'

He tried not to appear disappointed—yet disappointment indicated that at least *his* decision was made. Yet arguably it hadn't. Transient physical desire wasn't the same as carving a future path, let alone embarking on a relationship *without* a view of how it would last.

'There is no rush, I agree. If it is the case that our future has been three years in the making, it would be silly to have a misstep now.'

'Exactly. I don't want my body making decisions when my mind and heart are still debating the issue.' She beamed. 'Anyway, I don't know that my body's concerned about much beyond hugs and kisses. But still. Those are a slam dunk for expressing where I'm at, okay?'

'And I too.'

'Good.' She checked the clock. 'I need my head on a pillow.'

'Likewise. It has been another landmark day.'

When he emerged from the ensuite, she was sitting on his bed.

He froze. 'What is it?'

She sprung up, perplexed. 'Nothing. What did you think? I had a problem?' Her eyes narrowed. 'Or I decided to renege on our no-bed-sharing commitment?' A smile played on her lips. 'Getting your hopes up?'

That hurt, just a touch.

She read it in his face. 'I'm kidding. This is goodnight, okay?'

He relaxed. 'Okay.'

She stepped in and put her arms around him. 'Kiss me.' Her eyebrows tweaked. 'You know, because it'll be part of the evidence in my decision.'

'For the defence or prosecution?'

She touched her nose to his. 'Depends how convincingly the evidence is delivered.'

He began softly, then broadened his affections. She gave an equal quarter in her kiss, stroking his shoulder blades. He held her head and lower back, pressing their two forms together like longtime lovers—although the truth was far from that.

Keeping his hands from her backside was a test of will, as it might begin a series of events he'd be powerless to control. Instead, he caressed her shoulders and neck, pushing this potentially innocent goodnight kiss into marking another step forward on their journey.

When they parted, she laid her head on his shoulder.

He didn't want to let her go.

'I think,' she murmured, 'no more goodnight kisses. Until I know what I want to do.'

'Okay.'

'Because I don't want to put too much store in them.' She moved her face close, inspecting every millimetre of his features. 'So, no more after tonight,' she whispered.

'Agreed.'

Her last look told him that she didn't want to go any more than he wanted her to, but still, she rubbed his upper arm, winked, and left.

# 41

They spent Sunday pottering around, tidying the garden and playing with the children.

Kennet was careful not to be too physical with Kayte in case Tomas asked awkward questions. Besides, it could be a phase.

Keen that the boy's summer holidays weren't spent indoors at home—despite the great break in the Loire—Kennet found an activity club for the upcoming week, brokered the arrangements, and Tomas agreed. It would also help the adults to focus on work and... other matters under consideration.

'He'll have to come with us to DC when I sort out things over there.'

Kennet nodded. 'So let's make that soon, before school restarts.'

'And before Olsson gets back. I want to be ready for the guy.'

'I don't think Tom will let us anywhere near him.' Her nostrils flared.

Kayte's shoulders fell. 'Yeah. Anyway, we've got other things to follow up on. And we should be getting the...' she swallowed, 'remains back soon, so I need to make arrangements for what she wanted.'

'Do you want to make a week of it? Dilute the... not nice parts... with a vacation?'

'Around and about DC? Why not? I can show you my old haunts. Find a... cabin in the woods, maybe.'

He clasped her hand. 'That sounds nice. Roomie.'

'It'll be a big cabin, yeah? Four rooms?'

'Absolutely. No assumptions made.'

'Good.' She bit her lip. 'You know what thought about yesterday? This... whatever we're doing. This decision. I know we're close, but if we're considering something... closer, then we should cover as many bases as possible. Rule out any red flags—that kind of thing.'

'We already know each other.'

She shook her head. 'There's scope for learning every day. It was five years before I found out Carey hated black-and-white movies. That's not a red flag, granted, but it was a... surprise. It was unusually... not her. Shallow maybe? Anyway, point is we should hang out and chat. Not about life now, or the cases or our lost loves, but just... stuff. Is that weird?'

'No. Not at all. It's information gathering.'

'For the "case of the curious relationship"!'

'Exactly. Would it be a thought for me to show you some "old haunts"? Local landmarks?'

'That sounds great. Around and about, you know? Where you had your first kiss, arrested your first perp. Play me your favourite song—that kind of thing.'

'And you do the same in America?'

She stuck out her hand. 'It's a deal.'

For the sake of efficiency, they engaged in police work, leaving time on Monday—when the children were elsewhere—for the "get to know you" time.

He found it curious to be doing something which close friends, couples even—though *they* weren't a couple—might have done much earlier in their relationship. Still, it was a positive step on one front because they'd made meagre progress on any casework.

There were three aspects to their lives—the painful but necessary actions and administration around the deaths, the frustrating yet empowering police work, and the tentative, exploratory Kennet-and-Kayte "journey".

He wondered which would be concluded first.

So, for a couple of days, they mixed personal chat and worked through Olsson's life.

They viewed a couple of potential houses for Kayte and Charlotte but ruled them out. They secured a permanent place for Charlotte at Bollnäs preschool—Sergeant Mikkelson's daughter was leaving at the end of the following week.

They talked to Janssen and Tom, but there was little news. Olsson's life seemed pretty much on the straight and narrow. The biggest lead was the calls to and from the unknown burner phone. Their best hope was to liaise with a small, dedicated squad in Stockholm which specialised in tracing 'off-grid' communications, so they made contact, and the squad said they'd keep Kennet updated with progress. Everyone knew it was like looking for a needle in a haystack.

Worse news came on Tuesday when Janssen revealed that he couldn't devote any more of his time to the investigations. With Mikkelson leaving the squad, and a flurry of other work, time was tight.

However, he confirmed that Kayte's transfer from Söderhamn was approved. To some extent, it was a relief for the Söderhamn superintendent, who'd never been fully supportive of Kayte taking time off domestic cases to help Fleet PD. Janssen was always more accommodating.

That evening, celebratory champagne was drunk, and Kennet received a fulsome kiss of gratitude.

# 42

Enna was pleased to be back at their villa in Fort Valley, VA. Whilst the gesture of friendship towards Kayte and Kennet had been an immensely pleasant experience, despite many travelling hours, there was nothing like home.

On Tuesday, she took Lexie to kindergarten, then began preparing for her next roster of lunar flights.

The problem was, after exposure to the conundrums and mysteries surrounding the plane crash and Eva Svensson's murder, she struggled to keep her inquisitive mind off the subject. Seeing what it had done to Kayte and Kennet made things worse.

All the same...

'Do you think there's anything... going on?' she asked Tom over dinner.

'With what? This whole mess is a huge list of "what's going on?".'

'I meant K and K.'

He frowned. 'Oh. Wannabe detective Dacourt is back. Leave them alone, Enna.'

She held up her palms. 'I am leaving them alone. Hell, the last thing I want to do is interfere in the course of true love.'

'I know,' he murmured. 'Too busy interfering in Fleet PD and a million other things.'

'I heard that. Rat.' She blew a kiss.

'Anyway, "true love"? Baloney. They're friends. Partners. They've been through a lot. Both very likeable. But, honestly, Enna? So they've erected a bubble of coexistence and support? They just need to be happy—or at least not bent double with grief, hollow inside, and examining their futures.'

'Whoah, back up there. I'm not denying them a right to mutual companionship. I want them each to be happy. I love them to bits—and I'll bet you want them back on duty, one hundred percent committed and awesome, as soon as possible.'

He shrugged. 'I do.'

'If I died tomorrow, would you let someone else move into this house so you could lean on their shoulder?'

He put down his cutlery. 'Stop judging, Enna. Stop hypothesising and extrapolating. They're our friends. Colleagues. Look what you did for them, taking their kids out from under their feet. Giving them time and space.' He eyed her directly. 'Hell, I could sit here and accuse you of helping to push them together, enabling that bubble. Okay?'

She sighed. 'Yeah. Sorry. I just want some good news, you know?'

'Then here's some. Olsson's on Mars. He took the bait. Flight leaves today.'

'What bait?'

'He has a sister. They're close. We've told him she was badly hurt when a window blew out on a construction site in Malmö, where she lives. We—well, Stockholm PD—have someone acting as her surgeon consultant. Sent a couple of messages. Olsson's scared as hell that she'll croak. Parents are already dead. She's all he has and vice versa.'

Enna cocked her head. 'Kinda like K and K.'

'Except this is a story, not real life.'

'You really think this will work, keeping him in the dark?'

'It damn well better. He's our best chance.' Tom tucked into his meal. 'And there's a bonus. Your buddy Gina is on the flight. Found out this morning. So, seeing as she's your mentee, and you think a lot of her, I asked Fleet if Gina could be the one to keep a special watch on him.'

'Like I did before?'

'Exactly. Treading in your footsteps.'

She grimaced, a bad memory returning. 'When I brought Danny Trello to Earth, he lasted under a day. I hope my curvy colleague has a damn sight better luck keeping her suspect alive.'

'She's a lot less of a tearaway than you, honey. Plus, Olsson doesn't know he's a suspect. He's not being treated like a caged animal.'

She slugged her beer. 'Let's hope it works.'

'Absolutely. You heard the call I got?'

'The car wreck? Yeah. Not all about Sweden anymore, I guess.'

'No. But it shows there are strong feelings. Fleet's Head of Infrastructure is bound to get it in the neck from OnePlanet—he's the lynchpin for major construction projects, pushing forwards your—our—reach and capabilities. OnePlanet hates that stuff. If they downed that plane—which is still a stretch—then targeting a bigwig in the hope of reversing key decisions is at least better thought-out.'

'You think they engineered that car wreck?'

'No idea. Too early to say. But for sure, Fleet wants us, as their in-house PD, to throw resources at this. Maybe it was an accident? Point is, I need Han and Ellie off the Svensson case and onto this new one. Which sucks for Kayte and Kennet, but they're back in the saddle—kinda—so I'm good with that.'

'You'll go easy on them? When Pascal died, I didn't stop grieving overnight. We may be six weeks down the line since Carey and Jana died, but they won't be themselves again. The echoes last.'

'I did lose my dad, remember.'

She sighed. 'Yeah. Sorry—again. Just want to get to the bottom of this, that's all.'

'Don't I know it.' He winked.

She ate for a minute.

'Who'd have the motive to kill both Eva and Anders?'

'That's the question, honey. Solve that, we're home and dry.' He grimaced. 'Or that's the way it looks.'

'So, who?'

'Potentially OnePlanet, if they'd put pressure on Wilmer already—gave him an ultimatum. Told him to reject the Spaceport bid or lose his kids.'

'That fails on two counts. You said he's a OnePlanet sympathiser, so he'd never agree to the project anyway. Plus, he hasn't reported any blackmail, pressure or criminal acts against him. And why have the Committee left his site on the shortlist if he's already indicated he's not interested?'

'Because it's technically the most suitable site. I think they're holding out for a change of heart. I don't see it, though. By all accounts, he's a stubborn guy. Matteo Svensson backed that up.'

'But you think Matteo is in the firing line too?'

'Makes sense. Not much of this does, but there is a pattern, and it leads to him. Or even Wilmer.'

'Hard job for anyone to get to the old man—plenty safe enough in that sprawling estate.'

'You forget—Anders thought he was safe enough with an alias, a bodyguard, and on a commercial flight. Whoever is behind this is sharp as a tack. Well-connected. Ruthless.'

'But what do they *want*?'

He drained his beer. 'Answer me that, darling, and I'll pin the commendation on you personally.'

# 43

On Wednesday, Kayte was unusually quiet.

They worked productively, side-by-side at his desk at Bollnäs PD, beginning the painstaking task of tracking Olsson's movements over the four weeks prior to his departure for Mars.

They used his shift pattern, Transit touch-ins, monetary spends, and scant information about his routine. It looked decidedly like he hadn't met any potential accomplice—but it was hard to be sure. He also hadn't exchanged messages with any secretive parties—though, again, it didn't mean that any one of his regular contacts wasn't the person they sought.

At least they were attempting to make progress, he consoled himself. They weren't lounging around at home, feeling sorry for themselves. They were trying to be part of the solution. Yet, she seemed pensive and guarded—not the vivacious woman he knew and... loved? Loved in some way, for sure. But romantically?

He felt sure it was this matter which occupied her thoughts, so he didn't try to winkle any information—or a brighter demeanour—from her. Instead, they finished the day's work, collected their respective children, then went home.

She spent time with Charlotte, he with Tomas, then he cooked, they all ate, and the evening routine took its course.

Without conference, she pulled a bottle of wine from the rack, poured them each a glass, then tentatively took his hand and led him to the sofa.

This felt momentous. He didn't know whether to be excited or worried. He tried to disguise his deep, calming breaths. This couldn't be a cataclysmic end, could it?

She kissed his knuckles. 'Kennet, I'm ready to talk about this now.'

'Truly?'

'Yes. We've known each other for what, four years? In that time, you've gone from stranger to colleague, to friend, cop buddy, close friend, lifesaver, soulmate, emotional rock and a kinda romantic roomie. We've lived together for the shortest few weeks ever. You've cared for me, Tomas has accepted me, and Charlotte, I'm sure, sees you as more than merely the biological father you are.'

His heart skipped. This didn't sound great—like there was a "but" coming.

'Kayte—'

She held up a hand. 'Please. This is tough, it took a long time to prepare this speech in my mind, and I don't want to cry.'

'Okay.'

Unarguably, her expression was earnest as well as somewhat devotional.

'We have lost what was our entire world. People we loved like crazy. To even entertain this... strange thing we have together, some would say it's madness. Disrespectful. A misguided emotional bounce-back that's guaranteed to come off the rails. Wouldn't they?'

'I'm sure some would. Not me.'

'Nor me. So, fate has shown us that one chapter of our lives has ended—there's nothing we can do to reverse or deny it. Another much less foreseeable chapter has started. In a country I don't really know, in a town where I have no friends or relatives. The polar opposite of the young girl—young *gay* girl—in the big city of New York, then the less young, more married one in DC.'

She drank, girding her loins, then retook his hand. 'What we have is unique. It always was, and your patience through it all is the cherry on the cake of the person you are. Now, please don't think anything about what I say is knee-jerk. These last few days of space have been vital, and I'm so grateful for them.' She smiled.

'You had as long as you needed.'

'Thanks. So, what's happened over the last few weeks has shown that I've changed—we both have. I've searched my soul, heart and mind, and, being honest, my essence, and I've discovered—admitted?—something. What I want in my life, and who I want to spend time with, isn't about gender. It's about the *person*. Someone who is smart, warm, kind, giving, grounded, funny, and, more than anything, can put up with my foibles. And, damn, do I have some—not knowing if I want to get romantically attached to women or men is—was—a pretty big red flag.' She sighed hard, closing her eyes.

He released his hand and squeezed hers, holding in any reply as she corralled whatever thoughts and words were coursing around inside.

'So, here's the thing, Kennet. Partner. Roomie. Pal. I'm as sure as I can be that the person I want to be with, going forward, can easily be a man. Is a man. And that man is *you*. In fact, maybe it's *because* it's you that the fact you're a man is almost secondary.'

He smiled awkwardly. 'I don't know how to take that.'

'Look, every day since this nightmare began has been a journey and a gamble. Mostly by you, that I wouldn't wake up one morning and wonder what the hell I was doing, betraying my sexuality. Especially lately. You must have thought the spell would break?'

'I try to take you at face value, Kayte. Hope for the best but prepare for the day when you realised the experiment isn't working. But it was never romantic, certainly not sexual, only companionship.'

'Yeah. Then I recognised I wanted more.'

'You do?'

'Well, if I could give a cast-iron, rock-solid guarantee, then I would, but I can't. I've explored deep, deep in my heart of hearts, looking for a reason to throw all this away. This... friends with benefits, or whatever we're doing. The hugs. The kisses—and man, I have to say they were great. Trying to discover the little voice, the devil on my shoulder.' She shrugged. 'It hasn't come. Not guilt or regret. But know that, even though the odds are very long that I'm mistaken, this is a gamble on your part.'

'I understand.'

'Look at me, Kennet, you sweet man.'

Jittery, he fixed her in a nervous contemplation of awe and appreciation. If a detective couldn't work out the answer to these clues, he was a poor detective. All the same, part of his mind wouldn't accept them at face value.

She blew out an apprehensive breath. 'I want us to keep living together, even after the worst of this storm has passed. I want us to share a bed every night, not just when we feel it's needed. Much more than hugs and kisses. I want to be with you. Completely. I don't want anyone else, man or woman.' She brought his hand to her cheek and looked deep into his eyes. 'I want us to try for a child in time. In summary, in case you fell asleep before, while I was pouring my heart out and issuing disclaimers, I am completely in love with you, and I want to spend all my time with you.'

His throat tightened, and his cheeks flushed.

'And if the answer is No, then that's logical because it's a heck of a punt, but I couldn't *not* ask you. We're not getting any younger, and hell knows we both deserve to have a happy *rest of* our lives. Please, *please*, don't tread water with me if you want to find someone who's more... your type.'

He processed that for all of two seconds. Then he rose, drew her up from the sofa, and took her in an embrace. He pulled her impossibly tight as contentment flooded every pore.

Then he let loose and cupped her face in one hand. 'Your honesty and consideration are as intoxicating as your beauty. You're all I want.'

She kissed him, and the physical bond was swamped by relief, symbiosis and unshackled desire. He could have cried but didn't.

They broke off, and she played with his soft fringe. He clasped her bottom, desperate for her not to leave.

'Did you notice a flaw in my wish list?' she asked.

He frowned. 'No.'

'When I said about having a baby, I meant through traditional conception this time.'

His heart fluttered. 'Okay.'

'You see the problem? We haven't made love. We haven't taken that step. Nor even come close. But I'm sure you've noticed.' Her eyes sparkled.

'We never knew how long this journey would be or where it would lead.'

'You have the patience of a saint, and most men would have snapped before now.'

He shrugged. 'Our relationship was always more than that one dimension. Plus, you know, your past preferences.'

'Past is past. We're talking about the future.' She explored his face, then tilted her head towards the bedroom. 'Do you want to start the future now?'

He laid his forehead against hers. 'You're gambling with this. I know that.'

She stroked the back of his head. 'Everything else we've done together has worked out pretty damn wonderful. I think this will too.'

'Are you sure?' he whispered.

'No,' she murmured. 'But it's the thing I want to find out most in the world.'

'If we do this now—or any day—everything changes. You know that?'

'Yeah. That's the whole idea. No more wondering. No more "what ifs". You want that, right?'

'I do.'

She took his hand. 'Let's go to bed.'

# 44

Kayte woke, her body did its natural start-up systems check, and she got her bearings. Odd, as she'd no reason to wake up anywhere other than the familiar and expansive bed at home.

The bedside display gently glowed 07:05.

In her peripheral vision was a figure. It only needed a microsecond's sense-check to know who it was.

Kennet was still asleep, his face half-tilted towards her.

She licked her dry lips and stretched her limbs. Then the recollection came. Fragments of pictures in her mind's eye, snippets of movements and reticent touches. Analysis snuffed it out quickly, a galloping through emotions and judgements, rights and wrongs, worry and fondness.

It felt like it went on for minutes, tormenting her not with its inherent negativity but with all-consuming reflection. She knew, it probably lasted barely seconds. What merited no debate was the veracity of the situation: it was real—the immediate present and the hours before.

When she jolted—more in consciousness than any bodily alarm—she found her right hand to be on her belly. Her index finger stroked her skin, then she moved her hand down below her waist and let it rest there as if a comfort.

There was a smile on her lips, which told her one undeniable thing. It meant her overriding emotion was contentment. So, she bathed in it, listening to him breathe, glancing around the room which was so normal yet oddly unusual. Something had changed—inside her. She let her thoughts range and parked those which merited investigation.

She needed the bathroom, so went as quietly as possible, then pulled on a pair of panties and slid carefully under the sheet. Not gently enough, however. His breathing pattern changed, and she watched his face with interest and affection as he joined her in the conscious world.

Whilst she wasn't schooled or gifted in the art, she'd become quite an expert at spotting the nuances of expressions—certainly his, what they meant, and sometimes what they deliberately or accidentally concealed.

His smile said, "Good morning", but his eyes said, "Ah". His Adam's apple moved as he swallowed—surely in a familiar tinge of embarrassment or self-consciousness. It was nothing more nor less than she'd expected, and it reinforced her affection.

'Morning.' She rolled to face him.

He moistened his lips. 'Morning.' He wriggled.

It wasn't the first time they'd woken up together, yet every facet of his behaviour reflected what they both knew—this morning was different.

'Did you sleep?'

'Yes. Did you?'

'Mmm hmm.'

In her head, she laughed because this was a cliché written large and painted in countless bright hues. Except, the situation wasn't a cookie-cutter Morning After. Nothing about their lives and love was everyday or predictable—which was utterly fine.

'Kennet?'

'Yes?'

'We need to talk.' She'd planned this in the interval between them waking, but now she'd said it, it had come out with more gravity—more cliché—than she'd wanted.

'Alright.'

She reached out, under the loose cover, found his hand and entwined their fingers. 'I'm still in love with you,' she said.

A sigh of relief, unseen, made his shoulders relax. 'I'm still in love with you too.'

'Is there a "but"?'

He frowned. 'No. Should there be?'

She pulled herself closer. 'I mean, do you want to withdraw your acceptance of my... let's call it "proposal"?'

He shifted on the pillow. 'No. Why... why would I?' His face swam with alarm. 'Do you withdraw it? Do you regret it now? After....' He swallowed. 'After what happened?'

That caused curiosity, and worry sparked in her belly. 'What did happen? Was it ... was it that... *bad*?'

His eyes widened in concern. 'Oh, heaven, no. Why would you think that? Did I...? I didn't mean....' He forced his eyes closed and open. 'I meant what we *did*, not how... it *went*.'

He let go of her hand and rolled onto his back. 'I am messing this up so badly.' He rubbed his forehead.

She shuffled closer, her heart welling, and drew his face back towards her.

'Listen. What we *did* is fine. This isn't an "Any regrets?" type of conversation. Certainly not a "Do you still respect me?" one. Two single, sober, consenting adults slept together with mutual agreement. Even better, two who love each other. Right?'

'Yes.'

'What I meant is....' She sighed and gathered a drop of courage—the one needed to voice the chief concern which had surfaced in those post-waking minutes. 'Did I spoil the illusion, or your expectation of the future, with how... I... *was*.'

That made him smile, which evaporated much of her anxiety.

He rolled onto his side. 'I knew you were apprehensive. I even knew you'd be worried here, now, in the morning.'

'Score one for empathy.'

'We have to be honest, don't we? Because we are—or I think we are—every other moment, how we live and work, as friends, partners, parents.'

'Honesty is part of what makes us tick, and why I love you.'

He brought her hand up and kissed each soft finger in turn. 'I think it was....' His gaze left her face, found a spot on the ceiling, then returned. 'Like being a teenager again. Even... like the first time.'

'In a good way?' She swallowed, on tenterhooks.

'The first time is the first time. You had a first time too. Even better that it was with a boy.'

'It was a while ago.' That was one defence. It wasn't as much of a slam-dunk excuse as her lack of practice—but both knew the situation, so it was pointless to raise it.

'As was mine.'

'Just tell me, Kennet, okay?'

He let go of her hand and stroked her cheek.

'Is it what you want, to analyse our... night? Our making love?' His expression betrayed the answer he wanted.

Except, this was important, and she couldn't rest easy until she heard at least *some* words, knowing she'd see any flannel behind them—although she expected none.

'I didn't mean "analyse". Just humour me. You know this was the kind of leap Aldrin would have been proud of.'

His smile reappeared. 'Kayte. My friend, my love. The first time is never perfect. Yes, this wasn't truly the first time, but that's how it felt. I remember unfamiliarity, the expectation, the awkwardness, yet with innocence and hope. There was a... giddiness. But I could no more score *you* out of ten than I would expect you to do to me. This is a journey, remember?'

'Which you want to continue?'

'Heavens, yes,' he said.

Then she saw the penny drop.

He smiled. 'You think you spoiled things by being... less than perfect—or what you judge perfection should be?'

He shook his head in faint amusement. Then he pulled her close, his hand warm and comforting in the small of her back.

'I will be honest and direct. And maybe a bit typical of how a man thinks. Okay?'

She felt his breath on her face. 'Okay.'

'You know I love you for many qualities anyway. For me, that was always necessary before we took... significant steps.'

'That's kind. But then, you are a gentleman.'

'Well, this *gentleman* thinks you are a beautiful, sexy woman, and I enjoyed making love with you. Does that answer your worries?'

She planted a soft kiss on his lips. 'If it's of any importance, I had a nice time too. Maybe nicer than I expected to have.'

'I think I should be flattered, no?'

'If you wish, but it comes from the heart.' She tapped her chest and watched as his gaze went there. She chuckled.

He snapped his attention to her face. 'Sorry. I can be a cliché. Especially in situations like this.'

'It's expected. And flattering, I guess.'

'But it probably doesn't come from the *heart*. You should know that about us men, we think with our....' He glanced down and winked.

'That's okay. "In situations like this".'

They exchanged a smile, and she leant into his kiss.

'So, we are agreed,' he said. 'We carry on. You stay, we grow, we learn.'

'And with this... situation, we learn through practice, huh? I'm sure I can get used to being with you. Probably get better, as well.'

'And I too.'

She kissed him, and the contentment bloomed inside. 'Do you want to start now?'

'Yes. But the children will wake up very soon.'

'Oh. Yeah.' Her libido's climb was halted.

'So, such is our life. Our fledgling but happy life.' He propped himself up on one elbow. 'There is always time later for... practice.'

She tapped his nose with one finger. 'That's a deal. But part of our fledgling but happy life is that the woman gets the first run in the shower.'

He gave an awkward shrug. 'That's fine with me.'

'Why?'

'No reason.'

But she spied a glimmer of something hiding there. 'Hmm,' she said, unsure, and climbed out of bed.

Halfway to the ensuite, she turned. He was gazing at her.

'Are you ogling my ass?'

He angled his head upwards. 'Not anymore.'

She put her forearm across her bare chest. 'You're a real mischief sometimes, Kennet Carlsson.'

'Is that one of my good "qualities"?'

She put her hands on her hips. 'Are you trying to turn this into a discussion, purely so you can get more time taking in the view?'

'You are a detective, sweet. I'm sure you can work *that* out.'

She shook her head in amused disbelief, and then locomoted to the bathroom with deliberate tease.

When he hadn't barged into the bathroom a minute later, keen for affection, she knew he'd gone to get the kids up, and that made her love him even more.

# 45

Kennet's head was filled with a gamut of emotions, feeling self-conscious, with sprinkles of guilt, yet like the cat who'd got the cream. He forced a mantra upon himself: this was a good development. It was right. It hurt nobody. It gave him and Kayte some clarity and a sense of purpose. It made the living situation less awkward. It gave them headspace to focus on other things.

He multi-tasked, making coffee and helping Charlotte with her breakfast.

Kayte entered the kitchen, fully dressed, and ran her fingers adoringly up his arm.

'Morning, Kennet.'

'Morning, Kayte.'

'Hej.' Tomas dug into his breakfast.

She ruffled his head. 'Hey, champ.'

Her gaze darted to the boy, whose back was now turned, then to Kennet, and she seized the opportunity to kiss him. It was brief yet unequivocal and also, frustratingly, had been noticed.

Tomas glanced back and forward between them. Kayte shot Kennet a nervous expression.

Tomas leant towards his father, lowering his voice, but not enough. 'Daddy? Is Auntie Kayte your girlfriend now?'

Kennet's throat emitted a short, nervous laugh.

Why deny it, he asked himself. Why try to gloss over it, like he had with Jana's death?

Kayte, because she was amazing, rescued him from inertia.

She crouched down. 'Would that be okay? Would you mind? I'd like to be daddy's girlfriend. I really, really like him a lot.'

'I don't mind,' Tomas replied cheerfully. 'Will you and Charlotte stay a longer time, then?'

'Yes, I think we will.'

'Okay.' Tomas pondered, eyeing both adults, as he finished the dregs of his breakfast.

Kennet offered Kayte a nervous smile. She winked.

'Daddy?' Tomas whispered.

Kennet perched on the adjacent breakfast bar seat. 'Yes, champ?'

'Will Kayte be my new mummy too?'

Kennet steeled himself against the tears which formed in his ducts. 'Would you like that?'

'Yes.'

He stroked the boy's head. 'Good, I'd like that too.'

'Okay!' Then he put his arms around Kayte's waist, squeezed, then hopped down and pelted out of the room.

Kennet let out a long-held breath. 'I think you pass muster... älskling.'

She frowned. 'Whatnow?'

'Älskling. It means... my beloved one.'

Her face lit with joy. She drew him close. 'Then... tack, *my* älskling.'

They kissed.

She ran a finger over his lightly stubbled chin.

'If we're going to be a couple, you have to promise to shave. I am *so* not used to scratchy skin!'

'Agreed. Why would I do anything to jeopardise the chance to kiss you?' He beamed.

'Smart work, Inspector.'

He squeezed her backside. '*Tack*, Sergeant.'

'But... and don't take this the wrong way, but this is not a public thing. Definitely not at work. I'm not embarrassed—not a bit of it. I just don't want... judgement yet.' She smiled. 'Besides, Enna will work it out soon enough.'

A thought occurred to him. 'And... would you still like me to help you find a house?'

A familiar impish smile appeared. 'Would *you* like me to live in a different house?'

'I would... like you to be close by.'

She pressed her cheek to his. 'How close?' she murmured.

'At least this close,' he whispered. 'At all times.'

'That'll be damn awkward at the polis station.'

The silence rang.

'I will tell the agent we are no longer seeking a house.'

Her lips brushed his earlobe. 'I think that's a good idea. It'll be... *cheaper*.'

He felt her snigger. 'You are incorrigible sometimes, älskling.'

'Yes. And you put up with it. Which is one of the many reasons I love you.'

He eased her away. 'Do you want to move in today? And terminate your Söderhamn lease?'

'Damn right I do.' She kissed him. 'No way back for you now, mister. You get me twenty-four seven.'

'But you also get me. We are equal, no?' He winked.

She poked him playfully in the belly. Her eyes darted. 'How about... a date night? To celebrate.'

'But we *are* dating.'

'I meant wine and dine me—candles, romance. Woo me, yeah?'

'Hmm.' He pursed his lips, considering how the evening was likely to unfold. 'It is a shame we couldn't do this when the children weren't here.'

'Are you turning me down, Kennet?'

'Never. I may outrank you, but outside the office, I am very aware of who... wears the pants.'

She tapped his nose. 'That's my guy.'

They went to the office, caught up with the team at Fleet PD HQ, then took a call from Juhani Koskinen.

Post-mortems on the remains of the cockpit crew showed the co-pilot had been injected with a paralysing agent. Doubtless, this was done by Hansen so his colleague wouldn't interfere in the plan and could be why the voice recorder had been tampered with.

There was more. The fingertip search of the scene yielded potential fragments of the trigger mechanism. The inescapable conclusion was that Hansen had remotely broken the voice recorder circuit immediately before he began the final stage of the plan.

Kennet seethed with hatred for the man.

Kayte must have seen it in his demeanour because she carefully—without overstepping protocols—gripped his shoulder, shot him an expression of support and love, and told him to focus on tracking down someone who could experience justice. Hansen had undeniably been a lynchpin, the root cause of the crash, but it was important to remember that whilst the disaster was personal to them, it was only one part of a larger puzzle.

They spent the afternoon trawling Hansen's life for anything that might have been missed. Hansen's Com records included calls to and from a burner phone—but not the same number as had interacted with Viggo Alban and Frans Olsson.

'You think there are *two* very secretive people out there?' he asked her.

'Or someone smart enough not to channel all their despicable communications through one number.'

'True enough.'

'I'll bet you one thing, Inspector.' She turned away from the glass partition so nobody could read her lips. 'Inspector *darling*. There is more than one person involved in this bullshit. Let's not get hung up on those burner phones. We need to work out all the moving parts which made this thing happen.'

Kennet pondered. 'The AirSweden resource woman was one. Anna Persson.'

'We should go see her.'

'Tom already did.'

'I know. And she lawyered up. Meaning she is guilty as hell.'

'She got Hansen to pilot that flight. Presumably so that Anders Svensson could be taken out.'

'So, she is the one with the grudge? Or the one who had the information that Svensson was on that flight?'

Kennet pulled a face. 'I'm not sure. But Sergeant Mikkelson didn't establish a link between Persson and either Olsson or Svensson.'

Kayte tapped the table. 'By phone or message, right?'

'Yes.'

'But what about in person? In public or in private? Or by another method that's off the grid?'

'That implies Anna Persson is underhanded, deliberately evasive and calculating. Tom didn't get that impression.'

'Well, I know he's the boss and all, but he's not infallible.' Kayte checked the clock. 'We'll take a fast train down and back tomorrow. Okay?'

'You're very... driven, suddenly.'

'Maybe I'm settled now. Maybe a weight is off my mind—I already wrapped up the case of the curious relationship, and I reckon the two perps are in for a *long* stretch.' She winked. 'Now I want to kick some ass.'

If the privacy partition's glass had been opaque rather than merely patterned, he would have kissed her. Instead, he checked the clock and began to count the minutes until he could.

# 46

The trip down to Stockholm was a washout. Anna Persson was doing a fine job of protecting someone. All they discovered—assuming she was being truthful—was that she didn't have any connection to Olsson or Hansen.

Over the weekend, she was being bailed and would be under house arrest, wearing a tracking tag to ensure she didn't leave the premises. Kayte ventured that Stockholm PD should station a guard at Persson's house. The case CI was unconvinced: she wasn't a career criminal, displayed no flight risk, and hadn't technically committed a crime. All she had done was roster a pilot who should have remained on standby. She'd broken AirSweden protocol, probably costing her job, but arguably she couldn't have known what would follow.

Kayte was visibly peeved, but Kennet urged calm. He suspected that her New York accent rang too much of foreign interference in a domestic case—though nothing was further from the truth—but wouldn't jeopardise their involvement by challenging a Chief Inspector in an unfamiliar PD.

Yet again, they were faced with a key cog in the wheel that refused to budge.

As they took the train home, they vowed to go over Persson's life with a fine-tooth comb—even tracing every movement captured on city-wide security cameras—in search of a chink in her armour.

After a downbeat day, "date night" was something to look forward to. He pulled out all the stops with dinner, dressed the table with candles and a rose, and picked out a rarely worn smart shirt.

There was an undeniable change in Kayte's demeanour as he watched her from across the table. A lightness, almost a girlishness. She'd dressed in a very fetching outfit with a plunging neckline and—a rarity—nail polish.

After the meal, replete with laughter and ranging conversation, the atmosphere gained a youthful nervousness.

'Where to now, Inspector, älskling?' Her eyebrows twitched.

He matched her beat. 'Dessert?'

'I think so.'

'Okay.' His mouth dried.

A silence descended, one that crackled inaudibly with expectation and yet restraint. How could there still be apprehension, with all they'd been through, mentally, emotionally, and physically?

Strangely emboldened by the knowledge that risks—of any kind—were vanishingly small, he stood, took her hand and led her to the bedroom.

Even the walk had a romance to it, a different feeling from the previous encounter's otherworldly nature. As his feet moved, they created echoes of that nervous walk, echoes which fast-forwarded through the liaison: the tentative embrace, morphing into a longing coated in reserve. The lights going off. An unspoken agreement to undress in the dark, slide under the sheets. His stomach knotted with fear of her rejecting such intimacy. The loose hug, his hands reserved for her back and sides, even as their lips met in terse waves. A sense of endeavour—that she was pushing through, heart battling head. He knew, as it unfolded, that it wouldn't be the stuff of his dreams—although it might be the gateway to them.

Then, limited foreplay done, things progressed quickly to conclusion. Pleasurable, yet tinged with her mollifying words for him not to worry and terminating in a ripple of guilt. In some sense, waking up beside her the following morning was the highlight, enjoying her beauty and the feeling that she wanted to be with him as time unfolded.

She closed the door behind them. 'That was a nice date, Kennet.'

'Possibly the oddest first date—which wasn't a first date—I ever had. And I only ever had two or three.'

She put her arms around his neck. 'Well, I wanted to do something different to before. Because that time was... odd—in a good way.'

'It was... a step, that is for sure. And would always be difficult. Despite all we have.'

'So, tonight was a chance to do things... maybe not *properly*, but better.'

'A real "dinner date".'

She nodded. 'One where you know I'm a sure thing. Which is the best kind, right?'

'Probably so.'

She unbuttoned his shirt. 'And where we don't need to be worried—because I know you were last time, like I was.'

He watched her hands. 'Only fear of failure, my lovely. Because we don't want that. At work, at home, at play.'

She winked. 'We're dealers in success.'

He kissed her, long and fulsome. Then she broke off, ran the lights down halfway—for atmosphere, he mused—then returned to him.

'Properly?' he murmured.

'Mmm-hmm.'

He slid off his shirt, then unbuttoned hers and removed it.

She must have seen his eyes widen. 'I thought I would wear... feminine, not functional, for our date.'

He admired her brazier. 'It's very nice.'

She tugged off her trousers. 'It's a matching set.'

'It's... *very* nice. Suits you. Makes you look even lovelier.'

She pushed up to him. 'Thanks.'

'Maybe I'll buy you more sometime.'

'That's a step, honey. Buying clothes for the woman in your life. Makes us a real couple, huh?'

'Would that be so bad?' he said impishly, stroking her back.

'Far from it.' She popped him a kiss. 'Shower me with lovely things. That'd be awesome.'

'You're a tease.'

'Well, in case I'm not teasing....' She put his hands on her waist. 'If you're buying—secretly—then I'm a size six here.'

He smoothed her skin. 'Okay.'

She laid his hands on her chest. 'And a 32B here.'

He ran a finger around the lace edge of the garment and gave a warm, throaty noise of satisfaction and understanding.

'Want me to shop for you?' she asked.

'Hardly the same.'

She caressed his chest. 'Size?'

'Forty-two.'

'Okay. Pants?'

He frowned, recalling. His waistline had fluctuated through the travails of the last couple of years.

She rolled her eyes. 'Men.'

'You're still a tease.'

She ignored that, unbuttoned his pants, and he stepped out of them.

She checked the label. 'And you're a thirty-four regular.'

He nudged her playfully. She discarded the garment and squashed into his embrace, a veritable marathon of unfettered longing. When they broke off, he held her, a stillness of contentment enveloping the room.

'What shop is it from? Your underwear?' he asked.

'I forget. It was in Stockholm. Last year. Not a brand I know.'

'Mmm-hmm.'

'Check the label.'

He clocked the naughty glint in her eye, then removed her bra. It had no label inside.

'Oh, yeah, I always cut them out. Can scratch like a swine.'

He ran his palm over her shoulder blades. 'Wouldn't want to scar this lovely landscape.'

'True.' Her eye line dipped. 'I don't cut that label out, though.'

'I see.'

She smiled, then looked down at his waist. 'You know where you get your underwear?'

'Suddenly, I forget. But I don't cut the labels out.'

'We should check, huh?' She pecked his cheek. 'If we're going to do this... properly.'

'For sure.'

Each removed the other's underwear. They checked the labels—although he knew her glimpse was for effect—then tossed the garments aside. He watched as she locked her gaze on his eyes, seeing that impish sparkle reflected in a blossoming smile. Then she looked him up and down, slowly and deliberately.

His heart pounded with desire. Following the previous night's cloak-and-dagger, being openly naked together for the first time was strangely without nerves or embarrassment.

He imbibed her figure.

She pulled him into an embrace.

He wished for eight arms, to be able to hold her everywhere. 'Let's have a fine time, my love.'

# 47

Kayte hung up the call. It wasn't even 10 a.m. on Monday, and the week was probably ruined already.

'We should tell Tom,' Kennet said.

'He's not awake for a while.'

'Ulrik?'

'I don't know, Kennet.' She pinched the bridge of her nose. 'It's not like anyone can help.'

Because they were at home, not in the scrutiny of colleagues, he pulled her close and kissed her neck. She inhaled his scent.

'Chin up, Sergeant. There are other leads. And maybe this is a new one. After all, it was unlikely she would have talked.'

'Yeah,' she grumped. 'If only everyone had such faith in her silence.'

Anna Persson wouldn't give up whoever had hired her—that was certain now. She'd taken in a groceries delivery on Saturday, and something had been poisoned. She was found dead by a neighbour on Sunday evening.

'Come on. See the positive side.'

'The positive in an innocent—well, fairly innocent—young woman being professionally killed?'

'Yes. It means our mystery perpetrator is getting nervous. They know we're onto them.'

'Except we're not. We're at a ton of dead ends.'

'Hmm.' He sipped his coffee. 'Alright, if you want good news, there are no reports of any more actions against the Spaceport committee.'

'There are protests at all four sites,' she pointed out.

'That was always going to happen. They may be OnePlanet, or they may be locals up in arms. So long as they are not killing people, yes?'

'I guess.'

'I'll tell you something positive. Somebody used poison to kill Viggo after supplying it to him so he could kill Eva. Now there is poison used on Swedish soil. It's another link.'

'True.' She toyed with her cup. 'I'll tell you what else. If there's a chance that Wilmer and Matteo Svensson are in the firing line, poison is a likely method. We should warn them.'

'That is a hard thing to guard against. If it is a contact poison, then using gloves to remove the packaging is fine. But how do you avoid ingesting poison in food or drink?'

She shrugged. 'You cook everything from scratch.'

'That is not one hundred percent foolproof.'

'Throw me a bone, Kennet,' she sniped. Then she softened her temper and rubbed his shoulder. 'Sorry. Älskling. You're right. But we should warn them anyway. I don't want us to get caught with our pants down or sued because we were party to information and didn't pass it on.'

A smile played on his lips. 'I am quite prepared for you to get caught with your pants down. At home, anyway.'

She patted his thigh. 'Easy, tiger. The sun will go down soon enough.'

They decided that Kennet should stay home with Tomas and Charlotte while Kayte took a trip down to see Matteo Svensson. She took Sergeant Mikkelson, partly to discuss the casework handover; Mikkelson was leaving Bollnäs on Friday. Kennet would endeavour to speak to Wilmer, perhaps even set up a meeting if the billionaire was feeling amenable.

Matteo had only reluctantly agreed to the meeting, and when they arrived—Kayte was encountering him for the first time—she had half a mind to turn around and head home without delivering the warning. The man was terse, guarded, and scrutinised their ID with undue diligence.

Mikkelson surveyed the entrance hall. 'I see you've had new security put in.'

'I told you—I'm taking precautions.'

'The bodyguard?'

Matteo's eyes flared. 'Running an errand. What's this about?'

Clearly, Kayte needed to tread carefully. She tugged down her uniform jacket. 'Somebody—a suspect—who is potentially connected with the plane crash which killed your brother has... become a victim themselves. I'm not at liberty to divulge details yet, but the case shows a worrying parallel with the death of your sister Eva.'

'Which I'll remind you remains unsolved.' He sneered, looking her up and down. 'Your countrymen, Sergeant Connors, are asleep at the wheel.'

She left that alone. 'I think that's because we're dealing with somebody very skilled in avoiding evasion. The point is, Mr Svensson, it's our duty to warn you that an assassination attempt is a real possibility.'

'Wow,' he mocked. 'Great police work.'

Mikkelson put a restraining hand on Kayte's arm—the woman had sensed that her colleague was getting riled. Good call, Kayte mused, knowing she was the ballsier of the two, lacking Mikkelson's more conciliatory demeanour. Besides, Kayte was more invested in this whole mess.

'You might just want to take extra precautions, Mr Svensson,' Mikkelson said. 'Make sure none of your food and non-food deliveries have been... tampered with.'

Matteo twitched, then frowned. 'You mean there's a *poisoner* running around?'

'Not "running around". But I think you and the polis are of the same mind—that there is a potential vendetta against your family. We don't anticipate anyone going to such extreme lengths as a plane crash—'

'You're *absolutely certain* that appalling disaster was a deliberate act to kill one passenger?'

Kayte took a step forward, keen to field this. 'Suddenly, you *don't* want explanations, or crimes solved?'

Mikkelson coughed. 'I think Sergeant Connors means that, regardless of the proof of the matter, the potential reasons for engineering your brother's death, or even the identity of the person behind it, we are investigating three linked cases where murder was achieved through poisoning. It's our *duty* to warn you about that.'

Kayte wanted to say that she didn't care if the objectionable asshole dropped dead in the next five seconds. Yet, everyone has a family, and Matteo's death *would* be felt—and she knew that dealing with the loss of a loved one was a godawful way to pass the time.

The guy took a deep breath, probably calming his frustrations. 'Okay. I consider myself warned.'

'You've not noticed anything suspicious? Crank calls? Threats? You've no family—that's correct?'

He flashed a patronising smile. 'No, Miss Right hasn't found me yet.'

'Then, is it fair to say that, as your mother passed some years ago, you and your father may be the only targets?'

His brow knit. 'I don't know—you tell me.'

Kayte glanced at her colleague.

'Why?' Mikkelson asked. 'Could there be... additional persons under threat?'

'You're the detectives.'

'Is there something we should know?' Kayte trod carefully, feeling thin ice underfoot.

'If I knew, it would be my civilian duty to tell you, I suppose?'

Kayte clenched her teeth, fed up with playing cat-and-mouse with this obstructive or evasive idiot they were trying to protect.

'Yes, it would,' she said calmly. 'But only if you also felt a *civil* duty to consider the welfare of anyone you may be related to. Anyone who might be considered a target for whatever godawful scheme someone has in mind.'

Matteo locked his gaze on her. 'I have my suspicions. That's all I'd say. If I knew for certain there were... others... then you'd have their names and addresses in a heartbeat.'

'Suspicions of what?' Mikkelson asked.

Matteo's lip curled in apparent distaste at what he was revealing. 'You should ask Wilmer about his affair. Once upon a time, I thought that... *I*... was a dirty little secret.' He scoffed. 'I may as well be, for the way he treats me. But is there another dirty little secret?'

'An undeclared child?' Kayte asked.

'Wilmer keeps very quiet about the whole thing. No names, no nothing. I tell you, Sergeants—I'd be as interested as you to know the answer to that situation. It cost our family enough heartbreak.' His jaw hardened. 'Maybe it's still doing harm today.'

# 48

Kennet didn't know whether Matteo's revelation was good news or bad news for the case.

If there was a fourth heir to Wilmer Svensson's estate—an individual out of the public eye, unknown to his or her siblings, and not openly acknowledged by their father—would those be reasons enough to exact revenge, perhaps try to destroy the family?

He and Kayte went back and forth over the matter without a conclusion either way. Unfortunately, the only way of being sure was to track down the person. This was difficult for three reasons: it was unlikely that Wilmer would give them chapter and verse, it could be merely rumour and supposition—meaning they'd be seeking someone who didn't exist, and even if they did exist, how to identify a person born over thirty years ago?

Wilmer—to maintain his social standing—would hardly have left his name in the birth records. If the mother's name wasn't forthcoming, they'd have to follow up on every birth within the three-year span of the affair, and if Wilmer had bribed the relevant officials, the offspring's name might have been expunged from the register.

They'd either have to get very lucky, win over the billionaire, or hunker down for a long trudge.

Still, as he looked across the dining table that Wednesday evening, at least he had company with which to do it.

'How long 'til you stop with the adoring gazes?' she asked.

'When I pinch myself and discover this is a dream—a dream on the heels of a nightmare. Or when I get my eyes tested and realise you aren't truly that pretty after all.'

She gently kicked him under the table. 'Love has certainly loosened you up, that's for sure.'

'Yes. But it does cause a problem. We will need to tell the Chief Inspector that we are... involved.'

Her head dipped. 'Yeah. All relationships are to be declared. But I can still transfer on Monday?'

'Yes. But I think our days of partnering on the streets are over.'

She sighed. 'That sucks. We're good together.'

'Yes. But if we had to choose, living, dining and... *sleeping* together make it worth it.'

'Absolutely.' She shook it off. 'Let's see what Janssen says. But we have to balance the childcare stuff anyway. We can work cases and split up the desk work. Hell, if we're still affiliated with Fleet PD, maybe Tom will take a different view. For those cases, maybe we can do legwork together.'

Reflexively, he'd fallen introspective—and she saw it.

'Shit—don't tell me.' She took his hand. 'You're going to come over all protective and say you don't want me in the line of fire.'

That was the nub of his concern. 'I don't mean to—'

'Am I allowed to be worried too? We both just lost someone. We also had close shaves in the past. You're no less at risk than I am. Don't tell me you suddenly want to wrap me in cotton wool? I'm not the stay-indoors, little lady type, right?'

'I know you aren't.' He smiled ruefully. 'Maybe I'm thinking that if I lost you, I would fear for myself because I didn't have you to help me get over it.'

She rose, then drew him out of his seat and into an embrace. 'We have to believe our bad luck is over. We've had more than a lifetime's worth.'

'I cannot stop you from doing what you love. To suggest that you come to this country, in the hope it would make you safer and happier, and then put qualifiers on that? It would not be fair.'

'No, it wouldn't. And be sure of this, Kennet—I love and worry about you equally as much.' She kissed him. 'Now, we're getting off-topic. One—we need to figure out what to do about the mystery heir. Two—we need to tell Janssen we're dating.'

She bit her lip, sighing. 'And we need to get through the next couple of days. The funerals will be damn hard.'

His spirits dived. 'That is true. And I think it is worse.'

'For why?'

'Because I don't think we can be openly together. If there is one time it might invite comment, it is when we are burying our loved ones. People will think it is inappropriate.'

'Yeah,' she said sadly. 'Ordinarily, I'd tell them to go fish, but you're right. It's impolite to be brazen about what we are. They can know in time.' She stroked his cheek. 'Their problem is not knowing this: you and I are three years in the making—not six weeks. We haven't suddenly jumped into bed to consummate some long-forbidden love. There's no scandal. All the same, part of me can't wait to get this over with. Not for forgetting what we lost, but feeling we're free to move on.'

'It's... another step on our journey.'

'Good. Look, this Svensson thing is a real minefield. This whole mess is like wading through treacle. Sometimes I wish it *had* been an accident—technical malfunction, whatever—then we could box up the episode, the pain, and not have it needling our lives at work too. But we didn't get that break. So, for the sake of trying like hell to move on with our lives—and I'm not making any judgements about what that looks like—I'd like to get mine and Carey's place in DC sorted out. No point in waiting. It's an albatross which'll only make me sad.'

'Agreed.'

'Here's the idea. We take next week as leave. Go to DC. I'll meet with Carey's folks, take the ashes. We'll get the wheels in motion to sell the apartment. I'll show you around. We can discuss the case with Tom. Enna, too—if she's around, and assuming she won't keep her nose out. Kids can spend a couple of days with Lexie?' She rested her cheek beside his ear. 'Plus, Carey's folks have a cabin up in Tuscarora. Remote. *Private.*'

Kennet didn't have a clue where that place was, but the idea was fine enough. His pulse quickened.

'Do I accurately follow the clues you are laying, *Sergeant*?' He squeezed her ass.

'I'm sure. But we can't offload the kids, go away for a recreational weekend to a cabin for two, with no pretence of it being work-related, and sell Tom and Enna a pup. We'll have to come clean. I think that's the only downside.'

He pulled her close. 'I can cope with that.'

# 49

The memorials on Saturday were tough, but Kayte was sure it was marginally easier for her.

Kennet's was very real, local and personal, with colleagues and family in attendance. She focussed on helping Tomas to cope.

Carey's ceremony was briefer—as this wasn't her native land. Janssen attended, as did a few of Carey's colleagues from the Uppsala orchestra and a couple of cops from Söderhamn. The wake in the US would be a harder grind.

On Sunday, they travelled to DC and stayed in a hotel. On Monday, they explored a few sights for Tomas' benefit. On Tuesday, Kennet stayed in the hotel with Tomas and Charlotte while Kayte met Carey's folks.

It was the first time she'd seen Mr & Mrs Maddison since the crash—in fact, the first time since she and Carey had left for Sweden the year before—so it was an emotional experience.

The Maddisons had planned a small wake, which took place on Thursday. She really wanted Kennet there for support, but the children had seen enough grief lately, so he kindly took them sightseeing.

So far, the getaway hadn't been much fun, but she'd succeeded in setting the wheels in motion for the sale of her apartment. Things picked up on Friday when they took their hired AutoDrive out to Fort Valley to meet Tom and Enna.

After the initial pleasantries, tempered by the awkwardness running through Kayte's bones about the need to reveal her new relationship—especially so soon after Carey's memorial—she noticed a familiar air of unsettlement in Enna. Tom too wasn't quite himself.

Were they reacting to any signs that she and Kennet were giving off?

They sat on the rear terrace, warm sun on their faces.

'Something's up, isn't it?' Kayte asked.

'Nothing that anyone can do anything about,' Tom replied.

'Not yet,' Enna murmured.

'Is it about the case—or labyrinth of our current matters?' Kennet asked.

'The Fleet brass?' Kayte remembered the incident with Fleet's Head of Infrastructure.

Tom shook his head. 'No. We tracked down the guy. No connection to Sweden. Just a very... active activist. He'll stand trial. Nothing else has happened locally that could be connected to Eva, Anders or the plane crash. Be good if it had, though, huh? Any more routes into the source would be good.'

'That's not what's bothering you,' she said. 'I've seen that look in Enna's eyes before, and when it happens, people tend to get their ass kicked.'

Enna's smile was clearly over-sweet. 'Well, that won't happen here because I'm an innocent Navigator, and I'm butting out of things that don't concern me.'

Kayte glanced back and forth between Enna and Tom, desperate that a domestic squabble didn't break out.

'The problem with that statement,' Tom said, 'As our esteemed colleagues know, it's damn hard to resist any wishes that innocent Navigators do have, especially when they are married to Chiefs who know which side their bread is buttered, and who are aware of the track record of their spouses when it comes to dishing out justice.'

Kayte laid a palm on the table. 'Enna. Tom. Due respect, tell us what the hell is going on.'

'It's no big deal—really. Especially given what else has happened in the last seven weeks. Olsson's upset the apple cart. He's not blown the ruse, but things... took a turn.'

Enna set down her coffee mug a little too hard. 'What happened is he got antsy because he noticed Gina taking too much interest in him.' She closed her eyes. 'Meaning, my mentoring has a way to go.'

'Gina Devine?' Kayte asked.

'Yeah. Again, not Fleet PD either, but volunteered to watch Olsson until they were back on Earth and in the hands of someone other than crew who aren't fully trained or equipped to deal with wanted felons.'

'So, what happened?' Kennet asked.

'The short version is that she kept her mouth shut, but because of her...' Enna rolled her eyes, 'looks, Olsson kinda made a pass at her. She declined. He hit her. She fell. Broke her arm.' Enna balled a fist. 'And I know it's not a good look for me to be mothering a woman only ten years younger, but goddamn if I hate assholes messing with people I've taken a liking to.'

She took a couple of deep breaths. 'First, the guy helps Hansen crash your plane. Then he assaults one of my colleagues—someone who's stood up for me. And herself found a coworker dead in a bathroom stall.'

She looked at Tom. 'So I have a moderate beef with the guy, and I'm counting the days until I can have thirty seconds to give him a piece of my mind.' She fiddled with her mug's handle. 'Probably stop short of kicking him in the balls or shooting him in the back of the head, though.' She beamed. 'Because I'm trying to be a nicer person nowadays.'

Tom roared with laughter. 'See—Kayte, Kennet—just because you live all the way over there now, and my wife is back in a shuttle cockpit for a living, doesn't mean she's not still the mouse that roars.'

'Not sure she was ever much of a mouse, Tom,' Kayte said.

'Lioness?' Kennet suggested.

She patted his shoulder. 'Not sure the analogy works, then, hon— Kennet.' She grimaced, pissed off at her misstep.

Enna eyed her, then Kennet. He darted an awkward smile at them both.

Enna tapped the table decisively. 'Connors—come see what we've done in Lexie's room.'

Kayte frowned, her tummy skipping with worry, sure that the cat was out of the bag. Still, she followed Enna upstairs to the child's room.

By the time they'd got there, she'd decided. She gently closed the door behind them.

'What do you think?' Enna spread her arms wide.

'Good diversion, honey.'

Enna's query was transparently false. 'Huh?'

Kayte took her friend's hand and looked at her without disguise.

'Enna, I'm telling you this because I value our friendship, and I don't want any whispering going on. Kennet and I are dating. It's serious. Very serious. If you have any objections or concerns, I don't want to hear them.' Her steely gaze was tempered by affection.

Enna pulled her into a hug. 'Good for you, honey. I'm not going to tell you how to live your life. Other than one thing. Be happy. Oh, and stay out of trouble—both of you.'

# 50

The two days at the cabin were a much-needed tonic at the end of a difficult week.

Enna and Tom looked after Tomas and Charlotte, while Kennet and Kayte indulged in what was unashamedly a romantic getaway.

They were back in Bollnäs by late Sunday, and Kayte pressed her uniform, ready for the first official day at the new PD.

Kennet really did sense a new life was starting—yet the spectre of unsolved cases weighed on their minds. The motives and personnel behind what was undeniably the murder of their loved ones.

Despite Mikkelson's departure, Janssen being busy, the crash investigation team no longer interested in ongoing criminal matters, Enna on Moon shuttle shifts, and Tom, Han and Ellie mostly tied up on other domestic cases, Kennet wasn't bowed by the task ahead. They had two weeks until Olsson—their best hope yet—landed at Washington Spaceport, and he and Kayte were determined to make concrete progress on other matters.

Their plan was to mix working at home and the office, get Tomas' usual childminder to watch him and Charlotte every other day, and conduct interviews together where possible.

They'd decided to delay telling Janssen about their relationship—which wasn't ideal, but they didn't want anything standing in the way of solving the cases.

When the children resumed school, Kayte was no longer registered as living in Söderhamn, and they were in the office daily, that was the moment to be forthcoming. Besides—it would mean more time had passed since the funerals, and people might not be so judgemental.

In the master bedroom, he noted the small display on the shelf. They had each put a small, framed picture of their lost loves, and in front of each were the respective wedding rings which had been recovered from the crash site.

They had vowed Jana and Carey wouldn't be forgotten or used as comparators, but he and Kayte were allowed to reminisce fondly. It was an anchor in turbulent times and a reminder of why they were pushing on with the police work. Justice, not tears, would make the difference to their heads and hearts.

She emerged from the ensuite, noted his introspection, sidled over and laid her head on his shoulder.

'New chapter tomorrow, älskling. I hope I don't drive you around the bend, being PD partners as well as a roomie.'

He kissed her hair. 'We are not truly ourselves right now. I hope our togetherness is not a product of that. I hope what we have is not based on comfort in grief, unusual proximity, anger and desperation.'

She eased into his arms. 'It would be very wrong and disrespectful to say that much of my love for you is many, many months old.' She stroked his chin. 'So I won't say that.'

'And I will *not* say that your actions in Paris were very much misplaced because of the effect they had.'

She smiled. 'Good. Some things have changed, but some haven't. It's not love that's going to put this all to bed. It's like before—one small-town Swedish cop and one big-city American gal against a conspiracy of malevolents.'

He slid his palms inside the back of her night shorts. 'Tomorrow—yes. Now, something else needs to be put to bed—Sergeant Kayte Connors.' He slid off her underwear. 'And no uniform, of any kind, is allowed.'

Over breakfast, they divided up the tasks. Chief amongst these was to discover whether there was a fourth Svensson child. They also wanted to find out why the proposed site on Wilmer's land was "the best option". This necessitated speaking to the Siting Committee head, Sara Lindström.

He'd try to secure a meeting with Wilmer Svensson while she assembled ideas on how to track down the mystery child—now an adult of around thirty-five—if Wilmer didn't spill his guts.

After Kayte left for the office and he dropped the children at the minders, he took a preparatory hour to conceive a plausible reason for Wilmer Svensson to agree to a meeting. Arguably, Tom had failed because he was an American or because his attempts came too soon after the deaths of Eva and Anders. Equally, it could be because Wilmer was a guarded character who was already too much in the public eye for his liking.

It had been impossible for the death of Anders not to make the news—once some unidentified source had clarified that an alias had been named amongst the victims. On top of Eva's murder, the press was starting to voice wild theories: how could two disconnected incidents take connected lives in such a short time?

Kennet was on their side—for once, the hyperbole was unlikely to be misplaced. Someone had it in for the Svensson family. In a stroke of genius, he decided to use a huge bluff as the basis of his request for "five minutes" of the man's precious time.

The billionaire's estate covered tens of square miles of Swedish grassland and plain near Knutby. The main house was located up a long drive, guarded by a manned security hut.

Kennet had seen images of the place but was still slightly awed by its grandeur. Eighteen windows looked out from the castle-like structure, built in pale brick, with towers at either end.

He suppressed an uncharacteristic flutter of nerves.

A valet, manservant, whatever—Kennet didn't care—let him in and showed him to a grand but soulless lounge.

After five minutes, Wilmer Svensson appeared. He was in good shape for a man of seventy-two, with blonde hair paled by age, strong cheekbones and jaw, and still wore his wedding band. He sported a polka-dotted collar shirt, sleeves folded towards the elbows.

He didn't offer his hand. 'So? You have a lead on who is behind the deaths of my children?'

Kennet felt like this interview was going to be trickier than his charge along the roof of a speeding train—and this time, Kayte wasn't there to cover his back.

'Your other daughter,' he said with baseless confidence. It was a fifty-fifty gamble.

Wilmer's eyes flared. 'I don't *have* another daughter. Eva was my only. And—'

'*Declared* daughter, Mr Svensson. Not the one you don't like to talk about. From the period when you... strayed from your marriage.'

'I may have to ask you to leave, Inspector Carlsson. I get enough gossip from the press. Now from the polis? It's unbelievable.'

'I will remind you, sir, that I am here on matters of a polis investigation—specifically concerning the murder of two of your children. I do not expect gratitude for my work—cooperation, at the very least. But obstruction is an offence.'

Wilmer's gaze lasered on Kennet's face. The latter put his shoulders back and chest out.

The man raised an index finger. 'I do not have an undeclared—illegitimate daughter. And to suggest that is—'

'A son, then?'

Wilmer tried to disguise his alarm and his half-step backwards, but Kennet caught both gestures—and their meaning.

Kennet held up a pre-emptive calming hand. 'Mr Svensson, I lost someone on that plane too. I won't claim we are kindred spirits, but you should know that nothing will stop my colleagues and I getting to the bottom of things. I have no plans to make enemies of law-abiding citizens, especially,' he gestured around, 'well-appointed ones.'

He stepped closer. 'I don't want to make your life uncomfortable. Quite the opposite. And be assured that not a word of this will go beyond secure case files.'

The man thought for a moment. 'I know. And your candour is appreciated. The bluff tactic, less so.' His brow arched.

Kennet's stomach squirmed. 'Sir—'

'Are you good at your job, Inspector Carlsson?'

'Of course.'

'Will you stake your career on your promise to be discreet with anything you uncover?'

'Absolutely.'

'Then I think you have a place to start.'

'With respect, it would be helpful—'

Svensson held up his hands. 'If you can discover what the press and gossip websites have failed to turn over in the last thirty-some years, and nullify a threat against my remaining family and me—if it exists—then I'll gladly call up your Commander and lobby for your promotion. Now, please let Lucas see you out.'

# 51

D on't do yourself down,' Kayte said. 'You may have broken this case. Hell, you basically got him to admit to a secret child. Feels like people have been trying to do that for years.' She pulled him close under the covers.

He sighed. 'I suppose so. At least I didn't annoy him too much.'

'You think he'd speak to us again?'

'Not about this. About the whole thing? Perhaps.'

She stroked his short sideburn. 'Look on the plus side—we've halved the list of possible offspring.'

He forced a smile. 'Yes. Now we only have the problem that it's a *male* with an unidentified mother, born on an unknown date in an unknown hospital. Probably with a false surname, a father who is falsified or unlisted, and living anywhere in the country—possibly the world.' He grimaced. 'Or on another colony if Wilmer insisted the child was banished.'

'It's a needle in a haystack—I get it.'

'And they may already be dead. Or not responsible anyway, even if we do find them.'

Her eyes twinkled. 'Sometimes, you're a real ray of sunshine in a gal's life, you know?'

'Whatever the case, you are a ray of sunshine in mine. No—the whole Sun.'

'Comments like that *will* get you access to this out-of-uniform colleague.'

He stroked her shoulder. 'Honestly, sweet, what I crave right now is your mind, not your body.'

She looked at him askance. 'Bed is for bedtime. Sleeping or... *not* sleeping. Not for casework. In the morning, okay? Nobody's going anywhere overnight.'

He inspected the ceiling. 'Do you think... ground engineer Olsson could be the mystery son? It would answer many questions.'

'Honestly, Kennet? Clock off, partner. Here,' she took his hand and slid it up inside her camisole. 'Remind me how good you are at frisking.'

He spent the day at Bollnäs PD—Kayte was home with the children—interrogating the list of births she had prepared. Firstly, he removed all females, then cross-referenced the remainder with any who'd died in the last 30 years: he didn't care *whether* Wilmer had had a son, only whether the son was still alive and able to orchestrate mass murder.

There were over 170,000 names.

He moved aside his coffee mug and laid his forehead on the table. This was so daunting as to be disheartening.

Where to start? Small, by assuming the person was born locally to Uppsala, or the father was undeclared, or the baby had been put up for adoption? Or whittle down the list, removing categories of people it *couldn't* be?

How he craved input from Han, Ellie or, ideally, Kayte.

The first concrete step was to check that Frans Olsson couldn't be the fourth heir. Kennet discovered he wasn't—which was a shame, although it would have been too neat anyway.

Next, he confirmed it wasn't Viggo Alban. Then he checked if anyone on the fated plane was of the right age and whose history was murky. As they'd already scrutinised this list, it was a cursory but necessary step, and predictably he came up empty.

Then he took lunch and called Kayte. She had secured a meeting with Sara Lindström, the Committee head, for the following day.

He spent the afternoon considering ways to get inside information about the woman Wilmer had an affair with—perhaps that would be easier than tracking a mystery child.

PD hadn't secured access to Wilmer Svensson's financial or Com records, leaving no way to check his history—which would be hard enough anyway, given the timeline. His wife was dead, and two other children who could have shed light on the affair were also now gone. Matteo wasn't alive at the time, so would have no first-hand evidence. Besides, he'd had plenty of opportunity to provide anything he did know.

What was needed was to locate someone who was in Wilmer's inner circle thirty years ago and might have been party to a word slipping out in conversation. His accountant, perhaps? A housekeeper? Security guard?

Kennet began to research and draw up a list of potential avenues. As a backup, he spoke to Tom, asking if Han had the time and headspace to find innovative ways to whittle down the list. Tom said they'd brainstorm it as soon as possible but concurred that Kennet's "close acquaintance" method was the best bet.

This time, rather than leave the "talking shop" until they were horizontal, he discussed things with Kayte over dinner.

They came up with a few new ideas, chiefly to talk—in confidence—to people Wilmer currently associated with, to see if they could offer insight into what the man's business and social circles were like three decades before. It required treading wisely so as not to alert the man that they were poking around his life. Certainly, the idea of a secret child must not even be mentioned. Kennet would have to spin a yarn, citing a fictitious investigation into people who may have held a grudge against the man for long-ago deeds or squabbles.

Kayte suggested it was unlikely that anyone would believe the yarn—who would keep a grudge for thirty years? He pointed out how scarcely believable this whole matter was—that anyone would down a plane to kill one person. Yet here they were.

Unless, of course, they'd been barking up the wrong tree all along?

# 52

Kayte was primed to head down to Gävle to meet Sara Lindström when her polis Com bleeped.

She took the call, her spirits sank, then she noted down the details and hung up.

'What is it, sweet?' Kennet looked up from his terminal, calling to her through the study doorway.

She entered the room.

'That was Västerås PD. A body's been found. It's a guy called Bob Gerhardt.' She rested a hand on his shoulder. 'He was on the environmental site survey team.'

'For the Spaceport?'

'Yeah. He helped put together all the reports.'

'I imagine from your expression that it wasn't an accident.'

'He was shot,' she said.

He played with her fingers. 'So this is it for certain now. Someone, or some group, is interfering with the mechanics of the Spaceport bids.'

'The thing Tom looked at? Probably isolated, but who knows? Definitely, there's a joined-up campaign over here.'

'You think the same person who killed Anna Persson?'

'Doubt it. That was an indirect link—more related to the plane. I think this latest murder belongs with Lindström's car being vandalised, Lena Ekström's dog being killed.' She shrugged. 'Maybe they're turning up the heat.'

'So what did Gerhardt do to deserve a bullet?'

She ruffled his hair. 'Not a clue, honey. But I bet Sara Lindström does—so there's luck, huh?' She pecked him on the cheek. 'I'll call you when I'm on the way back.'

He quickly stood, pulling her close. 'Take care. Lindström could be misdirecting us with that vandalism. It is hard to argue that she is in a prime position to make things happen the way she wants.'

'The Committee head is steering the decision?' She pulled a face. 'Doubt it.'

'I think, given what has gone before, nothing is certain. History is replete with inside jobs and payoffs from lobbyists. I mean... keep an open mind. Take her words at face value. If she doesn't already know Gerhardt is dead, perhaps tell her and see if she looks guilty?'

'She'd have someone connected with the team *shot*?'

'Or another party did—to scare her.'

'Okay. I hear you. I'll fact-find, no agenda.'

He kissed her. 'Good luck, partner. Best progresser today chooses dinner.'

'Then I'll start considering my choice.' She winked, then left.

Kayte took the car down to Gävle and met Sara Lindström at her house.

The forty-year-old was tall, athletic and personable. If she held any secrets, they were well-disguised. She was unmarried, financially comfortable and spent the first few minutes of the interview asking Kayte about her US origins.

Kayte steered away from the plane crash, not wanting to get tied up in emotion or give the impression that she had a hidden agenda.

She segued into questions about the Spaceport, the key drivers and objections, then asked about key personnel on the Siting team.

'Have the recent events and criminal incidents got people worried for their safety?'

'You mean my car, Lena's dog?' Sara shook her head. 'We went into this with our eyes open.'

'Do you get any sense that... people might be bowing to these kinds of pressures?'

Sara frowned. 'Being influenced. I don't think so.' She sipped her coffee. 'Not on the core team, anyway.'

Kayte heard something unsaid. '*Outside* the core team?'

The woman contemplated. 'These kinds of public enquiries don't always go smoothly, you know that, Sergeant?'

'Ma'am, my whole career is based on investigating things going wrong—accidentally or deliberately.'

'We found out that one of the environmental scientists was falsifying results. We had to fire him.'

Kayte got a bad feeling. 'How did he take it?'

'He screamed blue murder. He denied it.'

'What was his name?'

'Bob Gerhardt. He was one of yours—American, I mean. Very experienced.'

'When was he fired?'

'Two days ago, on Monday. Why do you ask?'

Kayte sighed. 'Ms Lindström, this is confidential, but... he may be in trouble.'

'In trouble, how?'

She swerved the question. 'In what way was he falsifying results?'

'He manipulated the soil composition tests at two of the sites.'

'Why?'

Sara threw up her hands. 'I have no idea.'

'What impact would the false tests have on the decision?'

'They would make two of the sites appear more problematic and less desirable.'

Kayte sipped her coffee pensively. This was a key development. There was no point in telling Lindström that Bob Gerhardt was dead. The takeaway was that claws were being sunk deeper into the Spaceport machine: there was definitely motivation to sway the result of the siting decision.

Still, this was nothing new—plenty of corporate backhanders had been uncovered during the siting of the Washington Spaceport. Livelihoods, profits and much more were always at stake. Vested interests and vehement opposition were always at war.

'The decision process is confidential, of course.'

'Unless we are compelled to reveal facts in support of a criminal investigation,' Lindström said.

'Hypothetically, if the results hadn't been falsified, would either of those sites be the preferred location?'

The woman wrestled with that. 'There are so many factors—hence the enquiry.'

'Can you say which way the Committee is leaning?'

'Do you mean gut feel or evidence-based?'

Kayte shrugged. 'Gut feel. Which would be ideal?'

Lindström, oddly, laughed. 'Well, the Knutby site has only one key objection. Unfortunately, it's the landowner.'

'Wilmer Svensson,' she inferred.

'Exactly. And not a man to trifle with. But from a lot of ways, that land is best.'

'Was that one of the sites Gerhardt tampered with?'

'No,' Lindström replied.

'What about the surveys on the Svensson land?'

'We can only do non-invasive surveys. Digital imaging. Work on and around the estate fence line. But it's all moot. If you ask me, we should never have put the site on the shortlist.'

'Why was it added?' Kayte asked.

'I got a tip-off that it was a good location. One or two others on the Committee did too. Then, when we examined it, we thought if Mr Svensson had a change of heart, there would be a lot fewer hoops to jump through than on the other sites.' She gave a sober chuckle. 'But the problem with dealing with a reclusive billionaire is that he's hard to get hold of and probably thinks he's rich enough not to need the settlement fee.'

'Which is worth billions in itself.'

'Exactly. And if we'd known his OnePlanet affiliation meant he'd be even less likely to sell up, I wouldn't have added the site to the shortlist. Now it sits there, mocking us.'

'And I suppose he's too busy grieving for his lost children to entertain discussions and compromises.'

Lindström nodded. 'It's becoming more trouble than it's worth. It does make me wonder why Bob Gerhardt would do anything to stymie other sites too.'

'Did he do it of his own accord?'

'He didn't say. I was merely interested that he did it. I suggest you question him, Sergeant Connors. It may not be criminal, what he did, but it's no less curious than other things that have gone on. You and your colleagues might find out the wool is being pulled over our eyes in ways we don't even know about. Our decision is supposed to be evidence-based and impartial. There are clearly people who reject that approach.'

Kayte merely nodded. She wasn't going to say that those rejections had a steadily increasing body count.

# 53

'How's Gina?' Tom asked.

Enna frowned. 'Okay, what gives?'

'She's your friend. She was hurt after volunteering to guard my suspect—something beyond the line of duty. So, I care, okay? I'm grateful.' He cocked his head. 'What—I'm not allowed to butt into *your* world, despite you butting into mine at every opportunity?'

She set down her cutlery. 'It's a damn good job I love you to the Moon and back, and I know you're yanking my chain.'

He took a breath. 'How's Gina?'

Enna narrowed her eyes but didn't rise to it. 'She's fine. Keen to get home, proper medical attention.'

'Good.'

'I'm sure she'd also appreciate knowing why her friend Eva was killed.'

'Wouldn't we all.'

'It's over *two months*, Tom. I can't believe Wilmer Svensson's not on the phone every day, wondering what the hell's going on.'

'Is that code for *you* are wondering what's the hell's going on? Or gently suggesting, in your adorable M.O., that Fleet PD would have cracked this case if you were on the team?'

She clasped his hand. 'You know I find it hard to stay away. I enjoyed my time on the team—'

'You nearly died too many times, honey.'

She shrugged with cheeky off-handedness. 'I fly into space every week. I know from danger. And I did plenty well enough cheating death before you rocked up on the scene, Tom Wagner. Remember Iversen?'

'I think you'll find that my rocking up at one particular scene—a crashed Porsche maybe?—at the right time was instrumental in your being alive long enough to cheat death a few more times.'

She had a flashback to lying on a snowy bank, having received the kiss of life. She shuddered.

'Bad memory?' he asked.

'And good, too. If you hadn't arrived, we wouldn't be sitting here having these... disagreements.'

'I wouldn't change it for the world.'

'But you still want me to butt out?'

'I want you safe, above all. And, yeah, that's over-protective, and no, I can't look after you while you're jetting round the stars, but I also know that beautiful mouth can get you into trouble.'

She beamed. 'Yeah—one minute you're pressing your lips to it, the next minute I'm a mom.'

'What can I say? You're irresistible.'

'Well, at least your detective skills aren't *totally* shot.'

He stood, drew her up from the dining chair, and pulled her close. 'You're a piece of work, Enna Marie Dacourt.'

'I am. And you do damn well putting up with it.' She stroked his cheek. 'I wasn't insinuating—'

He put a finger to her lips. 'We all want the two Svensson cases solved. Believe me, we've covered so many bases, hit a ton of dead ends. Kennet could be onto a winner, though, if there's a fourth heir. It would explain a lot.'

She led him to the sofa. 'You know I get a lot of time kicking my heels. It's not all glamour, what I do.'

'It's tough work. Point?'

'My mind wanders. A lot of the time to you, to Lexie. Lately, to Kayte and Kennet. Especially since they... hooked up.'

'Sweet, huh?'

She waved it away. 'Their lives. But yeah, they're good for each other. So long as it's not a rebound, fuelled-by-high-emotion thing. Anyway. My point.' She put on a serious expression. 'I wondered who knew Anders was on that plane? Sure, people from AirSweden. Maybe his father and brother—if they cared and if he'd told them. Clearly, the engineer and pilot.'

'The bodyguard.' Tom's eyes widened. 'Maybe he was the leak?'

'Not deliberately—because he died too. He could have told whoever happened to be targeting Anders.'

'But why Anders? We still don't know that. There's no evidence of ill-will anywhere we looked.'

'The people he was meeting in Narvik knew. Hell—they arranged it. Maybe it was a honey trap to get him on the plane. They'll have known, like everyone, that the guy was precautious and paranoid. Hard to assassinate on any given day.'

'Come on, Tom—killing a guy over a bad business deal?' She shook her head. 'I'm not sure.'

'So, why, then? And why Eva too?'

'It's about the Svensson empire somehow. Or the Spaceport bid. You said Matteo was all jumpy—he's smart enough to see the pattern.'

'You're missing the kingpin, Enna. If this is about leverage, Wilmer is the guy to target. He's the one with the money, the one who says yay or nay to selling up his land. His kids have no input.'

'If he's dead, they do.'

Tom nodded. 'Which is why Kennet is hunting down this missing son. Someone off the grid, and as likely as anyone to live in a bunker, have a burner phone, be angry at his father for abandoning him, and want a share of the family fortune.'

She smiled. 'Damn. And I thought I had a new line to follow.'

'It's okay.' He pecked her cheek. 'You can't be expected to be brilliant and insightful twenty-four seven.' Then he fell introspective, picking at his fingernails.

She recognised that. 'What?'

He shook his head. 'Need to know.'

'Because it's *actually* a secret, or you think I'll go off half-cocked? Huh?'

He examined her eyes. So, because he was damn handsome—albeit sometimes too guarded, oblique and untrusting—she gave him a long, passionate kiss.

'I like your bribery style, Dacourt.'

'Spill, Wagner.'

His shoulders fell. 'Okay. Actually, maybe I could use your amazing mind on this. Olsson sent a message yesterday. To the burner phone—which we reckon is whoever hired him.'

'So—bingo, right?'

'No. We still have no clue who it is.'

'Did you let it through to the recipient?'

'Yeah, unedited.'

'What did it say?' she asked.

'Just that he was back on Earth in a few days. Wanted to know what to do—because the plan had been changed.'

'He just has to lay low for a while. Or you think he'd try to get back to Mars immediately? I mean—as soon as he finds out he's been duped into coming home?'

'Clearly, he won't be going anywhere because he'll be in custody.'

'Well, duh.' She rolled her eyes.

He poked her in the belly.

'So, did the mystery recipient reply?' she asked.

'Yeah. And we left it alone. And, yeah, I'll tell you what it said. Something like, "We will take care of you".'

'Then *that's* the bingo. Someone will meet him at the Spaceport—or soon afterwards, if they have any sense not to be seen in public with a potential felon. Then, that's your guy.'

'Exactly. We'll track Olsson every step from the spacecraft. When he meets his handler, we have them bang to rights.'

A smile spread across her face, and contentment warmed her chest. They'd find the person who'd trashed so many lives. It was so close now, almost tangible.

A thought occurred. 'Guess what, Chief? My amazing mind *did* just come up with something.'

'I'm all ears.'

'Fifty bucks says this person will be flying in from Sweden to DC any time from now.'

'Or their partner, sidekick, lackey will—yeah.'

'So, I don't need to tell you the way to go here, right?'

He lifted her hand and kissed it. 'You know what? Your mind *is* as fine as your body—and everything else that's wrapped up inside it.'

'Why thank you.'

'I'll call Han in the morning. We'll scrutinise the hell out of everyone flying into the US from Sweden, starting immediately. Then, if we find out who's coming over for the welcome committee, we'll have twice the chance of tracking that rendezvous. We might not even need to squeeze Olsson to give up that name. The guy—burner phone asshole—will walk right into our net.'

She cocked her head. 'So, what you're saying is that sometimes butting in *is* okay?'

'What do you want, a medal?'

She pushed in tight. 'No. But you're welcome to remind me how much you enjoy this heavenly wrapper.'

# 54

Kennet had devised a not-too-subversive scheme in an attempt to beat Han to the discovery of the fourth heir—or even the name of its mother. Han would deploy his great intellect, data mining skills and lateral thinking. Kennet was trying an old-fashioned stakeout.

There were two entrances to the Svensson estate; the beautifully surfaced long winding drive and a shorter, more rudimentary access road which wasn't signposted and functioned as a tradesman's entrance.

Kennet had travelled in an unmarked PD vehicle and sat facing the gated entrance. He'd been there since six a.m. It was now eight-fifty, and his coffee flask was empty.

With nothing better to do, he was about to call Kayte and ask if she wanted him to pick up some reindeer steaks on the way home when the gate began to whirr open.

He stepped out of the car, ready to flag the vehicle down. He hadn't worn his uniform, to stay under the radar.

A pickup appeared—exactly the type of thing he'd expected. He hailed it, and mercifully it stopped before entering the gateway.

The driver ran down the window. 'Can I help?'

'You are the gardener for the Svensson manor?' It was a pretty redundant question—everything about the man and his vehicle confirmed it.

'Maybe. Who are you?' The guy was fiftyish but with a weather-beaten face and big hands.

Kennet glanced around. 'Polis. I spoke to Mr Svensson about the death of his son.'

'Uh-huh. And?' There was suspicion in the man's eyes.

'You've worked for Wilmer for a while, yes?'

'What's this about?'

Kennet gripped the door frame. 'You're not under caution, arrest or suspicion. Don't worry, Mr Dahlberg. You have been employed here for, what, twenty years?'

'I suppose.'

'You knew Mrs Svensson?'

'You're not implying—'

Kennet smiled, raising a hand. 'No. What I'm looking for is anyone who has known the family for longer—thirty years or more. Who might recall... events at that time.'

Dahlberg glanced around nervously. 'I don't have anything to say. I mean—I don't know anything. Only the rumours.'

'The affair.'

'Does Mr Svensson know you're asking people about that? He won't like it.'

'True,' Kennet replied. 'Which is why this is a casual chat between you and a passer-by. Because I'm sure if I told your employer you'd provided any incriminating information, he'd—'

'I understand. Except I don't have any information. I wasn't working here then, and nobody has... taken me into their confidence.'

Kennet nodded. 'I didn't expect so. All I wanted to ask was about the Svenssons' comings and goings. Who *might* have witnessed things the late wife didn't. I know the security firm is new, otherwise, I would ask the front gate attendant. The same with the staff in the house—although I don't suppose Mr Svensson's... special friend... would ever have come here.'

'No. He'd go to her place. Or somewhere else.'

'A man like he, with a public standing, would not go to another woman's house and maybe be seen.'

Dahlberg shrugged. 'You're the detective. Wilmer has a place on Singö—maybe he went there. It's his... getaway. He went a couple of weeks ago. Said he needed to clear his head after what happened to Anders.'

Kennet's eyes lit up. 'This place is like... a remote cabin? That he might have taken Mrs Svensson for romantic getaways?'

'Search me. But if I was a man like him, and I had a... special friend I wanted to spend time with, then a love nest would be ideal.' The gardener glanced around. 'I need to go. And don't worry about what we said. I know you're doing this for the right reason.'

'Yes—to find out who killed Anders and Eva.'

Dahlberg smiled forlornly. 'Eva was… a shock. Lovely girl. Lady.' He shook away a memory. 'Good luck.'

He closed the window, and the pickup purred away into the grounds.

Kennet went to his car, pointed the nose homewards, and called up his—and this still sounded odd in his head—girlfriend.

'Would you like to go to Singö for the weekend?'

'I'd love to. Sounds amazing.' A pause. 'Where and what the hell is it?'

On Saturday morning, they journeyed down to the coast north of Stockholm, having found a rental cottage that was available for one night.

Once they'd checked in, then taken the children for a seaside walk to clear their heads, Kayte stayed behind to unpack while he visited a couple of local stores and carefully enquired where the billionaire's cabin was located.

Having struck lucky, after a late lunch the foursome set off, heading for Svartklubbens on the east of the island. There, they buttered up Tomas by taking the tiny ferry across the short stretch of Åland Sea to the lighthouse, watched the waves and the birds, let Charlotte run around, then returned to the main island.

After half an hour of inspecting the hamlet's scattered properties, they located one which matched both the shopkeeper's description and their expectation of what the getaway would look like.

'Well, Inspector, darling, what are you expecting now? A miracle? That the mystery woman ended up living here?'

He loved the cheeky smile she wore.

'Sergeant, älskling, I think I am… "two for two" on canvass interviews? So I will ask at that property there.' He pointed.

'I'll keep my fingers crossed. And well done on the slang, honey.'

Five minutes later, he slid back into the driver's seat.

He tried to suppress delight, but with a detective in the passenger seat, it was impossible.

'You're three for three, aren't you?' she said, clasping his thigh lovingly.

'Mrs Lundin has had that house for forty years. She is a very nice woman. Also quite nosy. She looked out of the window and asked if that was my family. I said it was.'

'That's very sweet, and I love you too. But spill the beans, or I'll break your little pinkie like a twig.'

Kennet remembered his colleague was a black belt. 'Mrs Lundin barely spoke to Svensson when he was here. But sometimes, his lover came a day early.' He met Kayte's eye. 'We have no surname, but she was called Ebba.'

# 55

Kayte caged her enthusiasm over the weekend but was at her Com terminal with gusto on Monday morning.

Kennet took the children to the sitter's house, so the two cops could track down Ebba and—hopefully—find evidence that she'd given birth to a son about thirty-five years before.

By lunchtime, they had three matches.

They called Tom and gave an update. He was effusive in his praise and unrestrained in his excitement.

'I'd jump on a plane if I could, but Enna's on the Moon until tomorrow, and Olsson arrives on Saturday. If you need anything, shout. I don't need to tell you this but keep the Ebba thing locked down tight. It's not ideal, but we have to respect Svensson's privacy—and stay in his good books.'

'We'll tell you what we find,' she replied.

'Okay.' Tom's face fell serious. 'Now, above all else, I'm issuing a strict instruction about the Olsson flight. I do not want you there. Even if you wrap up the Ebba thing in time, I do not want you in DC. Understood?'

'Absolutely.'

Kennet leant in. 'You know, Chief, we might race you. We have a lead here. You have one there. Which of us do you think will find the culprit first?'

'You guys seem to be on a roll, so—you.'

'Want to wager on that?' Kayte asked.

'Not in the least.'

By late afternoon, they'd ruled out two of the matches—the mothers and sons had lives which didn't match what they were seeking. The final match ticked a lot of boxes. The son was going under the name Lars Öberg—after his mother—and was listed as living in a residential facility in Uppsala.

When she rang the facility to make an appointment, she was glad Tom hadn't agreed to a wager because things didn't look promising.

Nevertheless, they went to Uppsala on Tuesday and were shown to Lars' apartment. The man was slightly built, with crew-cut hair, sluggish eyes and a soft handshake. With him was his carer, Pernilla Holm. She was about Kayte's height, mid-thirties like Lars, smiley and gently spoken.

After staccato pleasantries, they left Lars in his favourite armchair, watching kids' TV, and stood in the small kitchen diner.

'There were problems during the birth,' Pernilla said. 'Physically, Lars is fine—no long-term conditions. Mentally?' She smiled sadly. 'You can see. He has a developmental age of five.'

A cloud passed across Kayte's heart. She considered herself lucky that Charlotte was as perfect a child as she could have wished for. If she and Kennet did decide to go ahead with another baby, she prayed it would work out well.

She jiggled her shoulders: this wasn't about her. It was whether Lars, as the secret fourth heir, could have masterminded the deaths of two siblings he probably didn't even know he had.

About as likely as Kennet taking up naked hang gliding.

'Do you live here?' he asked.

'In the facility, not the apartment.' Pernilla replied. 'I look after Lars most of the time, but I have another individual too. Older lady, very infirm.'

'Are you aware of Lars' heritage?'

'Yes. And I've signed documents to maintain his privacy.'

'At Wilmer Svensson's request?' Kayte asked.

Pernilla frowned. 'No. Mr Svensson has never visited. Certainly not in the decade I've worked here. The manager said he would be unlikely to ever come. Erik—the manager—has been here since day one. Apparently, Lars was given up by his mother when he was seven. You know she died the year after?'

Kennet nodded. 'So he, essentially, has nobody.'

'He has me.'

'Does he know who he is?'

'That his father is a reclusive billionaire who abandoned him at birth out of shame and self-preservation? No.' There was disgust in the woman's tone.

Kayte sighed. 'I suppose it's a blessing that he didn't know he had siblings—because to lose them....'

'Yes. Ironic that his father would have done better to build some kind of a bridge with Lars because he's outlived two of the three.'

'Do you fear for him?' Kennet said.

'No. He's essentially hidden away from everything and everyone. Besides, if any visitor was announced, I'd be on alert.' She smiled. 'Apart from the police, of course.'

They continued talking for a few minutes, then said farewell to Lars and went to the car.

Kayte patted Kennet's thigh. 'Sorry, honey. All that work for nothing.'

But he was deep in thought.

'What is it?' she asked.

'They seemed... close, yes?'

'They're bound to have a bond after so long.'

'They are the same age—physically, anyway.'

The penny dropped—and she didn't like it. 'That's a pretty dark suggestion, Kennet.'

He shook his head. 'If anything... physical was going on, I wouldn't care. That is their business.'

'He's basically a *child*.'

His gaze was direct and earnest. 'As soon as that apartment door is opened—yes. We didn't see any medical diagnosis.'

Her jaw fell. 'You can't honestly believe he's *faking*?'

'It is horrible, I know. Disrespectful. But it is the tiniest of possibilities.'

She wagged a finger. 'Sorry, honey. Hard disagree. Your radar is off. Besides, she'd have to be in on it, wouldn't she?'

He licked his lips and peered around outside. 'Yes, she would.' He took her hand. 'Unless it's *all* her. She seems like a bright woman. She cares a lot for him. Thinks his whole life is an injustice. Maybe it's just a platonic love—or even a deep friendship. But, Sergeant, sweet, Pernilla Holm knows that in another universe, Lars would inherit his father's fortune. Specifically, a universe in which all the other heirs were dead.'

# 56

Kennet's stomach was grumbling, so they headed into Uppsala for lunch.

'You're assuming that Wilmer Svensson would even include Lars in his will in the first place,' Kayte said. 'Which is a damn long shot.'

He glanced across. 'I agree. But you raise a question—what *is* in the man's will?'

'That sounds like issuing a warrant for his lawyer to hand over the information. Which I reckon will be an even longer shot.'

He tutted. 'I wish we'd done this before.'

She rubbed his knee. 'Hindsight is twenty-twenty. I wish the ladies had gone away a different weekend.' She punched her thigh. 'Damn. I'm sorry. That's insensitive.'

'Because it would mean you weren't with me?'

She grimaced. 'Yeah. Which I do like. A hell of a lot. Just....' She shrugged. 'You know.'

'Parallel universe.'

'Yeah.'

'We are where we are. Before, I had you as a friend and fine colleague. I still have that. The extra is... a bonus. And, yes, I do think about the bonus often.' He pushed hair from her temple. 'But at times like this, I value you as polis. Because while we don't agree on everything, you are as smart as you are beautiful. We should look at everyone's wills. And we should speak to Wilmer Svensson. And ask him whether he would ever, in any circumstance, bequeath money to Lars.'

'Agreed. And for good order, we should see what arrangement Lars has in place. If somehow he's been ushered into making a will, despite having no children of his own—'

'That we know about,' Kennet said.

Her eyes flared. 'Good point. Another thing to follow up. But if he has a will, then if Pernilla Holm really is the closest thing to family....' She gave him a "what do you think of them apples?".

'Kayte, sometimes your theories are a little too warped. Still, I rule nothing out. Except to say, what does this have to do with the Spaceport?'

She burbled her pretty lips, watching the urban landscape scoot past. 'You know what? No idea. Maybe it's a coincidence. Maybe it's a money grab. I'll agree that painting a car and offing a dog as protests are very different from downing a whole damn plane. And Lindström said—as did Matteo—Wilmer would never change his mind. He's a billionaire—why does he need the money from selling his land?' She eyed him. 'Just two problems with that. One—rich people always want to get richer.'

'He'd be compromising his principles.'

'True—my point two. Or, if he was dead, and the decision to sell up passed to Lars—Pernilla, assuming she has power of attorney—then maybe the deal would go through.'

'If, as we said, Lars is even *in* the old man's will.'

'Again, true enough, honey. But if he isn't, maybe Matteo is. Then, if Matteo meets an unfortunate end, and Wilmer hasn't made alternate arrangements, he dies intestate. And that's a big damn sum of money going begging.'

'Bigger, if someone agrees to sell the site to Fleet.'

She patted her thighs like a drum. 'A lot of this is looking like Wilmer *has* to be in the line of fire very soon.'

'The problem is if we tell him the theory from first principles—including tracking down Ebba and Lars—he won't be happy.'

'Then we need to put our thinking caps on because—' She jabbed the window. 'Look!'

He watched. 'It can't be.'

'He lives here. Of course it can.'

'And her? Holding hands?'

She bit her lip. 'I'm calling foul.'

'You might be right, Sergeant. I'll pull over.'

He took SelfDrive control and parked the car a hundred yards down the street from where the couple were walking. Then they watched the targets to ensure their assumptions were correct.

Kayte's tone was measured, conspiratorial. 'You know what she said, Kennet? She talked about impartiality. What a crock.'

'I think this may be a time to speak softly and keep the big stick in our holster. He is a difficult character. Let's not make assumptions, yes?'

'Agreed. And not a word about Lars.'

They hopped out and waited outside the adjacent café.

Kennet watched carefully and spied the moment Matteo Svensson noted the two uniforms. His hesitation was brief, and he didn't alter his course, but his body language became tightened.

'Ms Lindström,' Kayte said.

'Sergeant... Connors?'

'Hi. And Mr Svensson, isn't it?'

'Arvidsson. Andreas Arvidsson. I'm sorry, have we met?'

Kennet desperately wanted to clench Kayte's hand, seeking to convey that she shouldn't push the matter. Clearly, Matteo was bluffing or lying. He didn't think Matteo—or Sara, for that matter—were armed and certainly wouldn't want to start a conflict in a public space, but he was wary of showing more of their hand than they needed.

Sadly, Kayte didn't get the vibe that diplomacy was best for avoiding an incident.

'That's funny, Mr Arvidsson. You must get a lot of cases of mistaken identity.'

Sara was looking at the man, wide-eyed. If there was a lie going on, she wasn't party to it. 'I think you must... Andreas?'

'Is there a problem, officers?' Matteo/Andreas asked, nostrils flaring.

'Not specifically,' Kennet said. 'And I think we *are* mistaken because Matteo Svensson indicated he would not go out in public without a bodyguard. Are *you* a bodyguard, Ms Lindström?'

She shrunk back. 'I'm his... Andreas'... *friend*.' She let go of his hand as if it was a dead rat.

'I will ask again,' Matteo said through thin lips. 'Is there a problem? Am I, or Ms Lindström, needed for questioning about any matters?' He glowered at Kayte.

Kennet's pulse quickened. Now, he really did want to offer Kayte a protective arm. Matteo had already gained a reputation for abrasiveness and evasion. Kennet sensed guilt, fear, or both building in the man.

'No. Not at all.' Kayte's tone was suddenly breezy. She waved the couple on. 'Sorry for bothering you. Enjoy your day.'

Matteo shot Kennet daggers. Sara Lindström looked flustered and bewildered.

Kennet flashed a smile, let the twosome pass, then jabbed his head at the car. Within fifteen seconds, he and Kayte were seated.

He blew out lungfuls of tension and relief—hardly model polis behaviour, but he trusted his law enforcement partner not to raise the issue with Janssen. Firstly because he was sleeping with her, and secondly because she softly whistled, eyes like saucers.

'Well?' he asked.

'I think there *is* a problem. A big one. Like, thousands of acres big.'

# 57

Matteo was careful not to make any more of a scene on the street—things were bad enough already. Instead, he took Sara back to his place.

Hoping to gloss over the matter, he coaxed her into a tender clench and plotted a journey into the bedroom. He was a good lover; maybe that would take her mind off things.

She wasn't having any of it.

'I want an explanation, Andreas—if that is your name. You can't screw your way out of this.'

'Look, Sara, names are simply placeholders. Love is about people.'

She shuffled away from him on the sofa. 'And who *is* the person who's been dating me—playing me?—for nine months?'

His jaw worked. This seemed to have passed the point of being bluffed away or swept under the carpet.

'Let me tell you something about Matteo Svensson. He was an unwanted child. He was disowned by his father after a travesty of a prison sentence. Then, when he discovered his father's affair, the unholy row pushed his mother into a heart attack. Again, he was blamed for something that wasn't his fault. His siblings tolerate—or *tolerated*—him at best. And since his brother was tracked down and killed—despite his attempts to avoid attention—Matteo Svensson is pretty keen on not being stopped on the street by interfering cops, one of whom doesn't even belong here. Nobody cares too much about *that* man. But Andreas Arvidsson?' He cupped her cheek. 'Someone cares a lot for *him*.'

Her eyes were darting. He wasn't convinced the sob story had worked.

'What's this about a bodyguard?'

He snorted. 'I told them I was hiring a bodyguard, so they'd leave me alone. I know what I'm doing.'

'By lying about your identity?' She eased back. 'Or was that just for my benefit?'

'Would you have dated me if you knew different?'

'I don't know. I have no clue who this Matteo person is—was—is.'

'It's me.'

'You mean, the son of one of the key stakeholders in the Spaceport decision?' Her lip curled. 'Currying favours.'

'Tell me I've strongarmed you—go on.' His lips pursed. 'I haven't. What *have* I done? Brought you the best option. You've said it yourself. Even the basic location analyses tell you—and the Committee—that our estate is the frontrunner.'

She moved away. 'This isn't happening. Now you *are* pressuring me. What next—are you going to spray my car or shoot someone's dog?'

He gritted his teeth. 'I didn't do those things.' Which was technically true.

'I think it's best if we break up.'

'Because of your conscience? Or I'm not good enough for you?'

She jabbed a finger. 'Because I don't want to be investigated for bias and impropriety. How long did you expect to get away with this for?'

'At the start, until the decision was made. Then, I suppose part of me fell in love with you.' It was worth a try.

She scoffed. 'You expect me to believe that?'

He swatted a hand. 'I don't care anymore. But if you actively choose to dump our—the Svensson—site, then you're putting emotion and petty revenge above logic.'

'You know what, Matteo? That site is the logical choice. But first of all, he still shows no signs of wanting to sell up. And second, if it ever comes out that you and I were an item, nobody will believe that the decision was impartial.'

He grabbed her jaw. 'You're absolutely right. I don't want to do anything that stops the build going ahead on my land. Get your stuff and get out.'

When she'd cleared out her few belongings, he took a bottle of beer to the sofa, fished the burner phone out of its locked drawer, and placed two calls.

# 58

Kennet didn't have to bend the truth too much when he asked Wilmer Svensson for another meeting.

He and Kayte travelled down to the manor in a PD vehicle.

'I hope he'll let us be direct,' she said.

'I hope he doesn't ask for too much evidence.'

'Yeah. I mean, a lack of evidence doesn't mean there isn't any, but I don't trust Matteo. Pernilla and Lars? It's the longest shot.'

'We need a smoking gun. If it is Matteo behind all this, then what are we missing? He has achieved nothing so far.'

She took his hand. 'Except deprived us of our loved ones.'

'And he will pay for that. I hope Wilmer gives us what we need.'

The billionaire was less standoffish this time without being entirely amicable. He did at least allow the meeting to take place seated, and he had coffee brought through.

Kennet glossed over his methods but revealed that they had located Lars. It was important for the context of the discussion, and they didn't want to leave the matter alone in case it had a bearing on whatever information Wilmer chose to reveal. This was an "I show you mine, you show me yours" conversation—a vital piece of the puzzle was likely hiding in the shadows.

He told how they'd chanced upon Matteo and Sara, including the impression that Matteo was dating her under a false identity.

'I don't understand,' Wilmer said. 'I told the Committee I'm not interested in selling my land.'

'The impression we've got is that Matteo and Sara—independently—know that's the case.'

Wilmer ran a hand through his thickish hair. 'Then I don't know what the boy is up to.'

'Being honest,' Kayte said, 'Neither do we.'

'Which is why we're here,' Kennet added quickly. 'Because all logical lines of thought point to your safety being endangered.'

Wilmer's frown lines deepened. 'Those lines of thought, if I extrapolate them backwards, imply Matteo is involved in the deaths of his brother and sister.'

'And, by extension, our wives. Hence why we're raising matters that we would rather not. But all those deaths *are* criminal matters, and we want to prevent new ones from arising.'

'I agree.' Wilmer's head fell. 'And while I don't have much time for Mat—and you'll have gathered I've been a poor father to Lars—I don't want either of them hurt by whoever is behind this.' A faint smile appeared. 'And I'm not too keen on dying yet either.'

'So, sir,' Kayte said, 'It's all about your inheritance plans. We think that's the lynchpin.'

'A fair enough assumption.'

'Have you been pressured to alter your will in the last... three months?' Kennet asked.

'Only by my lawyer, Peter.'

Kennet flashed Kayte a query. She nodded. As so often, they were on the same wavelength.

'Then we need to find out if *he's* been influenced.'

'He would never be,' Wilmer replied.

'And nobody would ever coerce an environmental scientist into falsifying test results? Or hire a hitman to pose as a barista so he could poison an innocent woman?'

Wilmer covered his face. 'You don't have proof of that.'

'No, but those things happened,' Kayte said. 'And someone connected to all this did it. Paying off a lawyer would be mild in comparison.'

Wilmer sat up straight. 'I'll call him.'

'We'd prefer he came here,' Kennet said.

Wilmer picked at a stray cushion feather. 'Alright.'

While the lawyer was summoned—he'd surely drop everything for such a significant client—Kennet and Kayte took a walk on a tiny corner of the vast estate. When they were out of sight of the house, he took her hand.

'When the case is solved, and the reminders are gone, I will still miss her. I need to tell you that.'

'And I'll miss Carey too. It's allowed. It's normal. But I hope it doesn't hinder... us.'

He stopped, taking her in his arms, glancing around to be sure there were no prying eyes.

'Besides what I cannot fix, I love you more every day.'

'Back at you, partner.'

He poured his heart into the kiss they shared.

'Come on, Inspector,' she said when they were done. 'Ten kronor says this Peter guy has received calls from a certain burner phone.'

He hadn't.

Kennet watched the lawyer's body language and listened to what wasn't said but found no lies lurking.

Peter *had* advised Wilmer Svensson to alter his will—but only following Eva's death. After Anders' death, things had reached a stalemate: Wilmer didn't want Matteo to be the beneficiary of choice.

Kennet took Svensson aside and asked if it was permissible to reveal to the lawyer the existence and status of Lars.

Wilmer reluctantly agreed. After all, he was going to die sometime and didn't want his estate mired in legal wranglings if, for example, Lars contested the will because he felt legally entitled to something. Of course, he'd be acting under the counsel of someone—possibly Pernilla—but the future had to be secured as best as possible.

Peter reaffirmed his silence over anything that was said—especially regarding police matters.

As neither Eva nor Anders had children, and Wilmer didn't want his estate going to Eva's widower, the traditional and logical approach was to make Matteo the sole beneficiary or possibly leave Lars a share too. What if either son was in prison—assuming they were responsible for current events? What if they died childless too? It didn't matter whether Wilmer sold out to Fleet; a bequest would be forthcoming—irrespective of size.

There were two entwined matters to consider. What was Wilmer's ideal outcome for his estate?

The second was thornier. Assuming Matteo was hatching a scheme, how could they second guess what came next and, ideally, turn the tables before more people died?

# 59

Enna had felt out of sorts for a couple of days, but nothing would stop her from being at Washington Spaceport that Saturday morning.

She dressed in her Fleet uniform, then took pleasure in watching Tom get into his Fleet PD attire.

'Damn, you're sexy in uniform.'

He looked at her, reflected in the mirror. 'Yeah, well, I don't have the advantage of being sexy *out* of uniform.'

'You flirting with me, Chief?'

'If we didn't have somewhere to be, I would jump your bones, Lieutenant.'

She shot him her best coy expression. 'Honestly, you can show your appreciation of my brilliance by getting Olsson to confess and give up his hirer. Then our pair of Swedish lovebirds can get closure, and I can take Gina some flowers to show that her busted arm was worth the inconvenience.'

'And tell her that having you as a mentor doesn't mean she has to try dumb stunts. One of those is plenty.'

She went to him. 'You're regretting having me along for the ride—is that what I'm hearing?'

'Not a bit of it. A lot of the time, your logic is as flawless as your looks.'

'Sneak.'

He poked out his tongue. 'Caution is good. You've learned—we all have: trust nobody. So, outside of turning this into a SWAT team operation—which is overkill for some flight systems engineer who doesn't even know the cops are on his tail—I've de-risked this as best as I can. Olsson will be watched all the way from the ship, through Arrivals and Acclimatisation, until he meets us. Then Ellie and I—'

'And Thurmann.'

'—who I've known for years and whose background Han rechecked yesterday, will escort him to WPD, where he'll be interviewed and then remanded under Thurmann's guard. We won't let any unfamiliar faces near him until we have what we want.'

'The owner of the burner, and more.'

'Exactly. Then he'll go straight to WP. Plus, it'll all be kept on a need-to-know.'

'Okay. So, who's meeting him?' she asked. 'Our mystery paymaster?'

'Million-dollar question. There were no flags on anyone flying into DC from Sweden. Still, it doesn't mean the person didn't fly in via a third country. Or they were here already.' He shrugged. 'We've done diligence on this. Hell, getting Olsson back under false pretence is a miracle in itself—notwithstanding Gina's injury. And, giving credit, some of that diligence is due to what's inside that pretty head of yours.'

'Aw, shucks.'

'Hence why you can ride shotgun.' He fondled her backside. 'Plus, if you manage not to piss off the guy en route, you can sit in on the interview too. You've outsmarted a ton of people when you weren't trying to be an action hero.'

She grabbed his ass and laid her face into his neck. 'And I did pretty fine in the action hero parts, too, right?'

'You've more lives than a damn alley cat. But, yeah, you kick ass pretty good.'

'Yeah,' she murmured, fondling. 'I'm good with asses.'

They trundled up from Fort Valley to the Spaceport on the far side of DC.

There, they rendezvoused with the Spaceport duty Captain, Ellie and Thurmann.

Enna hadn't met Thurmann before. He was a bookish-looking cop, ginger-haired, with a weak handshake but strong shoulders.

The quintet passed a half-hour over coffee.

Gina Devine messaged Enna to say she was in Arrivals with Olsson, and the man was behaving. Enna couldn't help surveying the area for what they might have missed. *Surely* Olsson would be met? He hadn't arranged onward travel to Sweden, nor had he booked overnight accommodation in DC.

Sadly, they had no clue who might be meeting him. Kennet had updated them on the situation with Lars and Matteo Svensson, and neither had left the country.

Still, there *must* be a middleman. Possibly the person who had killed Viggo Alban after he murdered Eva? Again, they had millions of potential suspects, and the solitary link was a burner phone whose owner was anonymous.

Just after twelve noon, Gina and Olsson appeared.

They were accompanied by a Captain Parker, who'd helped Gina bring Olsson landside. Gina's arm was in a temporary cast, and Olsson wore Fleet-issue restraints—not handcuffs. Enna kept her greetings professional and her looks towards Olsson less-than-devilish.

Parker left. Tom, Ellie and Thurmann took the suspect in tow, and Enna insisted Gina get to her pre-booked hospital ride as soon as possible.

Olsson remained subdued. He'd realised what had happened and seemed resigned to his fate. Enna didn't see in his demeanour anything other than a man who'd been turned to an evil task but believed he had a foolproof escape route. Maybe if his handiwork had remained undiscovered, he might have returned to work after excusing an impromptu 'holiday' or found a more glamorous role on Mars, servicing spacecraft instead of aircraft.

Enna didn't much care. He was a guilty sonofabitch who'd taken the lives of innocent people, sent a shockwave through two cops, and broken the bones of a colleague who wasn't even *trying* to be the new, improved, younger and sexier Lieutenant Enna Dacourt—rabblerouser and colony-hopping kicker of scumbag ass.

All she demanded was justice. She wanted Olsson kept safe so he could spill his guts. After that, she didn't care.

Thurmann took point, Enna and Tom flanked Olsson, and Ellie brought up the rear. All of them continually scanned the vicinity. Enna saw nothing except travellers passing in dribs and drabs, uniformed Spaceport Fleet staff attending to queries, and the occasional Security officer who flashed a comradely nod in the direction of the mobile group.

At the front entrance, they exited onto the wide concourse. Thurmann walked away to bring the PD car up from barely a hundred yards away. Tom took point.

Enna grabbed Olsson's wrist restraint. This was his first opportunity to bolt for freedom—though he'd be unlikely to get far. She scoped out the environs. Firstly nearby, looking for anyone who might have been expecting to meet Olsson but was now making an about-turn. Secondly, further away, checking nothing untoward was happening with the PD vehicle. It's where Tom was focussed too. Lastly, she looked for drones—though none should be able to get this close to the Terminal building without being taken down.

A half-mile away, where Admin buildings were dotted, something on the rooftop winked. There was a blob of a shape up there. The reflection glinted again.

She didn't like it. With stomach-churning worry, she didn't like it. 'Tom!'

He turned.

The flicker this time was different. It was a muzzle flash.

She shoved Olsson violently sidewards, letting go of his wrist but toppling in sympathy.

Two impacts slammed into her chest, and she sloughed to the ground. Her skull connected with the marble apron, and she blacked out.

# 60

The world was a damn funny place.

She was on Mars, and it was snowing. Dr Iversen was there. Gina Devine was making eyes at her. Her shoulders felt heavy. There was an ion backpack there.

Nearby, Kayte and Kennet were playing Pattycake.

Tom's face appeared in front, larger than life, almost giant.

'Enna?'

*How is he doing that without moving those lovely lips? Man, I could kiss those lips. Hang on, isn't that Lexie crying? Go see what's wrong, husband. Leave me alone.*

*What the hell is this creature? Jeez, it looks just like me. Oh, hey, Emma. Didn't you drown—or whatever it is robots do? Rust?*

'Enna?'

*Leave me alone. I'm resting. I earned it.*

*Those were bullets, right? Sheesh, they hurt, too. Goddamn sniper. Why didn't we expect a sniper? Well, you didn't, missy, because you're a damn astrobiologist-turned-Navigator in SpaceFleet, not a freaking close protection officer.*

*What were you thinking?*

*Oh yeah—saving a life.*

*Man, that really does hurt.*

She became aware of true, deep pain.

'Enna?'

A real voice, not an imagined one. She felt her body come into existence. Her face. Her eyes. Her lips. Her throat.

'That's my gal.'

*Yeah, I married him, right? That was ages ago. What a trooper he is. Brave. Whoah, where did everybody go? I like Mars' snow. I'd go there.*

The snowflakes morphed into a sheet of white, which bloomed into undulating brightness beyond her eyelids. Something eclipsed the light.

'I bought chocolate pudding, Enna....'

Her eyes snapped open.

'Made you look!' He winked.

'You're a rat, Tom Wagner.'

'Hey, no insults.' His expression hardened. 'I'm furious as hell with you, and I'm only bottling it because the doctors asked me not to spike your blood pressure.'

She opened her mouth for a trademark witticism but reconsidered. 'I still have blood?'

'You still have everything. A little more Swiss cheese and a fraction less Enna than I'd like, but I'm calling it a win.'

Her spirits sank. 'I'm sorry, Tom.'

'I know. Do you want water?'

'I want coffee and chocolate pudding.'

'Doc says water. Water and sleep.'

'Buzzkill.' Her brow knit. 'What happened, Tom?'

He kissed her forehead. The touch was lovely, but beneath it, her head throbbed.

'You lived. Everything else is secondary. Drink water. Sleep.'

She swallowed. 'You really are cross?'

'I really am. But I also love you, plus I need a pee. I've been sat here for two hours.' He held a cup with a straw to her lips.

She drank. The water was like ambrosia running down her throat. Then a tidal wave of tiredness crashed over her.

'I have a crazy idea, honey. I'll get some sleep.'

'Finally, Enna does what she's told. Miracles do happen.'

She didn't know how long it was before she woke again—she hadn't checked the clock before—but it was dark outside, so at least ten hours since the debacle at the Spaceport.

Debacle? She hadn't done anything wrong except try to protect a valuable asset.

Maybe the wrong was only in Tom's eyes. After all, he could have been widowed.

There was nobody in the room, so she pondered that thought. Which was more important: doing right by the man of her dreams—and her family, or trying to do right by a criminal? Any one of thousands of people could have done that escort job instead of her, but she was the apparent one-woman army who could accomplish anything.

She toyed with the tube connected to the cannula in her arm.

*Last year, Tom wound up in a bed like this after playing the hero, and hell, was I mad and scared. He's bigger and cleverer than me, but none of what we did is big and clever. It's dumb and selfish, and misjudged.*

She sighed.

*I wonder how long before I can get coffee and chocolate pudding. I hope the doctor is a guy, then I can turn the charm up to ten.*

She lifted the water cup over and drained it.

Tom appeared, with a doctor at his shoulder.

'Hi, doc,' she said.

'Ms Dacourt.' He checked her chart.

He didn't seem like the kind who'd fall for charm. Besides, Tom was there and would tell her to cut it out.

'Your medical history is interesting reading, Lieutenant.'

'Yeah. Doesn't quite touch Tolstoy for length, but the drama? Sheesh.'

He smiled thinly. 'You were very lucky. Two high-velocity bullets pierced your chest and exited your back. One just missed shattering your scapula. The second almost nicked your lung. Few stitches in your scalp but no breaks.'

'In summary, I'll live.'

'You'll be fine. And so will the baby.'

She spluttered out a breath. Tom was beside her in a second. Relief and dread and surprise and love and self-admonishment coursed through her.

'Baby?' she said, in a dumb reflex statement of the obvious.

Tom stroked her forehead. 'Yeah. Helluva day, huh?'

The doc left them to it. She was too stunned to ask for indulgent refreshments.

'I'm sorry, Tom.'

'I'm still mad. I mean, I was mad anyway, then when he told me....' He shrugged.

'I'm *really* sorry.'

'Yeah. Well. Live and learn, huh? Especially the "live" part.'

She gave an anticipatory grimace. 'But I did good, right?'

He sighed hard, taking her hand. 'Here's the thing. He was a pretty fine shot, the guy. And bullets don't come in twos.'

Sadness and anger mushroomed inside her. 'Olsson's dead.'

'Hmm.'

'Goddammit to hell.' She wanted to cry.

'Took the words right out of all our mouths.'

'If I had the energy, I'd be as mad as you. You know, if the old veins were coursing with caffeine and cakey goodness.' She forced a smile.

'Slow down a while, okay?'

'I guess. So, give me some good news and tell me you got the shooter?'

He gently shook his head. 'BOLO is out, but nothing so far. Han is assisting. WPD is taking the case. We have enough on our plate.'

'*Any* good news?' she asked hopefully.

'Kayte and Kennet think they know who it is anyhow. Everything points at Matteo Svensson.'

She chuckled forlornly. 'So my crazy stunt was for nothing?'

'No. It was well-meant, instinctive, and damn near worked.'

'I'll take that as the only compliment I'll get from you, huh?'

'That's fair. Look, Han and Ellie are here. Want to see them?'

'They as pissed off as you?'

His expression hardened. 'This isn't a joke.'

'I didn't mean—'

'This is serious. Very nearly *deadly* serious.' His eyes blazed.

She waved it away. 'I don't need a damn lecture, Tom.'

He held up a finger. 'Yeah. You do. I can't do this, Enna. I can't keep almost losing you. If you're going to carry on this gung-ho, butt-in, superwoman approach to life, then,' he took a deep breath, 'Then I think you and I are done.'

He might as well have plunged a knife into her heart. Yet she knew it was said with an all-consuming love and designed as a last resort. Fortunately for him, she'd already seen this kind of ultimatum coming. Besides, getting shot was an excellent way to make a person examine their priorities.

She reached for his hand. 'Go get Ellie and Han.'

He frowned. 'Huh?'

'Please, okay?'

He tried to look behind her expression, then gave up and did her bidding.

Two minutes later, he was back with the young twosome in tow.

'What's up, Enna?' Ellie asked, worried.

Enna beckoned. Tom approached. She took his hand with her left hand, then laid her right hand on her chest as if pledging allegiance to the Stars and Stripes.

'You two hotshots are witnesses.'

'Okay,' Han said.

She looked up at Tom. 'I promise, and swear on the graves of my brother and everyone else we've known and lost, that I'll never get involved in Fleet PD ever again. Not beyond the dinner table or the bedroom. I've said before that I'm done. This time I mean it. You have my permission to throw me in a holding cell if I welch on this. Wife, mother, Navigator—nothing else. I'm getting off the rollercoaster now. I'm too dizzy, and the fun is gone.'

Tom perched beside her. 'When we met, you were plenty awesome enough. You didn't need to dial it up. Nobody remains undefeated forever. Now is *exactly* the time to stop.' He smoothed her belly.

She craned her neck, and he kissed her.

She looked at Ellie and Han. 'Because pretty soon, I'll want to be on maternity leave. You know—just so you're in the loop.'

'Congratulations, Enna,' Han said.

Ellie darted over and squeezed Enna's hand. 'We'd all rather you had babies inside you than bullets.'

'Thanks, Ellie. Does mean I'll be bored out of my mind for six months.'

'I'll come over.'

'Good. You too, Han.'

'Thank you.'

She fluttered her eyes at Tom. 'Now, honey, *please* ask when I can get a coffee.'

# 61

K ayte hung up the call.

It was Sunday afternoon, and Tom had been giving an update. After the gut punch of the previous day's news, nothing would be as bad, yet it wasn't all good.

She trudged down the stairs, drinking in the scene. Kennet and Tomas were playing blocks with Charlotte. Kayte was hit by an overwhelming love for the family she'd inherited. As she watched, briefly mournful for the two ghosts that might otherwise be here, she felt a greater kinship with Enna. She had a sudden pang to jump on a plane, rush to the hospital, and bear hug the crazy woman.

Kennet was looking at her, frowning.

She descended the stairs to him, and offered a loving kiss.

'Daddy?' Tomas asked. 'Is mummy Kayte sad?'

He patted the boy's head. 'I think she is worried about Auntie Enna.'

'You said she is not hurt too bad.'

Kayte plopped down on the floor. 'Enna is fine, Tomas. She's already talking about the cool scars she wants to show you.'

His eyes lit. 'Can we go to the castle again?'

'Maybe in the holidays, champ.' Kennet stood and helped Kayte up. 'Play with Charlotte for a while, yes?'

'Okay, daddy.'

Kayte led Kennet into the kitchen.

'Well?' he asked.

'Enna will be out in a day or so. She put Tom on the call afterwards. They found the shooter.' She clenched a fist. 'Dead. Contact poison, like Viggo Alban.'

He lifted her chin. 'Meaning they are connected. Which is good.'

'But a dead end. Anyway, no use crying over spilt milk. Tom's flying over. Enna practically insisted. He gave her chapter and verse on Matteo and Lars. On another day, she'd be digging out her knuckleduster and coming along too. Finally, she's seen the light.' Kayte instantly brightened. 'She's incubating another little one.'

Kennet pulled her close. 'That's wonderful. So... Tom likes our plan?'

She did a so-so. 'With reservations. Not as many as Wilmer has, for sure.'

'He clearly needed a couple of days to think it over.'

'Can't say I'd rather Olsson hadn't done the testifying. Easier all around.' She chuckled reflectively. 'Enna was always one for laying traps and outsmarting her prey. It's not really a mantle I want—not with her track record of playing chess with the Grim Reaper.'

'I wholly agree. I wish we had hard evidence against Matteo. He has probably been concocting this for months, and is a very smart man. Obviously, he is nervous now. Cutting all his ties.'

'But he still doesn't have what he wants. No concession to the Spaceport bid. No mention in Wilmer's estate.' She snarled. 'Just a body count and a handful of very pissed-off cops.'

'Sara Lindström was a step too far. That was unnecessary. She had a reason to keep quiet.' He sighed, gritting his teeth. 'But then, once you've killed your brother and sister, it's easy to murder someone you're only dating.'

She eased him into a seat at the breakfast bar and poured them a coffee.

'He's a coward, too. He doesn't have the balls to do it directly. Here's another ten-kronor bet—he met at least one of the shooters while he was in prison. Put the names in a little black book for when he was planning revenge on his family for kicking him into touch.'

'Two shooters?'

She frowned. 'Sure. One in DC, one here—who killed Persson, Bob Gerhardt and now Sara Lindström.'

He sipped pensively. 'True. So, tomorrow I'll tell the Chief to put a resource on that. Find out if there's someone common to all three times and locations. Maybe someone already on the database. Cross-reference it with all the inmates from Matteo's time inside.'

She kissed the top of his head. 'Wish we'd known this shit weeks ago. Too many tears, not enough clear heads.'

He held her waist. 'No regrets, partner. We said no looking back, remember? Only forward. Come on, don't beat yourself up. We have a big chance now.'

'Yeah—if Svensson agrees to the crazy plan. And if Matteo takes the bait.'

'He has to. Otherwise, like we said, he's got nothing.'

She bit her lip. 'But he is shrewd and sharp. I mean, you and are hardly chicken feed, but he's like a master watchmaker.'

'I disagree. He gets riled. Like when we saw him on the street. And now, to have Lindström killed? He must know he would be a prime suspect for that.'

She ran a fingertip around the rim of her mug. 'You're right. And if he's getting antsy, it means he wants this over—so offering him a quick way out should play into his hands.'

'Let us hope.' He smiled. 'And let us hope Wilmer remembered what he said about pulling strings to get me promoted.'

'And just when I was hoping I could put in for my own raise. Is this Kennet's plan to make sure his girlfriend is always duty-bound to salute him?'

He squeezed her backside. 'You already have the beauty and brains, älskling. Let me have seniority?'

'Fair enough. Now, enough work. What do you say we teach Charlotte the word "daddy"?'

'And Tomas, the word "sister"?'

'She technically is anyhow. But he's a smart kid. I think he gets the way things are going.'

'He likes you. A lot.'

'I know.' She winked. 'He's got great taste. Like his dad.'

That evening, as she snuggled up to Kennet in bed, there was something she needed to discuss. The bedtime routine had settled easily into a convivial, mature and loving coexistence—but had it been *too* easy? Too superficial, expected and masking unspoken concerns?

It was certainly different from nights with Carey but, even as she pondered it, probably more akin to Kennet's old married life. She'd always regarded him as more sensible, settled and measured. There was certainly no sign of things like pillow fights, late-night drinking sessions or impulsive silliness.

Yet, was that what she wanted from him? What she'd truly expected? Neither of them was the same person they'd used to be.

She stroked his chest. 'Honey?'

'Yes?'

'Forgive me, but I have to ask. It's been four weeks. Do you... regret your decision?'

He explored her eyes, and a smile broke. 'To become involved with you? Not for a moment. Why? Do you?'

'No. I just.... I don't know. Maybe I just expected more...' she smiled impishly, '*lovin*'.'

His brow arched. 'Because men want only one thing from their lady love?'

She growled at her insensitivity. 'Sorry. Pigeonholing you. And the point about you is that you're the best of everything.'

He pulled her closer. 'Now, älskling, the problem is that your appeal is beyond words. Yet it is easy to fall into that trap of conveying my love through... lovin' alone.'

She laughed.

When she stopped, he kissed her. 'We are still on your journey. Both inside the bedroom and outside it. I hope we have so very much time together still to come, so this is the reason I have not been... over amorous. Not because you are not a fountain I wish to drink from at every moment.'

She gently rubbed her nose against his. 'Thanks, honey. Your restraint is so sweet. And, for the record, I wouldn't want to spoil quality with quantity, if you know what I mean.'

'And I don't want to ruin what seems to be a perfect life with you by demanding sex.'

She put her mouth by his ear. 'Demanding isn't necessary. Asking nicely will do the trick.'

He nuzzled into a long kiss.

When they broke, she traced a finger over his jaw. 'Look, I only asked about the... us choice—and the sex—because I don't think we ever went over that part of our... decision evening... where I mentioned a baby.'

'No. I don't think we did.'

'And I think we ought to, because that one thing is a biggie when it comes to maintaining a perfect life. I mean—discussing and agreeing on it, not me necessarily getting for the decision I want.'

'I agree.'

'So the question is, do you think we could handle having three kids in this household? With our work and everything.'

His eyes caroused for a while. 'Probably. Do you?'

'Probably. If we both keep our jobs and find a way to work out all the childcare.' She stroked his temple. 'It does require plenty of *lovin'* though, älskling. Do you think you can manage that?' She smirked.

'I can,' he said, deadpan.

She laughed. 'Then I suppose the next best step—practical, sensible Kennet style—is to look at logistics and finances and see if it's doable.'

He slid a palm over her chest, stomach, and down. 'But the better, sparky, wild, Kayte approach would be to start getting some practice.'

# 62

On Monday morning, they put a tap on all Matteo's Com traffic. Whilst he might have used the burner for any new nefarious activities, they didn't want to miss the easy stuff.

They spoke to Wilmer Svensson—who was ironically at his getaway cabin, gaining perspective—about the planned honey trap for Matteo.

They took a long meeting with CI Janssen, who was providing manpower to support their approach. He'd instigated a deep dive into Lars and Pernilla's lives and discovered nothing to indicate they were involved in anything untoward. In parallel with the sting operation, he approved an investigation into Matteo's financial records and movements for the past six months: if the suspect didn't trip himself up, a weight of evidence was needed.

Tom arrived in the evening. They had dinner and a pow-wow. The poor guy was clearly shaken by what had happened at the Spaceport and wore Enna's heart on his sleeve. All three had received strict instructions to "think smart, be sharp, take care, and nail the sonofabitch".

They agreed to do that—and keep her informed every step of the way. This counted as Enna "butting out".

Kennet found Kayte to be oddly reserved and introspective when they retired for the night. He put it down to bottled nerves and the feeling that success was within their grasp.

He held her close. Spartan conversation ended up circling back to the reason why they were pursuing Matteo, and they cried silently, extensively and deeply. It had been a long time since such emotion had surfaced, but now it was understandable when—hopefully—they were on the cusp of justice for Jana and Carey.

In the morning, they took Tomas and Charlotte to the sitter, then rendezvoused with Tom at Bollnäs PD.

There, they set out the plan.

Tom and a Bollnäs uniform—Officer Ekberg—would be secreted within the Svensson manor. Kayte and Kennet would take a hidden position nearby. Janssen and a colleague would be in a car at the tradesman's entrance. A fourth unit would hide near the main entrance.

Everyone would be wired into an open Com channel from the room where Wilmer would meet Matteo. They could therefore follow things and be prepared to move into an arrest when Matteo had hoisted himself by his own petard. A helicopter—provided by Uppsala PD—would wait two minutes flying time away, should Matteo bolt.

The most important thing was that the suspect didn't get spooked—he must believe he was being invited to the manor by Wilmer, expecting a reversal of his father's position.

At ten-fifty, Wilmer called Janssen to confirm that Matteo had agreed to meet at two p.m.

Kennet patted Tom and Kayte's shoulders. 'The game's afoot.'

The unmarked PD car cruised along the minor road leading to the Svensson estate.

He and Kayte were in full uniform, their weapons loaded. He dearly hoped they wouldn't see action. She'd been unusually quiet, and it worried him: nerves were unlike her.

'What is it, sweet?'

'Pressure, Kennet.'

'We are not at the sharp end. Tom is. In fact, Wilmer is.'

'He's a loose cannon—Matteo. The things he's done.' She shuddered, gripping his hand.

Sometimes, her flashes of vulnerability were welcome, grounding and adorable. Sometimes they felt so out of place and circumstance as to be a potential liability.

He cared so much for her physical and mental well-being that it ached. 'Do you have a grip, Sergeant? You want to do this, right?'

'More than you know. For the ladies. The other passengers. For Eva, Anders, Sara. Definitely for Enna. She did a lot for us recently. I don't want her heroics in vain.'

'Then what's—?'

'Things *must* go right. They have to. I totally know where Tom's head is. I've already lost someone I loved dearly. I can't lose another.' She eyed him, supplicating—for what, he didn't know.

'I will take care,' he protested gently, smiling. 'Of us both. This is just another case, Kayte. Another day on the job. You and I. Partners. Don't get—'

She grabbed his jacket sleeve. 'Ask me.'

He frowned. 'Ask you what?'

'The question. Ask me now, please. Right now.' The words were firm, desperate, yet measured.

His stomach somersaulted. He tried to gaze into her heart and soul, sensing a mournful yet excited pleading. She squeezed his hand. Hers fizzed with either nerves or excitement.

'Now,' she peeped, eyes moistening.

Not much detective work was needed here.

He swallowed hard. 'Kayte Connors, will you marry me?'

She clasped her arms around him and buried her head in his chest. 'Yes. Yes, yes, yes—a million times, yes.'

He kissed her hair. 'You've done some crazy things in your life, älskling, but—'

She eased away and shook her head, beaming. 'This is the sanest, most logical thing in... ever. I waited too long to marry Carey. Years. I'm not making that mistake again.'

She pressed in so close their noses almost touched. The car swayed.

'Life is too damn precious. Time is short.' She touched his cheek. 'Marry me, Kennet. Soon. Very soon. We don't know what the future holds. Hopefully, nothing except togetherness and happiness.' She ran tender fingertips over his stubble.

He stroked her hand. 'Okay.'

He kissed her. The hope and harmony gambolled in the bond of their lips.

She inspected his eyes. 'You did want to ask, right? Is this my love's Swedish Reserve, or are there... true reservations? Did I put you on the spot? You have to say—you know that? I'm *deadly* serious about this. This is so not a rebound thing. Honesty is—'

He laid a finger on her lips.

'I have always disbelieved the crazy notion—the dream, the nonsense of it—that you would ever be with me. Now? I can't conceive of a day without you. If there was a priest in this car, I would marry you in a...' he smiled '...New York minute.'

'I love the bones of you, Kennet Carlsson.'

'And I you, Kayte.' He looked out of the window. 'We're nearly there. Let's make this work and go home alive. Together. Successful.'

She kissed him. 'Yeah. Let's throw this dickhead in jail.'

# 63

Tom sat, quiet as a mouse, in the smallest of the manor's three reception rooms. In front of him, the PD Com tablet showed a four-way split of the feeds from the camera units concealed in the main lounge. The audio came through his earpiece.

Both his personal wrist Com and PD handheld Com were muted. He'd told Enna that everything was set and ready, then said he'd speak to her when everything was wrapped up. The polis units dotted around the estate had checked in. Now it was down to a civilian to make this thing work. And he thought *Enna* could sometimes be a liability....

Wilmer was showing Matteo a sheaf of papers.

'What happened?' the young man asked, his eyes shifty, body language jumpy.

'I came to my senses, Mat.'

'Wow—that must have been hard to say. What next? You'll say you were wrong to excommunicate me from the family?'

'Take it easy, okay? This *is* hard. I've spent a long time thinking about it.'

'You mean my brother and sister dying *made* you think about it.'

Bile rose in Tom's throat. Matteo was basically asking his father to give him credit for the change of heart—to accidentally condone the murder of his two siblings.

A PD unit had been watching Matteo's house in Uppsala. As soon as the suspect headed to the manor, the squad gained entry, searched the premises, and located the burner phone. The confirmation had come three minutes before Matteo arrived at Wilmer's front door.

Arguably, the phone was sufficient evidence to plead a case, but Tom wasn't satisfied. Enna, Kayte and Kennet wouldn't be either. They wanted the whiny murderous shit to put his head in the metaphorical noose and kick the chair away.

'Alright, Mat, let's be civilised—or at least try. Read the will. It's all there. I'm a practical man. I'm not going down in history as an eccentric moneybags who gave all his fortune to a... sanctuary for three-legged reindeer. It should have been split three ways—I accept that. You made some bad choices—not ideal, but in the past. I suppose we all have our burdens.'

Tom thought he saw a thin smile on Matteo's lips. He gripped the chair arm.

Matteo was reading the documents. 'Why should I believe you?'

'Because Peter's signature is on there. He approved this—even recommended it.'

'Because he doesn't hate me like you do.'

'I don't hate you, son. I just wish... things were different between us.' Wilmer scratched his chest. Tom held his breath.

'Yeah, well, so do I.' Matteo dropped the sheaf on the table. 'Seems fine. I know what a will looks like.'

'You do know I'm not going to stop until I find out what happened to Eva and why.'

Mat waved it away. 'I'm sure. Now, what about the Spaceport?'

'What about it?'

'You need to change your mind.'

Wilmer laughed, but it was forced. 'Why?'

'Because it's the right decision.'

'For who?'

'For Fleet. For the country. For the neighbourhood.'

'You mean for you, Mat.'

'I couldn't care either way.'

'Then why ask? Why the big pressure?'

Matteo threw up his arms. 'Okay—you know what—I'll tell you. Because you deserve the extra few billion. What's the use of miles and miles of trees? Just sitting on that like a proud peacock? Nobody's impressed. I'm not. The Committee are dying to take that land off your hands.'

'Because you suggested it to them.'

'Of course I did. You might have disowned me, but there are your genes in here.' Matteo tapped his head. 'Your business smarts.'

'The problem is that I don't want a Spaceport on my back lawn.'

'You'll be dead, Dad. Why do you care?'

Wilmer put on a theatrical expression of recognition. 'Ah. So this isn't really about the development. You'd never move in here, of course. You'd be happy to flatten this place. Maybe get some more money for it. Or turn it into a fancy passenger hotel.'

'Maybe. Who cares? I'm the last one left, and you just signed everything across to me.'

Wilmer lowered his voice. 'I can *un*-sign it.'

'You wouldn't dare. I'm all you've got left. It's the reindeer or me. So, how about it? Say yes to the Committee, then take the cash and buy an island. Maybe the place where you shagged your mistress? Better place to retire to than this old dump.' He gestured around.

'I'm not selling out to them, Mat. That's final.'

'You asshole!' the belligerent toddler shouted.

'Get out. You got what you came for.'

'I came because you said you'd seen reason. Do I have to *make* you accept that money?'

'You couldn't.'

Matteo whipped out the gun with startling efficiency.

Tom sprung up, heart racing.

'Maybe I can,' Matteo said.

'You mean, shoot me like you had Sara Lindström shot?'

'Shut up.'

'Like you had your own *sister* killed?'

'Shut up!'

'Your own *sister*. Jesus Christ!'

'I told her,' he yelled. 'I gave her a chance. Anders too.'

'Put the gun down, Mat,' Wilmer held out a plaintive hand.

'Sell up, you over-principled asshole. Do something decent for me for once in your stupid life.' Matteo was jinking and bobbing, a ball of nerves and desperation. 'Give me something to make up for thirty years of being a duplicitous shit.'

'I'm not selling, Mat. You don't get to fatten your inheritance by killing fifty people and trying to make it look like an accident.'

Tom was wringing his hands. He decided. 'Get the ambulance up to the house. Quickly. Silent.' His voice was barely a whisper.

'Roger,' came a voice in his ear.

He returned his attention to the standoff showing on his screen.

'You've got no proof, *old man*. Now tell me you'll sell up—or they died for *nothing*. Is that what you want?'

'Get lost, Mat. Get out of my life forever. You're getting nothing. My inheritance can be changed in an hour.'

'Yeah? Well, you don't have an hour.'

He levelled the gun and put three bullets into Wilmer's chest, glanced both ways, grabbed the sheaf of papers and charged the patio doors.

Wilmer thudded to the expensive Persian rug.

Matteo slammed through the impromptu exit and disappeared off the edge of Tom's screen.

# 64

Kayte pointed. 'There he goes.'

Matteo rounded the front of the house a hundred yards away to their left. Immediately, he screeched to a halt on the pebbled turning circle. A PD car was coming to rest.

His head darted, then he locked onto a spot to Kayte's right and set off apace.

He hadn't seen them concealed in the shrubs.

'At least he didn't start a gunfight with Janssen,' she said as the CI jumped from the car. She grabbed Kennet's cuff. 'Come on.'

They burst out from cover, drawing their firearms. It was pointless to call out: they needed to gain ground.

'I'll cut him off,' Kennet rapped, panting.

'Don't take chances.'

'Love you too much for that.'

Their paths diverged, and she engaged another gear of sprint, pounding the vast lawn which spread out towards the arcing treeline Matteo was following.

Her heart thudded. She was way off the pace she could have mustered five years ago, but it was enough to slowly haul in Matteo, who was visibly tiring. She didn't know his destination, but he must have gathered that both road exits were sealed off. Perhaps he knew of a gap in the fence line. Maybe he'd dug a tunnel when he lived here as a boy? She didn't care.

She willed herself on, arms pumping, the gun heavy in her hand.

'Armed police!'

Matteo glanced over his shoulder, and his run faltered. He lost his balance, toppling to the ground.

Now she was only fifty yards away.

He rolled with commendable alacrity, got onto a knee and levelled his gun at her. She dived to the grass. Two cracks cut the still air. Something smacked into the grass nearby.

She raised her head a few inches. He was on the move again. Kennet was nowhere.

She scrambled up and accelerated away.

Matteo cut left and entered the thin woodland.

Knowing she was out in the open, a sitting duck, she veered left.

Three more pops in quick succession. She hit the ground and rolled. The impact almost dislocated her shoulder. She yelped.

At least I'm still two bullets shy of Enna's bodily total, she thought.

Matteo was weaving through the trees. She sprinted to the nearest trunk, leant hard, found aim, and cracked off a warning shot. He was barely a flash of colour a hundred yards away, but he got the message.

Two more shots came, but he was well wide.

She moved off, scouring for Kennet, who should be away to the right. When she returned her attention to Matteo's path, she saw nothing.

'Shit!'

Now it was cat and mouse. She flattened against a tree, panting hard, and listened. Nothing.

'Ah, screw it.'

She bolted away, easing left to form what she hoped was a pincer movement.

How many bullets were in his gun? she wondered. Can he reload on the move? Was he expecting this? Had he even planned to shoot Wilmer?

Her muscles were complaining, and it was hard to concentrate on the evasive target whilst not turning her ankle over on an exposed root.

Two shots: tap-tap.

She winced, but they weren't aimed in her direction.

Two more, but a different weapon: Kennet had found him.

She abandoned caution and pelted for the source of the sound, riven with anguish that Kennet had been hit. Her engagement was supposed to last longer than this! She hadn't even gotten a ring out of him yet.

She was desperate to call his name but needed to retain the element of surprise. If Matteo had downed her love, she needed to be able to catch the bastard.

As her heart pumped away, fuelling the final tens of yards, she begged that it wouldn't break when she reached the men.

'Drop it!'

Her spirits soared on hearing that voice.

She burst into the clearing. 'Drop it, asshole!'

She levelled her gun at Matteo. Risking a glance at Kennet, she saw he was fine.

Matteo had his arms out like a cross, gun still held.

Her pulse was a bass drum. 'Now, Matteo.'

He glanced over, sneering.

She dipped her aim and put a bullet between his feet. 'Goddamn now!'

Out of the corner of her eye, she saw Kennet, gun arm arrow straight, bring his left wrist up. 'We have him, Tom.'

'Make the smart decision, Mat. For once,' she said, gaze locked on his gun.

'Are you hit?' Kennet asked her.

'No. Did you count the shots?'

'Yes. Twelve.'

She smirked at the suspect. 'We know what gun you have, shithead. You're out. Drop it.'

Matteo sneered.

She fired. A leaf six inches from his foot spat up. 'I have plenty more. And believe me, I'm dying to put them in your smug face.'

Matteo glanced at Kennet.

'Chief Wagner says your father is fine.' Kennet tapped his chest. 'We can plan in advance too. *Shithead.*'

While the shithead's attention was on her partner, Kayte scuttled in, gun outstretched. Creditably, he didn't move.

She tore the gun from his grasp and tossed it away.

'Matteo Svensson, you're under arrest for—'

He swung his left hand round, fist readied like a club to deliver to the side of her face.

She ducked hard, put her left hand to the ground, took her weight, then kicked round with both feet, sweeping his legs from under him.

He smacked to the earth.

In a moment, Kennet was there, gun barrel aimed at Matteo's forehead. She got to her feet.

'Nice move, partner,' he said.

'Nice collar, honey.' She winked.

Kennet moved to Matteo's outstretched left arm and casually trod on his hand. He howled in pain.

'Inspector,' she cautioned.

He jabbed his head at her to be quiet, then fixed his aim on Matteo. 'You killed my wife. You killed my partner's wife.'

'Kennet,' she said.

'You had our colleague shot by a sniper. You ruined hundreds of lives. For what?' He flicked the gun. 'For what?' he yelled. 'Money?'

'Inspector Carlsson,' she rapped.

'What would you do with billions of kronor, Matteo?' Kennet's tone was suddenly calm yet unsettling.

Kayte didn't like it—despite feeling exactly the same about the man at their feet.

'Get lost, cop,' Matteo spat. 'Just arrest me and stop the lecturing.'

'Arrest?' Kennet looked at Kayte. 'What do you think? Tie up the courts, and allow him time to come up with excuses? Maybe pay off or kill a few more key parties? Throw himself on his father's mercy to get bail?'

He tweaked his aim and fired into the ground inches from Matteo's head. 'Or do people who've lost loved ones deserve *real* justice? Guaranteed and swift?'

This was too much. She grabbed his left hand and hauled him away.

'Sergeant—' he began.

'No, Kennet. Cut this shit out.'

His expression was plaintive. 'He killed them, Kayte. For money. Pure greed. We're here for Enna, too, remember. What does she hate more than anything? Greed.'

'Look—' Matteo snipped.

She levelled her gun. 'Shut it.'

'Our family doesn't need *two* cops in it.' His eyes searched hers. 'You can take seniority, älskling. I'll be happy to lose my badge. There will be the school trips to do, and homework, and I can cook for you and—'

'You damn well won't, Kennet.'

He gritted his teeth. 'He *cannot* live.'

'I'm not marrying a murderer.'

He studied her for an age. She glanced at Matteo. He wasn't dumb enough to go for his downed gun five yards away—yet she wished he would.

She couldn't judge Kennet for his behaviour. She'd done it once before, and she was a few ounces of sense from doing it again. She *really* wanted Matteo Svensson dead for what he'd done.

Except, she couldn't let Kennet throw away his career. However, there was another way....

'I'm the mom. I'm the outsider. Hell, I'm out of jurisdiction. A loose cannon. The big city cop with the vendetta agenda. Yeah—that'd work.' She levelled her gun at the prone man.

'You bitch!' Matteo snapped.

'Lower your weapon, Sergeant,' Kennet said.

'Come on, Kennet—you showed you feel the same as me. You want closure. Who's going to miss this asshole?'

He clasped her wrist, trying to shift her aim. She tensed, fighting it.

Inside her, loss, hate, fear, and relief fought with the possibility of a swift end to the affair.

'We cannot undo the past,' he said firmly. 'We cannot change it. We have a *future*. If you do this, you ruin it. And... I will retract my offer.'

She saw pleading and disappointment on his face. Vengeance wasn't worth losing all she had in the world. Yet....

'He has to pay,' she murmured. 'He has to know the damage he's caused.'

Kennet eyed her, his forehead working. He brought up his wrist. 'Tom. Get a paramedic to our position. There's a... problem.'

A pause. 'On our way,' came a voice.

'You crazy—' Matteo began to wriggle horizontally away.

Kennet stamped on his foot, pinning him. He yelped in pain.

'Do you know?' she snapped at the conniving murderer. 'How you hurt people?'

'Piss off.'

Kennet gritted his teeth. 'I think he's going for his gun, Sergeant,' he said, measured yet broken.

Then he raised his weapon, sighted, and shot Matteo in the right knee.

The man detonated into hellish screams of pain.

'Do you know understand now?' Kennet asked.

Her blood boiled. On the one hand, she didn't know this part of the man she'd just agreed to marry. On the other hand, she knew precisely how he felt—and that his response was, if anything, tame.

On another day, she could have emptied her magazine into Matteo's head. However, she'd forever have to live with that moment of utter insanity. Worse, Kennet would have to live with her feeling like that, possibly ashamed of her, perhaps jealous that she'd got the last word. Whatever, he'd never be able to experience her aftermath, not live it in her bones as she would. Their relationship might not even survive.

Here, now, she couldn't know whether he felt better for his actions. Yet, as he holstered his gun, she knew he was done. He blew the tension and anger from his lungs.

Matteo was sobbing, yet his eyes were devilish.

How long would Carey, Jana and the other passengers have screamed as the end approached? How torn up would Wilmer be for the remainder of his days, having lost his most-loved progeny?

How could she, Kayte, get closure? Every nerve and fibre crackled with the desire for a statement of her disgust. His knee could be mended. He'd walk again—only in prison, but still.

He needed to experience true loss.

She raised her gun, sighted carefully, and, as his eyes screamed in fear and protestation, she shot him in the groin.

He exploded into pain, hyperventilating, and then, mercifully for him and them, he passed out.

With a quivering hand, she holstered her gun. 'No heirs for you, you piece of shit.'

Instantly, Kennet pulled her into an embrace, and they sobbed.

Hearing footsteps on the brush, she broke off and dried her eyes.

Tom came to a halt, surveying the scene.

'Chief.'

Tom frowned. 'Sergeant. Inspector.' His tone was cautious, odd and confused.

'The suspect went for his weapon,' Kennet said.

Tom spied Matteo's gun nearby. 'Uh-huh.'

'My aim was off. It was a warning shot,' she said.

Tom noted the two bloody stains on Matteo's clothing.

'Mine as well,' Kennet said. He forced a smile. 'My fitness is not what it should be.'

Tom inspected their faces.

Expectation and nervousness prickled her cheeks. She willed her boss to see sense. She was desperate to walk away, soak in a bath, bawl her eyes out in relief and self-recrimination, and collapse into a never-ending hug with her fiancé.

Two paramedics, bearing a stretcher, burst through the trees.

'Understood,' Tom said. 'I'm sure your report will be... accurate.'

'Did he cop to it?' she asked.

'Yeah. And we have the burner. His instructions put bullets in my wife too. So....' He sighed. 'At least he's alive to serve time, right?' A faint smile flickered.

'Definitely.'

Tom's Com beeped.

The trio backed away, letting the paramedics attend to the wounded man.

She clasped Kennet's hand. 'I wanna go home.'

'That sounds good.'

Tom walked ahead of them. The identity of the caller was apparent and predictable.

'Tell her... we did the right thing,' Kayte called.

Tom slowed, and they caught up to him. He put Enna on speaker.

'You two okay?' came a familiar voice.

'I've been better,' Kayte said. Then she shook her head and squeezed Kennet's hand. 'Strike that. I'm fine.'

'Chief says you got everything you needed. Trap sprung.'

'Is this code for you wanting credit for suggesting Wilmer wear a vest?'

Enna laughed. 'Hell yeah.'

'Credit given, honey,' Tom said. 'Your last ever butt-in saved a life.'

'If only that wasn't a first, right?'

Kayte checked the time. 'It's late there. You rest.'

'From me, too,' Kennet added.

'Will do. Send my man home soon.'

'I'll put a bottle of brännvin in his flight case,' Kayte said.

'You're a gem, Connors.'

She smiled. 'Oh, I know.'

Enna laughed. 'Look after yourselves.'

'Will do.' She glanced across at her partner. 'Oh, by the way, Kennet and I are getting married.'

Tom's mouth hung open.

The line fell silent. Enna was temporarily—and unusually—lost for words. Leaves scrunched underfoot. Birds chirped.

'You going to give me any ultimatums or tell me how to feel?' Kayte added.

'No. You've had enough fighting for today. Hell, a lifetime. Me too, honey.'

'Thanks, Enna. So... you've got five seconds to tell me you don't want to be my maid of honour.'

Kayte paced onwards, listening intently. 'Enna?'

Tom shrugged.

'Damn,' Enna said finally. 'Guess my five seconds are up.'

# 65

The November dusk brought sharp cold to the Narvik afternoon.

Enna pulled Tom closer for warmth and tugged the woollen bonnet down over Lexie's ears.

On the hotel terrace, the heat lamps, dotted between the couple of dozen people, began to radiate with greater force. Away to both sides, the town lights winked. A few hundred yards ahead, the sea slopped.

Kayte and Kennet sidled up, arms linked. He'd buttoned his suit jacket to the collar. She wore an ivory-coloured shrug over her white dress.

'Hotel's not sure we'll get lucky tonight.' Kayte looked skywards. 'But at least we saw the whales.'

'You've got two more nights,' Enna said. 'Besides,' she gently jabbed an elbow into her friend's ribs, 'I'm sure Kennet's the one planning to get lucky tonight.'

'I am lucky every day and every night,' he replied.

'I do pretty well, too.' Kayte winked at him.

'Out of tragedy sometimes comes hope. And happiness,' Tom said sagely.

Enna smoothed her curved belly. 'And the patter of tiny feet.'

Kayte held Enna's hand. 'You have a name yet?'

She glanced at Tom. 'Pascal Stephane. Probably.'

'Stefan?' Kayte's eyes widened. 'After Iversen—after what he did to you?'

'Without him, I wouldn't have met Tom. And don't forget, honey, you wouldn't have met Kennet.'

'She is right, sweet,' Kennet said. 'Although the road has not been so short or so smooth.'

'It's been bumpy as hell, husband. But all the wheels are still on the car.' Kayte pecked his cheek.

Enna watched as Lexie scrutinised the inky canopy, which was becoming dotted with stars. Beyond her, on a bench, Ellie and Han laughed.

'They were dancing before,' Kayte said.

Enna wrinkled her nose. 'I think it's... him easing into things, nothing more. Besides, Wes has been in touch a lot, apparently.'

'He wants to give it another go?'

'He's not as happy as he expected to be after leaving Fleet PD for something more ordinary.' Tom shrugged. 'I get the feeling I'll be getting a call before long.'

'He would come back?' Kennet asked.

'I'd certainly have him. Now that supermom here is officially off the team.' Tom patted Enna's bump. 'We could do with reinforcements. These last months have shown there's a need for us. Actually, the brass indicated they were happy to double our budget.'

Enna gazed adoringly at her man. 'Looks like the great experiment continues.'

'If you ever need a hand,' Kayte said.

'But maybe in a year, sweet, yes?' Kennet said.

Enna saw something in the Swede's eyes. She inspected Kayte's face for unnoticed recent micro-changes in her complexion. The latent sleuth in Enna had missed something these past weeks—a sign she knew from experience.

'We won't tell,' she whispered.

Kayte glanced at Kennet, who gave the faintest shrug.

'What the hell,' she said. We were going to ask you anyway soon enough.'

'Ask what?' Tom said.

Enna rolled her eyes theatrically. 'The great leader of the crack police team. Sheesh.'

'Men, huh?' Kayte said.

Laughter broke like a wave across all four. Kayte noticed Kennet's sheepishness and embraced him hard.

'God, you're adorable,' she murmured.

'So, what?' Enna demanded with cheerful insistence.

Kayte stroked her belly. 'Which do you think works best—Carey Jana or Jana Carey?'

Enna's bloodstream flooded with joy. She gave Kayte the fattest kiss on her cheek. Then she checked Kennet's expression. He didn't seem reluctant, so she kissed him too.

Tom followed up with a kiss and handshake, respectively.

Tomas pelted over. 'Daddy, daddy!' He pointed northwest, above the horizon.

Enna was overcome with wonder. This wasn't the first time, but the sight never failed to amaze her and rekindle her love for the beauty and majesty of space.

Tonight, after Earth had taken too much from their lives recently, the planet was making up for it in spades.

'That's one off the bucket list,' Kayte said, gasping at the dancing colours.

'And almost as pretty as you,' her new husband replied.

'Oh yeah, he's a keeper,' Enna said.

Tom leant down and whispered in her ear. 'Not a patch on how amazing and beautiful you are, Lieutenant Enna Marie Dacourt.'

'Yeah. That's a fact.'

He whacked her on the ass.

Kennet raised his champagne flute. 'To those we love and to those we've lost.'

Four glasses clinked.

'To the future,' Enna said.


## THE END

**The Enna Dacourt series:**
Imperfect Isolation (2018)
Reprisals (2019)
Trip Hazard (2021)
Freeze Effect (2022)
Breaking Ground (2023)

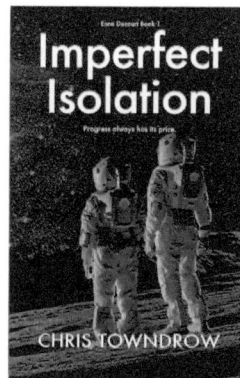

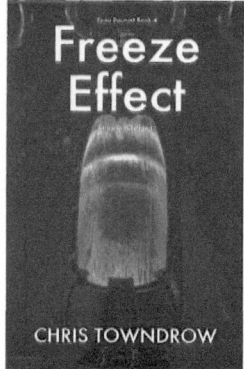

# About the author

Chris Towndrow has been a writer since 1991. He began writing science fiction, inspired by Isaac Asimov, Iain M Banks, and numerous film and TV canons. After a few years spent creating screenplays, in 2004 he moved into playwriting and has had several productions professionally performed. This background is instrumental in his ability to produce realistic, compelling dialogue in his books.

His first published novel was 2012's space opera "Sacred Ground". He then focussed on near-future sci-fi adventures, writing the Enna Dacourt pentalogy.

He has always drawn inspiration from the big screen, and 2019's quirky romantic comedy "Tow Away Zone" owes much to the Coen Brothers' work. This book spawned two sequels in what became the "Sunrise trilogy". His first historical fiction novel, "Signs Of Life", was published in 2023.

Chris now writes romcom under the pen name Chrissie Harrison. The first of these, "Floored", arrived in April 2024 and gained excellent reviews.

Chris lives on the outskirts of London with his family. He is a member of the UK Society of Authors.

Visit his website at: www.christowndrow.co.uk
Instagram: @AuthorCTowndrow

If you have enjoyed this book, please do leave an online review. An author's ability to generate valuable sales is enhanced by the reviews of kind readers.

# Also from the Publisher

ere's the complete list of books from Valericain Press.

Whether your reading taste includes sci-fi, romance, comedy, or something quirkier, there may be a story here for you.

Romantic Comedy                                      Historical Romance

Absurd humour        Quirky romantic comedy / cosy mystery        Post-apocalyptic

Near future sci-fi adventure                              Space opera